The Clover Girls

Center Point
Large Print

Also by Viola Shipman and available from
Center Point Large Print:

The Heirloom Garden

**This Large Print Book carries the
Seal of Approval of N.A.V.H.**

The Clover Girls

VIOLA SHIPMAN

CENTER POINT LARGE PRINT
THORNDIKE, MAINE

This Center Point Large Print edition
is published in the year 2021 by arrangement with
Harlequin Books S.A.

The text of this Large Print edition is unabridged.
In other aspects, this book may vary
from the original edition.
Printed in the United States of America
on permanent paper.
Set in 16-point Times New Roman type.

ISBN: 978-1-63808-027-5

The Library of Congress has cataloged this record under
Library of Congress Control Number: 2021939506

To my friends:
You make me laugh,
you make me do things I regret,
but mostly you make me believe
I can still do anything
and be anyone I dream.
You inspire me every day.

PART ONE

Letters Home

SUMMER 1985
EMILY

Dear Mom and Dad:

The first week at girls' sleepaway camp started out totally scary. I hid in an old barn where they store all the canoes and kayaks and cried for like an hour. I didn't know anyone, and I felt SO alone. But then something happened! Three girls in the same bunkhouse as me realized I was missing, and they came to find me. "It's going to be okay," they said. "We're all in this together." On the way back to camp, we took a shortcut through this huge clover field that sits off to one side of Birchwood Lake. It's sooo beautiful. The clover moves in the breeze like it's alive and breathing, the green and white matching the waves in the wind on the lake. On our way back, we all linked hands and walked through the middle of the clover. And that's when it happened! I found a four-leaf clover right in front of me. I just looked down, and there it was, this tiny little lucky charm in a huge field. Well, we all freaked out and ran back to camp. Mrs. Nigh told us there was clover in the Garden of Eden, and Eve took a four-leaf clover with her to remember the splendor and majesty of paradise. "You possess a piece of paradise now," she told us. "That's why I planted it there. So paradise will always be with you, even when you grow up and leave this camp." She told us the three leaves of a normal clover represent faith, hope and love. The fourth is for good luck . . . "The lucky clover."

Now we know! We were always meant to meet! And we're all, like, totally BFFs already. We're all SO different, but each of us has a cool part that completes the group, almost as if the four of us make one perfect person, like the four leaves make a lucky clover. Their names are Veronica, Elizabeth and Rachel, and we're all from somewhere different! Now, Camp Birchwood is totally rad! It's gone from lame to legit!

Like I said, I was so nervous in the beginning. The first night, I didn't know anybody at dinner. We sat at a big table, and all the older girls were laughing and talking about all the boys at Camp Taneycomo. You could even hear the boys calling across the lake for these girls, hooting like insane owls. Some of the new campers knew each other from school, but most of us just sat around and chewed on our hot dogs like dorks. Well, the counselors (ours is Dana, and she is SO nice!) had all the new campers introduce themselves by doing something artistic that represented who we really are inside. Some girls sang, some girls danced, some girls acted out scenes from plays, some drew pictures of themselves or their families, but the four of US?! We ALL did the same thing! We made friendship pins! And all of them were green! The counselors thought it was because we were all in the same cabin, and that's why we did green, but we did it because it is our favorite color. And when we were done, and I looked down at our tennis shoes, I totally freaked! Their laces were all covered in friendship pins, too!

The next night, at our first bonfire, we were toasting marshmallows, making s'mores and singing camp songs when Rachel started to scream, "Oh, my Gawd!" just like a Valley Girl. I laughed, but when I looked over, her eyes were like totally wide, and she started pointing at us around the fire. "Emily, Veronica, Elizabeth, and me, Rachel . . . !"

Veronica was like, "Um, yeah, we all know our names." Liz asked, "Are you okay?" and Rachel started pointing at herself, her arm shaking so hard that her marshmallow slid right into the fire. We all thought she was joking around, but she stopped and looked at each of us, her face all spooky through the flames. "You're Emily!" she said to me. "You're Veronica. You're Elizabeth. I'm Rachel."

"We got it." Veronica laughed.

"No, you don't," Rachel said. "The first letters of our names . . . E-V-E-R! Friends Forever! Get it? FOUR-ever!"

We all looked at each other, and that's when we got it.

Anyway, just as Rachel said it, "Girls Just Want to Have Fun" started to play on one of the older girls' transistor radio, and we all screamed at the same time, got up and started to dance, just like Cyndi Lauper does, all crazy, not caring what anyone else thinks. And right after that, "That's What Friends Are For" came on, and we all started swaying and singing to each other. Now we call Camp Birchwood Camp-Girls-Just-Wanna-Have-Fun, and all the camp counselors call us "The Clover Girls" because we all love green and wear green T-shirts, and because we're all going to be green in Color War. But especially because we're like the lucky four-leaf clover I found that first day. We're good luck charms for each other.

THE CLOVER GIRLS!
FRIENDS 4-EVER!

Let me try to describe the Clover Girls to you.

Veronica goes by "V," and she is beautiful. She looks just like Molly Ringwald, and she is so confident and funny. Even all the older girls are jealous of her, and the boys at Taneycomo already send her notes they float across Lake Birchwood on rafts. She's sort of the leader of The Clover Girls without even trying. I think I'd hate her if she wasn't my friend.

Liz looks like she walked straight off a Madonna video on MTV. Her hair needs its own bunk, and she wraps lace and bandanas into it and makes all of these wild slogan T-shirts in our art classes. She made us all "CLOVER GIRLS" T-shirts, but they won't let us wear them because we're Camp Birchwood first, Pinewood Bunk second and Clover Girls last. She has the coolest add-a-bead necklace—

with, like, a million beads on it—that she loves to wear with all her friendship pins and bracelets. She says she has Forenza sweaters in every color and that she wears them backwards—can you believe it? Backwards! I never thought to do that!

Rachel's our movie star. She's like the twin of that actress in Footloose. She can sing and dance, and she won the last talent competition! As a newbie! We made her up like a zombie, and she sang "Thriller." She even knew every dance move. Rachel wants to move to New York or LA and become a star. We all know she's going to make it!

I guess I'm like the mother of the group, just like you, Mom. I worry about everyone and just want them to be happy. I also feel like the glue for the group, like you, Dad. I want to make sure everyone feels safe. We've already made a pact: we've all agreed that, one day in the future, when we're really old (like you, ha!) we are going to buy Camp Birchwood and all retire here together. No boys allowed (we can talk to them, but they have to stay all the way on other side of the lake!). It would be PERFECT! Camp will be our forever home, where we'll take care of each other, always bring out the best in each other, always make each other laugh and feel safe. Most of all, we'll know each other better than anyone, and we'll always be there for each other, no matter what. Everyone laughs at us, but I don't care. We're friends 4-EVER, and one day The Clover Girls will all be together. Just watch!

Every night, before we go to bed, the bell chimes, and the entire camp sings "Land of the Silver Birch." It's so eerie and beautiful, and the way everyone's voices echo over the lake gives me chills but makes me feel safe.

Blue lake and rocky shore,
I will return once more,
Boom, didi, boom, boom,
Boom, didi, boom, boom,
Boom, didi, boom, boom . . . Booooom.

And then The Clover Girls all say good-night to each other, just like they did in The Waltons. And every time we do, right before I close my eyes and go to sleep, I understand why you both wanted me to come to camp. So I don't feel all alone. And I'll never be alone as long as I have friends. That's why you sent me here, wasn't it? To make friends.

I haven't told anyone about Todd yet. I mean, how do you tell people you just met that your brother died? But I will. And I know they'll understand. And it's weird, but I feel like he's with me here. And when I hear the boys from Taneycomo yell, I hear Todd's voice. He'll always be a little kid while the rest of us grow old.

I only let myself cry now when I inner tube into the lake and am far away from everyone. That's when I bawl, even harder than when I watched you drive away from camp. But no one knows. Only the lake and the fish and the hawks.

And Todd.

But I have friends now. And they make me cry less every day.

I love you, Mom and Dad. And I love camp! See you in August!

Em

SUMMER 2021
VERONICA

GROCERY LIST
Milk (Oat, coconut, soy)
Fizzy water (cherry, lime, watermelon,
    mixed berry)
Chips (lentil, quinoa, kale, beet)
Cereal (Kashi, steel-cut oats, NO GMOs!
    VERY IMPORTANT!)

Whatever happened to one kind of milk from a cow, one kind of water from a faucet and one kind of chip from a potato?

My teenage children are seated on opposite ends of the massive, modern, original Milo Baughman circular sofa that David and I ordered for our new midcentury house in Los Angeles. Ashley and Tyler are juggling drinks while pecking at their cells, and it takes every fiber of my soul not to come unglued. This is the most expensive piece of furniture I have ever purchased in my life. More expensive even than my first two years of college tuition *plus* my first car, a red Reliant K-car that would stall at stoplights.

I still don't know what the K stood for, I think. *Krappy?*

That was a time, long ago, when that type of negative thought would never have entered my mind, when the K would have stood only for *Konfident, Kool* or *Kick-Ass.* But that was a different world, another time, another life and place.

Another me.

Another V.

I steady my pen at the top of a pad of paper emblazoned with the logo of my husband's architectural firm, David Berzini & Associates.

Los Angeles is the latest stop for us. My family has hopscotched the world more than a military brat as David's architectural career has exploded. He is now one of the world's preeminent architects. David studied under and worked with some of the most famous midcentury modern architects—Albert Frey, William Krisel, Donald Wexler—and has now taken over their mantles, especially as the appreciation for and popularity of midcentury modern architecture has grown. Now he is working on a stunning new public library in LA that will be his legacy.

I glance up from my pad. A selection of magazines—*Architectural Digest*, *Vogue*, *W*—are artfully strewn across a brutalist coffee table. The beautiful models stare back at me.

That was my legacy.

"Mom, can I get something to eat?"

This is now my legacy.

I glance at my children. Everything old has come back en vogue. Ashley is wearing the same sort of high-waisted jeans that I once wore and modeled in the '80s, and Tyler's hair—razored high by a barber and slicked back into a big black pompadour—looks a lot like a style I sported for a Robert Palmer video when every woman wanted to look like a Nagel woman.

Yes, everything has made a comeback.

Except me.

I look at my list.

And carbs.

My kids, like my husband, have never met a Pop-Tart, a box of Cap'n Crunch, a Jeno's Pizza Roll or a Ding Dong. My entire family resembles long-limbed ponies, ready to race. I grew up when the foundation of a food pyramid was a Twinkie.

I again put pen to paper, and in my own secret code I write the letter *L* above the first letter of my husband's name. If someone happened to glance at the paper, they would simply think I had been doodling. But I know what "LD" means, and it will remind me once I get to the store.

Little Debbies.

You know, I actually hide these around our new home, which isn't easy since the entire space is so sleek and minimal, and hiding space is at a premium. It took a lot of effort, but I, too, used to be as sleek and minimal as this house, as angular and arresting as its architecture. Anything out of place in our butterfly-roofed home located in the Bird Streets high above Sunset Strip—where the streets are named after orioles and nightingales, and Hollywood stars reside—is conspicuous.

Even now, on yet another perfect day in LA, where the sunshine makes everything look lazily beautiful and dipped in glitter, I can see a layer of dust on the terrazzo floors. Although a maid comes twice a week, the dust, smog and ash from nonstop fires in LA—carried by hot, dry Santa Ana winds—coat everything. And David notices everything.

Swiffers, I write on the pad, before outlining "LD" with my pen.

David hates that I have gained weight. He is embarrassed I have gained weight.

Or is it just my imagination? Am I the one who is embarrassed by who I've become?

David never says anything to me, but he attends more and more galas alone, saying I need to watch the kids even though they no longer need a babysitter and that it's better for their stability if one parent is with them. But I know the truth.

What did he expect would happen to my body after two children and endless moves? What did he expect would happen after losing my career, identity and self-esteem? It's so ironic, because I'm not angry at him or my life. I'm just . . .

"Why don't you just put all of that in the notes on your phone?"

"Or just ask the refrigerator to remember?"

"Yeah, Mom," my kids say at the same time.

I look over at them. They have my beauty and David's drive. Ash and Ty lift their eyes from their phones just long enough to roll their eyes at me, in that way that teens do, the way teens always have, in that there-couldn't-be-a-more-lame-uncool-human-in-the-world-than-you-Mom way. And it's always followed by "the sigh."

"I like to do it this way," I say.

"NO ONE writes anything anymore," Ashley says.

"NO ONE, Mom!" Tyler echoes.

"Cursive is dead, Mom," Ashley says. "Get with the times."

I stare at my children. They are often the sweetest kids in the world, but every so often their evil twins emerge, the ones with forked tongues and acerbic words.

Did they get that from me? Or their father? Or is it just the way kids are today?

The sun shifts, and the reflection of water from the pool dances on the white walls, making it look as if we are living in an aquarium. I glance down the long hallway where the pool is reflecting, the place David has allowed me to have my only "clutter": a corridor of old photos, a room of heirlooms.

My life flashes before me: our family in front of the Rockefeller Center Christmas tree in New York at the holidays, eating colorful French macarons at a café in Paris, lying out on Barcelona's beaches, and fishing with my parents at their summer cottage on Lake Michigan. And then, in the ultimate juxtaposition, there is an old photo of me, teenage me, in a bikini at Lake Birchwood hanging directly next to an old *Sports Illustrated* cover of me. In it, I am posing by the ocean where I met David. I am crouched on the beach like a tiger ready to pounce. That was my signature pose, you know, the one I invented that all the other models stole, the Tiger Pose.

I was one of the one-name girls back then: Madonna, Iman, Cher, V. All I needed was a single letter to identify myself. Now V has Vanished. I have one name.

"Mom!"

"Lunch. Please!"

My eyes wander back to our pool. I would be mortified to wear a bikini today. I am not what most people would deem overweight. But I have a paunch, my thighs are jellied and my chin is starting to have a best friend. It was that photo in all of the gossip magazines a year or so ago that did it to me. Paparazzi shot me downing an ice cream cone while putting gas in my car. I had shuttled the kids around all day in 110-degree heat, and I was wearing a billowy caftan. I looked bigger than my SUV. And the headlines:

Voluminous!

V has Vanished Inside This Woman!

If you saw me in person, you'd likely say I'm a narcissist or being way too hard on myself, but it's as hard to hide fifteen pounds in LA as it is to hide an extra throw pillow in this house. I get Botox and fillers and do all the things I can to maintain my looks, but I am terrified to go to the gym here. I am mortified to look for a dress in a city where a size two is considered obese. The gossip rags are just waiting for me to move.

My eyes wander back to the photos.

I no longer have an identity.

I no longer have friends.

"Earth to Mom? Can you make me some lunch?" Tyler looks at me. "Then I need to go to Justin's."

"And you have to drive me to Lily's at four, remember?"

I shudder. A two-mile drive in LA takes two hours.

"Mom?"

Ashley looks at me.

There is a way that your children and husband look at you—or rather don't look at you at a certain point in your life—not to mention kids in the street, young women shopping, men in

23

restaurants, David's colleagues, happy families in the grocery.

They look *through* you. Like you're a window.

It's as if women over forty were never young, smart, fashionable, cool . . . were never like them, never had hopes, dreams and acres of life ahead of them.

What is with American society today?

Why, when women reach a "certain age," do we become ghosts? Strike that. That's not an accurate analogy: that would imply that we actually invoke a mood, a scare, a feeling of some sort. That we have a personality. I could once hold up a bag of potato chips, eat one, lick my fingers and sell a million bags of junk food for a company. Now I'm not even memorable enough to be a ghost. This model has become a prop. A piece of furniture. Not like the stylish one my kids are stretched out on, but the reliable, sturdy, ever-present, department store kind, devoid of any depth or substance, one without feeling, attractiveness or sexuality. I am just here. Like the air. Necessary to survive, but something no one sees or notices.

I used to be noticed. I used to be seen. Desired. Admired. Wanted.

I was the ringleader of friends, the one who called the shots. Now, I am Uber driver, Shipt delivery, human Roomba and in-home Grubhub, products I once would have sold rather than used.

I take a deep breath and note a few more grocery items on my antiquated written list and stand to make my kids lunch.

They are teen health nuts, already obsessed with every bite they consume. Does it have GMOs? What is the protein-to-carb differential?

Did I do this to them? I don't think so.

Even as a model, I ate pizza, but that's back in the day when a curve was sexy and a bikini needed to be filled out. I pull out some spicy tuna sushi rolls I picked up at Gelson's and arrange them on a platter. I wash and chop some berries and place them in a bowl. I watch my kids fill their plates. Ashley is a cheerleader and wannabe actress, and Tyler is a skateboarding, creative techy applying to UCLA to study film and directing. Ashley wants to go to Northwestern to major in drama. They will both be going to specialty camps later this summer, Ashley for cheerleading and acting, Tyler for filmmaking and to boost his SAT scores. My eyes drift back to my photo wall, and I smile. They will not, however, spend their days simply having fun, singing camp songs, engaging in color wars, shooting archery, splashing in a cold lake, roasting marshmallows and making friends. A kid's life today, especially here in LA, is a competition, and the competition starts early.

There is a rustling noise outside, and Ashley tosses her plate onto the sofa and rushes to the door. In LA, even the postal workers are hot, literally and figuratively, and our mailman looks like Zac Efron. She returns a few seconds later, fanning herself dramatically with the mail.

"You're going to be a great actress," I say with a laugh. Ashley starts to toss the mail onto the counter, but I stop her. "Leave the mail in the organizer for your dad."

Yes, even the mail has its own home in our home.

"Hey, you got a letter," she says.

"Who writes letters anymore?" Tyler asks.

"Old people," Ashley says. The two laugh.

I take a seat at the original Saarinen tulip table and study the envelope. There is no return address. I feel the envelope. It's bulky. I open it and begin to read a handwritten letter:

Dear V:

How are you? I'm sorry it's been a while since we've talked. You've been busy, I've been busy. Remember when we were just a bunk away? We could lean our heads over the side and share our darkest secrets. Those were the good ol' days, weren't they? When we were innocent. When we were as tight as the clover that grew together in the patch that wound to the lake.

How long has it been since you talked to Rach and Liz? Over 30 years? I guess

26

that first four-leaf clover I found wasn't so lucky after all, was it? Oh, you and Rach have had such success, but are you happy, V? Deep down? Achingly happy? I don't believe in my heart that you are. I don't think Rach and Liz are either. How do I know? Friend's intuition.

I used to hate myself for telling everyone what happened our last summer together. It was like dominoes falling after that, one secret after the next revealed, the facade of our friendship ripped apart, just like tearing the fourth leaf off that clover I still have pressed in my scrapbook. But I hate secrets. They only tear us apart. Keep us from becoming who we need to become. The dark keeps things from growing. The light is what creates the clover.

Out the cabin door went all of our luck, and then—leaf by leaf—our faith in each other, followed by any hope we might have had in our friendship and, finally, any love that remained was replaced by hatred, then a dull ache, and then nothing at all. That's the worst thing, isn't it, V? To feel nothing at all?

Much of my life has been filled with regret, and that's just an awful way to live. I'm trying to make amends for that before it's too late. I'm trying to be the friend I should have been. I was once the glue that held us all together. Then I was scissors that tore us all apart. Aren't friends supposed to be there for one another, no matter what? You weren't just beautiful, V, you were confident, so funny and full of life. More than anything, you radiated light, like the lake at sunset. And that's how I will always remember you.

I've sent similar letters to Rach and Liz. I stayed in touch with Liz . . . and Rach . . . well, you know Rach. For some reason, you all forgave me, but not each other. I guess because I was just an innocent bystander to all the hurt. My only remaining hope is that you will all forgive one another at some point, because you changed my life and you changed each other's lives. And I know that you all need one another now more than ever. We found each other for a reason. We need to find each other again.

Let me get to the point, dear V. Just picture me leaning my head over the bunk and telling you my deepest secret.

By the time you receive this, I'll be dead . . .

My hand begins to shake, which releases the contents still remaining in the envelope. A pressed four-leaf clover and a few old Polaroid pictures scatter onto the tabletop. Without warning, I groan.

"Are you okay, Mom?" Tyler asks without looking back.

"Who's that from?" Ashley asks, still staring at her phone.

"A friend," I manage to mumble.

"Cool," Ashley says. "You need friends. You don't have any except for that one girl from camp." She stops. "Emily, right?"

The photos lying on the marble tabletop are of the four of us at camp, laughing, singing, holding hands. We are so, so young, and I wonder what happened to the girls we used to be. I stare at a photo of Em and me lying under a camp blanket in the same bunk. That's when I realize the photo is sitting on top of something. I move the picture and smile. A friendship pin stares at me, E-V-E-R shining in a sea of green beads.

I look up, and water is reflecting through the clerestory windows of our home, and suddenly every one of those little openings is like a scrapbook to my life, and I can see it flash—at camp and after—in front of me in bursts of light.

Why did I betray my friends?

Why did I give up my identity so easily?

Why am I richer than I ever dreamed and yet feel so empty and lost?

Oh, Em.

I blink, my eyes blur, and that's when I realize it's not the pool reflecting in the windows, it's my own tears. I'm crying. And I cannot stop.

Suddenly, I stand, throw open the patio doors and jump into the pool, screaming as I sink. I look up, and my children are yelling.

"Mom! Are you okay?"

I wave at them, and their bodies relax.

"I'm fine," I lie when I come to the surface. "I'm sorry. I didn't mean to scare you."

They look at each other and shrug, before heading back inside.

At least, I think, they finally see me.

I take a deep breath and go down once more. Underwater, I can hear my heart drum loudly in my ears. It's drumming in such perfect rhythm that I know immediately the tune my soul is playing. I can hear it as if it were just yesterday.

Boom, didi, boom, boom . . . Booooom.

RACHEL

TALKING POINTS
CONGRESSIONAL CANDIDATE
RALPH RUDDY
DISTRICT 47/MICHIGAN

–Do NOT engage anchors if angry
–Always say "As a woman" to humanize
  yourself
–We must be seen as equals to men!
  We do not need a "handout," we need
  "hands clapping"!
–Women CAN and DO do it all!
–Small business CANNOT afford paid
  maternity leave; how can we raise a
  family when we don't have a job?

"How's my hair?"
  "Perfect."
  "Makeup?"
  "Ditto."
  "Teeth."
  "Clean."
  "Thanks, Lisa."
I check my notes, stand, tug my jacket and then
sit on its tail so it will appear taut on camera, my
clothing streamlined and unwrinkled.

Like me.

"Are you ready, Rachel?"

I look into the camera.

"Hold on! Hold on!" I say. "We specifically stated that I was to be shot in front of the turquoise graphic with Ralph's logo."

Dana, the director, looks at me, checks her notes and nods. She talks to production, and a few seconds later I'm surrounded by the color that research has proven not only is most appealing to women but also perfectly complements my eyes and outfit.

"Thanks, Dana," I say.

She gives me a faint nod.

"Remember *Sorority Sisters*?" I ask.

An imperceptible smile crosses her lips.

"Fun times, huh?"

She doesn't respond.

Dana doesn't like me. In our early twenties, I was cast in a comedy about a group of very different college students who join the same sorority and become friends. I still don't know if I was hired because of my audition or the fact that the summer camp I attended became a *Life* magazine cover story and they used that backstory—and all the retro Polaroids—as publicity.

It certainly wasn't because of *she who has no name,* I think. My mind wanders to the recent tabloid photos of her, and part of me feels a sick sense of satisfaction and part of me feels sorry for her.

Even after everything she did.

Sorority Sisters was so low-budget in the beginning that viewers could see the sets move when we slammed a door. I was just thrilled to get a real acting job right out of college. And then the show took off. How we were able to remain in college and the same sorority until our early thirties was beside the point because we had a cult following. It ran for nearly a decade, before two of us got a spinoff, *In A New York Minute*, that followed our lives as hard-partying new career gals in NYC. It lasted only one season. Dana was a production assistant on *Sorority Sisters* who eventually worked her way up to directing the show. We all made a lot of money, but the show made us Hollywood jokes. My career was over, pardon the pun, in a New York minute. Dana moved to broadcast news, and I moved into politics. My good looks and girl-next-door persona made me a great spokesperson for conservative male politicians who had difficulty wooing suburban, independent women voters.

Dana was a hard worker, driven and passionate. We used to sit up late at night and talk about how we were going to change television by creating and promoting content by and about women.

A jagged pain jolts my brain, and I take a sip of water.

Dana may not like me now, but she knows I make damn good TV.

"Gotta love Hollywood." I grin.

"This is news," Dana says.

"Keep telling yourself that." I wink, my false eyelash fluttering like a butterfly.

A commercial about a new heart drug with happy balloons comes on the air, and I take a deep breath to steady myself and check my notes one last time. The anchor, Chip Collins, takes a seat and nods at me, and a trio of makeup artists powder his face, spray his hair and adjust his tie. Chip's hair is a work of art, a waterfall of arcing jet-black waves. Chip used to be one of America's best investigative journalists. Now he hosts a UFC match that pretends it's a talk show.

If I were a betting woman, I would estimate that I've made over a hundred appearances on *Red, White & You*, Chip's national TV morning show that discusses politics. But I am not a betting woman. You can't change your odds when you bet. They are what they are. No, I am a magician. People can watch me and truly believe they understand how my act works, but then—*voilà!*—I fool them. I make them believe. I change the odds.

"Okay, everyone," Dana says, getting the attention of the crew as the news station returns from commercial break. "Three, two . . ." Her finger signals *one* and then she points at the host.

"Welcome back!" Chip Collins says. "I hope you haven't had too much coffee yet, because our next guests are sure to get your heart racing. Joining us from Washington, DC, is Tanya Nebling, an attorney and professor focusing on women's rights, and live in studio is one of our regular political commentators, Rachel Ives, who is currently serving as spokesperson for Michigan's Ralph Ruddy. Let's start there, if we may? Rachel, Ralph has come out strongly—very strongly—against paid maternity leave for women. Why is that?"

"Good morning, Chip! It's nice to be back. First, let me start by saying that you really are a chip off the old block, spouting the same ol', same ol' Fake News. Ralph Ruddy is pro-woman . . ."

"Whoa, whoa, whoa, let me stop you right there, Rachel," Chip says, his blue eyes blazing. "Can we put up the quote your candidate just made yesterday about paid maternity leave? There it is, Rachel, right in front of you. Mr. Ruddy said, and I quote, 'Men already pay enough when women are pregnant.' "

"That was a joke, Chip. And you know it. No one has a sense of humor anymore."

"But Mr. Ruddy has not only voted *against* paid maternity leave for women every single time, he's voted against women's *rights* at every turn, from equal pay to job protection to health care."

"As a woman, I wouldn't support a candidate

who didn't see women as equals, Chip. Ralph believes women don't need a handout, we need hands applauding for all we do!"

"Can I say something please?"

"Go ahead, Tanya."

"The United States is the only industrialized nation without a paid leave policy. Twenty-five years ago, President Clinton signed the Family and Medical Leave Act, which included a provision giving eligible workers twelve weeks of unpaid leave to care for a new child. Emphasis on *unpaid.* The United States remains the only country in the developed world that does not mandate employers offer paid leave for new mothers."

I take a deep breath and pounce. "Liberal claptrap from an out-of-touch deep-state *lawyer.*" I draw the last word out and sigh.

Tanya shakes her head and continues. "The typical household income falls by ten percent at the point of childbirth in the United States and doesn't fully recover until several months later when parents are back to work. For households headed by single women, the drop is even more drastic: 42 percent at the time of childbirth, with decreases happening in the months prior because of pregnancy-related reductions in hours worked."

"Small businesses comprise 99.9 percent of all US businesses," I say, speaking quickly but succinctly. People have the attention spans of gnats. "Small businesses employ nearly 50 percent of the country's total workforce. It would break these companies to do what you're asking. Is that better? You'd rather women have no jobs and be on unemployment than be able to take time off to care for their families AND have a job? You liberals amaze me."

"You're comparing apples to oranges, Rachel," Tanya says.

"An apple a day keeps the doctor away," I say. "Hopefully, an orange or two will keep the libs at bay. You need to get out of DC on occasion, Tanya. Talk to some real Americans."

"We're running short on time, I'm sorry to say." The camera cuts to Chip. "I'd like to thank my guests today for joining us. Back after the break."

"Thanks, Tanya," Dana says to the monitor.

Chip stands up and leaves without acknowledging me. I start to take off my mic, but Tanya says, "How do you live with yourself, Rachel?"

I don't answer.

"You don't have children, do you? You don't know what it's like to work your way through college holding down two jobs, be the first in your family to earn a degree, walk out thinking you can change the world and be confronted every day by self-loathing women like you who spout hate and whose only interest is in making themselves richer."

"You don't know me," I say.

"Oh, but I do," Tanya says, looking directly through the monitor at me. "My mother was a hospice nurse, and she used to say nearly every person she cared for at the end of their life was filled with regret. You won't just be filled with regret, Rachel. You'll be eaten alive by it."

Tanya stands and pulls off her mic, and the monitor is empty.

I remove my mic, stand and force a smile at Dana.

"We used to have some great late-night talks, didn't we?" Dana says.

For the first time, I realize how tired she looks. Dark bags are under her eyes.

"We did," I say, relieved she's remembering our years when we were a team.

"What happened to that girl?"

I feel as if I am paralyzed.

"What happened to all those friends you had growing up? The ones who used to check you and keep you down-to-earth, no matter what was going on in your life?"

My breath hitches, and I feel dizzy.

"The press is under siege these days," she continues, her voice filled with fury. "*Women* are under siege." Dana stops and looks at me for the longest time. "And you're leading the attack with knives disguised as alternative facts."

"Thank you for having me, Dana," I say. "Can't wait until you have me back."

Dana smiles sadly. "The question is, which side will you be on when you return, Rachel?"

I rush to the green room, grab my bag and a bottle of water and head to the car that is waiting for me outside the studio. "I'll meet you all in Michigan," I say to my staff, who will be following me to events later in the week.

"Airport?" the driver asks.

I nod and lean my throbbing head back against the seat, ignoring my buzzing cell. Once on the plane, I order a glass of wine and take an Ambien. In fitful spurts of sleep, I dream that I am Tanya, the opposite of who I am. When I open my eyes, a little girl is staring at me from across the aisle. Her hair is pulled back in a too-tight pony, giving her the look of a sprite.

"What do you do for a living?" she asks. "My dad is an author." She grabs her father's arm and gives it a tug. "He's on tour. People like to listen to what he makes up."

I nod sleepily. "I'm a magician," I say. "People like what I make up, too."

"Coooool," she says. "I'm going to visit my grandparents on Lake Michigan while my dad tours. My mom has to work."

"That will be fun."

"Have you ever been to Lake Michigan?"

I smile and nod. "I grew up in Michigan. When

I was a kid, I spent summers at a camp by the lake."

"Coooool," she says again. "It's like summer camp at my grandma and grandpa's."

The voice of our flight attendant comes on. "Prepare for landing."

When the plane lands, the girl waves good-bye, and I get in yet another car that will take me to yet another TV interview and hotel. My cell is buzzing endlessly, my head is screaming, and I pop two aspirin and slam a water, but nothing helps. I try to think of something to calm me. I think of the games I used to play as a kid with my parents when we'd drive up to Camp Birchwood, games like "Slug Bug," or the "Alphabet Game."

I see a sign for a U-Pick.

Apples, I think. How ironic.

Buick.

And then I see another sign that screams—even more ironically—CAMP! It's for a camp in northern Michigan, much like the one I attended as a kid. There are four girls jumping off a dock, arms intertwined, about to splash into the lake. They are screaming, laughing, happy. "Take A Leap Into A Summer Experience That Will Change Your Life!" the billboard says in giant letters beneath the picture.

As the car flies by, I stare into the girls' faces, and I am jolted back in time.

D, I think. Dad.

I feel sick and shut my eyes.

My phone buzzes and buzzes and buzzes.

"You received this letter," my assistant says. "Didn't have a return address. I scanned and emailed it to you. Thought you might want to read. Don't know if it's a scam or a letter from someone who hates you . . ."

"That doesn't narrow it down," I say.

My assistant doesn't laugh. "Oh, and remember, you're on air at 8:00 p.m. ET. Bye."

I hang up, open my email and begin to scan the letter, reading faster and faster, the words blurring, my heart racing.

. . . Let me get to the point, my dear Rach. Just picture me leaning my head over the bunk and telling you my deepest secret.

By the time you receive this, I'll be dead.

One of my hospice nurses—a mom of six who works nights so she can be at home with her kids before and after school—told me not to die with regret. She said the majority of her patients—no matter their age—are filled with regrets before they die. They regret working too much, not spending more time with their families, not traveling enough, not having more fun, not having more friends. I regret what we all did to each other. You,

V and Liz were my best friends and my entire life.

Let me ask you a question: What happens to friendships as we age? What happens to the people we used to be and the people we dreamed of becoming? I guess I was silly to hang on to all those memories, silly to believe that those were the best years of my life. But they were, Rach. They were. I became a different person, a better person, because of you, because of all of you. You made me whole. You made me feel safe, protected, loved. After I lost my brother, you made me feel like I had a family again. I didn't just save your life, Rach. You saved MINE!

Your life didn't have to turn out the way it did. We both know why you're doing what you do. But you have to forgive, Rach, or you, too, will end up filled with regret in the not-too-distant future. I thought of something while I was sick in bed and holding that four-leaf clover I found when we all first met: like forever, you can't spell forgiveness without our initials either.

Forgive, Rach. I know it might be the hardest for you to do, but you need your friends again, or you will end up even lonelier than you are now.

My phone trills. My assistant has attached a bunch of photos. I click out of the letter and open one, and a friendship pin stares back at me, a row of green beads hugging our initials as if we were all right beside each other once again.

I open another. It's the four of us jumping off the dock into the water, just like the photo on the billboard.

And another: a pressed four-leaf clover.

"Pull over," I suddenly say to the driver. "Please. I feel sick."

The driver pulls off to the side of the road, and I stumble out of the car and into a ditch filled with clover. I shut my eyes to stop the world from spinning. I think of camp. I think of Tanya's words this morning. I think of Em. I think of my dad and my mom. I take a deep breath, the Michigan summer air filling my lungs, and then bend over and put my hands on my hips.

The thumping of the car tires as they drive across a nearby overpass are rhythmic, like a song. My heart stops. I know this tune. Because it's a part of me. A part of me that I forgot a long time ago.

It was the best part of me.

Boom, didi, boom, boom . . . Booooom.

LIZ

PLEASE DON'T TOUCH
MRS. ANDERSON'S CLOTHES!
FAMILY WILL DO LAUNDRY AT HOME!!
LEAVE THEM IN BASKET FOR DAUGHTER!
THANK YOU!!

I stick the marker in my mouth and look over at Mrs. Dickens, who is wearing one of my mother's purple nightgowns. It is covered in food.

"Hi, Mitheth Dickensth!" I say with a faux chirp despite my irritation, the marker distorting my words.

Mrs. Dickens doesn't notice. She waves at me. She waves at everyone.

A bird lands on a feeder outside, and Mrs. Dickens turns toward the window and waves at it.

The piece of tape that held up the last sign I made still dangles from the tiny closet that sits across from my mother's bed. I stick the new one onto the door, open the top drawer to her wobbly cabinet and grab the new gowns I just purchased for her. I yank the marker from my mouth and write ANDERSON in big letters in the back.

My mother begins to cough, and I drop a gown and the marker. I rush to her side, pick up her giant tumbler of water and place the bendable straw in her mouth. My mom sputters and hacks before finally calming. She looks at me, her eyes soften and she lifts her hands—now hard, clenched stones—a few inches off her body and shakes them excitedly.

"Hi, Mom," I say. "You know me today? Liz? Your daughter?"

Her blue eyes, once as vibrant as a Michigan summer sky and now the color of a faded hydrangea, blink quickly.

"Oh, I love you, too," I say. I set the water bottle down. "Do you know how much I love you?" I spread my arms. "To the moon and back!" I say, and then rain her head with kisses. My mom smells like a baby.

My mom is a baby again.

She sighs and drifts off. The rag doll she loves to clutch has fallen to the floor, I now notice. I go to the other side of the bed and pick it up. I nestle it into the crook of my mother's arm.

Mrs. Dickens waves at me as I cross back to the closet.

"Hi, Mrs. Dickens!" I say.

I pick up the dropped gown and marker, and start anew.

Mrs. Dickens was my third-grade teacher here in Holland, the little Dutch town I grew up in and thought I would leave. I never did.

She was the sweetest woman in the world, and the one who taught me how to walk and dance in wooden shoes for the famed spring Tulip Time parade, where kids dress up to celebrate the town's heritage. Mrs. Dickens, it finally dawns on me, taught all the kids in her class to wave majestically at the crowd while marching.

They're here to see you, she would tell the class. *Wave to welcome them.*

I step inside the closet, shut the louvered door and begin to cry. This is my secret hiding spot when I need to release all the emotions that build inside me and then burst. To the world, I am Mount Rushmore; in here, I am Niagara Falls.

I press my face against my mother's new nightgown and weep. I cannot allow anyone to see me cry. I cannot allow anyone to know that I'm vulnerable. I am now the only remaining link in our family's chain, the final narrator of our family's history, the solid patch on my family's old quilt.

Sometimes, I think I'm the only strong one left in the world. Sometimes, I think I'm the weakest one in the world.

I open the closet door, and the rush of cool air—along with the smell of—*what is that today, meatloaf?*—fills my nose. I inhale and steady myself.

I fold my mom's nightgowns and arrange them in her drawer. I swear these have legs, because they walk constantly, no matter how many I buy, no matter how many times I write my mom's name in them, no matter how many signs I post on the closet door.

My mom used to love purple. It was her signature color. Even the flowers she planted—petunias, tulips, salvia, lavender—had to be purple. When she first moved into Manor Court, I used to embellish my mom's clothes. I'd add a pretty collar to her sweatshirt, or shiny crystals down the sides of her pants. Now those would rip her tissue-paper skin apart.

I take a seat by my mother's bed. I open my cell and check my messages. There are a million texts from work as well as my kids and grandkids:

> The Olsens want to see the home at 421 Lakeshore Drive at 5:30 p.m. instead of 5. Does that work?

> Mom, can you pick up my dry cleaning?

> Grandma, would you buy me a new phone?

I don't answer any of the texts. Instead, I click on my Etsy shop.

VINTAGE GIRL IN A MODERN WORLD

I am a real estate agent, caregiver, mother and grandmother. Only one of those allows for any flexibility. I am the baloney in the sandwich generation. But I still fancy—and always have fancied—myself a designer. I have designed my own clothes forever and am fascinated by the resurgence in the popularity of vintage clothing. Kendall, Kylie and all the Coachella girls wear the things I wore in the '70s and '80s. And don't even get me started about high-waisted jeans and tiny belts. I invented that look.

Not you, V.

"Oh!" I say, looking at my site. I have four new orders. Two people want the knockoff Members Only jackets I'm making.

"Hi, Mrs. Anderson."

An aide rushes in carrying a tray of food my mother won't eat.

"Hi, Mrs. Anderson," she says again to me.

I still have trouble responding to my maiden name after so many years of being married.

"Hi, Tammy."

The aide pulls my mom's bed table across her lap and sets the tray down.

Mrs. Dickens waves at her.

"You're next," Tammy says.

I watch my mom sleep. She is rail-thin and rarely eats. Often she will knock the spoon from my hand and scream, just like a toddler that hates its first taste of carrots. She is my mother, and she is not my mother. She is dying, and—though it sounds awful and I despise myself for even thinking it—I am not only coming to peace with that but I am also praying the end comes sooner rather than later.

The aide whisks back in and leaves the tray for Mrs. Dickens, who tries to feed herself, dropping half the food on the way to her mouth on the gown I purchased for my mom. I get up and take the spoon from her hand. I feed her, slowly, and Mrs. Dickens coos her happiness. I look out the window, and I have a vivid memory of sitting in her class. As part of her history class, Mrs. Dickens used to have an international food day, when she would cook foods from around the world. Growing up in Michigan, we were pretty much used to meat and potatoes, so many of the children did not react well to tasting cumin, garlic or curry. She would always hold up a spoon with a tiny bit of a tamale, lasagna, paella or butter chicken and ask us to try it.

What's the worst thing that could happen? You hate it, she would say. *And what's the best thing? You'll love it and change the way you eat forever.*

To this day, I adore all of those things she made.

I hold up the spoon, and Mrs. Dickens smiles.

I have the urge to run to the closet and weep yet again, but I smile, too, and tell her of my memories.

Mrs. Dickens had a husband who passed, and a daughter who lives in Detroit. She shows up a couple of times a year, with great fanfare, her kids sometimes in tow, and stays for maybe an hour.

"Bye, Mom," she always says, before looking at me. "I don't know how you can do it."

I don't know how I cannot do it.

I wipe Mrs. Dickens's mouth when she's done, move the tray and return to my mom. She is still sound asleep. I pick up her spoon, take a bite of meatloaf and mashed potatoes, and then another.

Stop it, Liz, I tell myself. *You don't need to eat this.*

My phone trills again, and I pick up the spoon instead. The potatoes are buttery and salty, the meatloaf rich with ketchup. I finish and start on the chocolate pudding.

"Wow, your mom was a good eater today," Tammy says when she returns.

I nod.

I planned and planned and planned, but I never planned for any of this: I didn't plan for my husband to leave me after our kids were grown. I didn't plan to stay in my little hometown forever. I didn't plan for my father to die and have my mother fall ill immediately after that tragedy. I didn't plan to be the caretaker to a family who doesn't seem to care about me or its history.

Friends offer more support to me and my mom than family. The people she touched randomly at church, in her neighborhood, in the women's club or volunteering have deeper affection and connection than her own children and grand-children.

I look up, my heart racing. Mrs. Dickens waves yet again at me.

I see this as a privilege. There should be a dignity in the way we age and die, and to care for someone at the end of his or her life, as they did for us when we were babies, when we were growing up, when we were ill, is a blessing. I also believe it shows the character of who we truly are.

I text my daughter, Lisa.

> With grandma. Can't get your dry cleaning. Have a showing after this. Are you coming out to see her this week?

My heart begins to race as little moving dots on my phone show Lisa is already texting.

> Can't. Too busy.

More dots.

> And you know Dan and I don't want the kids to see her like that.

Like what? I think. *Like an old woman who still needs love?*

Why do I still ask? Why do I do this to myself?

They have never come to visit. *Ever.* Not to see the woman whose back was bent like a peony stem because she spent decades sewing overalls in a factory. Not to see the woman who saved pennies so I could go to camp and be the first in our family to go to college. Not to see the woman who helped raise you and who cared for your children countless nights. Not to see the woman whose sacrifices helped you have the life you have now, the one that is better than the one she ever had, which is all she wanted in this life.

How dare you!

My voice echoes in the little room, and I jump. I have yelled this out loud.

"Everything okay?"

Tammy peeks her head in the door.

I nod.

She leaves, and I stand and walk into the closet. I shut the door and cry.

I know my mom knows. Deep down, she knows her family has not come to see her. I think that's a reason she holds on. To see them one more time.

But I have already come to the saddest realization of all: not only will they never come to see her, but they will not come to see me either.

What keeps me up at night, what makes my soul shudder is not the question—because that was answered long ago—but the reality: my children will not be there to care for me when I'm old. They've already proven it.

They will shuffle me off, and I will be forgotten. They don't even want the heirlooms I
have—my handwritten recipes, Grandma's hutch
and cameos, my desert rose dishes and charm
bracelets—the things that tell the story of our
family, the things that have been passed down
for generations. They are already boxed away,
useless, like my memories. Things of the past—
elders, heirlooms—are no longer valuable. We
want new and fresh. To be reminded of the past
means we are not immortal, and today's generation does not like that. If we are not in the
moment, if we are not current, we are useless.

My phone trills, and I reach for it reluctantly.

I smile.

Another sale in my Etsy shop. For a pair of the
plastic geometric earrings I make.

And yet, I think, everything old is new again
because no one remembers our past.

I open the door, and Tammy is staring at me.

"I thought you'd left. Are you sure you're
okay?"

"I got stuck," I say, "putting up my mother's
gowns."

"It's okay to cry," she says kindly. "I do it every
night on my way home." She winks. "Buy you a
cup of free coffee?"

I smile. "I have to run to a showing," I say.
"Next time?"

She nods.

I take the back roads to my office, located in downtown Holland, a quaint historic district filled only with independent businesses that feels pretty much like it did when I was growing up. The streets still bustle with shoppers, and the sidewalks are heated, so that—in the winter—the snow melts. Downtown is a throwback, but real estate prices are not. I park and get out of my car. In fact, half-acre lots alone on the lakeshore run a million dollars today.

I should have bought lots of lots in 2008, I think.

My agency sits on the second floor of an old brick building above a coffee shop. I've spent more than one of my commissions on lattes, but it's a luxury I love and the smallest of comforts for me these days.

"White chocolate latte," I say to the young barista with purple bangs and cat-eye makeup. "Coconut milk, please. And three shots of espresso."

"Whip?" she asks.

"No. Yes. No. Yes. No."

She laughs.

"Maybe I should ask the Magic 8-Ball."

A puzzled look covers her face. She has no idea what I'm talking about.

"I'll write *light whip* on the cup? How's that?"

"Perfect."

"That'll be four-fifty," she says.

I should have taken Tammy up on that free coffee, I think.

I grab my latte and head upstairs. My agency is small. I am a boutique real estate agent representing fine homes on Lake Michigan and historic cottages on Lake Macatawa and Castle Park, which inspired the setting for *The Wizard of Oz*. I have only one other agent, but I'm the town elder, and I know who owned what and when and where before most of the other agents in town were even born. In fact, I grew up playing in a lot of these homes before I started going to summer camp every year.

"Lots of calls," my assistant, Annie, says.

"People want to take advantage of these low mortgage rates," I say.

"And lots of people just want a slice of Pure Michigan," she says.

I sip my latte. Annie looks at the side of my cup.

"Sure you need three shots?"

"Yes," I say.

"And should I start calling you 'Light Whip'?"

I laugh. "I'll be in my office."

I turn, and Annie says, "Oh, wait. The mail."

She hands a stack to me. "There's a weird letter in there, too. No return address."

I hold it to my head and start to do a Carnac the Magnificent impression, just like Johnny Carson used to do with an unread envelope. But Annie is only slightly older than the barista, and I know she wouldn't get it much less know who Johnny Carson was.

"Thanks," I say.

I head into my office and close the door. I take a seat in my swivel chair with a big sigh and take an even bigger sip of my latte. The caffeine jolts me, and I feel emboldened enough to tackle my calls. When I finish a half hour later, I turn my attention toward the letter.

I open it warily. It has the look and feel of letters I receive from passive-aggressive clients who are upset after the fact—often years later—that a water pipe has burst or the dishwasher has gone on the fritz, and they want me to know how disappointed they are in me.

The letter is thick, and I steel myself for what awaits.

I open it, and a friendship pin—screaming E-V-E-R!—tumbles forth, and I immediately know who the letter is from: Emily.

How sweet, I think. A letter from Em. She loves writing them. I bet she's on vacation.

> . . . I thought of something in bed, while I was holding that four-leaf clover I found when we all first met. Like forever, you can't spell forgiveness without our initials either.
>
> Forgive, Liz.

Start with yourself.

After all we went through, why did The Clover Girls end up losing touch? I know, I know, we tell ourselves that's just what happens when we grow older and become adults. And I know how deeply we hurt each other. But are those the only reasons? Or does pride have something to do with it, too? We all know the truth.

I stop, my heart catching. I take another deep breath and continue:

I think of you and your mom often, Liz. You are as kind and wonderful as she is. And I hope that you will never give up on your dreams of being a designer. Thanks for sending me all of those friendship bracelets you designed a few years ago. Where did you EVER get such an idea? Ha!

The last few years have not been easy. I was diagnosed with metastatic breast cancer two years ago, and though I underwent treatment, I've decided not to fight any longer. I'm sorry I lied to you about my health all this time. Believe me, it wasn't easy. But I know how overwhelmed you are, Liz, and I just didn't want to add any more stress to your—

or V's or Rach's—life. As you know, I never married or had kids, so I got used to being alone. But being alone isn't so great when you're sick. So, while I was still feeling okay, I opted to spend my last few summer weeks at camp. I guess I just wanted to be surrounded by friends, at least in spirit.

I jumped in the lake and screamed like a girl when my body hit the cold water. I made s'mores over a campfire. I painted watercolors of beautiful white birch, I hiked the dunes, and I watched the sun set. And on an evening walk back to camp, I found a four-leaf clover. I knew it was a sign, a sign of hope, a sign that paradise still exists and a sign that perhaps—just perhaps—The Clover Girls could be whole again.

I finally realized it's the little things that are the biggest things in life.

Like friends.

Mostly, I realized that life is as short as one blink of God's eye, and it's what we make of that single blink that matters.

My friendship with The Clover Girls was what mattered most to me.

Though I've long been the stem that tenuously held the four of us together, I know deep in your heart—despite everything that happened—you still consider Rach and V to be your best friends. And do you know why? Because we were all our best when we were together. We felt like we could be anything we dreamed.

I have one final request: I've written to ask the three of you to scatter my ashes at Camp Birchwood. Toss me into the summer sunset, and let the wind carry me onto the lake. Scatter me over the field of clover so I can rest forever with the FOUR-evers. I'm already there. You just have to show up. The funeral home has delivered my ashes to Camp Birchwood. I will be sitting at the entrance to our old bunkhouse waiting for you.

Don't worry. No one will disturb me. Camp Birchwood is for sale. Did you know that? It hasn't been a camp for a few years now. Family has it in their estate, and the kids are fighting over what to do with it. I stayed a couple of nights in Pinewood Bunk. It was just me, the owls, a few mice, a couple of raccoons, some curious deer and a nosy bear. It wasn't scary at all. In fact, I've never felt safer. I thought a lot about my brother, Todd, and how nice it will be to see him again. I wonder if he's still the same little kid. Like we used to be. I also thought a lot about my parents. They're the reason I met all of you. And you're all the reason I became strong again after Todd's death.

Now I want you all to be strong again after mine.

I love you, Liz, and I always have. More than anything. Whenever I hear "Girls Just Want to Have Fun," I dance. And whenever I hear "That's What Friends Are For," I cry. And whenever I hear girls giggling with their best friends, I smile.

If you, or The Clover Girls, decide not to come, I understand.

I'll still be there.

Waiting for you.

Until we meet again.
xoxo,
Em

I am crying so hard that my tears are staining the letter.

She didn't forget. She never forgot. I chide my kids for forgetting, but what have I done? I hid my memories away just like all of those Polaroid pictures.

I hook the friendship pin onto the lapel of my jacket, grab my binder about the home I'm showing and walk out.

"Who was the letter from?" Annie asks as I

scurry past so she won't see my puffy eyes. "Who writes letters anymore?"

We do, I want to say. *Us old people.* When words —and friendships—meant something. When we wanted to say something deeper than a four-word text.

I don't answer. I speed to the old shingled cottage with my For Sale sign in front, unlock the front door, and rush from room to room, turning on lights and opening windows. It is a stunning late summer day. The wind is from the east, and the lake is as flat, shiny and iridescent blue as a piece of beach glass. After years of living and selling on Lake Michigan, I know *this* is the main selling point. And a day like today is the reason we all want to live on the lake. I head out the sliding doors and down the winding beach steps to the deck overlooking the water. The lake looks drenched in diamonds, and on this cloudless day, you can see for miles, the shoreline arcing its back like a sleepy dog, the dune grass its fur blowing in the breeze.

Boats zip by in the near distance, the smell of gas on water. I shut my eyes, and the sun on my face transports me back in time. The lapping of the water moves in sync with my heart. The waves sing a song I packed away long ago like an old mix tape, but—like a favorite old tune—I still remember every word, no matter how much time has passed.

Blue lake and rocky shore,
I will return once more,
Boom, didi, boom, boom,
Boom, didi, boom, boom,
Boom, didi, boom, boom . . . Booooom.

PART TWO
Candles on the Lake

SUMMER 1988

"Where's Rachel?"

Liz ducks her head and quietly takes a seat on the beach in front of Birchwood Lake.

"Do you know, Liz?" V asks innocently, sitting down in front of Liz, who's uncapping a lipstick tube.

Liz shrugs.

"No clue," V says. "She can be a total space cadet. Not reliable at all. Right?"

Liz nods and applies brick-red lipstick to V's bee-stung lips.

"We can't wait any longer," the photographer says. "The light is already fading."

It is dusk, and an entourage from *Life* magazine mills about the lake. Each has a specific task: one mans the lights, one holds a light reflector, one is lighting candles and setting them onto the lake, one is even herding fireflies to move closer to the shoot.

"Ready, V?" the photographer asks. "Just you now."

V stands and moves toward the shoreline. A young woman hands her a candle. Lights pop on.

"Act like no one is around," the photographer says. "It's just you. At camp. Leading the ceremony."

V holds the candle to her face. Its flame flickers in the breeze off the lake. She smiles, slightly, as if she's holding a powerful secret, and angles her face back so the light shimmers in her eyes. V slowly moves into the water, until she is waist-deep, and the green camp T-shirt she is wearing—which Liz has torn to fall down over one shoulder—is wet at the bottom.

V places the candle on the surface of the lake. She gives it a little push with her hands and then raises them as if she is saying a prayer, water trickling off her fingertips.

The candle drifts into the middle of the lake, along with all the others the crew has already released. Fireflies blink, and as if by magic, one lands on the tip of V's perfect little nose and flashes.

"We have our cover!" the photographer yells, his voice echoing over the lake. "V, you're a natural!"

V emerges from the lake, and a woman instantly wraps a cushy towel around her body.

"Are you chilled?" she asks, her voice alarmed.

"No, I'm fine," V says.

"We can't have you get sick," she says, drying her off and rubbing her shoulders to warm her body. "We need you tomorrow. You're our star!"

The words warm V's body even more than the towel, and she can feel herself leave her body and drift high above the camp where she can see not only the entire world but her whole future in front of her.

"Sorry I'm late!"

Rachel rushes onto the shore.

"Where do you need me? What do I need to do?"

The photographer looks at her and shakes his head.

"Timing is everything in this business," he says. "Time is money."

"But there was a note on my bunk," she pleads. "To meet on the point of the big lake instead. I waited. On my way back, I saw all the lights."

"We're already done for the night, sweetheart," an assistant says. "V handled it all. Beautifully."

Rach looks at V, who shrugs innocently.

"We won't need you tomorrow either."

The photographer's voice is void of emotion.

"That's a wrap for tonight," he says.

Rach's eyes fill with tears.

"It's a wrap," another assistant calls. "We need some music to celebrate!"

"*If You Leave*" by Orchestral Manoeuvres in the Dark from the movie Pretty in Pink begins to play.

"I love this song!" someone yells.

Rach looks from V to Liz and back again, her face shattered.

She takes off running.

No one moves.

"Dance, V!" someone yells.

V moves in the twilight, the words of the song breaking her heart.

SUMMER 2021
VERONICA

"What are you watching?"

"A John Hughes marathon."

"Who's that?"

I sigh. My daughter is standing in the doorway watching me watch *The Breakfast Club*, an expression on her face that is partly bemused and partly concerned.

How do you explain your childhood to your children? How do you explain what these seemingly silly comedies meant to you growing up? It's like explaining rotary phones, TV antennas, Walkmans, mood rings, typewriters and handwritten directions.

They meant *everything*.

And even more now.

You know what I hear when I discuss idols from childhood—John Hughes, Erma Bombeck, The Go-Go's? Crickets. You know what I see? Blank stares.

I sneaked into a Starbucks the other day, and when the barista asked a young man for his name, he said, "Walter." I replied, "Oh, wow! I haven't heard that name in forever. I adored Walter Cronkite." Crickets. Blank stares. From both the young man and the barista. I babbled, explaining who he was, but when I left, I became angry. I understand pop culture changes. I understand that there are massive differences between generations. I understand that kids are kids. But, with a world of information at our fingertips, why aren't we more curious? I mean, I knew who Frank Sinatra was growing up. I knew the Beatles, just as I knew Madonna. It almost seems lazy that there is so little intellectual curiosity despite everything just a Google search away.

"Mom? Who's John Hughes?"

I can hear the soundtrack from his movies echo in my head. My heart breaks.

How do you explain old ghosts that continue to haunt you?

"A guy who directed a bunch of very successful teen comedies when I was a kid," I say.

"What's this about?"

"A group of teenagers from different high school cliques who have to spend a Saturday together in detention." I stop and look up at her. "They really get to know about each other and why they are the way they are because of their lives and their families. It's about how we get stereotyped without people ever knowing us."

"Do they become friends?" she asks.

I lift my shoulders. "For the day," I say. "They understand one another. Then they go back to who they were." I stop. "Like life."

I think of Rach, Em and Liz, and I will myself not to cry. I pat the couch. "Want to watch a little bit with me?"

Ashley looks uncertain. "Okay," she says.

I move my legs, lift up the blanket, and she slides in beside me. This is not common in our home. Lying around watching TV. Slacking, as we used to call it in school. Our television is hidden in a den at the back of the house. Sliding frosted glass doors close off the space, which is filled with my favorite things: a TV, beloved books, a comfy couch, McCoy vases, candles that smell like pine and campfires, and one of my grandma's old quilts. None of these things are midcentury modern. I take that back: I'm definitely midcentury these days. Just not so mod anymore.

"Want a Little Debbie?" I ask.

Ashley looks at me. "What?"

I reach into the cushions and pull out a box of Swiss Rolls.

"Mother!" she says. "You are a sneak."

I open a packet. "They are so good," I say. "And, look, if you chew the chocolate just right on the bottom, you can unroll it and lick out all the crème filling."

My daughter stares at me.

"Stop it," I say. "Just try a bite."

She takes a Swiss Roll and has a teeny bite. And then a bigger one. She downs the Little Debbie in four bites.

"Attagirl!" I say, laughing.

"What else do you have hidden around here?" she asks.

A lot of secrets, I don't say.

We watch the movie, before my daughter suddenly sits up on the couch and exclaims, "Oh, my God, Mom! You look just like her!"

She is pointing at the TV, her finger jabbing the air.

"I know," I say.

"Who is that?"

"Molly Ringwald," I say. "She was *the* actress of the '80s. *The Breakfast Club, Sixteen Candles, Pretty in Pink . . .*"

"Mom, no, this is, like, really weird. She looks just like you!"

"Wanna hear a story?" I ask. Ashley nods. "I rarely tell anyone this, but it was hard for me in school."

"You? The model?"

"I wasn't always a model. I was once a red-haired girl with freckles who wasn't blonde and pretty and hippie-chic like all the other girls. Everyone—and I mean everyone—thought I was ugly. They called me Carrot Top, Pippi Long-stocking, Ember, Big Red, Gingersnap . . ." I stop, remembering a nasty nickname, my face flushing.

"Are you okay? You can tell me."

"No, it's too embarrassing. Let me just say boys said even cruder things to me."

Ashley puts her hand on my shoulder. "Mom," she says softly. "I'm so sorry."

"And then along came Molly Ringwald," I say, nodding at her on TV. "She not only made redheads cool, she made them pretty. I went to summer camp not long after *Sixteen Candles* came out in theaters, and Molly was all the rage. And just because I looked like her, everyone at camp immediately thought I was beautiful. Girls were jealous of my looks. Boys liked me. Everyone wanted to be my friend." I stop, thinking again of The Clover Girls. "It changed my life and gave me confidence. I realized that being different was cool." The movie goes to commercial, and I reach for the remote and mute the TV. "I know I've told you some of this story before, but not everything. My last year at summer camp, I was a head counselor along with all my best friends from there. When we got to Birchwood our last summer, we learned that *Life* magazine was coming to do a photo essay on the fading appeal of girls' sleepaway summer camps in America. I was chosen to be the face of our camp. When the article was published and I got home from camp, every major modeling agency in the US wanted to sign me. That launched my career. I worked very hard, but I know I was also lucky. And I know that my friends believed in me."

Liar! You still can't tell the whole story. You

73

still can't be honest with yourself. You duped your best friend to get ahead.

I take a breath and continue: "You know that letter I got the other day?"

"The jump-in-the-pool letter? Yeah." Pause. "You know, I was really worried about you."

"I know," I say. I grab her hand. "I'm sorry." I look toward the TV. "The letter was from Emily, my old summer camp friend. The one who stayed in touch with me over the years. Remember?"

"I remember."

"She died of breast cancer."

"Oh, Mom. I'm so sorry."

"Thanks, honey. I wasn't such a good friend, though. I didn't know she was sick. I wasn't a very good friend to any of my friends actually." My voice trails off. "We all lost touch with each other after camp."

"That happens, though, right? Everyone grows up and moves away."

"Yeah, it does," I say. "But it shouldn't. Especially not with these friends. In her letter, Emily had a final request for all of us: she wants us to reunite in Michigan and scatter her ashes at the camp."

"Oooh. That sounds creepy."

"I know, but it's not. It's where she says she was the happiest. It's where she went to spend some of her last good days, to be surrounded by happy memories." I stop. "To be surrounded by her friends."

"Are you going?"

"I don't know yet. I need to talk with your dad, and see if he thinks it's a good idea. You and Tyler will be away at camp, so the timing is good."

The Breakfast Club comes back on, and I turn the volume back up. As the movie continues, I watch Ash settle into the couch. Her eyes are riveted on the TV, and we watch it until the very end. Ash tears up when the letter the teens have written in detention—about conforming and how society stereotypes us before we've even dis-covered who we are—is read.

"Can I ask you something?" I say as the credits roll.

"Depends," Ash says with a laugh.

"Do your father and I put too much pressure on you? I mean, that's a lot of what this movie is about."

"Truth?"

I nod.

"Sometimes," she says, shifting her weight and sitting up on the couch. "I'm still figuring things out. So's Ty. Sometimes, we feel like we're already adults, competing, running full sprint to get ahead. You know what I mean? But some-times we just want to be kids still. Blow off a day, have fun . . ." She stops. "Like we're doing right now." She stops again. "Can I ask *you* something?"

"Shoot."

"Do you feel like Dad puts too much pressure on you?"

I inhale sharply. My child is very perceptive and empathetic.

"Sometimes," I say. "Sometimes I think he wants me to be as perfect as his designs or as perfect as this house. I spent my career trying to be perfect. And there's no such thing." I stop. "He has very high expectations because he's been so successful, and that can be a good thing. It can also be a bad thing."

There is silence for a while as Simple Minds sing and the credits continue to roll.

"I think you're perfect, Mom," Ash finally says.

My heart leaps.

"Thank you, honey," I say. "But, believe me, I'm not."

"You're you, and that's cool," she says. "And you've been a great mom. I mean, for us to move so many times for Dad's career, for you to sacrifice your own career and make me and Ty always feel safe, is pretty amazing." She stops. "You need to know that."

"Thank you," I say.

"And you want to know something else, Mom? You're really lucky. To have friends like you did is special. I mean, I have friends, but they're not ones who know everything about me, all my hopes and dreams and secrets. We've moved so much, I don't know if I'll ever have friends like that. And maybe you need them in your life right now. Maybe that's what the universe is telling you." She stops and laughs, before adding, "And *The Breakfast Club*, too."

Ash reaches over and hugs me, and then leaves me on the couch.

I curl up in a little ball and remember Em at summer camp. The Clover Girls thought we would always be friends. We thought we would never die.

Why did I walk away? Why didn't I call?

"Em," I whisper, finally allowing myself to say her name. I take a deep breath and say the other names, too, for the first time in ages. "Rach. Liz. I'm so sorry."

"Are you sick?"

I wake with a start.

My husband is standing over me, arms crossed, a look of disapproval covering his face.

I sit up, panicked, feeling around my body for the Little Debbies.

I've hidden them, thank goodness.

"Not sick," I say. "Just . . . sad." I pat the couch and pull the blanket around me. He doesn't sit. "One of my friends from camp died. Emily. Remember?"

"The one who stayed in touch with all of . . . What was that nickname you had for each other?"

"The Clover Girls."

"I'm sorry to hear that," he says. "It had been forever since you talked to her, though, right?"

I nod even though I want to shake my head at him. *Typical David.* He can box everything up neatly and put it away so it doesn't clutter his mind or world. I mean, he's the only man I know who can wear linen all day in the heat without it wrinkling.

"It was my fault," I say. "I was a bad friend to her. I was a bad friend to all my friends. I stopped trying." I look at him. "Listen, I want to talk to you about something."

"Yes."

"Em sent a letter, and her final request was for the remaining Clover Girls to meet at our old summer camp in Michigan and scatter her ashes. I think I need to do it, David. Not just for her but for me."

"You need closure?" he asks. "You need to say goodbye?"

"I need to say hello, too," I tell him.

David cocks his head at me, not understanding.

"This is an insane time for me right now, V."

"It's always an insane time for you, David." My voice rises. I didn't intend for it to do that. "I'm just asking for a few days. Maybe a week, okay?"

"A week to scatter some ashes?" he asks.

"Don't do this, David. The kids will be gone. I don't ask for much, David. You know that."

He takes off his glasses and rubs his eyes as if he's considering my request.

"I'm not asking, David," I say.

"Then maybe you need this time." There is a long, awkward pause. "Maybe *we* need this time. Apart."

The last word is riddled with nuance.

"That sounds ominous."

"Time will tell, won't it?" he says, before taking the blanket from me, folding it perfectly and tossing it at an angle across the arm of the sofa, a soft but overt signal that my time doing nothing is officially over.

RACHEL

I have the '80s station on the satellite radio blasting, windows down.

The wind is blowing my hair around my head, I am nearly makeup-free—so *not* TV-ready today—and I'm singing at the top of my lungs.

I am heading north, and that is the ideal direction to head in summer in Michigan. But the irony and tragedy involved with this sudden road trip—and the fact that the timing couldn't be worse with midterm elections right around the corner—makes me feel as though I should turn the car around.

I already know they hate me. And they know I hate them. Our glue is gone. There is no reason to make amends after what they did to me.

I slow the car.

And then I think of Em.

Do it for her. Only her.

There's something I have to tell you, Rachel, I can still hear Em say our last summer together. *Just promise that you won't let it destroy everything.*

Just north of Manistee, there is a discernible change in the scenery as well as the temperature. Dense pines fill the countryside, and the forests darken. Rivers and little lakes dot the hills, and paper birch stand at their shorelines drenched in sunlight, their beautiful white bark peeling as if they just experienced a bad sunburn. When my parents would drive me to camp, my mom would make my dad stop nearly every time she saw a stand of birch so she could gather the bark for DIY projects. She made birch bark lamps, candle holders and coffee tables.

"Your mother would wrap me in birch if she could," my father would joke, our trunk filled with white bark.

"Just your mouth, Harold," my mom would reply.

The sight of birch nearly makes me cry. My heart aches, and I can't make it stop hurting, so I turn up the music even louder.

How long has it been? I think.

My dad was a Detroit auto executive, a union man who started on the assembly line and worked his way up. My mom campaigned for JFK. My father was my hero.

What would he think of me now?

I know what my family thinks: to see consistently blue Michigan turn red—and to realize that I had a lot to do with that—was a divide most could no longer bridge. In fact, it *was* as if the Mackinac Bridge had collapsed, and I was the Upper Peninsula of Michigan and my family was the Lower Peninsula.

Politics has not only divided families into

different camps, it has also driven a wedge between the entire country. And I've made a living—a good living—exploiting that divide. It used to be that the two parties could come together in the best interests of the country, but today's political system is like *The Hunger Games*.

My car continues to head north, and it chugs up a hill. As I near the top, Walloon Lake— where Ernest Hemingway spent his boyhood summers—stretches out beneath me. It is a deep, glacier-formed lake that is ringed with historic cottages, eventually flowing into Lake Michigan. I inhale the air on this perfect summer day, where the sky is so blue it seems as if God has Photoshopped it Himself. I think of Hemingway. He once wrote of this area, "It's great northern air. Absolute freedom."

I know, because I've used his words—and his alpha male persona—to promote many candidates in these northern Michigan districts.

"Why no women, Rachel?" my mom asked me a few years ago when we were still talking. "Maybe that's something you ought to ask yourself. Why aren't you out there seeking and nurturing women if you actually care about changing the world?"

I shake my head and realize I'm in need of junk food. It's not a road trip if there's no junk food. Twizzlers. Combos. Funyuns. That's my dirty travel secret.

"Fuel?" I ask my car.

"The distance to your destination is ninety-two miles. You can drive seventy-four miles with your current fuel."

"Thank you," I say to my car for some reason.

I think of driving up to summer camp as a teenager. I used to put in five bucks of gas and see how far it would get me in my big tank of a car. There were summers when gas was eighty-some cents a gallon. Back then, my gas gauge was like a spastic butterfly, the needle flittering back and forth from empty to a quarter of a tank, me praying I could make it to the next station to put in another couple of bucks and buy some Hot Fries.

I pull over at a rural gas station. Junk food hasn't changed. Like gas, it's only gotten more expensive.

I fill up my tank and then head inside to stock up on sugar and carbs.

A pack of girls in still-wet swimsuits race around the store. They have Drumsticks and bottles of Vernors, Michigan's favorite soda, the gingeriest-ginger pop that tickles your tongue.

Pure Michigan, I think. Hemingway knew. It was magic to be a kid in Michigan during the summer.

For a moment, I am lost in memories. I think of all the times The Clover Girls would sneak away from camp in the middle of the night. Sometimes, when we were still girls, we would inch our way out of our bunks and tiptoe to the kitchen, where we'd steal Lucky Charms and Count Chocula and shove them into our mouths as if it were our last meal. When we got older and became counselors, we'd sneak out after all the campers had gone to bed and bike to the party store a couple of miles away in the woods—the ones hunters went to— and beg strangers to buy us beer.

V would always ask why they called it a "party store" in Michigan and not a "liquor store."

Party stores are where you buy party supplies, like for Halloween, Mardi Gras and birthdays, she'd argue. *Liquor stores are where you buy, you know, liquor.*

Welcome to Michigan. We'd laugh. *We party. But it's a secret.*

Michigan "secrets."

I gather my supplies and head to the counter.

"Oh, my gosh, I just love you on TV."

I'm always startled when people remember me from my old show, *Sorority Sisters*, although it's a mainstay on late-night cable TV these days.

I look up. The cashier, an older woman with a smock emblazoned with I GOT GAS! written in big letters across the front, is pointing at me. That's what people do if you're on TV: they point at you as if you're an inanimate object or a zoo animal.

"Thank you," I say. "Can't believe that old show is still on the air."

"What old show?" she asks, her eyebrows twitching. "I'm talkin' about all those dang news shows. Man, you give those city folk a hard time." She raises her head and hoots.

For some reason, this catches me off guard.

"Thank you," I finally manage to say.

She bags my junk food and pushes it toward me.

"How much?" I ask.

"On the house," she whispers conspiratorially.

"Thank you," I say again.

I grab the bag and walk away.

"Love you!" she yells.

I begin to head out the door, but stop. "Why?" I ask. "Why do you love me?"

"Because you're one of us," she says. "Because you say what we're all thinkin'."

"Which is what?" I ask.

"You know," she says, before looking around. "Women don't belong in the White House. We shouldn't be CEOs and doctors and leaders and all that. We should let the men do that. They know better."

My heart sinks. This is a good woman, who is working hard to have a better life. It's not about politics, it's about setting the right example for people. I think of my former camp directors and the influence they had on so many young girls.

As I walk to my car, I watch the little girls in swimsuits load into their mom's SUV. A massive inflatable rainbow unicorn is tied to the roof.

They girls wave at me as they leave the station. Little girls who still believe in magic and that they can do and be anything they dream.

Just like I once did.

I pull my car back onto the road and reach for my Twizzlers. I dangle one in my mouth, and I remember how much Em loved red licorice.

She was the one who encouraged me to be an actress. She was the one who encouraged me to forgive and forget. She was the one who told me the truth and changed everything.

You're so talented, Em said. *You can be one of our greatest actresses. Like Ally Sheedy. Prove to everyone that you can do it.*

She wrote me letters nearly every month while I was on the set and she was earning her master's degree in library science. She always loved to write letters. She loved to read. She believed in the power of words. She sent me scenes from plays for auditions.

I think of the last letter she sent me years ago, when I first started appearing on the news.

You're still acting, but I know this is a role you don't believe in or want to play, she wrote. Sorority Sisters *was harmless. This isn't. Go back to acting. Make people smile. Like you used to do at camp.*

Em had sent a photo of me performing Michael Jackson's "Thriller." I don't know if she was trying to tell me I had become a zombie now, if I used to be talented, or both.

I sent Em her letter back, my own words written over hers in a bright red Sharpie.

ACTING.
WE ALL DO IT.
IN RELATIONSHIPS.
IN CAREER. IN LIFE.
YOU'RE STILL ACTING.
LIKE A CHILD.
REMEMBER THIS FROM CHILDHOOD?
LIAR, LIAR, PANTS ON FIRE!
GROW UP, EM.
WE'RE NOT KIDS ANYMORE.

I never spoke to her again, though she still tried to stay in touch. I never spoke to any of those traitors again. All I wanted to do was prove them wrong: I would make it on my own.

I inhale, and the scent of Michigan—pine, water, summer—fills my lungs.

I now realize that Em never acted. She never pretended to be anyone other than she was. Maybe the loss of her brother made her realize how short life is, and she didn't have time to play all the games we play as adults. Or maybe she knew her time here was limited.

In the distance I see a lake and am suddenly back at camp. Em's arms are around me, holding me, saving me.

The landscape spins, and I get dizzy. I slow the car and try to slow my heart. I can't get her letter out of my head. Or this memory. I can't be released from Em's grip.

Guilt has eaten me alive for years.

How many times did she try to save my life?

I try to drown out my thoughts, so I turn up the radio on the '80s station.

Tears for Fears is singing. "Everybody Wants to Rule the World."

The irony is literally too much for me to bear.

I reach for a Twizzler and then another—the licorice as red as the last words I wrote to Em— hoping the junk food will fill up the gnawing, empty feeling in my gut that just won't go away.

LIZ

I am alone, but I am never alone.

And it's almost uncomfortable to have time with myself and my own thoughts.

I may be a divorced empty-nester, but every block of my daily calendar and every moment of my day is jammed with taking care of someone else's needs: caregiving, errands, babysitting, shopping, endless questions from and meetings with clients. It's ironic that I make a living selling homes, because I am rarely at mine.

It's also rare I have days like this all to myself, especially in the summer, when the real estate market is the busiest in Michigan. I think of my mom, and my heart pings with guilt and worry.

Guilt and worry, the hallmarks of being a mother, I think. *And daughter. And friend.*

What if something happens when I'm gone? What if she needs me?

I am listening to a podcast about reinventing your life after fifty. Women are sharing their experiences about overcoming loss, handling grief, finding love and embarking on long-buried dreams, be it travel or starting a new business.

I often listen to these podcasts with an equal mix of hope and cynicism. I am riveted for a while, and then I get a text or twenty, and I say to my virtual spirit coach, "Right, honey. Just believe, and it happens. Maybe I can just twitch my nose to make it so like in *Bewitched*."

I switch off the podcast, and my radio begins to blare "Holiday" by Madonna.

Is this a holiday I'm embarking on? I wonder. *A time to celebrate an old friend and reminisce? Or is it a time to reopen old wounds?*

My heart begins to race as I think of saying goodbye to Em and seeing Rach and V for the first time in ages.

To be honest, I don't even know who they are anymore. I used to see V on magazine covers all the time, and—as a young mom—I would be consumed with jealousy. Same with Rachel. I mean, who graduates college and lands a TV show?

How did they manage to do it, when I had just as much talent?

Advantages, I think. *More money. Rachel acted like her parents were blue-collar, but at least they had collars. My family had nothing.*

Perhaps I am still consumed with the jealousy from my camp days of the two rivals who were so admired that girls forgot there were two other leaves to The Clover Girls.

I grit my teeth thinking of seeing Rachel. How did she go from being one of the most beloved people on TV to one of the most hated? I turn off the TV whenever I see her mug or hear her obnoxious voice.

Perhaps it's because I can't forgive what she did to me.

And vice versa.

This will be torture, I think.

I gaze down at my outfit, which fits perfectly with the station I'm listening to: All '80s, All the Time. I'm wearing an outfit I designed and made: a white, lightweight puffy-shoulder top, tucked into a pair of high-waisted acid-wash jeans shorts, statement earrings banging around in the wind, my curly hair pulled back in a scrunchie.

Is it age-appropriate? *Let's not poll the jury,* I think, before deciding, *Yes! Why not?* It's all back in style again. And I look good enough to wear it. Why do we let society—and men—dictate what is and what isn't appropriate for us to wear at a certain age? I may be a grandmother, but I certainly don't want to look like Granny from *The Waltons*.

My heart pings again, as I think of how we all used to say good-night to one another.

The little town near where Camp Birchwood sits is located in the pinky of Michigan. Ask any Michigander where he or she lives, and—if they were born and raised in the state, or are long-time transplants—they will raise a hand into the air. Visitors always wince, tending to think the question has offended us, and we are either going to backhand them or slap the snot out of them. But our hand is a map: Michigan is shaped like a mitten. We point at our hand to show where we live. Glen Arbor is in the pinky.

As such, the drive into Glen Arbor is storybook. The tiny town sits on a small strip of land that runs between Glen Lake and Sleeping Bear Bay. It lies just beyond the bend of the famed Sleeping Bear Dunes National Lakeshore, which features mammoth—and I mean mammoth—sand dunes, which media outlets from *Good Morning America* to *Time* have called the most beautiful spot in the world. And it is. From the tops of the dunes, some four hundred feet up, you have panoramic lake views that make you feel as if you're no longer in the US but perhaps on the Amalfi Coast of Italy. The water isn't just blue, it graduates from aquamarine to midnight blue, like the Mediterranean. The water laps at white sand shores, and the winds whisper across the dunes and through the aspens, as if they are trying to impart all the secrets of this sacred spot.

And there are many.

The dunes were the location for some of our Color War competitions at camp, and—even as a kid—I felt I might die trying to make it to the top of Sleeping Bear, my feet churning on the hot sand, my body going nowhere, as if I were running atop quicksand.

I head into town and decide to stop for a bite

to eat. I certainly don't want to be the first one to greet Em's ashes.

Or, worse, V and Rachel in the flesh.

If you want to know what Glen Arbor looks like, just Google *adorable.* The entire town is kitten-puppy-cuteness-overload-perfect-vacation-town adorbs. Its streets are lined with quaint shops and restaurants, and the air is filled with the smell of butter and fudge. As I stroll, I stop and look over the menus at the restaurants. People pack outdoor patios, enjoying a sandwich, salad and glass (or two) of wine. This area of northern Michigan is now famous worldwide among tourists and wine connoisseurs for its wonderful vineyards and reds and whites, and it lives up to its name, Glen Arbor, which was supposedly given by the wife of an early French settler who admired the beautiful landscape and trees adorned with grapevines.

I consider a glass of wine to steel myself for the evening's events, but worry it will either make me sleepy or surly—*ah, the things you now worry and think about as you near fifty*—so I opt for another fun option, just behind wine: ice cream. The coastal towns of Michigan are filled with ice cream shops, and the ice cream is always good, fresh and local, since dairy farms sur-round the resort towns. I order two scoops—one of Michigan blackberry and one of cappuccino chocolate chunk—in a homemade waffle cone and continue strolling the streets, twisting and licking the cone continuously to keep the ice cream from melting down my arm. This was a trick I perfected as a girl, but my adult hand and wrist do not seem as flexible anymore.

I stop in front of a shop, which has its doors wide open on this glorious day, and admire a beautiful scarf of green and blue.

"Handmade," says a woman standing on the front steps, her face to the sun.

"It's lovely."

"Thank you. I made it."

I look up at the sign. Smitten with the Mitten.

"All products from Michigan artists, including me. I'm Lynn." She reaches out her hand. Mine is covered in ice cream.

"Liz," I say, wiping my hand on my shorts and then shaking her hand. "I'm so classy. And that is so cute. How long have you had the shop?"

"Five years," she says. "I hit forty, got divorced, wanted to start over."

"Are we twins?"

She laughs. "Best thing I've ever done." She pauses. "Stupidest thing I've ever done."

This time, I laugh. "Can I ask you something?" She nods. "How did you do it?"

She looks up into the sky, as if she's considering the direction of the puffy white clouds. "I stopped overthinking everything. I stopped letting fear rule my life." She looks at me. "Life is short. None of us get out of here alive. I was an accountant. I was good with numbers. But I was also an artist. I wanted to create something with my life. Leave a legacy besides numbers. My skill sets actually work well together. It's not easy. I just turned my first profit last year. But it's all been worth it. I believe that you can always go back, but you can never go forward."

Her words move me deeply. She reaches out and touches my blouse. "You made this, didn't you?" I nod. "It's gorgeous. I love how retro it is. My clients—younger *and* older—would eat this up. You're on to something. Leave me your card, if you want."

I start to reach into my purse but realize I'm still holding on to my cone. I polish it off and wipe my hands on the napkin. "Think you can sell an ice-cream-stained top?"

She laughs as I hand her my card. "I'm a real estate agent."

"No, you're an artist who sells real estate," she says. "Stop overthinking." She winks at me as a gaggle of women head into her shop, oohing and ahhing. "I have to go. Good luck."

As if in a trance, I walk farther downtown.

I have always overthought everything. Fear has ruled my life, and where has that gotten me? I didn't pursue fashion because I never thought I was good enough, I never believed I could make a living, I always put others before my own dreams. Rachel and V always thought they were good enough. Always.

In college, when I declared a major in fashion design and merchandising, my college friends asked how I would ever make money. When I swallowed my pride and reached out so long ago to V and Rachel—apologizing for all I had and hadn't done wrong—hoping and praying they might consider using their influence to get me a start in the industry, my calls went unreturned. Every time I tried to start a business, my husband asked where dinner was, or why the house was dirty. When I tried to start a business when my kids were in school, I felt guilty. I should be attending their soccer practices. I should be room mother. I should be doing anything other than what was truly important.

To me.

And that thought made me feel even guiltier.

My husband never said, "Oh, honey, you spend the weekend creating, and I'll take care of the kids." And as young adults, my kids never said, "Oh, Mom, don't worry about us for a while. You focus on you." My mom would tell me that, but she can't any longer. And I have so little time left with her. When I finally embarked on starting my own business, fear knocked out my heart and reason won the wrestling match over passion. I knew I could make money in real estate. Fashion? Not so much.

Why has no one stood up for me?

No, Liz: Why have you never stood up for your-self?

Lost in thought, I suddenly look up to find myself standing in front of The Cottage Book Shop, a bookstore I consider the cutest in the world. It's an antique log cabin that looks as if it should be sitting in the middle of the woods with smoke streaming out of its chimney. Instead, it's jammed with books. The Clover Girls always came here, led by Em, whenever we'd escape camp. Em was obsessed with books. I always told her she should be a writer instead of a librarian.

Did fear stop her, too?

I walk inside and feel as if I'm on a field trip in school, exploring an old homestead. I browse through the selection of new books before I head into a corner of the old log cabin.

I wonder if they have a copy? *Oh, Em,* I think. *Can you imagine?*

I head to the front of the shelf, my fingers moving across all the *A* authors.

There it is!

A paperback copy of *Flowers in the Attic*. I smile, grab the novel and hold it to my heart.

Em sneaked a copy into camp one summer because her mom didn't want her to read it. She'd tried to convince her mom it was a sweet little book about a girl who loved flowers, but her mother didn't buy it: she'd already heard about it and didn't want Em to get nightmares. So, after all the other campers went to bed, Em crawled into my bunk and we read *Flowers in the Attic* with a flashlight under the covers.

And you had nightmares, Em.

I buy a copy and decide it's time to head over to Birchwood. I take the famed M-22 highway, a snaking, scenic roadway out of Glen Arbor and up to the picturesque point between Sleeping Bear Bay and Good Harbor Bay. Though Camp Birchwood is located a few miles off M-22 down a bumpy, narrow dirt road, I don't need GPS. I release an unexpected *whoop!* when I see the big sign for Camp Birchwood: an old wooden sign, white birch logs spelling out the camp's name against a peeling, dark green background, a carving of two girls paddling a canoe along the bottom. Many of the logs creating the logo have fallen, and Camp Birchwood now reads, "am i ood."

Am I odd? Am I old?

Am I both?

Is this, literally, a sign? I wonder.

My tires kick up dust. It's been years since the pines have been trimmed, and they are encroaching upon the road, their green branches scraping the side of my car as I drive.

My heart leaps when I see the camp. I stop the car in a parking area, now littered with broken tree limbs and pine cones, and step out.

I inhale deeply. It smells just as it did when I was a girl. Fresh pine and water, old wood and must . . . *and what else,* I think. *Oh, yes. Summer.*

The old bunkhouses, still the same rusty brown, dot the camp. Their names remain: Pinewood, Birchwood, Sugar Maple, Hemlock, Sassafras. As do faded rectangles on the wood where American flags were once draped over the cabin doors. The Lodge sits in the middle of the camp, and paths—now overgrown—still meander like spokes from the center. I leave my things—I haven't brought much, just an overnight bag and some food—in the car, and I follow the path that leads to Lake Birchwood. Monarchs flit in the sunshine as I walk, crickets hopping out of my way, and I gasp when I see the lake.

It has not changed, I think. *Unlike me.*

The lake is very deep, and campers used to freak out during their annual swim test when the water turned from blue to black once they reached the middle. *Friday the 13th* had come out in 1980, and it changed the way we all thought about summer camps. *Watch out for Jason!* some of the older campers would yell during the middle of a swim, scaring us young girls.

The camp sits on a hill, with Lake Birchwood set down a bit from the main grounds. On the opposite side of the big lake sat the boys' camp, which I heard is still going strong.

"I still remember your name: Billy Collins," I

say to the breeze. "I still dream about you asking me to dance."

Beyond that was what we called The Lookout: steep dunes led to a view from the top that was spectacular, Lake Michigan spread out before you. We would sprint down the dunes, our legs churning, and run directly into the water.

I take a seat on the sandy shore at the edge of Lake Birchwood.

The camp is located on the forty-fifth parallel, a line designating the latitude halfway between the earth's equator and the North Pole. Many Michiganders believe there is an invisible force—a migrational pull, if you will—that draws people here not only to vacation but also to settle. That pull has created a mecca for artists and photographers. Many are drawn here by the forty-fifth's magical light.

I look over the woods and water as the late afternoon sun illuminates the cattails and reeds, the loons and birds, the sand and the birch. It is a soft light, almost ethereal, and everything looks draped in golden gauze.

I shut my eyes. I can see all of us together, in our too-big camp T-shirts and too-big hair for our little bodies, gathered on the dock for our first camp photo. I can still hear the campers and counselors yelling, *Birchwood forever!* I can still remember the day we all met, Em finding that four-leaf clover, which began a legend and a downfall as fiery as any from Greek mythology. I can still hear us singing our camp song.

"So now I come to you . . ."

I jump out of my skin, screaming, but then I stop just as quickly and know immediately who it is.

"With broken arms . . ."

I stand and wipe the sand off my rear. I turn. *V!*

"I still sing that Journey song exactly the same way after all these years."

"Me, too."

"Same with 'Hold Me Closer, Tony Danza.' "

In the past, I would have held out my arms, and V would have come running into them. We would have swayed back and forth in the fading sunshine, as bullfrogs moaned a dramatic accompaniment.

Instead, we just stare at each other for the longest time, the bullfrogs' moans a noisy soundtrack to our uncomfortable silence.

"How long's it been?" she finally asks.

I don't know if she's asking about the last time we were here or the last time we talked, so I take the easy route.

"Over thirty years since I've been back," I say. "I can't believe I'm here."

"Me either. It's surreal."

"When did you get in?"

"A few hours ago. Flew into Traverse City,"

V says. "The traffic was terrible. This area is booming."

"Yeah, northern Michigan has become a famous tourist destination now." I look around. "I guess we knew something."

V tilts her head as if my words have knocked her off-center. "Maybe we did," she says, her voice soft as the breeze.

I stare at my old friend as she scans our former camp. To be honest, I don't know if I would recognize her if I stumbled across her on the street. She's gained weight as the decades have advanced. Her leonine body is now more Rubenesque, her angular face more shadowed. And her signature red hair is still red, but in a harsher, salon-made way. But she is still beautiful, and the photos in those tabloids did not do her justice.

She is a lot like me, I realize: still hanging on gamely, although the game has changed dramatically, say from Centipede to . . . well . . . Words with Friends.

"You look great," she says. "Still a fashion icon. I should have you start dressing me again. I feel like I've lost my mojo." V smiles, and her eyes sparkle.

I look into those gorgeous eyes, the ones that gazed off the covers of endless magazines. Everyone talked about her tiger pose and red hair, but I always believed it was her hazel eyes that made her famous. Grass green with flecks of gold that could seemingly match any color she wore or product package she pitched: blue, green, yellow, gold.

"I never had the opportunity to dress you after camp," I say. "I would've liked that."

Her face falls, and her eyes lose their sparkle. She looks toward the lake. I have swatted away her attempt to be nice like an irritating mosquito.

I start to apologize, but I stop.

"How's your mom?" she asks. "And your kids?"

"The same," I say.

"That sounds ominous," V says.

"It is."

There is an awkward pause.

"My mom is dying," I say.

"I'm so sorry, Liz."

"I probably shouldn't have even left her. I shouldn't be here. I just came for Em."

She nods. "Me, too."

There is a long silence.

"How's your family?" I ask to fill it.

"Busy," she says.

"That sounds ominous, too."

"It is."

We stand awkwardly for a few more moments, pretending to look at the lake, before heading back to the camp, both of us avoiding walking through the field of clover to take the dirt path that is still worn but weedy.

"Have you found Em?" V asks when we make it up the hill.

"I haven't looked," I say. "I'm a little freaked out."

"I feel the same way," V says. She lowers her voice as if she's telling me a secret. "About seeing Rach, too."

"What *happened* to her? I actually turn the channel whenever she comes on."

"Me, too!" V says.

For an instant, I feel better, but I know V's game: turn everyone against Rachel before we realize it. And I know what happened to Rachel: *we* happened to Rachel.

We both begin to wave our hands around our faces and slap our arms and legs.

"Mosquitoes!" I cry.

We race to our cars, grab some water and our jackets. "Bug spray?" I ask.

"No," she says. "I didn't really give this much thought. I just came."

"Me, too. Where are you staying?" I ask.

"Hotel on the bay in Traverse City," V says. "Thought it might be nice to spend a few days on the water with just me. I haven't been away from my family in ages."

"Same here. I booked a little B and B in Glen Arbor." I stop, and guilt pings again. I'm staying in a cute B and B while my mother dies alone.

"Oh," I say, attempting to remain light and airy.

"Look what I bought for Em at The Cottage Book Store." I grab the copy of *Flowers in the Attic.*

"Is that for me?"

V and I yelp at the same time. Rachel appears out of nowhere. We didn't hear her car pull in. She is holding an armful of birch bark.

Neither of us reach out to greet her immediately.

"I take it you both want to lock me in the attic, just like in the book?" she asks, trying to make a joke to cut the tension.

No, I want to say. *You're more like the horrible grandmother.*

Instead, we all play nice like adults do. V and I finally extend our hands, and Rachel sets down the wood and shakes them politely as if we're new business colleagues she's meeting for the first time. Kids are honest. They tell you the truth. It's grown women who play the games. We all learned that firsthand. We went from sharing secrets to hiding them here.

There is silence, long enough for us to hear the whoops of boys at Camp Taneycomo. Long enough for the first fireflies to appear as dusk settles on the camp. I watch Rachel watch V as fireflies dance around her. Her face is pained, as it was so long ago. The irony—and memories—are still too much.

"None of us came here to fight," I finally say, before taking a very deep breath. "We came here to say goodbye to Em. So, let's do that and move on with our lives."

"Agreed," V says.

Three decades later, and we still can't reach out to hug a friend when they're in pain.

"I actually came bearing gifts," Rachel says. She nods down at the birch bark. "Remember how my mom loved to collect this?"

I look at Rachel. I truly see just how vulnerable she is.

Still.

"How is your mom?" I ask.

"Not speaking," she says. "Thanks for asking."

Silence falls again.

"Listen," Rachel says. "We may not like one another anymore, but we all liked Em. She was our mom. She was our glue. And I think it says something that we all took time to honor her memory and what she meant to us." She pauses. "She asked us to scatter her ashes, but I thought of something that would mean even more to her. Remember how at the end of every camp we'd all gather for the Candles on the Lake ceremony? And we'd place them all on little birch canoes.

"Em loved that ceremony," Rachel continues. "She'd always cry."

"Yeah," I say, smiling.

"Candles on the Lake represented what was best about Camp Birchwood," Rachel says. "That we all grew closer over the years."

"That's lovely, Rach," V says. "Really." She extends her hand and touches Rachel's arm tentatively.

Rachel flinches at her touch, moving back like when you encounter a snake while hiking. She then looks at V for the longest time as if to say, *I knew you'd remember Candles on the Lake.*

"What'd you bring?" I ask, trying to avoid an incident.

"I bought candles and have them in a bag. I thought we could light one for each of us, put them on these little makeshift birch canoes and float them into the lake."

"Beautiful," I say. "Let's do it before it gets too dark."

"And we need to get her ashes," V says, making a face.

We head to camp and walk as if on instinct to our old bunkhouse. I open the screen door and there, sitting on the bottom left bunk in the far corner where Em always slept, is a large box. It is wrapped, like a Christmas present, but in vintage paper, with old writing on it. And that's when I notice that there is an indention in the old pillow on the rickety bunk, a camp blanket tossed haphazardly at the end. I grab the box and nearly fall running out of the door and down the stoop.

"I think she was in there!" I squeal.

"What? Now? Her ghost?" V half screams.

"No, no. I mean, she was in there, in there.

Like, not too long ago. There's a pillow and a blanket." I look at them. "She was waiting for us, just like she said."

We all jog to the lake. I set the box down. Rach hands out candles, and we each place one into a little birch canoe and set it at the edge of the water. Rach adds one for Em, and then she lights each one. We give them a push into the water and take a seat on the sand. The sun tilts behind the dune, and the world is cast into sudden darkness. The candles catch the current and float into the lake, spreading out as if they are going their separate ways. I remember what we used to say at the ceremony: the lights, like each camper, shine individually, brightly on their own. But as they move farther away from the shore, they swim together, getting closer and closer. Finally, in the distance, they become one unified light, shining even more brightly together as a beacon, a sign of hope, a symbol of the fact—as we used to recite—that we all may be individuals who arrive alone but we end up coming together. As a result, we are stronger, brighter, better, even more beautiful.

Did our lights dim over time because we swam apart, didn't come together?

There was a day when we were the candles, when we were brighter together.

"We better do this now," I say, gesturing at the box. I grab my cell and turn on the flashlight. I begin to open the box, when I do a hammy double take, my bad eyes finally realizing in the light that it is not wrapped in gift paper, it's covered in a letter.

In Em's handwriting.

"Oh, my God," I say. "This is a letter from her! Hold the flashlight."

I peel the letter off the box. It is four pages long, in her cursive, and taped onto each side of the box. Once I have it in hand, I look inside and pull out a little vase.

"Holy crap!" Rach says. "That's the pot she made our first summer here. Remember?"

"You're right," V says. "It's all coiled and lumpy. She rolled all those pieces of clay like little snakes and then just laid them on top of each other without ever smoothing it out. We all made fun of her."

There's a tiny lid on her vase. I remove it and tilt the vase toward the flashlight. Em's ashes, gray and sad, sit inside.

"Read the letter," V says. Her voice is trembling.

I look out over the lake. Our candles are a single light. My eyes fill with tears.

"Okay," I say, "but first we need to scatter her ashes."

I tilt the vase and pour some ashes into our hands.

"To Em!" I say, tossing her ashes onto the lake.

"To Em!" V and Rachel repeat.

Some of her ashes catch in the breeze and float toward the dunes. The rest float into the lake, and I watch until they disappear, become one with the light.

And then I start to read the letter, but it's as though Em is sitting right here, reading it to us in her own voice. I can hear her, clear as day, feel her spirit next to me.

EMILY

My Dear Clover Girls:
If you're reading this, we're together again! FINALLY! AFTER ALL THESE YEARS! Thank you!

How does it feel to be back at camp? I know that one leaf—me!—is now missing from our good luck clover, but I'm hoping there's still some magic left in our group.

As I wrote to each of you, I spent a few weeks here early this summer, when I was having a few of my last good days. I knew it was my last summer, so I wanted it to feel like my best summer. And that was always here. I slept in my old bunk in our cabin. No one was here, just me, but I felt like I was still surrounded by all of you.

Remember that pact we made a long time ago, that very first summer at camp? We promised that we would all retire here together one day. Did you know we were way ahead of our time? Everyone these days is talking about what we planned so long ago. People in their forties and fifties want to ensure that their lives down the road are lived on their own terms: privacy and space of their own while being surrounded by their friends and enjoying shared and communal spaces like dining rooms, kitchens, fitness rooms, gardens, TV rooms and libraries. What kind of place does that sound like to you?

Camp!

Why am I telling you all of this?

As you know, I didn't have children, and I don't have any next of kin, so I've been wondering what I would do with my estate. And this is it.

I bought Camp Birchwood before I died. And I'm giving it to all of you.

What better place—and memories—to leave as my legacy, right?

In short, the camp is paid in full, and I've also established a small endowment (invested, so it will grow) to pay for future capital projects as well as help with the taxes. Like you, the camp needs a lot of love: roofs need to be repaired, cabins need mortar, there's no AC or heat, plumbing is a mess, all the appliances are from the '80s, there are virtually no modern conveniences. But I did turn on the water and power in The Lodge and stocked it with some necessities. I also invested wisely and lived modestly. My only children were books. I didn't know what I was saving for . . . until I returned here.

I was saving for this. I was saving for you!

You're all lost. Face it. You are.

Since I can only imagine how awkward it is to be together again after everything we went through, let me ask each of you some questions so you can remember how fragile, human and desperately in need of friendship each of you are.

V, you gave up your career for your husband's and lost your self-confidence as a result. And your kids are so incredible, but are they happy? Are you?

Liz, you've given your entire life for everyone else, but you've lost your own dreams. You are such a talented designer. When are you going to fashion a life for yourself?

And Rach, our superstar, you're the most lost of all. You're still acting, but it's a role I know you no longer want to play. It's not about politics. It's about being true to yourself. What do you believe in anymore? Anything? What about us?

I know, I know, you all have families, careers and busy lives, and I know we've each hurt one another so deeply, but I ask you this: Why can't this be the paradise it once was? Why can't this be the place where you find out who you once were? Why can't this be the place where you come together, forgive and brighten one another's lives again? It's all up to you. Because it's yours.

But, there's a catch.

In order to inherit the camp, you must all spend a week together here at Camp Birchwood. The only stipulation is that by the end of the week you must commit to the camp TOGETHER. It can't just be one or two of you. The only goal is that you have fun and reconnect. There can no longer be any secrets, pacts, petty jealousies or grudges. This is a week for you to decide whether you want to do something better and more important with your lives as friends. Sounds simple, right? At one point in time, this would have sounded like a dream. I bet you're not thinking that right now.

When you're dying, everything finally becomes as crystal clear as the lake on a sunny day. The simplest of things—the things that we take for granted each and every day—are the most important: our health, our family and our friends.

If any of you choose to leave or walk

away, then the camp and its endowment will be turned over to the State of Michigan for future generations to enjoy.

Those are my only rules. Have fun! It's so easy, but it will be so hard.

As I mentioned, you'll find some basic necessities here that I've already purchased: pillows, blankets, kayaks, a canoe, firewood, some food and coffee, all the things we had at camp (okay, coffee has replaced our love of Jolt soda! Remember?).

Really, the only things you need are already right beside you: each other.

And although I'm not with you physically, I am there with you in spirit. And, should you agree to this, I will be with you FOUR-ever!

Speaking of which: I've enclosed the four-leaf clover I found our very first day together. Yes, I've kept it forever. It's dried and fragile, just like our friendship. But it's a symbol of what was and what could still be.

Do you remember what Mrs. Nigh told us about it? The clover represents faith, hope and love. The four-leaf clover is imbued with luck.

You'll need it. You'll need all of those things.

But Mrs. Nigh also told us that the four-leaf clover represented paradise.

"That's why I planted the clover," she said. "So paradise will always be with you, even when you grow up and leave this camp."

Well, we left. And it was never the same.

Now you're back. You can choose to leave forever, or you can choose to recreate the happy memories from our camp days and remember what it was that made us friends, made us whole, made each of us unique.

Paradise surrounds you. So do your best friends.

What you decide to do with that is now up to you.

I love you all more than anything!

Em

PART THREE
Talent Night

SUMMER 1987

"That's boring to the max!" Rachel yells.

"No duh! Do *something* for once! Don't be lame!" V says. "It's Talent Night."

"My talent *is* fashion design," Liz protests. "I just want to show the girls what I can do. That I can make something cool out of anything." Her voice rises with emotion. "Em, what should I do?"

Liz looks at Em, who lifts her head from the book she is reading. Her body is halfway off the bunk, her legs helicoptering in the air. She stops and twirls her hair, taking the question very seriously.

"I think you should do what makes you happiest," she says, her voice calm like a soft rain. "If you try to do something you don't want to do, your heart won't be in it. People can see through that."

"Not even!" Rachel says. "You have to do something that gets everyone's attention. You have to stand out." She looks at Em. "Don't listen to her. She never wants to stand out."

Em shakes her head. "No, Rachel. I just don't need to be the center of attention like you and V all the time. You'll see one day." She ducks her head back into her book.

"You can pretend you're in another world all you want, Em," Rach says, "but I know talent." She stops. "Oh! My! Gawd! I just had the gnarliest idea! Didn't you used to twirl, Liz?"

"When I was a kid," Liz says.

"That's what you should do, right, V?"

"Totally!" V agrees. "Not just twirl. But a fire baton routine! Can you imagine?"

"We'll totally help you!" Rachel says. "Right, V?"

"Right!"

The two grab hands and run out of the bunk-house, giggling.

Em looks down at Liz.

"Don't," she says. "Don't do it. Those two may be your friends, but they always think of themselves first, especially if it's a competition. They don't want anyone else to win besides them. They may act like rivals, but some girls are always bonded by the things they have in common. Rach and V are beautiful, popular and born leaders. They don't think anyone can beat them. Ever." Em puts down her book and hops off the bunk. She grabs Liz's hand. "They're not doing this to help you, Liz. They're doing this to help them. They may be my BFFs, but they can be selfish. You may not win, but people will respect you, Liz."

Liz shakes her head. She already has made her decision.

The night of the talent contest, Liz walks out onto the tiny stage in The Lodge. It is pitch black. The music for "Burning Down the House" by Talking Heads comes on, and then all of a sudden, a spotlight shines on Liz. The campers explode in applause. Liz is performing a fire baton routine. It is going perfectly. The baton nearly touches the rafters. Liz even does a cartwheel and catches every toss. The sequined twirler outfit she'd fashioned for herself—in green paillettes!— sparkles in the light. Rach looks at V, both of them silently cursing themselves for encouraging her. Everyone is mesmerized. Until . . .

Whoosh!

Liz's hair briefly goes up in flames. Everyone screams, and Liz nearly knocks herself unconscious trying to put out her hair with her own baton. Even though her hair is no longer aflame and only the ends are singed, a camp counselor still turns a fire extinguisher on her, and another tosses a bucket of water over her.

The Lodge explodes in laughter.

Liz is devastated. She rushes offstage, where her friends are waiting. They hold her as she cries.

A counselor walks over. "It's time for your performance, girls," she says.

They let go of Liz.

"You're performing together?" Liz sniffles. "Why didn't you tell me?"

"Wanted it to be a secret!" they say as one. "Wish us luck!"

They perform a dance routine to "Walk Like an Egyptian" by The Bangles, and win Talent Night.

Devastated, Liz hides in the costume room, her secret space, where all of the clothes she made and was going to showcase for Talent Night hang lifeless. She hears voices whispering outside. She cracks the door. Rachel and V are just offstage, feet away.

"Burnin' down her hair!" Rachel sings.

"Shhhh!" V says in a stage whisper.

"I actually feel sorry for her," Rachel says. "She tries so hard."

"Desperation is not a good look," V says.

"Like her clothes."

"I actually think she's talented," V says. "But you can't teach confidence."

"Right?"

Liz stands at the door. Her heart is beating out of her chest. Her head is spinning. She wants to move, confront them, yell at them, but her feet and mouth are paralyzed, as if in quicksand.

She is wounded so deeply by her friends, but it would hurt even more, she knows, to lose them.

Or worse, have them turn against her forever.

Liz closes the door.

SUMMER 2021
VERONICA

Why are darkness and quiet so unnerving to adults? We spend nine months in a womb and cry like the dickens when we encounter light for the first time. As kids, we loved to camp outdoors, even in our backyards, with only a flashlight. We yearned to head to summer camp in the middle of nowhere, or crawl under our covers to snuff out the reality of the world.

And then we become addicted to light, be it fluorescent office lights or headlights of passing cars through our neighborhood. Today, we are addicted to technology's light: cell phones, laptops, TVs. A constant glow surrounds us that makes us feel so safe, protected, connected. Only when we remove that glow do we realize we're alone.

I take a sip of water from my bottle and close my eyes.

My career was spent in the light. In fact, I was an expert in light. I learned how light was angled, reflected, diffused. I understood where shadows fell. I knew how to cast it in my eyes. I knew how to spread my limbs apart so that light would flow around my body. When that light was removed, I had to learn to live in the shadows.

Although my life is still bright—my children are miracles—I feel like I've lost my balance between dark and light.

I felt basked in light early in my marriage, and now it feels as though twilight is drawing close. The dark, the unknown, is unnerving.

"Let there be light!"

I jump. Liz has started a fire.

The irony is unbearable. She used Rachel's birch despite the fact Rachel has gone AWOL since we read Em's letter together and stopped to scatter some of her ashes over her beloved field of lucky clover. We all seemed ready to say goodbye to Em and each other, forever, but now it just feels too hard to leave here again without some semblance of closure with one another, as Em wanted.

Without some semblance of light, just like Candles on the Lake.

"You could be on *Survivor*," I say.

"For one night only," Liz says. "I need my hairspray."

"Me, too," I say. "And my lip gloss."

I smile at her in the glow. Her hair has not changed. It's a marvel unto itself. It not only still requires its own zip code, but it is still Madonna circa "Lucky Star" video days. She is even wearing a giant bow on her head. She bends down to stoke the fire.

Whoosh!

Liz screams, and I smell the horrid stench of something burning.

I look up. Liz's hair explodes, ever so briefly, into flame. It resembles burning tumbleweed.

"Do something!" Liz yells.

I stand, and Liz is running around the campfire, smashing her hair with her hands, as if a thousand bees were upon her. I rush over to assist, tossing the remains of my water bottle onto her head. Her hair sizzles, and she stops moving.

She looks up at me, water cascading down her face. "How's my hair?"

I move closer and take a look. "Some singed ends, but I think it's all intact."

I look at Liz, trying to act upbeat as she always did, even when something was hurting her. Memories of her past Talent Night disaster flame through my mind. That summer, campers called Liz "Carrie," because the memory of that night on stage was so unbelievably monstrous and horrific. She never performed in another Talent Night. She spent the rest of her camp years offstage, designing other girls' costumes and doing their hair for their performances.

I now wonder how much that Talent Night nightmare impacted her psyche and confidence.

No, V, be honest: you've always wondered how much your impact had on her psyche and confidence.

Was she afraid everything would end up in flames?

"Since Em wanted us to bury the hatchet, I have a question that's haunted me for a very long time." Liz looks at me, and I hold my breath. "Why didn't you ever take me up on my offer to help style you when you were a model? I mean, I helped you before."

My heart stops. I think of what she did for me so long ago. Not just lying to Rachel but styling me for the photo shoot that launched my career and changed my life.

Why didn't I? She deserved some form of payback, didn't she, V?

"I thought you weren't serious," I say. "You were in college. You were just starting out. And then you got married soon after that."

"Did I *ever* act like I was joking?" she asks. "You know that was my passion."

Liz touches her hair, nervously, and comes over to take a seat beside me on vintage lawn chairs—the webbed kind, in green, of course—that Em left in the shed next to the kayak and canoe.

"Did you ever think I was talented?" Liz asks. "Be honest."

"Oh, Liz," I say. "Of course." I hesitate, dreading the question I'm about to ask. "Where is all of this coming from?"

"Because I kinda always thought I was a joke," Liz says, her voice barely audible. She looks at me. "I heard what you and Rachel said about me after my Talent Night debacle. Do you even remember that?"

I shut my eyes. I think back in time so long ago. Images and words flash, just like bulbs from my modeling days. My face flushes, and I can feel it turn as red as my hair.

"I do," I say. "I'm sorry. We were just kids."

She looks at me. "C'mon, V. That's no excuse. You and Rachel may have acted like rivals, but you could be the mean girls. Everything came so easily to you two."

"But it didn't always for me. I think that's why I acted the way I did."

I tell Liz the story I told my daughter of being picked on in school. "It felt good to be popular for once. It felt good to be the leader," I say. "It felt great to be the girl everyone thought was beautiful. It *was* nice that everything—for once in my life—came easily. Maybe I got off on that power."

"But it didn't come easily for me," Liz says, mirroring my own words. "Why did we hurt each other so much? Why did we lie to Rachel? I mean, I lied for you. That launched your career. And when you made it big you didn't even have time to give your supposed best friend in the world one opportunity. *One.*"

"I had managers and handlers, Liz. I didn't have as much power as you think I did."

"I had nothing!" Liz yells suddenly. "You had everything!" She stops and there are tears in her eyes. "I just needed someone to see me. It was not easy leaving here—leaving your light—and being invisible."

I reach out my hand.

"You don't know how much I needed you," she continues. Liz takes my hand and grips it tightly. "Everyone was going someplace, and my dreams died after camp. And you didn't do a damn thing to help my confidence. Do you know how much a simple call asking how I was would have meant? Or that asking me to design a dress for you for some stupid premiere you no longer remember would have changed my whole life? You had designers clamoring to make clothes for you. You had men clamoring to be with you. You traveled the world. You could have tossed a scrap to the girl who sold her dignity and a friend to make that all happen."

I feel cold, despite the fire, and begin to shiver. Tears fill my eyes.

"I'm so sorry—"

"Stop saying that!" Liz spits, dropping my hand. "It's not enough."

We watch the fire crackle for the longest time. I don't know what to say because she's right. In my heart, I know it because it is shattering into tiny pieces.

"I tried to design in college. Everyone told

me I was silly. Then when I was newly married, my husband told me it was silly," Liz continues. "He asked me to choose, my career or his? Mike wanted a family. Mike wanted dinner on the table at six. It didn't seem realistic. I was so jealous of you and Rachel. I mean, the world just opened up for you. In the blink of an eye, you both were stars. You were seeing the world. I was back in the little town where I grew up, and instead of the world opening up, the walls closed in on me. I saw the faces of my little camp friends everywhere, and I thought, 'Why isn't that me?'"

"It could have been you," I protest.

"Could it?" she asks. Her voice drops and turns cold, and, as if on cue, the fire dims.

"Maybe it's your turn now," I say. I look at the fire. "It's not all so perfect anymore, Liz. My marriage is rocky. My dreams have dwindled. That's not even true. I don't even dream anymore. Em's letter rocked me to the core. My husband didn't even think I should come."

Liz stands, grabs a big stick and stirs the fire again, this time from a distance. She looks at me and gives me a sweet, but faint, smile. "But at least you had a dream come true. As far as mine goes, I'm gettin' up there in years. I think my time to become a designer has passed. I have an online shop. And I have a successful career as a real estate agent. I may not be able to make all my own dreams come true, but I can make everyone else's. And that makes me happy."

"Does it?"

We are silent for way too long. The fire crackles, and I'm thankful for any type of noise.

"Do you think Rachel will come back?" she finally asks, not answering my question.

"No," I say. "Why would she? I think she sees us as co-conspirators every time she looks at us. Em was the concrete. We were the sledge-hammer."

"I think Em's dreams are over, too," Liz says. "Her whole plan is over before it even began. I guess that's life. Being an adult. We're not kids anymore."

I think of Em and her final weeks here. I can feel Em's spirit. She loved this place with all her heart and soul. Like a great book, this camp was filled with characters, life and storylines. It pulsed with narrative highs and lows. It was a saga of childhood, and the coming-of-age story of four strong women.

I think of her being alone, not just here but during her illness. How much inner strength did that take? Could I be alone at this stage of my life, much less face it if I were sick? She may have been the quietest of The Clover Girls, but her actions continue to speak volumes.

"It's getting late," Liz says. "I'm glad we stayed a little while longer. Not only for Em, but for us. I'm glad we had a chance to talk. Finally. I didn't mean to unleash. It's just . . ."

I nod. "Me, too," I tell her. "And I promise not to say I'm sorry again."

Liz chuckles.

"You ready to head out to our hotels?" I ask. "We can follow each other until we hit M-22."

"Okay," Liz says. "But could we wait until the fire starts to die. I can't leave just yet for some reason. It doesn't feel right. It's as if something is telling me to stay."

"Sure thing," I say.

There is silence for a moment. I shut my eyes and listen to the logs crackle, and the bellows of the frogs rise and fall like a symphony.

Will I get used to this quiet once my kids are gone? Could I be happy alone if David and I are unable to iron out our differences?

"Boo!"

I scream. Liz stands and begins chopping at the air like a crazed jujitsu fighter.

Rachel is standing in front of us, holding an overnight bag and a sack of groceries.

"Psych!" she says.

"You scared us!" I say. "Where did you go?"

"For a drive," she says. "I needed time to think."

"We thought you were gone," Liz says. "For good."

"Still undecided," she says. "Let me be blunt."

131

"As usual," I say.

"I don't want to do that right now," Rach says. "I don't want to yell at both of you and get angry for what you did to me."

"I could say the same thing to you," Liz says.

"What is going on?" I ask.

"Can I finish?" Rachel says. "Please."

We look at one another, nodding.

"I just feel like I need to take a moment in my life to honor Em. I think I need to take a moment to assess my life. Just a moment to slow down. I don't ever do that. I'm sure neither of you do either. But what does it say about us as people— much less friends—if we can't stay a night in a place that meant so much to our best friend? She deserves that."

Rachel looks at me. Out of nowhere, she smiles.

"I got lost, too," she says.

I stare at her, waiting for her to expound, but she doesn't. I don't know if she's saying that literally or figuratively. All I know is she's back. For a night. I smile back at her.

My mind races, and my heart follows suit. I don't even know if we're up for a night together, but I'm bone-tired, and I need a hot minute to stop and assess, too.

And honor our friend.

We still might leave and never speak again, but, for one night at least, we're together.

And that just feels right, doesn't it, Em?

"Oh, and I brought dinner," Rach says. She pulls Jiffy Pop Popcorn from a bag and shakes it at us. "From the party store."

Liz and I clap wildly.

"Just like camp!" I yell.

"Who wants to do the honors?" Rach asks.

I grab it. "I don't trust you getting too close to the fire," I say. It comes out fast, without any warning, just as it might have decades ago. "I'm so sorry. I didn't mean that."

"It's okay," Liz says. "I'm not a baby." She stops. "And you just said you wouldn't say you were sorry anymore."

"Okay, what'd I miss?" Rach asks.

I don't say a word this time.

"Does 'Burning Down the House' mean anything to you?" Liz asks.

Rach laughs. "I missed Fire Baton Redux?"

"You missed 'Burning Off My Hair' 2021," Liz says, patting her curls.

"Liz heard what we said after that happened," I say.

"Oh." Rachel's shoulders slump. "I'm sorry," she says.

"There's certainly a theme tonight," Liz says. "I have a feeling we might be saying that a lot this week . . . if we stay."

Rachel takes a seat.

"Really, I am."

Liz nods.

I remove the instruction cardboard top of the Jiffy Pop, grip the handle tightly, sit on the edge of my seat and hold the popcorn over the fire. I shake it and shake it and shake it so the popcorn won't scorch until I hear the first kernels pop. Slowly, steam begins to pipe from the hole in the middle and the foil begins to rise, higher and higher, like Aladdin from the lamp.

"Looks like your hair," I say to Liz as the foil balloons.

"Ha ha," she says.

"My children would think this is absolutely barbaric," I say.

"They don't know what they're missing," Rachel says.

When it's done, we wait for the Jiffy Pop to cool a bit and then rip open the foil top and tear into the popcorn.

"Tastes just like I remember," I say.

"Me, too," Liz says, closing her eyes.

We shovel popcorn into our mouths without stopping, just like we did as kids. I look around the campfire at my oldest friends, now people I don't even know. And yet I can still feel something. It's as real as the fireflies, the stars and the campfire.

After we finish the Jiffy Pop, Liz asks, "What now?"

Life's million-dollar question, I think, *no matter what age we are.*

No one responds.

I watch the flames flicker and the embers burn, and then I look around the fire at my old friends and realize that we—for the first time today—look perfectly balanced, between dark and light.

RACHEL

"Why is there no service out here?"

"Because we're in the middle of nowhere," Liz responds.

"What are you doing, Rach?" V asks.

"I have a client going on a late-night news show out of Detroit. I want to make sure they understand the talent."

That last word—*talent*—echoes in the Michigan night. A bullfrog belches by the lake, and I see Liz and V give one another a secretive glance. Liz giggles.

Are they laughing at the frog or my use of the word talent? I wonder.

"What's so funny?" I blurt.

I look over, and Liz is glaring at me. "Really, Rach. I get—what?—a few nights a year when I'm not wiping my mother's butt, running my grandchildren all around town or showing houses for lookie-loos at every waking hour. I think it's okay for me to giggle."

I'm about to apologize when Liz adds, under her breath but for me to hear clearly, "Talent. Spare me."

This, I know, is aimed at me.

"Spare me your sob story, Liz," I blurt again. "You're a martyr. You always have been, and you always will be. That's why your life is the way it is."

Liz stands up, so quickly and with such anger, her chair tumbles backward. "And you're an ego-maniacal, self-centered woman-hater. You always have been, and you always will be." Despite her anger, she says this calmly, as if she's in a spelling bee. She marches off. "I'm going to bed. One of us needs to be gone by morning. And we all know who that is."

Silence. Total, complete silence. Not even the bullfrogs' mournful croaks can match the way I feel.

"You did it again," V says. "You and your mouth."

"I can't help it," I say.

"You can," V says. "You just don't want to. We were having a moment of honesty and calm and you blew it. As usual."

"Aren't you going to go after her?"

"Me?" V asks. "You two are the ones who have always had the secret bond. We may have been the leaders, but you always had more of a connection with Liz and Em. I think they spoke to something deeper in you, the sweet girl you hated to show the world."

"Wow," I say. "You sound like a mom."

"I am. A damn good one."

There is more silence, but then V says, her voice as low and rumbling as the frogs in the distance,

"You know, I never thought I was pretty. I was just telling Liz that. I don't think I ever shared what my life was like *before* Birchwood. Before I was a leader."

"What? No."

"Truer words were never spoken," she says. "Before I came to camp, I was teased nonstop at school for being the ugly redheaded girl. Coming here was the first time I was really accepted and popular. I was going to be a teacher, remember? Becoming a model was the last thing I ever thought I'd be."

I look at V. All of the memories come flooding back. She's right: we were having a moment of clarity, and I blew it. I keep my mouth shut. After all these years, I think, she is finally going to apologize for what she did to me.

V continues. "I became an expert at modeling. That sounds like such a joke, doesn't it? But I took it very seriously, as seriously as any business, because it was *my* business. I studied the companies and products I sold. I stayed in shape. I didn't drink or smoke or stay out late. I arrived early to every single shoot, no matter if it was at dawn or the middle of the night. I was professional with photographers, even those who treated me like a piece of meat, and I was kind to every single person who was on staff. And do you know that's what got me as many jobs as my looks? Just being a good person." She stops.

"I mentored so many young women who have turned out to be great models but even more amazing role models."

I am staring into the dying fire. I find it too hard to look at V. She is not going to apologize. I bite my tongue. I am tired. I just want to get through tonight and go on my way. I am not good at placating, but if that's what it takes, then I— for once—will continue to keep my mouth shut.

She continues. "I knew my looks would fade. I knew I'd eventually be replaced by the next Molly Ringwald or Brooke Shields. I also realized I was talented. I knew how to make a photo memorable. And I always knew I was secondary to the product I was selling. I may have worn a bikini and leg warmers to sell potato chips and jeans, but I also intentionally never took a job I knew might harm someone. I didn't sell cigarettes or alcohol."

She stops and glares at me in the firelight.

"And I never set women back. Ever."

"You hypocrite!" I hiss, my facade of playing nice shattering. "How dare you try to turn the tables on me! You set *me* back. Don't I count? You lied to me about the *Life* magazine photo shoot, leaving that fake note. You got the others to go along with you. And you never apologized because you got what you wanted. So don't sit here and act all high-and-mighty about your contributions to feminism when you set the bar pretty low for how women actually treat one another. At least I'm honest about what I do. You are the worst kind of liar, V, because you lie to yourself to make you believe your own worth."

A log collapses into the fire, mimicking my complete emotional collapse, and I exhale all the air out of my body. "You crushed me, V. Do you know that? My best friend stuck a knife in my back. You were my Judas." I stare at her. "But you want to know something? That actually motivated me to act. I was so filled with rage, I would walk through fire to make things happen for myself. I would never be duped by anyone again." I stop. I will myself not to cry. "You know the worst thing of all? I actually stopped believing I had a special talent, too," I finally say, my voice barely audible. "I lucked into a TV show that turned into a blockbuster. I starred in a sitcom for years, a gift to any actor. And I thought for the longest time I was a joke. But I was good, V. I was a *damn* good actress to make such a silly show so successful and such a shallow character so beloved and believable. I worked hard at my craft. But when the show ended and my next one was short-lived, I learned I *was* a joke in Hollywood. I couldn't get an audition much less a job shilling toaster ovens at midnight on local cable. Remember I got on that reality show, *Where Are They Now?*, about young stars whose careers died. I spouted off about how much I hated Hollywood, and that's when conservatives came calling. I had no job, I had no opportunities, I was running out of cash and I was offered a lot of money to be an attractive face that people knew and trusted. I've built a brand doing this. I've become one of the most influential women in politics." I look at her. "What would you have done?"

V ducks her head, and her red hair glows even brighter in the firelight.

"I don't know," she finally says. "But what you're doing now willfully denigrates women. You're against everything that we've fought for, that makes us equals. Everything we learned and celebrated here at camp. How can you do that every day?"

"Being an adult isn't as easy as being a kid," I say.

"Why not?" V asks, her voice shaking. "Shouldn't it be?" She is quiet for the longest time but looks at me intensely in the firelight. "And you still didn't answer my question. Do you actually *believe* in the candidates whose campaigns you promote? Do you actually believe what you're saying? I have a daughter who sees you on TV, and she wonders why you hate yourself."

"I wonder the same thing sometimes," I say, too low for V to hear.

"You *are* immensely talented, Rach," V

continues. "I'm not saying that I don't have conservative values as well. I mean, most of us grew up as Reagan Republicans. But times have changed. We've lost touch with the importance of meeting in the middle, of talking, of recognizing and respecting each other's differences and backgrounds and all the beauty that brings to this world. There are more women than men in America, and yet we continue to be treated like second-class citizens. Next time you campaign or talk about women's issues, think about my daughter. Think about Em. Think about your mother."

My mother hates me, I want to tell her. She is embarrassed by me. Em was the glue that held us together, and my father was the glue that held our family together. His death left two headstrong women not only adrift but to do battle. It is hard to grow up an emotionally fulfilled woman when you grow up eating dinner every night next to an empty chair at the family table. You always seek to fill that void, often with the wrong things. And to not have my friends . . .

I look at V. "And the next time *you* decide to lecture *me* about women's issues, think about what you did to me. Tell *that* to your daughter. You can't even say you're sorry for what you did."

"You can't even say you're sorry for what you're doing."

"I think it's time for bed," I say, standing.

Suddenly, I'm exhausted. Too tired to fight. Too tired to counsel a client. Just dog-tired, as my dad used to say.

"I'm going to sleep in one of the other cabins tonight. You and Liz are staying in town, right?"

V nods.

"Take care of yourself," V says.

"You, too."

I grab my stuff and head back to camp, turning on my cell's flashlight to guide my way.

I stop at Pinewood. I can see a tiny light illuminating the bunkhouse. I turn off the flashlight on my cell, creep onto the stoop and look through the window. Liz is on the top bunk, her old bunk, crying. I feel the pull to enter, but instead I turn away and walk to Sassafras.

Our rivals. Fitting.

For all the summers I spent here, I rarely, if ever, entered the Sassafras cabin. It seems as if I'm on an alien planet, although the bunkhouse is pretty much the same as ours was: same number of bunks lined in rows across the floor, same mattresses, same pillows. Except the bunkhouse is red. And the paint is peeling away.

Like our friendship, I think.

I peek at a lower bunk in the far corner. I throw the covers back and scan the mattress for bugs with my flashlight. *All looks good.* I kick off my shoes and crawl into the bed fully dressed, pulling the old sheet and blanket over my legs. They smell musty. They smell like they always did.

I scan my light around the bunkhouse. I can't even remember when, or why, the camp closed. I think of the former owners, Cy and Guy Nigh. We loved that their names rhymed. Everyone yelled, "Hi, Mrs. Nigh!" or "Hi, Guy!" or "Hi, Nighs!" whenever we saw them.

They started the camp because they felt like kids were losing touch with nature, being outdoors, being self-reliant, being around friends.

They were ahead of their time, I think. *All we had then was TV and radio.*

I guess their kids—I think they had four, two boys and two girls?—no longer wanted to run the camp. Or maybe some did. Maybe there were too many memories, good and bad. Or maybe they just ended up engaged in their own Color War.

I get it, I think.

I lay down my cell, put my head on the pillow and try to still my mind. My heart is fluttering, my brain twitching, my mind flying from thought to thought: candidates, campaigns, Em, Liz, V.

How did I get here?

How did I get so far from who I was here?

Suddenly, I am angry at Em for putting us all in this spot. What was she thinking? For such a sweet girl, her little plan seems very mean.

Did she think coming back here would just wipe everything away like dusting away all the cobwebs everywhere? Did she think we would somehow change when we smelled the lake? Or did she just hold out hope?

Scritch. Scritch. Scritch.

I open my eyes. My heart goes from butterfly flutter to hummingbird wings. I sit up in bed.

"V?"

Scratch. Scratch. Scratch.

"Liz? This isn't funny. Are you pulling an old camp trick on me? I'm freaking out here."

That's when I realize they are probably long gone by now.

Scritch. Scratch. Scritch.

The noise is close. Very close. Too close.

I grab my phone, which is sitting next to me, and flip on my flashlight.

A raccoon is scavenging through my backpack. The not-so-little scavenger has it wide open, contents scattered across the floor, and its tiny mitts are elbow-deep in a can of Pringles, eating them four at a time, just like I do.

I scream.

The raccoon doesn't budge. It looks at me and continues to eat.

I pull my knees to my chest and scream again. The raccoon grabs a lipstick from my purse, considers it and throws it aside as if it knows Perfectly Pink isn't its shade. It grabs a container of breath mints, opens it, tries one, seems to like it and tries another one.

You've discovered the wonders of fresh breath, I think, before yelling, "Scoot! Scoot!" at it.

V and Liz appear at the door. The raccoon, knowing it's outnumbered, grabs my Pringles and scurries through an opening in the log wall, which I hadn't noticed this late at night in the dark.

"Are you okay?" V asks, hurrying over.

"Yes. No. I don't know."

Liz stands at the door wearing a bemused expression.

"Why aren't you gone by now?" I ask. "On your way to your hotels?"

Liz looks at V.

"It's getting dark," Liz says. "We don't know the roads well. We didn't want to take any chances."

I give Liz a wary look. *I saw you crying,* I say to her telepathically, a way of communicating we've long had in common. We always said we could read each other's minds.

"I decided to stay for Em," she says. "She deserves it." She looks at me and cocks her head at where the raccoon has just been. "You held the Pringles back from us," she says.

I know this is Liz's way of saying, *Truce.*

For now.

"Come stay in Pinewood," V says.

I don't move. I look at Liz.

She shrugs.

I gather my belongings, throw stuff back into my backpack, and scurry out of the bunkhouse faster than the raccoon.

"Your old bunk awaits," V says, gesturing once we're inside Pinewood. "We've already checked for bugs and critters. We're safe for now."

I jump into the top bunk, above V. Liz gets into her top bunk next to me, above where Em always slept.

I feel like I should get up and wash my face and brush my teeth, wash all this nastiness away, but—for a night—I will be an exhausted camper who just collapses into her bunk. I turn onto my side and pull up the covers. Everything is green. It feels like home.

I shift my eyes and see Liz glaring at me from her bunk. It's a face-off.

This exact scene causes more memories to flood my mind. I turn away. I can't face the truth either. And I've never apologized to Liz for what I did.

V flicks off her flashlight, and darkness engulfs Pinewood.

I think of that cute Taneycomo camper Billy Collins with his mop of blond hair, and his legs covered in those too-high tube socks. Billy didn't want to dance with me because he liked Liz. He always did. And I never pursued him again because I didn't want to hurt Liz. She meant more to me than any boy.

She still does.

But she never knew all that because I never told her all that.

Secrets.

"I'm sorry," I whisper into my musty pillow.

LIZ

Billy Collins is looking at me, searching not just my eyes but my soul.

We are in a tiny boat off Capri. Billy puts his hand in my hair and unties my bow. I watch it fly away and catch on a rocky cliff.

"Are you ready?" he asks.

I nod.

He dips me, and our boat captain yells, "Watch your heads!"

With one swift, deft push, we are inside the Blue Grotto, pulled along chains attached to the cave walls.

I sit up from the bottom of the boat, where we've been lying flat, and feel as if I've entered another world. The cavern is dark, but the sea glows electric blue, as blue as Billy's eyes.

"This is the effect of sunlight passing through the underwater cave," the captain says. "It's magical. It's rare."

Like our love, I think.

I look into the water. It's a color that defies explanation. Billy leans toward me. I put my hands onto his back, feeling the muscles through his tank top. Billy takes my hand, and we stand in the tiny boat. Billy steps onto the blue water, and I start to scream, but he doesn't sink. I step onto the water, and it is solid.

"Would you like to dance?" Billy asks.

"Finally," I say. "After all these years."

The captain begins to sing "O Sole Mio," and it echoes throughout the cave.

The sunlight is beaming into the cave. I don't shut my eyes because I want to dive into the blue of his eyes, sink into the depths of the Blue Grotto and stay there forever.

Billy shuts his eyes.

"No. Keep them open."

My eyes open, and light is streaming into them. I rub my eyes to stop them from watering.

Where am I?

I sit up on my elbows, the sun beaming through the wavy old glass panels of Pinewood Bunk. The light through the windows makes the world look warped, as if I'm in a time machine, or one of those old TV shows where someone is placing a magic spell.

I hear V yell, "Play it again!", and the music pumps even louder.

The Bangles. "Manic Monday." 1986.

I *am* in a time warp. And I *was* just in the middle of a dream.

The Bangles sing again, V and Rach singing backup, and my mind wanders to that Talent Night so long ago. Those buried feelings of hurt rise again like lava in the pit of my stomach, and it burns.

And then I remember where I am again. Caught between two worlds: 2021 and the 1980s.

I've been stuck between two worlds for a very long time: the girl who had so many dreams, and the woman who had to push them aside to be a grown-up.

I'm also now—and have always been—caught between two friends who are more alike than they would ever care to admit. Despite V's sabotage, despite their rivalry, she and Rachel have much more in common than I ever had with them— looks, personality, leadership, popularity, lives that ordinary folk like me aspired to live—and I still feel that jealousy that I tried so hard to bury. They also had more opportunity than I could ever imagine. When your world is small, your chances are, too.

The lava bubbles.

I sit up, and the bunk creaks like a scrub pine in the winter wind.

That's not the bunk, it's my back.

I grab my lower back and massage it. It throbs.

How did I ever sleep on this? It's literally an egg carton on top of box springs.

I toss my legs over the edge of the top bunk. My eyes grow wide.

And how did I ever jump off this? It looks two stories high.

For a moment, I think about doing it, but then I think better: I think of my knees. I think about breaking a hip. I think about all the things you think about now as a middle-aged women.

I smell coffee, and that motivates me.

I edge my body to the end of the bed, turn all the way around and feel with my feet for the wooden posts at the end of the bunks. Slowly, I crawl down the makeshift ladder.

I slip my still-stockinged feet into my shoes and head out the door. I follow my nose. It leads me to The Lodge.

"Oh, my God. It's freezing."

Even though it's the height of summer, mornings are brisk in northern Michigan, probably a good ten to fifteen degrees colder than my mornings in Holland.

"Morning, Rip Van Winkle."

V turns the music off.

She is hunched over the stove in the camp kitchen. She has multiple pans going. Rachel is behind her, stirring.

"This is like *Top Chef*," I say.

"Em thought of everything: arranged access to the kitchen and really stocked us up," V says. "Pancake mix, syrup, coffee. Rach got up early and went back to the little country store to pick up some eggs, milk and creamer."

Rachel walks over and hands me a cup of coffee. It's in a speckled mug with Camp Birchwood spelled out in logs on the front.

"Thank you," I say. "You didn't leave."

She looks at me and shakes her head. "Not yet."
A partial answer.

"Em loved her camp breakfasts, didn't she?" Rachel continues. "The whole shebang: said it reminded her of weekends at her grandfather's cabin."

I lift my mug to toast her and take a big drink. The coffee is strong, very strong, and quite tasty.

"Where did you get this mug?"

"The Lodge is still stocked," Rach says. "It's almost as if the Nighs' kids just closed the camp and left it as it was, ghosts and all."

"That's so sad," V says.

"I bet Cy and Guy would be thrilled to know what Em has done," V continues.

"But it's not a camp," I say. "It's just . . . us."

"But we're keeping the memories alive, at least for now," V says. "Right?"

"Right," I say.

But we're keeping the memories alive, at least for now.

I take another slug of coffee to warm and wake my body, but V's words chill me.

Does it matter?

I think of all the traditions my mother kept alive. She put up seven Christmas trees in a tiny house, she gifted me with charms for my bracelet, she taught me how to make a perfect pie crust and strawberry preserves, she taught me how to sew. But my kids want none of that. They can buy new ornaments online, clothes at any outlet, have their food and groceries delivered to their doorstep. Our society has advanced in so many ways and declined in so many others.

My grandkids don't really interact with the world anymore. They play alone, they don't have hobbies, they don't seem interested in anything beyond their cells, laptops, TVs or games, anything that sits right in front of their own noses.

I don't even talk to my children or grandchildren anymore. I've almost forgotten what their voices sound like. All we do is text.

I look around the overgrown grounds. *Have summer camps become dinosaurs, too?*

My mom sent me to Camp Birchwood for the simplest of reasons: to have childhood summers like she used to have, floating on the lake, catching fireflies, roasting marshmallows, telling ghost stories around a campfire, sharing secrets with friends. She didn't like me slumped in a beanbag chair eating Doritos and watching soaps all day.

More than anything, she wanted to open my world up to new people, things, opportunities.

I shut my eyes and see my mom as a young woman. Time passes so quickly.

Especially when you're lost.

I shake my head to erase that thought, and guilt overwhelms me.

"I need to check in with my mom," I say.

"Pancakes first," V says. "I didn't get up at the crack of dawn and do all this to have no one eat." She stops. "I already get that at home." V looks at me, those eyes flashing. "Do you know how long it's been since I've made pancakes?" She stops again. "Been allowed to make pancakes? I can't even remember. All I make now is oatmeal, acai bowls, green smoothies, kale salads and berry parfaits with no parfait."

I laugh.

"Maybe that's why I closet-eat," V says, smacking her stomach under her Dodgers sweatshirt. "Little Debbies. Still my favorite."

"You are not fat, V," Rach says, flipping two pancakes out of the skillet and onto a red speckleware plate. She slices two pats of butter, smears them across the hot cakes and then drowns them in real Michigan maple syrup. She hands the plate to me. "Stop doing that to yourself."

"I am heavy," V says. "I'm not saying I need to look the way I used to look in my twenties to be happy. I just need to understand why I binge-eat bad food."

I look at Rach. Rach looks at V. We both look away.

"Oh, no," V says. "None of that secret code stuff you used to do."

"What secret code?" I ask.

"That twin thing you two had, where you could talk to each other just by looking at each other."

I look at Rach. She looks at me.

"I forgot about that," Rach says.

"Me, too," I say.

"Jinx!" we say at the same time, laughing.

"See!" V says. "You two always had that bond."

We did? Maybe we had more in common than I think.

Then why did she hurt me so badly? And why did I hurt her? And why did I think I was always the outsider looking in? Why didn't we just talk?

I eat and think about when this all started. It was—*what?*—our second Talent Night, when everyone was pushing Rachel to sing Madonna, and I could tell she wanted to do something more serious. When someone would press her, she would look at me, as if she were desperately seeking advice—and I would just stare back . . . not at her, but into her soul. Without saying a word, we realized we could communicate almost via ESP. She told me once she had that secret, silent bond with her father. Rach ended up doing a very funny scene from *Plaza Suite* by Neil Simon, one that changed everyone's perspective on her talent, and she was the first girl to ever win Camp Birchwood's Talent Night *without* singing. And the first girl to win two years in a row.

Maybe that's why we're so volatile, I think. *We're like family.*

I look at her. *But why did you want me to*

humiliate myself on Talent Night? And why did you steal the only boy at camp I've ever liked?

"Okay, weirdos," V says, breaking our trance. "As *I* was saying, I just want to get a grip on why I eat to deal with my emotions."

"You're bored or unhappy," Rach says, in the only way she can. She looks at V, and her face drops. "Sorry. It's hard for me to turn down the volume. But it's true: you used to be one of the most recognizable faces in America. Now you're a mom and a wife. I'm sure you feel a bit invisible."

"Hey," I start, trying to cut off Rach before she goes too far.

"No, it's okay," V says. "I haven't had a real adult conversation with a friend in decades."

She continues. "You're right. My husband is über-successful. My kids are thriving. And I've been instrumental in all of that. But soon, I'll be an empty-nester. What is it that I want to do for the rest of my life that will make me happy? Not them. *Me.*"

V's honesty chills me. I polish off my pancakes and hug my mug of coffee.

Rach flips two more pancakes onto a plate. She looks at V. "But, if I'm reading all of this right, the biggest question of all is, is your family happy, or is it all just pretend?"

"Okay, okay," I say. "Enough."

Rach turns and looks at me. We stare at each

other for the longest time. I nod my okay for her to finish.

"I'm asking because it's what I'm asking myself right now," Rach says, wiping her hands on her hoodie. "What is happy? When was I happy? How did I lose it? And how do I get there again without losing everything I've worked to become?"

Rach's voice cracks, the only time I've actually witnessed her all-too-familiar brave facade show vulnerability.

"Why do we have such incredible friends when we're young, and then we lose touch with them?" Rach says. "We rarely recreate those same bonds. Is that natural, or learned behavior? Do we grow up and get too busy, or are we just scared of sharing our true selves as adults? What happens to friendships? And, as a result, what happens to us?"

"All of that," I say. "And we just don't want to get hurt anymore. It's easier being alone than being broken."

Only then do we realize that V is crying, softly, like she would do when she'd crack a knee getting out of a canoe or whack her head getting into a bunk.

"I'm okay," she says. "I'm just going for a little walk before I pack up and head home. You check on your mom."

"Go on," Rachel says. "Both of you. I'll clean

up." She looks at us. "I need to start cleaning up my act."

V heads toward the woods, and I head toward my car.

No reception.

I continue walking, up the dirt road, until I get a single bar of reception. I call Manor Court.

"Your mom is the same," Sue, a nurse stationed near my mom's room, says. "You deserve a few days away. Enjoy."

I hang up and call my office.

"Everything is fine," Annie assures me. "Have fun with your friends. Drink some wine. It's beautiful out . . . go hike, go for a swim, get physical. Ooh, the other line is ringing. I gotta go. Enjoy!"

How? I think. *I'm used to doing anything but relaxing. I'm used to taking care of everyone else.*

I sigh and look up. The sun is filtering through the pines, white birch and sugar maples, my three favorite trees. The wind whispers through the needles of the pines, and it reminds me of my mom reading to me at night, her voice as soft as the sheets. The broad leaves of the sugar maples, the stereotypically perfect leaf to me, are a grand green, and the sunlight literally x-rays through them, bathing the woods in an otherworldly glow. And the birch contrasted against the arcing green leaves, the deep shadows of the dense woods and the glorious, humidity-free blue of the sky, a blue that can only be found in Michigan during the summer, makes me feel like I'm in a Glen Arbor gallery and all the watercolors have sprung to life.

As if pulled by their beauty, I wander into the woods. I shed my sweatshirt and tie it around my waist. That's the thing about Michigan: it can go from fifty-five to seventy in the blink of an eye in the summer, and the reverse in fall. I inhale the musty scent of the woods. I remember running through these woods. Em and I would find massive, twisted grapevines to swing on, and we'd climb onto them as if they were rope swings and leap off hillsides and dunes, screaming in both glee and horror the higher we'd fly.

I used to take chances, I think. *I used to live in the moment.*

I think of my mother, bedridden, unable to even stand and walk. *What chances does she wish she would have taken? What chances did Em wish she'd taken when she still had time?*

I see a grapevine, thick and gnarled, hanging over a dry creek bed. My heart races. I grab it on the fly, screaming, my hands already sliding down it, and I jump off just as I cross the creek bed.

"I did it!"

It feels good to move, I think. *Good to be in the moment for once.*

It feels good to get physical.

I stop, nearly tripping over my own feet.

That's it!

I suddenly take off running, leaping over downed tree limbs, mossy branches and stones. Out of breath, I race back into The Lodge. The smell of pancakes and coffee remains, but V and Rachel are gone. I look around, really for the first time.

Large, two-story windows line the huge space, and I run from window to window, opening the curtains. Dust motes dance in the sunlight, just like we used to do. The Lodge served as Birchwood's great hall: it was commons, kitchen and dining room; game room and gathering place; auditorium and theater. Sunlight fills the massive, wood-beamed building, which has the feel of a grand—if dilapidated—lodge where Hemingway may have tossed back a few whiskeys after a day fishing. The banners of each of the bunkhouses still hang from the rafters, and the long tables, stacked with chairs, fill the dining room, the kitchen hidden behind a swinging door that now hangs sadly from a missing hinge. At the far end sits the small stage, and old wooden seats are lined up as if Talent Night is about to start.

I rush up the stairs to the stage, my heart racing in excitement, and head backstage.

My old stomping grounds!

After my infamous fire baton debacle, I

channeled my energy into design, and I spent countless hours backstage designing campers' costumes for Talent Nights: from *Cabaret* to Cher, Wham! to Whitney, I made the costumes that transformed the Birchwood girls into stars.

At least for a night.

The clean freak me is mortified by the mess: backstage is filled with lights, rope, painted backdrops on wheels—starry nights, a park bench before a white gazebo, a café in Paris with the Eiffel Tower in the distance—that set scenes and moods from long-forgotten songs and plays.

The nostalgic me saddens as I open trunks still filled with feather boas, sequined dresses and too-big heels for too-little feet.

Memories, I think. *Forgotten.*

The creative me is bursting with excitement, though, as I tear through the trunks, my heart racing even faster as I toss inspiration pieces left and right like a dog digging a hole in the sand.

I grab armfuls of clothes and fabric and run to my old design room, a closet that I turned into my "design studio."

"No!"

An old door sits atop two sawhorses.

My makeshift table still stands!

On it are my Tupperware bowls of varying sizes filled with needles and multicolored buttons and spools of thread. Scissors are propped into more bowls, and my old pink Singer measuring tape hangs from a nail on the wall. My old Singer is no longer on the table, though. It wasn't mine, it was Cy Nigh's, who brought it to me the summer after my debacle.

"Use this to express yourself," she told me.

I pray that Cy, or one of her daughters, took it, and the old sewing machine has a place of honor and duty in one of their homes.

I take a deep breath and blow on everything, dust flying, and I use my sweatshirt to wipe off my table. I set to work. I am so lost, in fact, that I scream when V and Rach appear.

"We thought you had left until we saw your car still here," V says. "We were packing up to leave."

"You scared the daylights out of us," Rach says. "You've been gone for hours."

"What are you doing in here?"

"Shut your eyes!" I say. "I want to surprise you!"

They look at each other but do as instructed. I lay their outfits in front of them, as if they're backstage and only have a few seconds for a quick costume change.

"Okay, open!"

"What in the world?" Rach asks.

"Hear me out," I say. "I went on a walk, like you did, V, to think. I thought about my mom, Em, my life, the chances we collectively never took. I thought about the Talent Night so long ago that really affected me for so long. It punctured my confidence, not only in myself but in my friendships and taking chances. I had an epiphany: I needed to take a chance again, even if it were only for myself. And I needed to find some way to forgive you. We were just kids."

I realize my voice is trembling.

"I want us to redo a Talent Night."

"What?" Rach asks.

"For real?" V adds.

"For real," I say. "I think I need this. To believe in myself again. Humor me. Please. Then we can all be on our way."

"From the looks of all this, you already have something in mind," Rachel says.

"I'm the one who's choosing the talent for everyone tonight," I say. "No winners. No losers. Just us. Just trust."

V and Rach glance at one another again.

"Okay," V says.

"Okay," Rachel agrees. "But will you trust us, too?"

"I will," I say, nodding.

"Okay then," Rachel says. "Let me make a few calls first to let my staff know I'll be staying another night."

"Then try them on," I say. "Then we have to practice."

"Then we need wine," V says. "To pull this off."

Three hours and two bottles of good northern Michigan sauvignon blanc later, I take a seat in the auditorium. Two battery-powered floodlights we found in a closet, miraculously still working, are aimed at the stage.

"Ready?"

"Drunk? Yes. Ready? No."

I laugh at Rach's honesty.

Conservative Rachel walks out onto the stage dressed in shocking pink tights, a white leotard, a razor-thin purple belt cinched over the leotard, an electric-blue blouse tied in a knot around her middle, electric-blue leg warmers and a white headband. I've ratted her hair to the moon, and she's wearing blue eye shadow and my big white triangle-shaped earrings. I hit Play on my cell to the song I have cued and ready.

I snort so loudly it echoes when she belts out the chorus to "Let's Get Physical" by Olivia Newton-John—inspired by my conversation with my assistant. In fact, it sounds as if a wild pig has entered The Lodge. Although Rach is doing '80s exercises while she sings, including using a Suzanne Somers ThighMaster I found in a trunk, I've forgotten how talented she truly is. Her singing voice is worthy of winning *The Voice*.

When she finishes, I jump out of my seat, screaming and applauding.

I swear I see her eyes mist. "Thank you," she says, before calling out, "Next, sucker!"

I wait for Rach to join me and then click off the floodlights. I hear V's heels click across the stage. When she stops, I turn the lights back on.

V is standing high atop red pumps in a giant-shouldered, black-and-white polka-dot dress. A bright red, wide-brim hat sits atop her auburn hair, and she is wearing a matching red leather belt cinched through a gold circle belt buckle. V is angled dramatically in the center of the stage, one white leather-gloved hand perched on her hip, the other behind her, as if she's a beautiful bird about to take flight. Her legs are turned, ankles bent, elbows pointed, light beaming through her limbs. She is staring at us, her glossy red lips barely parted, like she's going to tell us a secret, and her eyes turn gold, blue, green in front of our very own.

"She looks exactly like she did on her first *Cosmo* cover," Rach whispers.

I grab her hand and stare at her. *I'm glad you understood my vision,* I tell her without saying a word.

"Girls on Film" by Duran Duran begins to blare from my cell, and V struts around the stage, striking poses, like the supermodel she was and still is. When Duran Duran sings about smiling wider and making a million bucks, V drops to the floor and hits her signature tiger pose, and we go crazy.

When the song ends, Rach and I rush the stage.

"That was amazing!" I say.

"I didn't look like a dancing hot dog?" V asks. "Like the one in the concession stand trailer the drive-in theaters used to play?"

"Oh, no," Rach says. "You were radiant." She holds out her hand. "You were born to model." V takes it and grips it.

"Thank you for making me feel beautiful again," V says. "Thanks for giving Em's dream a shot, even for one more night."

"Oh, no, there's one more performance!" Rachel says.

They grab my hands and lead me onto the stage. V runs offstage, her pumps click-clocking on the wood. She returns holding a baton. Series of marshmallows have been taped onto the ends.

"I don't think I can," I say.

"You told us you'd trust us," Rachel says. "We trusted you."

"This Talent Night was your idea!" V says. "The marshmallows were ours! Safe but effective."

"Says who?" I ask.

"Marshmallows burn," V says as if she's Bill Nye the Science Guy.

"I just don't want to get burned again," I say. "By anything. Or anyone."

"It's time to erase that memory," Rachel says. "For all of us."

"What if it erases my hair?"

"That's a small price to pay for redemption," Rach says.

They hand me the baton.

"Where did you find this?" I ask.

"In the back, with all the other stuff," Rachel says. "It's the one you used that night. I think everyone was scared to touch it. I think everyone thought it was cursed."

They look at me.

"This is insanity!" I say.

"No, it's a new start!" Rach says. "Trust. Starting now."

"Okay," I say.

"Hold on," Rach says. She returns with a glass of water.

"Gee, thanks," I say. "But I'm not doing that dance number from *Flashdance*."

"For your hair," she says, deadpan.

"That inspires confidence," I say.

They run to the side of the stage. "We have a short window," V says. "Marshmallows burn quickly."

"How do you know?"

"We've already tried it out," V says.

"Unsuccessfully," Rach adds.

"Great. Me, drunk, with fire. I don't see how this couldn't end well."

Rach holds up the water. "Go!"

V produces a fireplace lighter, ignites the

marshmallows, and then starts the music. It's already cued to the chorus.

I take a huge breath, throw the old baton into the air, marshmallows flaming, and as it rotates down toward me, I shut my eyes and say a prayer.

For my life.

It's then I can feel Em beside me.

I say another prayer.

For forgiveness.

For new starts.

For taking chances again in life.

For trusting my friends once again.

You got it, I can hear Em say.

The music blares.

Burning down the house!

Suddenly, I hear V and Rach cheering, and when I open my eyes, the baton is in my hand, my arm extended into the air. I pull it down, blow out the marshmallows and pop one in my mouth.

"Our Talent Night winner!" Rach yells as V applauds.

They hug me tightly.

"We are so, so sorry for what we said about you," V says.

"Sometimes those who seem the most confident are really not," Rachel says. "We say things we don't mean to make us feel better. Believe me, I've become an expert at that."

"Thank you for saying that," I say. I let them go and look at Rach. "I do have to ask you one more question, though: Did you try to sabotage me by making me do that fire baton routine?"

"Oh, Liz. No. Never. I just wanted you to take a chance. Step into the spotlight. I still do. I never would intentionally hurt you."

Then why did you try to steal my boyfriend? I think but don't say out loud.

I nod.

"I haven't had this much fun in ages," V says.

"Me either," I say. I realize my voice is shaking. "Ages," I whisper.

I tilt my head and smile.

Me either, I swear I can hear Em's voice say.

PART FOUR
Friendship Rock

SUMMER 1986

It is a rainy day, thunder booming and echoing off the lake, the kind of humid summer afternoon when even the sheets are damp. Rachel is playing Uno with Em in her bunk when Mr. and Mrs. Nigh enter, followed by nearly all the counselors. Rachel knows it's bad. Even the youngest camper knows it's bad when everyone comes to get you.

"Rachel?" Mrs. Nigh says, her voice as soft as the rain. "We need to talk to you about your father . . ."

Rachel's father had a heart attack at work. Dropped dead on the spot. No way to revive him. Gone, in the blink of an eye. Mrs. Nigh was going to drive her back to Detroit.

My childhood is officially over, Rachel knows.

She remains calm until everyone leaves, and then she blazes out of Pinewood Bunk and runs directly to Birchwood Lake. She sprints into the water—still wearing her jeans, tennis shoes and green hoodie—and swims toward Friendship Rock.

Thunder booms, rain pours, and it is dark as night. She is sobbing so hard, she can barely breathe.

"Rach? Stop! Come back!"

A voice calling from the shore.

Em.

Rach continues to swim. The farther she goes, the more exhausted she becomes, weighed down by her grief as much as her waterlogged clothes. When she finally looks up, searching the lake, she cannot find the rock. Rachel stops, rain pounding her head. Lightning flashes, and she looks up into the sky.

"Dad?" she yells. "Dad!"

The last memories she has of her father are of him tucking her into bed, singing, *You are my sunshine, my only sunshine . . .* , eating cherry pie on their way to camp and holding her high in his arms so she could put the topper on the Christmas tree.

Rachel stops fighting. She gives up and begins to sink.

"I've got you, Rach! I've got you!"

Rach is in Emily's arms. Emily is kicking with all her might.

"Em, I'm so tired."

"Hold on!" she hears Em yell. "Hold on, Rach! Do you hear me? Don't let go!"

"HELP!" Em yells. "Somebody, help!"

But it is so loud between the rain and the thunder, and the buzz of camp.

Rachel is tired. She now only hears splashing. She sees a lump in the water, Em's wet hair trailing behind. And then Rach passes out.

The next thing she knows she is on shore, and

Em is beside her. A nurse is blowing into Em's mouth. "Breathe, Em! Breathe!"

Rachel tries to sit up, but someone holds her down.

"No!" she screams. "Em! No! It's all my fault!"

Suddenly, Em spews water, and everyone sighs with relief. Rachel goes home, Em goes to the hospital, and when they both return the next year, neither is the same.

Rachel seeks to fill a void left by her father. She seeks to battle others as she does her mother. She seeks to gain attention from men, and overpower other girls, rather than earn respect from either one.

Em becomes even more of a loner, lost in her books, clinging to The Clover Girls as if she were drowning, and they were her Friendship Rock.

Em seemed to understand that all of this—like the four-leaf clover she found that first day—was a sign: she would be the first to die and yet the only one with the strength and the power to keep the others alive and together.

SUMMER 2021
VERONICA

My head throbs, and I search for my phone. I know it is somewhere around me in my bunk. I feel left and right, back and forth. I sit up and finally feel something odd on my body. I squint, trying to adjust my eyes, and that's when I find it: my cell has been taped in my cleavage. There are words written in red lipstick above and below it. I adjust my eyes yet again to try and read upside down what has been written on my chest.

DON'T BE A BOOB!
CALL ME!

I laugh and then slap my hand over my mouth so as not to wake the others.

I haven't acted this silly since my college drinking days. I haven't had pranks pulled on me since camp. And then a question hits me: How drunk was I last night?

I slowly—and with great agony—free the phone from my skin. I illuminate my cell.

6:00 a.m.

My body clock is completely off. I wish the time on my cell was, too.

My mind and body have yet to adjust to the time change. I am still on Pacific Time, which means it's the middle of the night there. But I'm used to going to bed very late, long after David and the kids, and still rising early. My internal alarm just won't turn off.

And it's way off.

I shut my eyes, and last night flashes in my head, in strobes, like it did when I was modeling. It was a stupid night, filled with lots of laughter and wine, a night where time slowed and the only thing that mattered was having fun.

Just like we used to do in camp.

I think of Ashley and Tyler ensconced at their camps, which are nothing like Birchwood. They are more boot camp than summer camp, with an intensive focus on improving a certain skill set. Tyler is not only working to bump his SAT scores at one camp, but will be working on a short film at another to bolster his chances of admission to college and demonstrate his talent in film-making. Ashley is at cheer camp and then acting camp, competing against stunningly beautiful and talented girls whose entire lives revolve around both, girls who've been in gymnastics since they were three, or already have agents and have landed commercials or roles off-Broadway. I was lucky to have been discovered.

Discovered? I think. *Or disloyal?*

I think of Rachel and what I did to her. Would

the outcome have been the same had I not lied to her? Would I have been discovered anyway? The question still haunts me.

Because my gut says no.

I was clueless about the time, effort and money other families spent on their children, or how long many models had been working in the industry just to get their big break. Many of my colleagues despised me for my good luck. Just as many despised their families for pushing them down paths they didn't want to tread.

I think of my children.

Are they really doing what they love? Or are we exerting too much force? Are they happy? Or are they doing this to make us happy?

Another director and actress in LA, I think. *How cliché.* I stop. *That's about as original as having an architect and former model for parents.*

Did they miss out on just being kids? Isn't it important to be well-rounded? To do things they may not be good at, but learning how to fall, fail and bounce back up again? To work together as a group and understand the world is bigger than just yourself?

Enough questions, V. Stop already.

It is still dark. I lie down and try to go back to sleep, but I can't.

I nudge myself out of bed without making the entire bunk shake, a near impossibility. Every little move I make feels as if an earthquake is occurring, a near-weekly event in California, a near impossibility in Michigan.

I feel in the dark for my shoes and my Dodgers hoodie. I baby-step toward the door and my foot bumps something. It rattles. I hold my breath and then click on my flashlight.

Em's vase and ashes. A glass of wine sits beside them.

I forgot we all talked with her last night, as if she were still with us here. We toasted her life. I raised a glass to her vase. And kindness.

You're still such a little girl in my mind.

My heart begins to race. I pick up her vase, as if I still need my friend beside me to hold me tight, and I slip outside and down the steps. It is already starting to get light. I look around.

It's a ghost town.

Em is gone. This camp is gone. Is summer camp dying everywhere, too? Are our traditions fading? I glance at my phone. Everyone is a model now. They think Instagram makes them famous.

All it does is make them like everyone else.

Are my children individuals or clones?

My feet crunch over the dirt. It is quiet, so quiet, as if time has stopped. I look up. Behind me, to the west, the sky sparkles. In LA, the sky—despite the clear weather—is often murky, the night sky cloaked and choked. I've forgotten how clean the world is in Michigan. I reach out to touch the emerging morning sun to the east with my free hand. That's how close it feels. I chuckle at my reaction. In Michigan, you are at one with Mother Nature. It's similar to how I feel when I leave the city and head to the desert of Palm Springs. The skies clear. The stars sparkle. The mountains hold you in their embrace just like the lake does here.

Embrace.

I miss being embraced.

By friends . . . by my husband.

David and I have become business partners. Our children and his success are the foundation of our marital LLC rather than our love and companionship.

I have let this happen. I gave myself over to him and our children and by the time I looked up again, the person I was had been consumed. I had become someone else, someone I no longer recognized.

I think of what I did to Rachel. Did I allow David to sabotage my career in order to subconsciously make up for what happened? I never thought I was deserving of my career, my husband, my home, my life.

I did not sleep well last night. Part of it was the tricks the wine played on my tired body, restless mind and grieving heart, but part of it was despite all our troubles—and I hate to admit it even to myself—I missed sleeping next to my husband.

After all these years of marriage—David's constant travel, our ups and downs—it is still hard for me to sleep in a bed without him. The warmth of his skin. My head on his chest. The way his breath eases when he falls asleep and ruffles the top of my hair. The way the outline of my body fits perfectly with his. How when we first get out of bed in the morning I notice the imprint of our bodies on the mattress and how it seems to make one complete person.

I walk toward the lake. I take a seat, the sand cool and damp on my rear, sending a shiver up my spine. I lay down Emily's vase beside me. I look again at the time on my phone. I know I shouldn't, but I hit "David" on my cell. It rings and rings, and I think it's going to voice mail when I hear, "Is everything okay?"

His voice is husky and panicked, and I already feel bad for calling.

"Yes," I say quickly. "I'm so sorry for waking you up." I stop. "I just needed to hear your voice. I didn't like how we left things."

"What time is it?" he asks.

"Middle of the night for you. Dawn here," I say. "I'm sorry."

I don't say, "I missed you. I couldn't sleep." I'm tired of being the one to say it. I want him to say it.

Say it!

"I've got a bear of a day tomorrow. Big meetings with the city. A lot of press."

"I'm sorry," I say again. I hesitate, waiting.

Say it! Please, David. Tell me you're sorry. That you love me and miss me.

"V, I've got to get some sleep."

My heart, like my head, aches.

"Have you talked to the kids?" I ask, adding time in hopes that . . .

"No," he says. "They're fine. They're nearly adults." David sighs.

"Okay," I say.

Tell me you love me. Tell me you miss me. Tell me you can't sleep. Tell me anything. Please.

He hangs up.

I stare at my phone as it fades to black, just as the world around me brightens.

Did I call to hear his voice? Or was it really a test? Why do I test people to prove their love?

I've long known I was codependent, but I've always considered that a good quality. Shouldn't you be intimately intertwined into the fibers of those you love most in this world? Shouldn't their dreams and desires be yours as well?

Who am I without him? Who would I be without him? How would David be if our roles were reversed? Am I the worst of all clichés, a woman who gave up everything for her husband? Did I follow my own path, or what I felt society expected from me?

I shut my eyes to calm myself and when I open them again, the world comes into focus. Moment by moment, Michigan awakens, and she seems as if she has been lit from within.

Maybe, I think, *it's good to get some clarity. Even if it brings pain.*

It takes a few seconds for my eyes to adjust as the sun begins to rise over the dunes. The birds begin to chirp, and the lake sparkles. Everything comes alive.

There is something magical, peaceful about being the first one up, as if the world is yours and yours alone. I see something move in the lake, and I squint. I am not alone, it seems.

A blue heron is standing statue-still a few feet into the water. The bird is a majestic sight. Though it stands nearly as tall as a child, its plumage is gray, and it tends to fade into the world. I noticed it only because of the tiny ripples it was making. At Birchwood, we once had to write a report and draw a picture about a camp creature, and I chose the blue heron. I search my memory for facts about the bird, and I laugh at the ones I pull from my mental card catalog: the blue heron is a solitary bird, except during nesting season when they make homes in treetops, which become the center of raucous communal living.

"Ahh, the irony, right, Em?" I say out loud.

All of a sudden, the heron's long, drainpipe

neck lunges forward. It pulls a small fish from the water crosswise in its bill and then flips it around to swallow it whole, head first. I move my hand over my mouth. The bird takes flight, belly full, its incredibly long wings expanded. It resembles a plane taking flight, and I watch it soar, its image reflected in the still water. The blue heron glides over the water and then settles on a giant rock in the very middle of Birchwood Lake.

I stand. I forgot. Especially in all the emotions of yesterday.

Friendship Rock.

A huge boulder, smooth and as gray-blue as the heron, still sits in the water as it has seemingly forever. Birchwood Lake is very deep, nearly black in the middle, a rarity among inland lakes, and the camp rumor was that it was connected to Lake Michigan by a channel that ran beneath the dunes. Many say the lake is bottomless.

How did the rock get here? we used to ask the counselors. *How big is it? How could it just sit in the middle of the lake if the water is so deep?*

Counselors used to tell us over campfires that the rock was either formed from an ancient lava flow or it's the top of a mountain peak that used to stand next to Lake Michigan.

When you touch it, you're touching a billion years of history, they'd whisper.

Friendship Rock was the point we'd have to

reach to pass our annual swim test. In my first years, I believed it would be easier to reach the moon than Friendship Rock.

It still seems like reaching the moon, I think, looking at it in the distance.

We could not continue at camp unless we passed the swim test. One at a time, we would swim to the rock, campers cheering. A counselor would be waiting in a canoe in the middle of the lake just in case any of the campers got tired or ran into trouble; another would be seated atop the rock, waiting with a marker. When we'd reach the rock, we'd sign our names and swim back. Once on shore, we would be mobbed by campers, and another counselor would hang a medal around our wet necks.

I take a step toward the water, and my heart races. There was never any trouble, until . . .

The heron stares at me for the longest time, its body perched on Friendship Rock. It cranes its long neck toward me. And that's when I see, written underneath its long legs in the burgeoning sunlight, all the campers' names we wrote so long ago on Friendship Rock. The names—Christi, Melinda, Becky, Sammi—are faded but have survived time and the constant push of the waves.

I stare at the rock and realize the water level has risen gradually and steadily over time— *what climate change?*—and that underneath the surface lie even more names, more secrets.

I turn, grab the vase and pour a handful of my friend's ashes into my palm. I walk back into the lake and scatter them into the water. It is my time to say goodbye now, alone.

"Goodbye, my friend," I whisper. "I love you."

A tear hits the water and sends her ashes moving toward the rock. The heron tilts its head at me and then takes off.

Alone.

RACHEL

Light has a life all its own during summertime in Michigan.

It is magical in the Mitten, but along the forty-fifth parallel, it's downright miraculous.

Light is important to Michiganders. We soak it up when it's available, like a thirsty dog taking in water. It's only available a few precious months a year before winter and the clouds come to call, and Mother Nature closes the curtains and turns off the light switch.

V's rustling woke me up early, too. I am standing atop The Lookout, just post-sunrise, the dune overlooking Lake Michigan and Birchwood Lake. Snuggled in the woods behind me is the camp, and to my right at the base of the dunes is Camp Taneycomo, the boys' camp, still going after all these decades.

A sad band of smoke puffs its way heaven-ward from Birchwood. *Is V or Liz making break-fast?* Meanwhile, Taneycomo is ablaze with light: bunkhouses glow like jack-o'-lanterns, campfires blaze and campers stream around like Day-Glo ants, the reflectors on tennis shoes and shorts beaming in the first rays of summer sunshine.

But the real light show is over Lake Michigan. In the early morning hours, the sky goes from blue-black to orange, then purple, gold and, finally, blue. The water puts on its own performance as well, the waves tipped in a rainbow of color, before the lake turns aquamarine. When the sun gets high enough in the sky, it resembles a pot of melting gold that God has turned upside down, and a trail of golden lava is streaming toward me.

Have I lost touch with my light? Have I lost touch with God?

I speak of religious and conservative values nearly every day, but the two no longer connect in my personal and political lives. I have a successful career. I have a platform. But do I have a purpose?

When I was acting, my soul was filled with light. I felt as if it was what I was born to do, and every day was a gift. I couldn't wait to get my day started. Now I dread mornings. I feel as if I'm playacting, and every day is a burden. I have more power, more money, more clients, but I have no home and no friends. I live out of hotel rooms. My best friend is my cell phone. I surround myself with people who only want what is best for themselves.

I think of my mom and dad. The children of working poor parents, my mom and dad worked hard to achieve a middle-class life in Detroit. Having a steady job with good benefits and a nice little house in a nice little neighborhood was a dream come true for them. Did I turn my back on their values? Or did I simply want more? My dad worked hard. My mom worked hard. I've worked hard. But I've largely done it on my own, and I value that entrepreneurial spirit. I don't need a helping hand.

I turn toward Birchwood Lake. It glows like a little lantern.

And then I see it. Friendship Rock gleaming in the sun.

I lurch forward, hands on my knees, and I feel as if I suddenly might throw up.

It should have been me, I think. *It should have been me.* Not just back then, Em, but now, too. I'm the one who's still not worthy to live. I drag down everyone I'm around.

Without warning, I start running, straight down the dune, without abandon, as I used to as a camper. The dune grass slaps at my jeans, my tennis shoes fill with sand, and yet I keep running, faster and faster down the narrow path, the world rising and falling, until I am standing in front of Birchwood Lake, staring at the rock, confronting my past.

"It should have been me!" I yell at the rock.

I shut my eyes and scream.

After my father died and Em saved me, I fell into a depression. I refused to leave my room, my grades sank, I didn't audition for school plays. I became a ghost.

My mother begged me to talk. She had a grief

counselor come to the house. I even went to a therapist with her.

Mom was a lot like me: headstrong, independent, outspoken, confident. With my father gone, there was no buffer. The fun seemed to die along with him.

I saw her as the enemy. She had always encouraged him to work more hours, get the next promotion, get involved in civic activities to boost his career. *Did she push my father too hard? Did she cause his early death?*

It's what I had done to Emily. My selfishness had nearly cost my best friend her life.

I began to see my mom and my friends through a different lens: we all hurt each other. Women were not nice to one another.

I used to keep a diary with a lock on it. After my father died, I started a good and bad list about my friends, writing it all down with my pink Paper Mate pen:

RIGHTS & WRONGS

The "wrongs" list was quickly much longer than the "rights": all of the squabbles The Clover Girls had over boys, clothes, friends. The petty jealousies. The rivalries. We were friends, but under the surface—like in *Jaws*—the sharks circled.

I added my mom to the list of "wrongs."

Please, Rachel, my mother said one night at the dinner table. *Can we talk? I need my daughter back. I need a friend, too.*

I looked at my uneaten plate of meatloaf, mashed potatoes and corn, my untouched glass of milk and then at the empty chair next to me.

It should have been you who died! I said to my mother. *You!*

Our relationship—like the one I had with Em—was really never the same after that.

I stare at Friendship Rock.

They all tried to save me. Why did I try to hurt them?

The letters and calls from Em and my mom went unreturned, or worse, returned with the venomous red pen that had replaced my pink one.

All I wanted to do was run away from the past, disappear, like Em, into another world, a pretend world of make-believe where everything before never existed.

Friendship Rock seems to wink at me in the sun.

And now Em—in either her great wisdom or her love of irony—has made me return to the world I left to confront my own rights and wrongs.

"Rach!"

"What the hell are you doing? Are you okay?"

I don't realize I am waist-deep in the lake until I hear V and Liz behind me.

"It should have been me who died," I say. "Em was a better person than me. What if I was the one responsible for forcing her to retreat even more, scared to reach out and love someone for fear they might die in front of her? She died alone. Like my father. It isn't fair! It isn't fair! I miss them so much!"

V and Liz race into the water, fully clothed, running and splashing until they reach me.

"Oh, Rachel!" V says. She grabs me and holds me.

"You hate me, too," I say. "Don't pretend. You hate who I've become. You hated who I was. But I became the person I am today because of you both. You turned on me. My best friends sabotaged me. The only good Clover Girl died. The only good one in my family died. It should have been me, long ago. Then none of this would have turned out this way."

"Stop it!" V yells. She shakes me, hard. "Rachel, I am so, so sorry for hurting you. I can never take it back. And I have to live with that every day. But you are a good person, Rachel. You're just lost. We all are."

I stare at the rock. "Am I?"

"You need to find the good in you again."

"Em saved your life for a reason," Liz says.

"What is it?" I ask, bawling.

"To be a good friend," V says. "To be a good person."

"To make a difference," Liz says. "Like she did."

"Like she's still doing," I blurt.

I fall into the arms of my friends, still weighed down by guilt after all these years. I stare at Friendship Rock, gleaming in the light, revealing all of the names written on it, all of the people that have touched it, touched my life.

Maybe I—maybe we all—need a helping hand. Maybe none of us can survive this world alone.

Maybe, I think, *my friend did save my life for a reason.*

Twice.

LIZ

"Oh, my God! I look like I should be in a Whitesnake video!" I say. "But for AARP."

V and Rach double over laughing. With my hand, I wipe off more of the dust covering the mirror on the wall of the Pinewood cabin. I do not look the same as I did decades ago. The old, wavy mirror has a funhouse effect, and it's not very funny at all. Everything looks bigger, out of proportion, and I fear it's not the older mirror. It's the older me.

After we calmed Rach down, dried her off, got her a cup of hot coffee, and held her as she cried, we all decided to stay just a bit longer, have a little summer fun and help get Rachel over her longstanding fear and remorse.

And thus, the 2021 Swim Test was born.

I can't help but feel as if Em were here, trying to tell us something, teach us something, by not only bringing us back here but also continuing to give us ghostly signs that we're meant to be here, right now, this very moment, for big reasons.

My mom used to call such signs *God winks.*

For instance, whenever I looked at a clock at home when I was little, and its number was repeated—1:11 p.m., 5:55 a.m., 12:12—my mom told me it meant I was exactly where I was supposed to be at that very moment.

It always made me happy, and made me feel so safe.

"We just have to be present and aware to notice God winks," she used to say. "But too many of us don't, unfortunately. We're too often lost in our heads, simply trying our darnedest to keep up with all that's going on around us. But Liz, that's like trying to walk on quicksand. Sometimes we need to stop, assess, lift our heads—and our hearts."

Why did we all come back to Camp Birchwood? Why are we all still here? Is this a game Em is playing with us? Or are she and God winking with all their might, hoping that the three of us lost, little sheep will finally pay attention?

A talent show. Now a swim contest. This can't all just be fun and games, can it?

I think of my mom then, and I think of her now.

Time passes so quickly. Aging can be so cruel. We take too little time for fun and games as adults.

"Life is as short as one blink of God's eye," my mom used to say.

Wink.

I look in the mirror again. I am wearing cutoff jean shorts and a green Birchwood T-shirt—sleeves cut off—tied in a knot around my waist.

I did not bring a swimsuit, nor would I wear a bikini, so I made one.

I wink at myself.

"Attagirl," V says.

Rach smiles.

Are they paying attention, too?

"You know," I start, "I've spent the last decades packing for everyone else: juice boxes, back-packs, real estate signs, weekly pill organizers, baby seats and strollers, walkers and then wheel-chairs. I don't even consider myself a priority anymore. Maybe that's why I'm single."

V and Rach nod. "Me, too," Rach says.

I pat my stomach. "What happened to me?"

V comes over to me. She lifts her shirt and rubs her tummy. "Back at'cha, sister." Her voice is wobbly. I turn from the mirror and stare into her pretty eyes. She looks as if she might cry.

"You okay?"

She shakes her head. "I haven't considered myself to be a priority either, and look what's happened." V stops. "It's not that I need or want to look the way I used to look. I don't need or want a perfect body. But why, as women, do we put everyone else ahead of ourselves? And when we even consider doing something for ourselves we feel guilty? We feel wrong?"

"It's how we're raised," I say. "We are the foundation. Everyone stands on us. We support the world."

"My back hurts," V says.

We laugh.

"After all," Rach continues, "Ginger Rogers did everything that Fred Astaire did. She just did it backwards and in high heels."

V and I stare at each other, incredulous.

"You're quoting Ann Richards?" V gasps.

"A Democrat?" I gasp.

I stare at Rach, in that way that we do. She tilts her head just so, as if to say, *I'm starting to understand that women need to support women.*

I nod. She nods. And then I ask, "Are we ready for this?"

"No," V says. "The last time I swam this far was in Aruba. Photographer wanted me to pose on a sandbar that magically appeared in the middle of the Caribbean. It was so windy, I didn't know if I'd make it."

"Was that for the famed photo shoot for the *Sports Illustrated* swimsuit issue?" I ask.

"You remember?" she asks.

I nod. "I used your cover as a dartboard in our game room. Your face was the bull's-eye. I used to toss darts with one hand and hold a baby *and* eat pizza with the other. I was very talented."

"You're not joking, are you?" V asks.

I shake my head. "Gotta admit. It sucked seeing you both in magazines and on TV, when I had two babies on my hips and a husband who never helped. I was insanely jealous, to put it mildly." I turn and look in the mirror. "I kept asking myself, 'What if?'"

"I should have helped you," V says. "I was not as good a person as I thought I was back in the day. I was consumed with making it." She looks at Rach. "And I should never have hurt you like I did."

"Thank you," Rach says. "I appreciate you saying that." She turns to me. "I truly thought you were happy."

"I tried to pretend I was happy. But jealousy and regret are like ingesting poison. There's a constant gnawing pain that just won't go away. It's maddening. It literally eats you alive from inside."

"You *are* talented, Liz," V says.

"Stop trying to suck up," I say.

"You are," she says in unison with Rach, who adds, "And you're still a young woman."

"Define young?" I ask. "I need to start using your calculator."

"There's still time to do anything you want," V says.

"What if I said the same thing to both of you?" They look at each other and then at me, but do not answer.

"Thank you for still believing in me," I finally say. I glance at my shorts again in the mirror. "Maybe one day," I whisper, before thinking of my mother, clocks and time. "Okay, time's a wastin'. Let's do this!"

We head to Friendship Rock, and I suddenly feel like I did when I first started camp. There are as many butterflies in my stomach as there are monarchs swooping through the nearby field of Indian paintbrush in bloom.

"Remember how scary this was?" V asks.

"Was?" I respond.

We had a few chances to pass the annual swim test each summer, and many of us needed every single chance we could get. It sounded so innocent: jump in the water and swim to Friendship Rock. The only rule was that we weren't allowed to dog-paddle; we had to swim, no matter how uncoordinated we were. When we reached the rock, we had to show that we could tread water and float on our backs. Once those goals were accomplished, the counselor waiting on Friendship Rock would hand us a waterproof marker, and we'd write our names on the rock. When we returned to shore, the whole camp cheered and then rushed in to congratulate the swimmer. The bigger part of the swim contest was that it also determined the areas of the water in which we could swim. Believe me, it was humiliating for older girls to be swimming with younger ones.

Em was always the best swimmer. She'd taken swim lessons, and the isolation of swimming seemed to suit her personality perfectly.

"Em was like a duck, wasn't she?" I ask.

The girls nod.

I was a very good swimmer, too, having been raised along Lake Michigan and spending a childhood on the beach. The test was always a challenge for Rach and V, though, who preferred lying on the beach slathered in a mixture of baby oil and iodine, tinfoil-wrapped cardboard in front of their faces.

"You wanna know something sad?" I ask. "I sell Lake Michigan homes, and do you know how many times I've actually stepped foot into the lake the last few years?" I form my hands into a big goose egg. I look down at myself. "I don't even go to the gym."

"Me either," V says.

V is wearing a long-sleeved T-shirt with her husband's company logo over her swimsuit.

"Take it off," I say. "I'm showing my tummy. You show yours. It's time we, quite literally, have guts."

V grabs her shirt, hesitates and stops. "No," she says. "I can't."

"You used to model," I say. "You were used to being nearly nude."

"That was when I had a good body."

"Stop it," Rach says. "You still do. You have curves. That used to be considered sexy. And never forget that's a body that has had two children, moved around the world nonstop and helped build a business with your husband. That body's a beautiful blessing."

V looks at Rach, who is wearing a bikini, not an ounce of fat on her body. "You haven't had children, though. You're still in great shape."

"Women supporting women, remember?" Rach says in her inimitable way.

"I'm sorry," V says, before ripping off her T. "You're right."

"You look amazing," Rach says. "We *all* look amazing."

"Ready, Em?" I ask, nodding toward the rock. "Ready, girls?"

I glance at Rach. *Are you ready?* I ask with my eyes. She nods.

I toss my towel onto the sand and then my phone on top of it.

We grab hands, form a human chain, and slowly walk into the water. When we're waist-deep, we begin to swim, very slowly, toward Friendship Rock.

A few minutes in, I am laboring, my body not used to exercise. I pop my head up and search the water.

Don't look until you get there, Liz, I tell myself. *Focus.*

My shoulders ache, my breathing is ragged. I want to stop, but I look over at my friends. V and Rach are going just as slowly as I am. I lower my head, the cool water splashing my face, the sun on my back, and I am a girl again, swimming with my best friends on a beautiful summer day.

If I pass this test, we can swim together all summer, no questions, just like we used to do.

My hand brushes something, and I lift my head, my heart racing.

I made it!

I look around.

No, we made it!

I clear the water from my eyes, lift a hand out of the water and scream. Rachel clambers up on the rock, stands and yells even louder, her voice echoing across the water. V is laughing. She splashes me with water, and I splash back, and we play like kids.

"Hey!" Rach says. At first I think she is admonishing us for being silly, but she says it again with even more urgency. "Hey! Look!"

Rach helps V onto the massive rock, and then the two of them yank me out of the water, my knee scraping the rock as I go northward.

"Ow!" I say. "What is it?"

Rach is pointing at the top of the rock.

What we first believed were only names still written on the rock is actually something more.

CLOVERS 4-EVER! The writing is fresh, new, written in green, the words encircling a four-leaf clover, each of our initials written in a leaf.

Below that is written:

You did it! Made it this far! TOGETHER!

"How did she . . . ?" I start, my voice trailing

off, water dripping off my body. "She was so sick."

I look at Rach and V, my mouth wide open.

"I don't know," Rach starts, but V cuts her off. "Love," she says. "Emily wanted to show us how much she loved us and this place."

For a moment, we are silent, staring at the clover, the water softly lapping at the rock.

"Hold on!" Rach says out of the blue. "Look!"

She crouches, and I finally notice a long arrow—the kind I used to draw as a kid, the kind we just drew on V with lipstick—trailing around to the back side of the rock. We turn and kneel atop the stone.

You saved my life, too, Rach!

You all did!

xoxo!

Rach collapses atop the rock, and we sit, holding her, until her sobs subside.

We sit like that, in silence, for the longest time, our only companions the hawks that circle overhead, the curious fish swimming beneath the surface and the loons floating in the reeds. Without warning, Rach leaps up and dives into the water. She rubs the rock and then leans in and gives it a kiss, whispering something into its surface. V and I follow suit—friends jumping off Friendship Rock hand in hand, and then we swim, in perfect rhythm like synchronized swimmers, back to the shore.

"We passed!" I yell when we return.

We collapse onto our backs and soak up the sun.

I lie for the longest time, not moving, and then sit up on my elbows, staring at Friendship Rock. I think of Em—so sick when she was here—somehow finding the strength and courage to swim out to that rock and leave a message of hope, strength and love for all of us.

She was alone. But she was not alone.

I turn and look at my friends, their eyes closed, half-asleep.

Em left all of us a sign. But we had to find it. We had to be aware enough to see it.

"Lunch, anyone?" Rach says, startling me. "I'm starving. I think I can whip up some PBJs just like in the old days. Liz, you still like a few potato chips on yours?"

I laugh and nod. "You remember?" I ask.

"You can't forget something that gross," V says.

We stand and look at Friendship Rock. Then V and Rach head toward the camp.

I reach down to grab my shoes, and pick up my phone, blowing off sand. That's when I see the time, the numbers sparkling in the sun.

1:11.

PART FIVE
Coed Social

SUMMER 1987

There were only a few times a year when Birchwood was this silent: when the rain fell in torrents and quieted not only the girls but also the world around them. Campers read, slept, played games, but everyone and everything was hushed, like when it snows in Michigan, and Mother Nature turns down the volume on the earth's remote.

The only other time it got this quiet was . . .

"Coed Social."

Liz says it aloud, in a whisper, to make it real.

And then she whispers, "Billy Collins," to make him real, too.

Liz giggles and shakes her head at herself, her poufy hair falling around her face. She pushes the yellow-and-lime bandana back farther on her head to keep her locks in place and again shakes her head at her immaturity, sending her plastic triangle earrings jangling.

In the days before Camp Birchwood's annual Coed Social, which included Birchwood and the three nearby boys' camps—Taneycomo, Caribou and Golden Arrow—the girls were uncomfortably quiet. With only a select few boys for a lot of girls, the competition was fierce.

Who will ask V? (Everyone!)

Will Em ask anyone to dance?

Will Rach sneak in an older boy who didn't go to one of the camps?

Will Billy Collins sway with Liz to "Crazy for You" under the construction paper stars and then kiss her under the real ones? (No. He always has a different girlfriend.)

At such a young age, the girls placed so much pressure on themselves to be wanted, liked and loved.

This year, V is desperately in love with a boy from Golden Arrow, who broke his arm horseback riding and had to have surgery. Rach's crush, who is working on a salmon fishing charter to earn money before his freshman year of college starts, just told her he had to work and can't make it.

"We're going alone!" V announces out of the blue one afternoon in Pinewood, as if it is an edict.

"Alone but together!" Rachel says.

"Easy for you two to say," Liz tells them.

Rachel stares at her in that way they do, a look that says, "The queen has spoken."

Bye, Billy, Liz thinks.

Em sighs, secretly relieved to have the pressure removed.

"The Clovers are over boys!" V says.

Word gets out, and The Clover Girls become the talk of the camps. That's what happens when you're the popular clique: you set the trends, no matter how silly. All of the other campers decide to go alone, too, which results at first in a cultural uproar but ends with the boys inspired and hopeful they can swoop in and make V or Rachel theirs on a single magical night, just like Sam and Jake in *Sixteen Candles*.

The anticipation makes the days leading up to the Coed Social feel even more like a balloon being overfilled with helium.

In an attempt to make this date-free Coed Social more exciting, Liz spends every waking hour she has making dresses for The Clover Girls. She is fascinated with the Gunne Sax collection of prom dresses that recently took teenage girls by storm, a sort of romantic Little Bo-Peep style. Liz makes Em a long white dress with a frilly overlay at the top and a matching choker from the fabric. For Rach, she creates an emerald-green gown with ruching in the midriff, three tiers of ruffles that end above the knee and asymmetrical sleeves. For V, Liz designs a sophisticated-looking strapless gold lamé dress with gold sequins on the bodice and belt. But Liz saves the best design for herself: a version of Gunne Sax's famed full-length pink taffeta confection featuring puffed sleeves and a draped overskirt fastened with little pink bows. She makes it in hopes that Billy will be her Jake.

Are the Clover Girls overdressed for a camp Coed Social? Yes.

Does V weep when she sees her dress? Yes.

Does it establish the Coed Social for future generations as a summer prom? Yes.

The night of the Coed Social, The Clover Girls march inside as if they are entering the Met Gala.

But for the first hour, as the music plays in the barn near the lake that serves as the make-believe wonderland, the boys are too scared to approach them.

And then . . .

Liz sees Billy Collins striding over, his blond hair slicked back. The entire social comes to a stop.

He is the first boy to approach the clique.

The four Clover Girls line up, the hay bales behind them their thrones.

Billy approaches. Liz sees he is wearing seersucker shorts and a matching jacket and bow tie, like James Bond's son come to life. Her heart spins like a top.

He wore that for me, she instantly knows. *He made an effort.*

Each girl holds her breath.

Liz shuts her eyes. *Dreams do come true,* she thinks.

When she opens them, Rachel has taken a step forward into Billy's path, exposing one long leg, that perfect leg of hers that stops boys in their tracks, the one that instantly turns them into little, demented men.

I can't compete with you, Rachel, Liz thinks. *I can't. Don't make me. I'm begging you.*

Billy stops. And reaches out his hand as Madonna's "Crazy for You" starts to play.

Rachel takes his hand, and the two make their way to the dance floor.

Liz's eyes fill with tears.

As Rach turns in slow motion in Billy's arms, Liz catches her eye.

I'm sorry, Rachel says to her silently.

I hate you, Liz says in return.

And then, as they sway, Billy faces Liz and catches her eye.

He smiles the sweetest, saddest smile at her.

Liz reads it as, *You will never be good enough.*

Billy is actually trying to say, *I'm sorry, Liz. I was coming for you.*

Liz runs out of the barn and back toward camp, tearing apart her gown, leaving a trail of tears and little pink bows.

"Stop! Liz! Stop!"

Liz turns. V and Em are chasing her, their gowns dragging in the dirt, getting dirty, poufy sleeves catching on tree branches.

They grab her.

"You can't run away from us!" Em says.

"Are you joking? With what Rachel just did to me?"

"She doesn't know any better, Liz," Em says, her voice calm. "She's still hurting."

211

"So am I!"

Liz sobs hysterically.

"Come back," V says. "Show them you're stronger than they think. Show them you're a Clover Girl."

"I can't," Liz says.

"You can," V says.

There is silence.

"Just look where we are," Em finally says.

Liz glances down. They are standing in a field of clover.

They return to the barn. When they enter, everyone turns. The song stops, and the world grows quiet. Another song comes on, and V smiles. She walks into the middle of the dance floor, shoulders straight, and holds out a hand. Em rushes toward her and puts her arm around her waist. The two turn and hold out their hands. Liz runs over and joins them. And the three Clovers dance in a circle to "Open Arms" by Journey.

"So now I come to you with broken arms," V sings.

Liz laughs, and the construction paper stars above once again seem to shine as brightly as the ones outside.

And the three dance together as friends all night long.

SUMMER 2021
VERONICA

"Do you hear that?"

I look at Rach and tilt my head, listening.

In the distance, a bugle plays.

" 'Reveille,' " I say with a smile. "Camp Taneycomo."

"I can't believe the boys' camp still does that," Liz adds with a husky chuckle, joining us at the campfire, rubbing the sleep out of her eyes with the end of her hoodie.

"Here, Sleeping Beauty," I say, handing her a cup of campfire coffee.

"Beauty is a stretch these days," she says. "I'm glad we stayed a little while longer."

"Me, too," I say.

"Me, three," Rach adds. "Thank you for yesterday. It . . ." She stops. "It saved me in a lot of ways."

I nod.

"Speaking of the lake, I think I need a good, long, hot shower," Liz says. "Bathing in the lake is exhilarating, but it's not quite as fun as it was when I was seven." Liz takes a big slug from her cup and looks at us. "I'm worried I'm going to find a minnow somewhere I shouldn't."

We laugh, and then the bugle sounds once more.

"Why haven't we noticed that before?" Rach asks.

"Hangovers?" I ask. "Although I'm going to stick with my original story and continue to blame the direction of the wind."

"The boys of Taneycomo," Liz says with a sigh. "Remember?"

As if on cue, we begin to chant in unison:

Camp Caribou boys you marry,
Golden Arrow boys you miss,
but the boys of Taneycomo
have the gnarliest bods
and lips you want to kiss!

The three of us toss our heads back and laugh, so long and loudly, tears fill my eyes.

"Totally gnarly," I finally say.

"Bangin'," Rach adds.

"No duh," Liz says.

I take a sip of coffee and lean toward the fire, the heat warming my face. For so many years—even at a girls' camp where there were no boys and which prided itself on making us independent—our lives were still defined by boys: *Who liked us? Who might like us? Who would totally like us if they weren't seeing that girl back home?*

Em always liked the shy, smart guys, the ones who read books behind trees instead of playing flag football, the ones whose bangs slid behind their glasses and whose faces turned beet red when you'd make her talk to them. Rach went for the bad boys, the ones she knew would never call her back or meet her after school at the Orange Julius at the mall as promised. Liz liked the all-American boys, the blond cutie-pies who your parents wouldn't bat an eye at twice if they asked you to go to the movies.

And me? I liked the rebels. Not the bad boys, but the guys who looked, thought and acted outside of the box.

If I were Andie in *Pretty in Pink*, I would have chosen Duckie over Blane. He had his own style and personality. He was funny.

David used to be like that, I think. But over time his work consumed him, and he put his soul into his career, leaving him a shell.

As I sip my coffee, I look around the group. In many ways, our girlhood crushes defined us. The boys Em liked never had the guts to make a first move, so she remained alone. The boys Rach liked treated her like crap, and that has seemed to continue, especially in her professional life. Liz's boys were so safe, so by-the-book, that you never realized they weren't happy until they walked out the door.

Have I—have we all—allowed ourselves to

continue to be defined not just by men but by men who are actually wrong for us?

Growing up, I could never be a skeezer—that's what we called the girls who were always all over the popular guys—because I wasn't in the clique. Being on the outside looking in for so long forced me to like boys who weren't in the in-crowd, guys who also had to discover who they were at an earlier age, just like me.

That's not a bad thing, V, I think to myself.

But to be defined by men our whole lives? To romanticize their every move, word and deed?

That is a bad thing, V.

"Boy on the premises!"

Liz yells so loudly that I jump out of my skin and toss my coffee into the campfire. That's the phrase all the Birchwood girls yelled when a man of any age showed up unannounced at camp. Many a visiting dad was startled into dropping his car keys in the woods, and many a horny boy ran in the other direction when Birchwood girls yelled that warning.

"Are you insane?"

I stand and turn to look at Liz, but she is pointing in the opposite direction, repeating "Boy! Boy!" just like a nervous girl whose crush is approaching.

A figure, tall and lean, hidden in shadows thrown by the pines and the bunks, approaches at a fast pace.

"V?" he calls in a deep voice. "V?"

Oh, my God, I think, *it can't be.*

"David?" I say.

I hand Rach my mug, and begin running at him, just like in a cheesy rom-com. I nearly knock David over.

You passed the test! I scream to myself, thinking of our phone call the other night. *You passed the test! You came all this way! For me! Because you love me! You were worried about me!*

"That's quite the welcome," he says. "I missed you, too, honey."

I kiss him, hard. Again. And again. I hold him at arm's length and then shake him to make sure he's real.

"What are you doing here?"

"I was worried about you," he said. "That call so late. You didn't sound like yourself. I hopped on a red-eye to Detroit and a puddle jumper to Traverse City."

"Planes, trains and automobiles just to reach me," I say.

"Just no John Candy," David says.

"Those aren't pillows!" we suddenly say at the same time, referencing one of our favorite holiday movie moments.

"What about your meetings?"

"They went well," he said. "And I postponed a couple. Said I had a family emergency."

"I don't know what to say." I kiss him again.

"Oh! Come meet the girls." I turn, and nearly bump into Liz and Rach, who are standing mere inches from us. "I see you've already met," I joke.

"Hi! I'm Liz!"

David extends his hand. "It's so nice to finally meet you."

"Rachel."

"Oh, yes," he says. "I've heard a lot about you."

Rach's eyes narrow. "I bet," she says.

"Let me show you around," I say to David, averting any conflict.

I grab my husband by the arm and drag him toward The Lodge and then to our bunkhouse.

"And this is Pinewood," I say. I take him inside and begin pointing. "Where we all met. Where we all bonded. I slept here, Em slept down there, Rach and Liz slept up there."

My voice is high and excited. I feel like I'm sharing a part of me with David that he never knew.

"This is who I was," I say. "I'm starting to realize all of this made me who I am." I stop. "These girls . . . these women . . . these friendships . . . I am me because of them." I stop again. "I don't think I realized that until Em asked us to come back here."

I turn to look at David, suddenly feeling vulnerable, as if I've just dropped my clothes and am standing naked before him.

David looks at me, his face softening.

You know how you look at someone you love, be it your husband, wife, child, parents—when you're on vacation, or sending them off to their first day of school, or witnessing them winning an award—when they're completely out of context, and it's as though you see them fully for the first time?

This is one of those moments.

David is more handsome than I remembered even a few days ago. His floppy dark curls—the roots tinged in silver—his dark eyes behind his hip glasses, the five-o'clock shadow already forming on his angular face, his lithe body in a tight shirt and formfitting dark jeans.

"I'm so glad you've had a chance to reconnect," he says.

"Me, too," I say.

"I have to admit this place is pretty cool," David says, turning slowly in a circle to take in the bunkhouse. "Totally nostalgic. I feel like I've been dropped off on the set of *Dirty Dancing*. I mean, the architecture of these buildings . . . the old camp blankets and nostalgia and vibe . . . it's very special, V."

I beam. "I know, right?" I say. "I'm glad you think it's cool."

I fill him in on Em's letter and her hopes for all of us to reconnect.

"We already had a Talent Night and a swim

contest, if you can believe it. It's like I'm reliving my childhood camp days. And I'm making friends all over again."

"Well, from what you've said, at least the state will be able to keep it," David says. "Your friend planned well. The state can maintain it the way it needs to be. It should be on the historical register."

I cock my head. There is a buzzing in my ears. It's not mosquitoes.

"We haven't decided what to do yet," I say. "I feel like everything's evolving in real time. I know it sounds crazy, but I feel like there's a reason we're all here."

David smiles at me, in the way parents do at their kids who don't understand why you can't just lasso the moon for them, or buy them a pony. "V, you haven't talked to these people in decades. They're not your friends. They're strangers. What do you know about them?"

I suddenly feel like I'm in shock.

David continues: "They probably Googled me. They know how successful I am. They certainly know how successful you were. Who knows what they might be after?"

"No," I say. "No. You don't know them. They don't need money. We need . . . each other. We need . . . this place."

"What you need is some rest." He stops. "I think you're emotionally exhausted. And, by the looks of all of you, it's been a taxing—and shower-free—few days." He laughs. I don't. "Where's your stuff? Let's pack it up, and go have some fun."

I am having fun, I think.

"I canceled my hotel," I say. "We all did. So we could be together. Stay a few extra days. Figure this all out. That's really what I wanted to tell you the other night."

"I booked a room at a beautiful lodge in Leland," he says.

"Fishtown," I say.

"What?"

"That's what they call Leland."

"Oh," he says. "Anyway, I was lucky to get it. I can pack your stuff while you say your good-byes, okay?"

He turns.

Did David come here for me?

Or did he come here to control me?

"No," I say. "Not okay."

"What?"

"I feel like I should stay." I stop. I try to keep my emotions in check. "No, I feel like I need to stay." I look at David and reach out my hand. "I hope you understand. This is really bringing up a lot of important stuff about our lives, who we became and why." He looks at me. "And I love that you came," I continue, taking his hand. "Really, I am. It means the world. But I wish you would have called to let me know. This is so unlike you. It's just that I want to be with my friends right now. I need closure . . . or a new start . . . or something. Stay for a few days. Fall in love with this area like I did. We'll show you around . . ."

"We'll?"

". . . but we have to stay here for a week together if we want to keep this place."

"Have you lost your mind, V? Do you hear yourself? Your 'friends'? 'Keep this place'? You're exhausted."

"No, I'm not!" I protest. "I have clarity."

"But what about us? We never have us-time."

Everything shifts. The last sixteen years of my life have been lived on David-time.

David knew when he wanted to have children and how far apart he wanted them. He uprooted our family's lives every few years for his career. I woke every few hours to care for the babies because I knew he had to rest. I got up at dawn with him—while he worked out and readied for work—so I could press his clothes and make his breakfast. I took the kids to soccer and dance and baseball and band because he was always so busy. I ate fast food because my life was spent in the car running errands to make his life as easy as possible.

Us-time? I made countless dinners that went cold when David said he was "on his way." I sat by myself in restaurants because David got hung up. Vacations were canceled because work got in the way. Weekend plans were consumed by phone calls and "Don't disturb Daddy!"

There was never us-time.

"That's not my fault," I say. "I didn't ask you to come."

"But I did. And I came all this way, even with all I have going on, for you."

"For me?" I ask. "Or for you?" The tone of my voice surprises me. It is ice-cold and tinged with sarcasm. "Why?"

"Because I love you," he says.

His sentiment comes out sounding like a question, and I release a staccato laugh that echoes in the bunkhouse.

"Do you?" I ask. "Is that why you came? Were yo͏ truly worried about me? Or did you come ḥ vou didn't like that I was showing my ͏ independence since we met? Did ͏ love to control me more ?"

ht now, V. I flew across you. Do you know how et away?"

I suddenly yell. "Do you was *for me* to get away? To ͏ felt like I had to ask for your come. When did that become

223

dates listed below:
s are due on the
When ghosts come home : a novel
Title:
Author: Cash, Wiley,
Item ID: 00005242023264
Date due: 12/4/2021 23:59
Renew Your Items
we247.org
Willowick Public Library
(440)943-4151
Total Items: 1
Date Printed: 11/13/2021 9:46:?? AM

normal? Why did I let it?" I take a breath. "I love you, David. But I don't think you even like me anymore. My weight. My looks. You married a model, but I don't think I'm the model of what you desire any longer." I realize I am still holding his hand. I give it a squeeze and shake. "Do you understand how important this is for me right now? I hope that you do. If so, just give me a few days."

David drops my hand.

"I don't actually," he says. "These people are virtual strangers. I was just being polite to your friends when I said that you talk about them because you don't, V. You never did. And that Rachel . . . she makes my skin crawl just to see her in person."

"I never talked about them because we all had a falling out," I say. "Did you know that? No. Because you never asked. Do you know how many times I tried to broach the subject with you, and I got a finger wag to stop me from talking? Did you ever wonder why I didn't have any close girlfriends in my life? No. Because you never asked. Did you ever consider I may have been lonely and depressed, and so I ate because I wasn't happy? No. Because you never asked."

"So now everything is my fault?" David says. "I gave you a life any woman would dream of—you have a beautiful home, beautiful children . . ."

"*You gave* me that life?" I ask. "*I earned* that

life. How do you think your entire career got off the ground? It was my money, success and notoriety that helped make you."

I stop, nearly panting for air.

For a moment, I just want to make it all okay, like I always do. But the ghosts on my shoulders begin to whisper, the forgotten whispers from male photographers who asked me to lose more weight, the voices of boys who wanted me to act stupid even though I was smarter than they were, the echoes from men who made all the decisions.

And I always allowed it. I always allowed it.

"So I ruined your life?" David says. "Wow."

"No," I say, my voice shaking. "You didn't ruin it. You just erased it. And I was dumb enough to hand you the pencil."

The shadow of a pine slides across the bunkhouse and suddenly covers David in darkness. He, too, is erased before my eyes.

David spins on his heels, storms out of Pinewood, the screen door banging behind him. I stand paralyzed, expecting him to return.

What just happened?

"V?" Rach calls.

"Are you okay?"

They both rush in, and I burst into tears.

In the distance, I hear gravel spit, a car engine roar away, and then a bugle. It's no longer "Reveille" being played by a skilled musician and counselor, but a rather sad incantation, a blur of hair-raising bleats—like a crazed goat being goosed. I know an annoying boy has confiscated the instrument and is now creating chaos for everyone around them.

Boys, I think. *It's always boys causing the problems.*

And it always has been.

RACHEL

From The Lookout, Camp Taneycomo resembles an episode of *Survivor*.

Boys paddle kayaks or learn to sail on Lake Michigan, run on the dunes and race on the shoreline. From a distance, they look as if they are creating complete chaos in the world.

I look at my cell, dreading the call I have to make.

To a chaos-making boy.

The Lookout is one of the highest spots around, with one of the best vantage points for miles. It's also one of the few I know will have more than just spotty reception.

I stare at my phone. I have two bars and—as my dad used to say when he was angry—zero shits to give.

The boys yell at the top of their lungs—just like boys always do—and I shake my head. They sound the same as they did in the '80s. Times change, boys don't.

Have I?

I look at my cell again. There was a time not that long ago when you could go away and not be reached. Now we are accessible to one another 24/7. We expect others to be accessible 24/7. We are online, constantly connected, but oh-so-divided and alone. There is no downtime. My eyes wander back to camp.

Maybe they call it the good ol' days for a reason, I think, sounding just like my dad again.

I think of when parents would call Birchwood. A counselor would come and get us, and we'd have to walk to The Lodge to use one of the two rotary phones available.

I smile and think of the giant red rotary phone I had growing up that hung from the wall in the hallway between my bedroom and my parents'. I called it the Bat Phone because it was so big and bright. I stretched that phone cord into my bedroom, pulling it until the coil disappeared and the cord turned as long and limp as an over-cooked noodle of spaghetti, talking to my friends and whispering to boys who called. It was, literally, my lifeline back then.

One Christmas break, I got hooked on those party lines, where teens paid a buck a minute to talk to—and flirt with—other teens from around the country.

Hi, this is Tanya, I would say, lowering my voice into a husky tone. *I'm seventeen, and I like bad boys.*

I invented lots of personas for myself—I was head cheerleader, I was a gymnast, my parents had a home in the Hamptons, I once guest-starred on *Dynasty*—not realizing that everyone else was doing the exact same thing: lying to be liked. And we still are.

My dad was furious when he got the bill. $283.15. Like my childhood phone number, I can still remember the exact amount vividly. He handed the bill to me and said I had to pay it back myself. I did. I got a job at Baskin-Robbins, scooping ice cream.

Looking back, though, I think that's when I got the acting bug. I was good at creating characters, inventing storylines, being someone else.

That's when I got the lying bug, too.

Have I ever been myself?

I lift my face toward the sun and inhale.

Here, I think. *I was here.*

My friends encouraged me to sing and act. I was told I was talented. I was nurtured and loved. Even V's deception taught me to fight. Would I have been willing to walk through walls, handle rejection and face such harsh judgment if I hadn't had to work just a little bit harder?

There is something about the way Michigan smells in the summer—the scent of the pines, lake, flowers, heat off the sand—that makes me feel like a kid again, that transports me back in time, like when I wore Love's Baby Soft, my mom wore Obsession, my dad sported Old Spice, or a boy wore Drakkar Noir. I miss all of those things: being young . . . my mom . . . my dad . . . boys.

Screams echo across the water. The massive dunes inhale the sound, as if that's the youthful elixir that keeps them ever-strong, and then it exhales as sand into the breeze, whispering its secrets into my ears as it whistles by.

I shut my eyes, and I am a girl again. Not that much has changed, really. It's the same world in a new format: kids create perfect images of themselves on social media; they Photoshop pictures that end up looking nothing like themselves; we outdo one another with our *I'm-happier-than-you-are!* Facebook posts; kids invent worlds where they are social influencers but have had no real role models or the knowledge and experience to influence anyone about anything.

If I looked closely in the mirror, really closely, I'd know I've contributed to this. I know I would have to take responsibility. But instead, when I look, I see a character, a role I'm playing, a life invented.

My father was my role model. My friends and my mom were role models, but we hurt one another so deeply.

I, on the other hand, am not a role model. And this proves it: I lift my phone, take another deep breath and dial.

"Where the hell have you been? And where the hell are you?"

"Good to hear your voice, Ralph," I say, my words dripping in sarcasm.

He laughs. "Haven't lost your edge, I see. Good, good."

"Family emergency," I semi-lie.

"My poll numbers are trending down, Rachel. Not good, not good."

He doesn't ask about my emergency. He doesn't ask about me.

"Don't panic," I say. "We're in the dead zone right now. People are on vacation. Your voters—the ones with money—are at their summer homes. They're not picking up phones and responding to polls."

He sighs. "Okay, okay." That's his MO—short phrases that he repeats over and over. It's all his brain can handle. "Wofford is all over my ass, though, right now. All over my ass. See her signs everywhere: Women for Wofford."

"She's raised a lot of money, Ralph. Not as much as you have in the vault, but a lot. We have commercials set to air in September and October. The airwaves will be flooded with your face and message."

"If I lose to a woman, Rachel, your career will be over. Over."

I don't respond.

"The whole equal pay, maternity leave BS is killing me."

"Ralph, I knocked that balloon out of the air on *Red, White & You*."

"My supporters don't like all this women's

libber nonsense. You, as a woman, need to reiterate how much women love me."

The world begins to spin, and I feel as if I might be sick. It's like talking to a real-life Archie Bunker decades later. It takes every fiber of my body not to scream, *You're a thrice-divorced man whose grandfather invented street cleaners. You're the one who needs to be swept into the gutter where you belong.*

"Women do love you," I say instead. "I love you, Ralph."

I can hear him exhale. "Women love me," he says. "Women love me."

In the near distance, boys scream.

"What's that noise?" Ralph asks.

"My stomach," I say. "My clients never give me enough time to eat."

"Camera adds ten pounds," he says, not joking.

You're 5'7", 280 pounds, Ralph. Cameras have to move back to the suburbs of Detroit to fit you on screen.

"I will be in touch," I say.

"You better, you better."

"Bye, Ralph."

I hang up before he has a chance to reply or I say something I'll regret.

I lift my head and scream—something I've been doing way too much of lately—my anger catching in the wind before being consumed by the dunes. I shut my eyes, and the sand whispers something to me.

A secret message.

Make amends.

"I know, I know," I say to the sand. "You're right."

I hear a boy scream. I swear his voice says, "Apologize."

"I know, I know," I say to the echo. "You're right."

I think of V and her husband, and my mind turns to Liz.

I can still see myself step in front of her, extend my leg and take Billy from her.

My mind turns to my mom. *Why didn't I confide in her?* She could have helped.

The wind whistles a sad song. *Was she as lonely as I was?*

Is she as lonely as I still am?

I take a deep breath, inhaling summer, the smell of my youth enveloping me, past memories wrapping me in their warm arms.

I know there is one call I must still make in order to honor the dunes' secret advice, but it's not to any boy. I lift my cell, begin to hit Call, but stop.

I cannot make the call.

"Make me stronger," I whisper to the dunes. "Make me stronger."

LIZ

The camp is eerily quiet. V is in her bunk, and Rach stomped off toward the lake, cursing under her breath about "boys." I am sitting in The Lodge, which is also silent, save for the squirrels or raccoons—or who knows what—skittering around in the rafters.

There were only a few times a year when Birchwood was this silent: when it rained or was nearly time for the annual Coed Social.

I say it aloud, in a whisper, like I used to do, and then I giggle, before shaking my head at my immaturity. I wrestle my poufy hair out of my face, pushing the yellow-and-lime bandana back farther on my head. My plastic triangle earrings, also lime, slap my face. I stop shaking my head.

I have changed so much over the past decades, but so little.

I'm still the same ol' Liz, and I don't know whether that's a good thing or not.

I think of all the men in my life, and Billy Collins pops into my head. I shut my eyes.

Why do boys from our pasts—old flames, bad exes, but particularly our secret crushes, the ones we never had—still crowd our minds, like ghosts crashing a party?

I open my eyes again, and see cobwebs draped from the lights, dust coating the tables, leaves strewn across the floor.

Because they're not real, I think. *They never were. We just want to dream of a life that might have been better than the one we've lived.*

I think of my family and my marriage.

All ghosts.

How does our past affect our present? Does it make us want to see things that aren't there? Are we scared of what we might discover? In others? In ourselves?

I think of my husband. *What was it like in the past?* We did love each other, but then it faded and finally disappeared. Getting married just seemed like what I was expected to do. I didn't even question it. And then I believed that parenthood would complete a perfect picture, but obligation, work, bills and exhaustion erased the border, then the background, finally our images entirely.

I tried. I really did. I juggled children, a career I hated, laundry, cleaning, cooking, errands, carpool, practices and still crawled into bed— stifling bone-tired exhaustion—reaching for my husband, feeling for his hand, tucking my body into the curve of his, only to have him yawn and roll away. I made dinner reservations and hired babysitters. He would not even turn off the football game and set down his beer to consider it. I begged him to go to counseling. I begged him to talk to me. I begged him to kiss me.

And then, one day, you just stop. You go numb. Routine becomes comfort. Love turns into complacency. Spouses become roommates.

The hardest part? He left *me*. Remarried a year later. Now he goes out on date nights to dinner and on beachy vacations. I know because I'm *that* girl. Yes, I've stalked them on social media. I even saw the bastard holding her hand in our grocery store. It wasn't even the fact that he was holding her hand that was the most galling part to me. It was the fact that he *actually went to the grocery store.*

In the days I've been away, I have not heard from my kids. They have not checked on me. They will not check on their grandma. *Why is it me always holding things together?*

How did you do it, Em?

I stand, pushing my too-little chair back too quickly, and it clatters behind me. I am bigger and stronger than I was as a girl, I realize a bit too late. I head to the kitchen, as if by instinct. It is the same as it was: '80s appliances. A trash compactor. A microwave—big as a UFO—that says LOW RADIATION across it.

"I'm amazed we're still alive," I say to it. "I'm amazed anyone could make a meal in here."

But we did. And we still are.

This kitchen used to be buzzing with people,

adults and kids alike, all chopping, washing, cooking as a team. When we became counselors, The Clover Girls had full run of the kitchen. If any of us were feeling down, Em—the mom— would make us slice-and-bake chocolate chip cookies.

I study the kitchen. Though Em got some things working—electricity and water in here— most of the light bulbs are burned out, there is no water in the bathrooms, and we have to use the old outhouses scattered about the property that the Nighs kept for "emergencies."

This place has a lot of *potential,* I think, a phrase all real estate agents love to use for decrepit, problematic properties that should probably be torn down but have a unique history. I've sold countless creaky cottages on the lake-shore that were built a century ago and loaded with charm.

And mold. And dry rot. And bats. And sewer issues. And knob-and-tube wiring.

I do the math in my head and wonder how much it would cost to get this camp up and fully running again.

A lot.

Would Em's endowment cover the repairs? I'm sure there are updated building codes, and Birchwood likely meets none of them.

I know something about home repair. I've duct-taped washers, I've unplugged disposals, I've cleared drains with wire hangers, pulling out clumps of hair as big as Garfield. I've installed pull bars, grab bars and shower seats in my mother's home, and then taken them all down, all while overseeing the city as it trenched up her collapsed clay pipes and installed new ones before I could sell her home. As an agent, I've fixed sticky windows, cleaned bathrooms, chased snakes out of garages, doing it all in high heels.

I don't—and will never—need a man's help again.

But this?

I look around again, and the critters having their own Coed Social in the attic answer my question for me. I may not need a man, but I do need help. And this . . . this is beyond my pay grade, skill level and allotted time frame—I mean, who knows how many more days or hours we will all be here considering the current emotional terrain? How fun would it be to surprise the girls with running water in the shower before we left, even if it's on the last day we're together? What a sendoff that would be!

I open cabinets and rifle through drawers. In the catch-all drawer—the one every house and kitchen has—is a warped, yellowed, water-stained manila folder.

"Bingo!" I whisper.

The folder is filled with business cards, pads of paper jotted with contacts.

I yank one out that says, fittingly, *Ed Yankton, Plumbing,* and dial the number.

"The number you've dialed is no longer in service."

I try another and another, but my phone drops service and I realize that none of these numbers will work since they're nearly forty years old. I look at the card again. Fax numbers are listed at the bottom. These cards are from the age of dial-up, when you could take a shower, do your hair and make dinner in the time it took to secure a computer connection.

These men probably aren't even alive anymore, I think. *But I know where some are.*

I march out the kitchen door of The Lodge and beeline toward the lake, following the sound of boys yelling.

I circle around the lake and take the well-worn path that the Taneycomo campers used to walk to Birchwood Lake. That connects to another path—half dirt, half sand—that sits along a ridge, the dividing point between the towering dune that heads to Lake Michigan and the thick woods that have always separated the girls' camp from the boys' camp.

The noise level grows as I near.

It's so much louder than Birchwood ever was, I think.

And then I see the Camp Store.

Still there, I think.

The Camp Store is a log cabin commissary that dispenses toiletries, batteries and snacks. Birchwood didn't have a Camp Store, per se; girls were too embarrassed to have to go to a Camp Store to buy "necessities," so we just asked our counselors or went to see Cy Nigh. We also had nightly "sweet treats": cookies and milk, or s'mores by the campfire, or—my favorite—Doughboys, which Rach called a Stick Biscuit, that consisted of cooking dough on a stick over a campfire.

"Hello," I call, walking up to the Camp Store.

The window is open, but I don't see anyone in the tiny little cabin.

"Hello?"

I lean on the ledge, lift my hands to my eyes and peer inside. The old Camp Store now resembles an Apple store lodged in a log cabin: at least fifty cell phones are plugged in and charging, along with a dozen laptops. A teenage boy is wearing headphones and playing a game on his cell.

"Hello!" I call again.

He looks up at me.

"Hi!" I say.

He doesn't react, just stares. I pantomime removing headphones from my own head, and it finally dawns on him that I might want to talk since I'm standing in front of him.

"Um, yeah?" he says. The boy is lanky and wears a glazed expression on his face. He sports a mess of Justin Bieber hair, which nearly covers his glassy eyes, that sweeps all the way from the back of his head into a perfect feather over pretty much his entire face. I wore my hair like that in a cute bowl cut when I was little and my mother was obsessed with Dorothy Hamill.

"I'd like to buy a Tab, a canister of Planters Cheez Balls and a box of Quisp," I say, deciding to mess with him.

"What?"

"Those were snacks we used to buy at the Camp Store in the '80s," I say. "I was a Birchwood girl, and we'd sneak over here and buy stuff."

He stares at me, completely confounded, as if I had just plunked a rotary phone in front of him and asked him how to use it.

"Sorry," I say. "I have a question. My friends and I are camping at Birchwood . . ."

"Isn't it like closed or haunted or something?" he asks.

"Closed," I say. "Not haunted." I stop. "Is it haunted? Why do you say that?"

" 'Cause it's creepy," he says. He whisks his hair out of his eyes in a quick motion, and seems to see me for the very first time. "Are you famous?"

"What? Me? No. Why?"

" 'Cause you look like that woman my mom likes who used to sing in the olden times, and now she's, like, really old but still tours and

241

my mom goes to see her every time she comes to Detroit, and I'm like, 'No, Mom. Stop.'" He takes a big breath and continues. "So, are you her? Or like not? So . . ."

I stare at him, mortified. He could be talking about anyone, from Rosemary Clooney to Madonna, Cyndi Lauper to Cher. I mean, he probably thinks Taylor Swift is ancient.

"I'm not her," I say.

"Oh. What's your question?"

I'd forgotten I had one. I open my mouth when I hear, *"Girl!"*

Two young boys are pointing at me. I'd forgotten girls aren't allowed—or they weren't back in the day—at Taneycomo, but I'm just so flattered to be called a girl after Bieber here suggested I may be Ethel Merman that I'm not at all scared.

"May I help you?"

I turn, and the most handsome man is standing before me. He's ruggedly attractive, like the boy-next-door-who-grew-up. He's wearing a Taneycomo T-shirt and beneath it looks to be reasonably fit, in a very Midwestern, outdoorsy, I-like-beer-and-brats-and-football-and-mowing-my-own-yard sort of way.

Not that I'm noticing, mind you.

"I'm so sorry to intrude," I say. "But I have a question."

"You came to the right camper," he says. He

242

turns and points at his back. HEAD HONCHO is scrawled on the back of his tee.

"Cute," I say, immediately embarrassed by my double entendre. "My girlfriends and I are camping at Birchwood . . ."

"It's closed," he says, his face and voice now very serious.

"I know, I know," I say. "Long story. I grew up going to summer camp at Birchwood, and one of my friends, Emily, passed away recently and we came back to scatter her ashes, and we've ended up just staying on a few days . . ." I stop. My face turns red. "This sounds like a Lifetime movie, doesn't it?"

"I don't know what that is, but if it's on one of those channels north of ESPN, then yes, it does."

I laugh, my face turning even redder.

He's clever. I like clever in a man more than anything else. Humor is the hottest feature a man can possess. I married a man who was about as funny as a nun in study hall at a Catholic girls' school.

"Wait!" he suddenly says. He is staring at me. Really staring. "No way."

I put my hand to my face, thinking I have old marshmallow stuck to it. I spit through my teeth. I feel for leaves in my hair. I look down.

I'm wearing pants. Yay for me!

"No way what?"

"Liz?" he asks. "Liz Anderson?"

"Yes?" I tilt my head back. "That's me."

"It's Billy. Billy Collins."

I am free-falling. And time traveling. Like Michael J. Fox in *Back to the Future*. I stumble for words.

I don't know whether to hug him, ignore him, or slug him in the shoulder, all of which I might have done back in the day after he did what he did to me. I try to play it cool. Which is usually not my smartest move.

"Billy?" I ask. "Billy Collins?"

I stop and actually scratch my chin like a total doofus.

"Oh, yeah," I finally say with total nonchalance. "Now it's ringing a bell. What have you been up to?"

His face falls.

"Well, I was an attorney, then I bought Taneycomo—and the two other boys' camps up here—over ten years ago. I hated my career. Now I love it." He stops. "Most of the time."

"Wait, you do this full-time now?"

He nods. "We have winter camps as well. It's really about restoring what we had as kids: being disconnected from the world but connected to what matters most, friends, nature, fun."

He makes a living out of camp?

I tilt my head. "I see a lot of cell phones. I thought those wouldn't be allowed."

"Boys earn points for good service or behavior. They can spend those points to use their phones for up to one hour a week. But that's it. It's a new world," Billy says. "And I felt it was important to acknowledge that without changing the old ways. We can have both. What about you?"

"Real estate agent in Holland. Divorced. Kids and grandkids. Boring story."

"You?" he says. "Never." He stops and stares at me. "My gosh. Liz Anderson. How long has it been?"

"A long time," I say.

"Too long. Man, you look great," he says. "Still have that great fashion sense."

It is just me and him again. No one else matters in the world. My heart is in my throat. I feel clammy.

Then why did you pick Rachel? I want to ask him. *If I'm so cool?*

"Thank you," I say instead.

He stares at me. I shift my feet. I start to open my mouth to ask him about the past when someone yells, "Mr. Collins!"

"Listen, I have to go," he says, "but we're having a Coed Social tonight. Remember those? Want to come? Bring your friends!"

I feel as if I might pass out from the irony.

Not funny, Em, I think.

Before I can say no—much less anything at all—Billy is trotting away. He turns at the last minute. "I'm really sorry to hear about Emily. She was a sweetheart, wasn't she?"

He jogs away.

I stand in the middle of Taneycomo lost in time. I can see the barn where Rachel stole Billy. I can see the clover where my friends grabbed me. I can feel all of my old insecurities coming back.

When I return, Rach and V are talking quietly, stretched out on blankets in front of the beach, a bottle of wine open between them.

"Guess who I saw? Billy Collins. He owns and runs Taneycomo now. All of the boys' camps, actually."

They bolt upright at this news.

"And he invited us to a Coed Social tonight."

"What?!" they say in unison.

"I'm not going," I say. "No one is."

I begin to march away, and V yells, "Stop!" like she did so many years ago.

"We don't run away from our problems or our past anymore," she says. "Em said that so long ago. I think we're all just starting to listen."

"Look." Rach stands. "I won't go. But you should."

"No," I say. "Let's actually talk." I pause. "For once."

She sits back down, and I take a seat on the end of her towel. Rachel fills her glass with wine, takes a sip and then hands it to me. She takes a deep breath.

"I'm so sorry for that night, Liz. And I can never take that away." She stops. "After I lost my dad, I had a huge hole in my soul. I still do. And I've tried to fill it in all the wrong ways. I've stolen boyfriends. I've been the mean girl. I work with snakes. And I've stepped all over women." She stops again and reaches out her hand. I give her back the glass of wine, and she takes another big sip. "I thought attention and success would fill that void, but it never has. I walked away from the women—all of you and my mom—who were my role models. I was so mad at myself for nearly killing Em. I was so mad at all of you for having a father. I didn't know what I was doing. I still don't. I didn't mean to hurt you, Liz. I didn't mean to steal Billy. He didn't even like me. Do you know what he said to me when we were dancing that night?"

I shake my head.

"He said, 'I was coming for Liz.' "

Tears spring to my eyes.

"Why didn't you ever tell me that?"

"I don't know. I think it was a way for me to make myself superior, or better, or more wanted, even though I knew I wasn't. I wish I could take it all back."

"Me, too," I say.

She cocks her head. I hold out my hand, she passes me the glass of wine, and I nearly polish it off in a single gulp.

"I have something to confess." Now I take a deep breath. "That's why I helped V sabotage you for the *Life* magazine photo shoot," I say, staring at the water, unable to meet her eyes. "I was so jealous of you. I hated that you stole Billy. I just wanted you to know what it was like to feel for once in your life that no one liked you." I stop. "I was the one who wrote the note about the change in location and left it on your bunk. Not V. Me."

Rachel shakes her head and stares into the water.

"I'm so sorry, too," I say.

She looks at me. A big, fat tear rolls down her face and shimmers in the light.

"I've spent much of my life thinking women hated me," Rachel finally says. "I wanted them to hurt, too."

"And I've spent much of my life thinking I wasn't deserving of a really good guy," I say. "Someone who loved me for me."

Rachel reaches out her hand. I hold out the glass.

"Not that, Liz. You." I scoot over, and we hold each other for the longest time, before V shuffles through the sand on her knees and joins the group hug.

" 'And now I come to you . . .' " V starts to sing.

" 'With broken arms,' " I sing.

"I think I'm missing something," Rachel says.

"Not anymore," V says. "None of us are. Let's do this Coed Social like we're The Clover Girls again. I think we all need a night of stupid fun."

"*Another* night of stupid fun," I add with a laugh.

Five hours, two bottles of wine and lots of wardrobe changes later, the three of us are standing in the corner of Camp Taneycomo's barn-turned-dance hall along with a throng of teen and tween girls who have been bussed in from camps miles away since Birchwood is no longer operating.

It is déjà vu all over again.

The barn doors are open on both ends, allowing a summer breeze to dance alongside the campers and make the construction paper stars draped from the wooden rafters sway, too. Hay bales are stacked in the corners, adult counselors serve punch (and, on occasion, I notice, sneak a hidden flask to their lips), and the room is filled with bad cologne and nervous energy. The only thing that has changed is the music. One rap song after another fills the barn, lyrics I can barely distinguish, not a DJ or turntable in sight.

And, in many ways, nothing has changed since I was a girl: I'm still standing in a corner with all the other girls, waiting for a boy to notice me.

I search the barn. I can't see Billy anywhere. I thrust my hands into the pockets of a long-sleeved minidress I fashioned from knockoff Lilly Pulitzer fabric I found in a trunk.

"I might be wearing curtains," I say to V and Rach. "If Carol Burnett could pull it off . . ."

"Better Carol Burnett than a call girl," V says. "We look like hookers in our outfits."

"Shhhh," I say. "Keep your voice down. There are children present."

Rachel begins to drunk-laugh.

"Well, we do," V continues in a stage whisper. "Teen boys are circling us."

"And look at the girls," Rach adds in her own dramatic whisper. "They're staring at us like we're competition. This is viral video end-of-my-career weird, Liz."

"Then get this on tape!" V says.

I stop and actually look at the three of us. V is wearing the same giant-shouldered, black-and-white polka-dot dress she wore for Talent Night, a bright red, wide-brim hat perched atop her auburn hair, a red leather belt cinched through a gold buckle around her waist, and red pumps. Rach refused to wear the workout outfit from "Physical," so I altered the white, lightweight puffy shoulder top I wore up here, took in the high-waisted acid-wash jeans shorts quite a few inches, and threw my statement earrings onto her lobes.

"People should be staring," I say. "It's like we jumped out of an episode of *Saved by the Bell*."

I grab my cell from my pocket and take a picture. "Smile," I say.

"Delete that!" V orders.

"Now!" Rach adds.

I look at the picture and begin laughing so hard, I can barely breathe. "You do look like hookers," I gasp.

They grab my cell, look at the picture, and double over in laughter.

I watch them. I can see that something is changing in all of us. The lying has stopped. The healing has begun. We're more like . . .

. . . *who we used to be.*

I stare at them and then around the barn. *Who would have thought just a month ago that we'd all be reunited at Birchwood and attending a Coed Social at Taneycomo?*

How did we get here? Was it luck? Or did Em have this all planned? Did she know it wasn't over for The Clover Girls? Did she know that friendships don't ever die even when someone does? Did she want us to know what was truly important in life before it was too late?

And then . . .

I see Billy Collins, his blond hair slicked back, a little bow tie on, like James Bond come to life, stride over. The entire social comes to a stop around me.

V and Rachel nudge me with their elbows.

"Stop it!" I say.

Billy approaches. He is wearing seersucker shorts and a matching jacket just like he sported decades ago.

Billy angles toward me, and I shut my eyes.

Dreams do come true, I think.

When I open them, Rachel and V have drifted behind me. I turn briefly. Rachel nods and smiles.

Billy reaches out his hand just as Madonna's "Crazy for You" starts to play.

I take his hand, and we make our way to the dance floor.

"I'm glad you came," Billy says.

He looks at me, takes me in his arms, and my knees feel like they're going to buckle.

"How did you . . . Why did you . . ." I can't find words.

"Believe it or not, I've been thinking of this day for a long time," he says. "I needed a do-over."

"It was thirty years ago. You remember all of that?"

"Every detail," he says. "You know, I was coming to dance with you that night."

"I know," I say. "Rachel told me."

"I dressed up for you that night, just like tonight." We stop swaying on the floor. "Liz, I've thought about you a lot over the years. I wondered what happened. I heard you'd gotten married and had kids like me. I never dreamed I'd see you again. Especially today. Tonight. Like this." He stops. "It's like it's meant to be."

My heart is beating so rapidly, I know he can feel it in my body, in my hands, over the beat of the music.

"We're the only ones dancing," I say, glancing around. "What will everyone say?"

"That we have good taste," Billy says. "The music these days . . ."

I laugh.

"I sound like my father," he says. "Actually everyone will say, 'Mr. Collins has a girlfriend! Mr. Collins has a girlfriend!' "

"Does Mr. Collins have a girlfriend?" I ask, shocked at my sudden brazenness.

"No. I've dated on and off since my divorce, but nothing serious. You?"

"Me, too. Been single for a while. Can I ask what happened?"

We again stop dancing for a moment, as if my question has knocked him off-balance. Finally, Billy begins to move again. "The million-dollar question," he says. "I used to blame myself. I used to blame her. Now I don't blame anyone. We changed." Billy looks at me. "I lost who I was. She did, too. I think I've finally found myself at fifty."

"I'm trying to do that."

"I'm so sorry to hear about Emily," Billy says.

"Me, too. But she brought us together again. In a strange way, her death seems to be bringing us all to life again."

"The famed Clover Girls," he says.

"We were famous?"

"Infamous," he says with a laugh. "You all

253

changed the dynamic at Birchwood. That girls of every type could be best friends. I still use you all as examples to my boys."

"You shouldn't," I say, giving him the thirty-second synopsis about our fights and why we lost touch.

"No better place to find yourself than at summer camp, right?" he says when I'm done.

I nod. "Spent my whole life caring for everyone else," I say. "I'm not sure anyone even appreciates that."

"They do," Billy says. "Just don't know it yet." Billy stops and glances over at V and Rach, who I now realize are recording our entire dance. I glare at them, eyes wide, wagging a finger, just like a parent. "Isn't that what your friend did? Emily? She took care of everyone. And now you understand the impact of what she did?"

I stop moving and hold Billy at arm's length. "Wow," I say. "You are a great counselor."

"We're all still the same inside, Liz. Doesn't matter if we're fifty or fifteen. We're fragile souls. We all want love and to be loved. We make it so hard. We hurt each other when we don't mean to do it. It's very hard to forgive. Actually, it's one of the hardest things to do. I'm glad you all are doing that." He stops. "I mean, you were The Clover Girls."

I tilt my head at him. "Yes. What's that mean?" I ask.

"It means you all always seemed destined to have good luck."

"Really?"

"You all seemed to be better together . . . as if you were connected and meant to be one unit," he says. "Did you ever think that maybe you all are who you are because of your friendships? That even the fights and squabbles and rivalries shaped who you are? The good always comes with the bad. What you're doing right now is a pretty amazing testament to lifelong friendship, isn't it? How many people would put their lives on hold in order to reunite and honor a late friend like this? That's all Birchwood and the Nighs could have hoped for: Strong, smart, talented women who formed lifelong friendships that stood the test of time."

In the nearby distance, I hear a little boy and girl sing, "Mr. Collins and a lady sitting in a tree, K-I-S-S-I-N-G!"

Some things never change.

Billy laughs. My face reddens. "Do you want to kiss me?" Billy grins.

His blue eyes are sparkling, and he is even more handsome than the boy I adored, the boy I've dreamed of for so long.

"We hardly know each other," I tease.

"Oh, we know each other," he says. "Thirty years of knowing." He stops. His voice is husky. "And longing."

He looks deeply into my eyes and kisses me. I am soaring, flying among the construction paper stars and then out the barn and into the sky to fly alongside the real ones.

The song ends, a hard-thumping song I don't know comes on, and all the kids scream and rush onto the dance floor. I am knocked back into the present day.

A counselor yells, "Mr. Collins!"

We turn, and a drone is flying around the barn, kids ducking and yelling.

"Turn that off now!" Billy yells. The drone drops to the floor. Billy turns to me. "I'll be back . . . not sure when, but I will. I promise." I smile. He starts to head off but stops. "Wait. Didn't you have a question this afternoon? That's why you came over here today. What was it?"

"Nothing much," I say. "I just need a plumber, electrician, roofer, contractor and therapist."

"I'm a lawyer who happens to do much of that," he says. "If not, I know people."

I laugh. "That sounds ominous."

"I'll stop by tomorrow. It was good to dance with you, Liz. Finally." He heads off toward a group of boys, grabbing the drone. "Okay. Whose is this?"

"We recorded every second of that!" V crows.

"Yeah, I know," I say. "I'll rewatch it after another glass of wine."

"Can we bounce and go find some grindage?" Rachel says.

I laugh. "Boy, do I miss the '80s sometimes," I say. "Let's bounce."

"Not yet," V says, taking off across the dance floor. "I have one more surprise before we bounce."

"Where is she going?" I ask.

Rachel shrugs.

A few moments later, a familiar song begins to play, and I double over laughing.

I grab Rachel by the hand and drag her onto the floor, and we dance in a circle to Journey.

" 'I come to you . . .' " V sings.

" 'With broken arms,' " Rach and I sing together.

PART SIX
Capture the Flag

SUMMER 1986

There is a game The Clover Girls play in their bunks they call "YouTV." It is a riff off of MTV, and a play on the fact they don't have television at camp, and *everyone* watches TV in the 1980s.

The directions are simple. In their game, someone says the title of a popular TV show, and the girls call out the character they think the others are on the show.

"*Dynasty*?" Liz yells, trying on blue eye shadow she sneaked into camp in her tube socks. She doesn't wait for anyone else, interjecting her own answer instead. "V is Krystal Carrington!"

"No, V *is* Krystal Carrington," Em says.

"Rach is Alexis!" V yells.

"No, Rach *is* Alexis Carrington," Liz says, laughing.

"MTV veejay!" V calls next.

"Em is Martha Quinn!" Rachel yells. "She seems so sweet!"

"Then Liz is totally Nina Blackwood!" Em says. "She has rockin' hair and is so stylish!"

"*Facts of Life*!" Rachel picks.

Everyone sits up and starts shouting their opinions.

"Blair!" Rach and Liz answer, pointing at V, before she can even open her mouth.

"Jo!" V yells, pointing at Rach, before turning her finger to Liz and saying, "Natalie *and* Tootie."

"What?" Liz asks.

"You always know what's going on with whom, and you *are* just a wee bit impressionable, too?"

Everyone turns and points at Em.

"Mrs. Garrett!"

Pinewood explodes in laughter.

After the game, the lights dim, and the owls start to hoot outside, The Clover Girls lie in bed, tossing and turning, wondering why their best friends in the world don't see more dimensions in them, wondering if they will grow up believing every stereotype that has been instilled.

They dream of being someone else but wake to the same world.

SUMMER 2021
VERONICA

"*The Golden Girls*!" Liz says, before breaking into a fit of giggles.

Her face is almost as blue as her eye shadow, which is smeared—along with her mascara—everywhere, giving her the look of a hungover raccoon that wandered out of Studio 54.

"What was that game called?" Rachel asks.

"How could you forget?" I ask, tossing my hand over my face in faux drama.

"YouTV!" Liz and I yell at the same time.

"That's right," Rachel says. "Now I remember."

"So The Clover Girls are now the Golden Girls?" I ask. "We used to be *Dynasty* or *Facts of Life*. What happened?"

Liz points at herself. "Life happened!"

We laugh, and then—just like in the old days—begin to shout who we think the other is.

"Dorothy!" Liz and I suddenly yell at the same time, pointing directly at Rachel.

It takes her a second to put the pieces together, but she finally says, "Hey!" before pointing at me and yelling, "Blanche!"

"Hey!" I say.

Just as quickly, Rachel and I point at Liz and say, "Rose."

"Hey!" She laughs.

We all look at each other, nodding.

"Em was Sophia," Rachel says. "Always a bit more mature than the rest of us."

"And she had lots of wisdom," I say.

"And that concludes today's episode of YouTV," Liz says, "our throwback to the '80s."

I can't help but think of the irony of Liz remembering this game and choosing *The Golden Girls*.

Are we all destined to end up alone?

Or did life bring us—like them—together for an important reason? So the end of our lives will be filled with joy, laughter and friendship?

"No, one more," Rachel suddenly says. "*Sorority Sisters*?"

"Your old show?" Liz asks.

We all look at each other. Liz points at Rach.

"Well, you were Sam," Liz says. "It fit you to a T: the sorority sister who wanted to be a star."

"The girl who lost her dad, and needed her friends more than anyone," I say.

Rachel looks at me.

"You've watched the show?" She stares at me, hungover, but now fully awake. Her eyes are wide, her mouth open. "I know Liz did, but you?"

I nod. "I did. I still do. It's on all the time."

Rachel is just staring at me, like bigfoot has wandered through the middle of camp.

"Why?" she asks.

"Why what?"

"Why would you watch the show? You hated me."

"I never hated you, Rach. I was . . . jealous of you."

"Really?"

"Really." I stop. "You were naturally talented. You could sing. You could dance. You had a look that fit the time. And you were quite good in it. You should have been nominated for an Emmy. You made Sam seem so real and natural. Viewers took that for granted. I used to talk to my friend, Yola Phelps, about you . . ."

"The producer?" Rachel asks. "How did you know her?"

"From my modeling days," I say. "She produced some of the films and videos I was in. Yola did a lot of the behind-the-scenes segments for magazines like *SI* that were aired on ESPN."

Rachel is staring at me.

"What?" I ask.

She is nodding. "You did it, didn't you?"

"Did what?"

"You put in a word for me to get the role, didn't you? I auditioned with Yola about a dozen times. I thought Helen Hunt was going to get the part. It was down to the two of us. You knew Yola. You called her, didn't you?"

The emotions of the last twenty-four hours

overwhelm me. "I did," I finally say. "You were going to get the part anyway. She had already decided. I just told Yola how great you were." I stop. "I actually told her what a good friend you were, too. And you'd be great with the other actresses . . . a leader and a role model." I stop again. "I also told her what I'd done to you."

Rachel continues to stare.

"I didn't mean to interfere," I continue. "I just felt so awful about . . ."

Rach gets up and hugs me with all her might.

"Thank you," she sighs, as if the weight of the world has fallen from her shoulders.

"I thought you'd be mad if I ever told you."

"For being a friend?" she asks.

Rachel takes a seat and, for the longest time, we sit in silence. For once, it's a comfortable silence, like family. We sip our coffee. Out of the blue, Liz begins to sing the theme song from *The Golden Girls*. We laugh and join in.

"I'm glad we stayed a bit longer," Rachel says. "Not just for Emily, but for me. I can't tell you what the last few days have meant to me. Truly."

"For all of us," Liz adds. She looks at the two of us and fidgets in her chair. "So, I gotta ask the hundred-thousand-dollar question? How much longer do you want to stay? I know I'm worried about my mom. I have to check in on my clients. V, I know you need to work some things out . . ."

"You think?" I say, trying to make a joke out of the pain.

"And Rach, I know you're busy."

She doesn't respond.

"Can we play it by ear?" I say. "I feel both totally lost and totally found right now. I just need a bit more time to figure things out." I stop. "On a lot of levels."

"I think that sounds good," Rachel says.

"Are you going to talk to David?" Liz asks.

"I am," I say. "But I might consult my therapist first."

They both look at me questioningly.

"My daughter," I say with a smile.

The sun strengthens moment by moment, and I lift my face to it. As a model, the sun was my nemesis. I spent years avoiding it. I wore hats, zinc, sunblock, sunglasses. I regretted the summers I spent lying out with tinfoil in front of my face, the tiniest of lines and spots reminding me of my youthful stupidity. My goal was to be a ghost, so that my face could be recreated and reimagined in any possible way. Everyone avoids the sun in LA, too. But it feels good to feel the sun again.

And then, just like that, a cloud passes over, and my heart darkens, too. I can't stop my mind from thinking about leaving here, the real world, what waits.

David. My marriage. The end of my marriage.

I look around at the old camp.

Was I wrong to stay? Was I so angry that I intentionally meant to hurt my husband? Or did he intend for me to follow him, yet again, no questions asked?

The embers of the fire continue to smolder, and I realize my hair, my skin, my clothes smell like smoke.

"I'm going to bathe in the lake," I say. "I stink."

My words have deeper meaning than the girls realize.

"We'll be down in a few," Liz says. "I have a feeling I need to wash my face."

Rach laughs. "You look like Bananarama got caught in the rain."

"Which member?" Liz asks.

"All of them," Rach answers. "In a hurricane."

I head to the bunk and grab a towel, some shampoo and soap that Em had left us.

You did think of everything, I think, looking at Em's bunk. *Did you also know the chaos this would cause in our lives?*

"Since we're staying, we'll need to head to the store soon for food and rations to get us through the next couple of days," I yell to Rach and Liz as I pass.

If we—I—make it that far, I don't add.

"I might need some clothes that don't smell like smoke, too."

"You're smokin' hot, mama!" Liz yells as I pass. "Ow!"

I wave her off, yelling, "Put on your readers!" and head toward the lake.

The grassy-weedy trail, which we've already trampled into a well-worn path, glistens with dew. It is going to be a warm day, and the cicadas are already buzzing, providing a moody soundtrack to my emotions. I stop and follow the sound. I see a cicada resting on a nearby tree and watch it for a moment. It's prehistoric-looking—dragon in bug form—and the sound they make is the sound that always reminds me of Michigan summers at Birchwood. In a way, it reminds me of the sound a frog güiro makes when you play it. I bought a güiro with David during a trip to Puerto Rico. It's a Latin American percussion instrument used prominently in their music. Traditionally, it's an open-ended hollow gourd with notches on top over which you rub sticks or tines to produce a ratchet sound. As a gift, they are made to resemble frogs. The stick is held in the frog's mouth, and you remove it and rub it along its back to produce a sound. When I first played it, while sipping on a piña colada, I was transported back in time to my days here, the instrument's sound reminding me, ironically and exactly, of the Michigan chorus frogs that would lull me to sleep.

The cicada buzzes. Cy Nigh told me when the

cicadas buzzed, they were looking for a lifelong mate. The memory jolts me, making my heart ache so deeply, and my sudden movement causes the cicada to move to the far side of the trunk.

"I feel like hiding, too," I say.

I grab for my cell and David's number pops up. It was the last number I called. For the longest time, my finger hovers over his name, like the bees buzzing the wildflowers in bloom, but I cannot bring myself to call him. Instead, as I initially intended, I scroll and dial my daughter's number instead.

"Mom? Are you okay?"

This is the reaction I always get from my husband and children when I call: something must be wrong. Did I cause this by being overly protective? Did I cause this by not sharing enough about myself?

"I'm fine, Ash," I say. "I just wanted to hear your voice."

"So, you're not okay, then."

I laugh.

"I just needed to talk to my therapist," I say.

"This is so unhealthy, Mom," she says with a big laugh.

It feels good to laugh. And then I start to babble, to tell her of her father's surprise visit, my reaction, his departure. "I shouldn't be telling you this," I say. "It's not fair to you. You shouldn't be burdened by this. I'm sorry. I'm a terrible mother."

"Stop it, Mom. I'm glad you did. Listen to me, it was just a fight," she says, very calmly as if she's the mother and I'm the daughter. "I mean, it was a big one, but it happens all the time. Couples *should* fight sometimes. If they don't, it just all bubbles up . . ." She stops. "You know how if you shook a can of soda and then opened it, and it explodes? That's what can happen when relationships don't get real." She stops again. "I could kinda feel this coming, Mom. You bottle things up and then explode. I mean, just think of how you reacted to your friend's death. You dove in the pool fully dressed. That's not a normal reaction."

I think of Rachel doing the same thing when her dad died.

Maybe it's normal for us.

My daughter continues to talk, and I am so dumbfounded by the accuracy of her analogy and logic that I can't even open my mouth to form a sentence.

"You know in that movie we just watched together . . . what was the name of it?"

"*The Breakfast Club*?" I ask.

"Yeah!" Ash says. "You know at the end, the one guy is reading the letter they all wrote to the teacher in detention?"

"Yes?"

"That, no matter what they write, or say, or do, he—and society—will still see them in the same

271

way, as a jock or a burnout or a spoiled princess? Well, maybe you and dad need to do that."

"Write each other a letter?" I ask. "You said that was old-fashioned."

"No," she says. "Maybe he needs to stop seeing you as you *were* but who you are now and who you want to be. And maybe you need to stop seeing Dad as you always have."

My daughter's words jolt me, and I think of us playing YouTV earlier.

We all stereotype each other until that becomes who we see rather than who we are.

"Maybe you need to take off—what were those old sunglasses you used to wear?" Ash asks.

"Ray-Bans?"

"Yeah, take off your Ray-Bans."

"Thank you, Ash," I say. "For listening." I stop. "For everything."

"No, Mom," she says. "Thank you. For everything."

"Hey?" I say, before she hangs up. "Are you okay?"

"I am," she says. "You make sure of that, don't you? Gotta go. I'm doing a scene from *Ladybird* in an hour."

I laugh again. The Greta Gerwig movie is one of our favorites. "Lots of personal inspiration there, right?"

"Feels sooo real," she says with a big laugh. "Later, Mom."

I hang up, and notice the cicada is eyeing me, buzzing.

And then I notice that I have wandered into and am standing directly in the middle of the clover field.

It is blooming, the clover blooms white, nearly purple.

It has changed from what I remember, as a girl and even from a few days ago. The clover is leggy, beautiful, reaching for the light.

I think of who I was when I was here. I think of who I became as a model. I think of who I was as a newlywed, then a mother, and now.

All very different people operating from the same soul and heart.

I take off my shoes. The clover is cool and still damp, and it awakens me.

I think again of playing YouTV with Rachel and Liz.

We are all very different people than we were, as varied as the multisided clover that grows before me.

None of us are like the stereotypes of the TV characters we yell. We are all deeper people. Maybe we too easily put one another in a box because it's easier to deal with others that way than deal with our own issues.

I reach down and pluck a piece of pretty clover and place it behind my ear. I pose in the sunlight, head up, like Twiggy might have done. I am a middle-aged, new age hippie come to life. The light dances around my face.

Maybe I need to see my friends and myself in a new light.

I take off running toward the lake, suddenly invigorated. I drop my towel, soap and shampoo, toss my shoes on the ground, take off my shirt and shrug out of my shorts just like a little kid. I grab the soap and shampoo and stand on the edge of the lake, soaping my body and hair. I toss them onto my towel and then race into the water, shrieking the deeper I go. I dive under the surface, rinsing my hair with my hands, and when I come up, the world looks shinier, brighter, newer, cleaner.

Maybe I do need to see my husband in a different light. No. Maybe he needs to see me that way, too.

I think back to when my husband and I first met. He was a free spirit, too, an artist who had no boundaries. He was funny, easygoing. We would go weeks without wearing shoes. He would cook for me. He would sing to me. He made me feel that I was more than my fame. He made me feel like a normal person. Most of all, he used to be my best friend.

I splash my face.

I did grow tired of modeling. I grew tired of trying to maintain a weight that was more appropriate for a teen than an adult. I grew tired of the travel and the hours. I was just plain tired.

I believed in David's talent. He was like Rachel: God gave him a gift. And I knew that he could be even more successful than I had been, and for a much longer time. I was the one who wanted to start a family immediately.

Did he ask me to stop modeling? Or did I want to stop?

Did he marry me for my looks? Or did I grow resentful that my looks helped launch him and he now enjoys the light in which I once basked?

The years have muddled things.

There is no doubt that he needs to change. He has become as rigid as the house in which we live. Life is not and cannot be as perfect as a photo shoot or a three-million-dollar home. It is often sloppy, lived in, comfortably worn.

If he wants to live in a perfect world, I am no longer the woman for him.

I need more than one room to decorate. I need more room to grow. I need friends. And I need my husband to understand and support that, or . . .

I look around the camp, the old cabins hovering in the distance.

Or everything will fall apart.

I go underwater again and come up for air. The water sparkles.

And I need to see the world in a different light, too.

I grew up in a world where girls who looked

like me—red-haired and freckled—were not considered beautiful. How many girls of every different race and size still feel that way? And how do we change that?

How do *I* change that?

I head back to shore, dry off, dress and lie back on my towel in the sun.

I think of YouTV once more. A different question pops into my head: What was our favorite camp game?

I have a feeling Rach would say Color War or Talent Night, and Liz might say Candles on the Lake. Me? I would say Capture the Flag.

The object of Capture the Flag is to cross into enemy territory, retrieve the enemy's base flag, and return it to your side without getting captured by any defenders.

I was always so good at Capture the Flag, so quick and deft at avoiding confrontation and capture.

I sit straight up, stunned by my epiphany.

Suddenly, an idea so grand and idealistic hits me that I have to shut my eyes to keep the world from spinning.

When I open them again, I notice that the bottom of my threadbare towel has a green flag Magic Markered on the end.

Emily, Pinewood, it reads underneath in faded writing.

Em's towel. Em's message. Em's flag.

RACHEL

"How was your lake bath?"

V stares right through Liz as if she's a ghost. She walks toward The Lodge, her hair still damp, and turns in a full circle. She walks into Pinewood and emerges with her bag. She pulls a pad of paper and pen from it and begins to draw.

"Still old-school?" Liz says. "Me, too!"

V acts as if she doesn't hear her, instead walking over to sit on the stoop of Sassafras Bunk and continuing to draw.

"You're sitting on the doorstep of our sworn enemy," I call.

V glances up. She looks dazzlingly beautiful right now, so natural in nature, the filtered sunlight giving her the oddly gorgeous but childlike expression of a paint-by-numbers picture.

"We need to stop stereotyping ourselves," she says, returning to her pad. "We need to stop stereotyping each other . . . all women."

Her words knock me off kilter.

Is she saying this to me? Or to herself?

"Me, next," I say, standing. "Nothing more old-school than bathing in a lake."

I grab the soap and shampoo, nab a fresh towel that Em left for us and head toward the lake. When I reach the knoll before the path that leads to Birchwood, the cell in my pocket begins to ding repeatedly, as if I'm standing directly beneath Big Ben at noon. My stomach drops.

I shouldn't have listened to Liz when she offered to recharge my cell in her car this morning. I shouldn't have brought my cell with me. I shouldn't have traversed over the only hillside that gets two bars of reception. Big mistakes.

I take a deep breath.

Have you seen this?

This is bad, Rachel.

Rachel! Please advise!

CALL ME! NOW!

I click the link attached to the first text.

A shaky video, obviously recorded by a cell phone, shows Ralph Ruddy outside of a bar. He's turned toward the person holding the cell, his face even redder and angrier than usual.

"Why do you hate women?"

"I don't hate women, young lady," he says, slurring slightly. "I love women. And they love me."

Oh, no, Ralph. Please don't.

The cell phone holder turns the camera on herself. It's a young woman wearing a university ball cap. "We do?" she asks. "What we demand is equal pay. We demand paid leave. We demand that you leave our bodies alone. We demand the same protections and rights that you have. More than anything, we demand respect."

Applause explodes around her.

Emboldened, the woman continues.

"You recently said men pay enough when women are pregnant. Do you even realize how disgusting that is?"

The camera rotates to Ralph.

"That was a joke!" Ralph yells, spittle flying from his mouth. "Women can't even take a joke anymore."

"Because it's not funny," a woman yells off-camera.

"You know what's funny?"

Please, Ralph.

"All of you angry women protesting for your rights and your bodies, like any man is ever going to touch you in the first place."

Boom!

The women boo.

"You will never be a man's equal. Because you aren't equal." Ralph walks toward the woman. You can see the camera moving backward. "And you want to know the really funny thing? Nothing's ever going to change. Check back in ten years, and let's see how you're doing."

All of a sudden, the footage shakes, and the

cell tumbles to the ground. You can see Ralph's foot come down on top of the camera as if it's quashing the young woman.

I fall to my knees. I am shaking harder than that young woman's cell. I am on sacred ground here. Birchwood raised women to be independent, strong, smart and fierce. Birchwood raised women who stuck together and supported one another.

I think of my friends watching this video. I think of V's daughter. I think of all the Birchwood campers whose voices rose and sang as one every single night before we went to bed.

I think of my mom.

Ding! Ding! Ding!

I stand, ignoring my cell, and race toward the water, kicking off my shoes and clothes until I'm just in my undies. I throw the towel and cell down at the last minute, jumping in the lake. I lather up and scrub my body and hair and clothing as if I'm trying to wash away years of dirt and guilt. I burst out of the water and swim out to Friendship Rock. I crawl atop it, setting the soap and shampoo in one of its deep crevices, and stand.

In the distance, I can see an American flag waving over Taneycomo. I am catapulted back in time, thinking of when we would all play Capture the Flag. I was always so good at it. So was V. No one could ever get me. I was too elusive. I think of how that has served me so well: I never get captured by my enemies. I always stay one step ahead of them. And I use that flag for my own goals.

And yet this lifelong game has also kept me a prisoner.

Without warning, I become emotional watching the Stars and Stripes flap in the summer breeze. It's such a simple flag really, and yet what it stands for—and those who have died for it—is so profound. That flag does not stand only for those boys, or just for men, or even just for women, but for all of us, every single one of us, no matter our gender, race, sexual orientation, religion, differences.

It unites us.

It does not divide us.

In the distance, my cell continues to ping. But over it, I hear birds singing, joyously, on a perfect summer day. They flit and they fly. They are free.

I am again catapulted back in time to a Talent Night when Em asked me to recite poetry rather than sing and dance. I had wanted to sing Pat Benatar, or "Bette Davis Eyes," but Em literally begged me to recite a Maya Angelou poem that had recently been published and that she loved.

"For me, Rach, please," she begged. "Please. Do it for me."

I did. And I lost. For the first time. Poetry and distracted young girls do not an ideal mix make,

I learned quickly. "It's okay you didn't win, Rach," Em told me. "You did in the big scheme of things."

"How?" I asked.

"You'll see," she said, before draping a home-made medal around my neck that said, #1 4-EVER!

It's as if Em knew those words would take root in my soul, just like friendship, and continue to grow, even if I didn't realize it.

Until today.

I stand atop the rock and yell into the Michigan sky, the words from "I Know Why the Caged Bird Sings" coming to me as easily as they did decades ago.

I suddenly understand the meaning of the poem, of why Em wanted me to recite it.

I am no longer caged.

The flag does not need to be "captured."

I can sing with my own voice.

I look at Birchwood glimmering in the distance, and I can see its infinite possibilities.

Just like mine.

"I am free!" I yell, my voice high and lilting and strong as an eagle's cry. "I am free!"

LIZ

Where is everyone?

I tilt my head left and right, holding it still for the longest time, just like the blue jay that is watching me, one single eye cocked on me.

"Shoo!" I yell. "Shoo!"

I suddenly think of my mom. She only disliked two kinds of birds: purple martins and blue jays. She had my dad install a purple martin house in our backyard when I was tiny, and they took over, acting as if the land were their own, dive bombing my mom every time she would head outside to pick tomatoes or hang laundry from the clothesline. I would laugh so hard watching her from the front window as she ducked and waved her arms, tossing tomatoes at them or dropping a bucket of clothes and running for the hills. It was one of the few times I ever heard her curse, and she would curse a blue streak—bluer than even the martin's belly—when they'd get too close. The martin house came down after a couple of years.

She hated blue jays even more because they would eat the newly laid eggs from a robin's nest. My mom adored robins, and when a nest was new, she would stand vigil by the window, watching, as protective as the baby birds' mama herself.

"Shoo!" I yell again, and the blue jay takes off with a flutter.

The camp turns still, and my mind returns to my mother.

I need to call. I need to check in. I know probably nothing has changed. And yet I know probably everything has changed. I can detect the tiniest of declines in my mother: the way she breathes. The color of her skin. The brightness of her eyes. How tightly she grips my hand.

In many ways, she is like this camp: a shell of its former self and yet still alive, still filled with memories, love and goodness. I can't save her, though. I know that. It's too late.

But Birchwood . . . ?

I look around.

This always happened to me here. I'd be lost in the day, designing in The Lodge or our bunkhouse while Em read, everyone else running around out in the world.

So much has changed. So little has changed.

I used to tell my parents that I would be nothing like them when I got older. And yet I am. The stupid phrases they used on me—*Were you born in a barn? If you keep making that face, it'll freeze that way. Turn your music down NOW! If all your friends jumped off a bridge, would you do it, too? Don't make me turn this car around!*—I used on my own children and still do to this day.

But there was something beautiful about my parents'—and this camp's—old-fashioned ways. I learned to respect those around me. I learned that my social influencers were my elders and not eighteen-year-old, half-dressed strangers on my cell phone. I learned to be incredibly self-sufficient. I learned that kindness and friendship were incredible gifts.

And yet, despite all of this, I am alone in this new-old world. When my mother dies, I will be the last thread tying the past to the future. My children and grandchildren are concerned about little else than themselves. It's not that they're busy. We all are, especially young parents. It's that they're selfish. They think only of themselves. And once my mother passes, I will be all alone, and I am not delusional about this reality whatsoever.

I stand without warning, as if to make sure my legs are still strong and sturdy, and scan the camp.

It's still as empty as I suddenly feel. But at my heart, I am a caretaker, just like Em was. I don't know how long the three of us will remain here, but I know that we need some supplies and groceries to keep us going.

I head into the bunkhouse and grab my purse, which is propped in an ancient bentwood chair. I scan my purse for my car keys and head out the screen door.

"Where are you going?" a deep voice asks.

I scream without even glancing up, throwing my purse toward the face of the intruder and giving the body before me a mighty shove.

When I look up, I see the words CAMP TANEYCOMO sprawled on the ground.

"Billy? Oh, my God, Billy!! I'm so sorry."

Billy Collins lies in the dirt, moaning.

"Is this how you sell a house?" he asks.

"Yep," I say. "That's why I usually get full asking price."

He laughs, and I reach out a hand.

"I came in peace," he says, pretending to flinch. "Uncle! Uncle!"

I grab his hand and help him to his feet. Billy stands with a groan, dusts off his butt and rubs his back.

"What are you doing here?"

"Just wanted to get beat up," he says. "I have to go now."

I laugh this time. "I'm so, so sorry. I was lost in my head. The last thing I expected was to see a man at my doorstep."

"Been that long since you've had a date?" Billy asks with a wink.

"You have no idea," I say.

"I felt badly about how things ended so abruptly the other night," he says. "I came over for a couple of reasons, actually. You said you needed some names and numbers. And a lot of therapy, which I can now understand."

I laugh.

"Do you have time right now?" he asks.

"I was just heading to the country store for some supplies. I have no idea where the girls are, or how much longer we're staying . . ."

"I hope for a while longer," he says, looking at the ground. "We just got started."

I blush and continue. ". . . but I thought we might need a few things." I stop. "You know, to survive."

Billy glances at the base of the bunk, which is lined with bottles. "You mean, other than wine?"

"Yeah," I say.

"Are you up for some fun?"

I look at Billy, raising an eyebrow dramatically.

"I have an hour," he continues.

I raise the other eyebrow even higher.

"What exactly are we talking about here?" I ask.

He laughs. "Oh, that didn't come out right! I can tell by your Groucho Marx brows."

I smile. *A witty man who uses old-school references.*

"Capture the Flag," he says. "I'm talking about playing a game of Capture the Flag."

"Is that a euphemism?" I ask.

He laughs even harder.

"Me and you?" I continue. "Don't we need teams? And must I remind you I'm not a kid anymore?"

"We're all kids at heart, Liz. Isn't that why you're still here?"

I cock my head at him, just like that blue jay.

Is he a good egg, or a bad egg? I wonder. *A nester?*

"Look, you don't need to go to the store if you play this game . . ." He hesitates. ". . . well."

I raise my eyebrows again.

"After you said you needed help the other night, I had an idea. So I planned something I thought you and The Clover Girls would like. I planned something I thought Emily would like. Sort of a memorial service in the form of a game." Billy stares at me, his hair fluttering in the breeze. He ducks his head and then smiles at me. "Summer camp is about playing games and having fun, but it's also about discovering our inner strengths and those of our friends. It's about believing that we're more than others think us to be. It's about the fact that we're better together. Em knew that, so I wanted to celebrate that." He stops. "Gather Rachel and V and meet me at the base of The Lookout in a half hour. If you don't show, I'll understand. If I don't show, I'll be in traction." He rubs his back dramatically and a hurt look covers his face.

"Okay," I say.

A half hour later, after tracking down the girls, who were lost in their own worlds—both wanting to tell me about their "big plans," "transformational ideas" and "epiphanies"—I am dragging them again in the direction of Camp Taneycomo.

"What's going on?" Rach asks. "Last time you dragged us somewhere, we were dressed like Julia Roberts in *Pretty Woman*."

"And you kissed a boy on the dance floor," V adds.

"I don't even know what's going on," I say. "Billy said it's sort of a memorial service disguised as a game. I'm just playing along . . ."

I don't even get a chance to finish because the yells of boys drown out my words. I suddenly realize that nearly fifty Taneycomo campers are cheering our arrival.

"What the . . . ?" V asks.

"Welcome, Clover Girls!"

Billy is shouting through a bullhorn. He is standing about ten feet up the giant dune, his feet wedged in the sand.

"What the . . . ?" I repeat.

We approach the group warily, and they stop cheering when Billy raises a green flag. There is a white four-leaf clover painted on it.

"What the . . . ?" Rach says.

"On behalf of the men of Taneycomo, welcome, and thank you for joining us!"

The boys cheer.

"Today is . . ." Billy shouts, before waving his hand in the air.

"CAPTURE THE FLAG!" the boys yell.

Billy beams as brightly as the sun. He is smiling, his white teeth juxtaposed against his tanned face. I now notice there is a series of smaller green flags dotted up the sand dune. Billy half scrambles, half slides down the dune toward us.

"What the . . ." the three of us say at the same time. We look at each other and then the boys surrounding us before finishing. ". . . heck is going on?"

Billy looks at us and then just at me. His blue eyes seem to cut through my steely exterior like the flame of a cutting torch. "I've been quite moved by your friend Emily's death and the reason you're all back here again," he says, his voice now as soft as the breeze off the lake. "I remember her reading under that stand of birch in the woods just outside camp. She told me once that books and smart girls were like generators: they could power the world." He stops. "I came back here, to this camp and this place, because I was lost. The lessons I learned here I'd forgotten. The lessons we all learned here are our compass." He hesitates again. "Emily was a bright, kind, sweet, humble soul. She knew, even in her last days, what too few of us ever realize: the simplest of things are the most important." Billy takes a deep breath. "Laughing. Having fun. Swimming in the lake. Warming your face in the sun." He turns and looks around at his campers. "Being a kid. Having a best friend. Going to summer camp."

Billy scans the dune. "I thought I'd honor Emily's memory—and her mission for all of you that Liz has told me about—by having you play Capture the Flag today. Well, a new version of Capture the Flag."

Billy points up the mountain of sand, and we start to protest. "Hold on, hold on! Just hear me out. See the series of flags going up the dune? Each one is numbered. And at each flag, I've placed a special object. Some are things you need, like more wine . . ."

"I'm ready!" V yells.

". . . more food, water, soap, shampoo, sweat-shirts, and even the names and numbers of the most trustworthy contractor, roofer, electrician and plumber around."

Rach and V look at me and then each other, but neither says a word. I shrug as if I don't know what Billy is talking about.

"And there are also a few items that you might want more than any of those," he continues.

"How do we play?" Rach asks, rubbing her hands together.

"Always the competitor," I say.

"This is not about capturing each other's flags," Billy says, "like we used to do. You're all playing on the same team and for the same goal, right?"

We look at each other and nod.

"The object is for each of you to gather as many numbered flags as you can and reach the top of The Lookout together in under five minutes."

"Five minutes?" I yell.

Billy laughs. "You must reach the top with your own Clover flag intact, and raise it to signal you've gotten there as one. I'll have boys at each flag, and at the top, to make sure you're all playing fair. If you drop or lose your big flag, you're out. You win together, or you lose together. Make sense?"

"You're an evil genius," Rach calls.

"Takes one to know one," Billy replies. "Ready?"

We look at each other for the longest time and, finally, nod.

"Boys!" Billy yells through the bullhorn. "Take your places!"

A group of campers scramble up the insanely tall dune as if they're ants scrambling up a small mound of dirt. Billy hands us each a Clover flag, and we raise them in the air.

"On your mark, get set, GO!" Billy yells.

I head toward the dune and begin to run up it. *Run* is a generous verb, I suddenly realize. I am moving, but moving as if I'm caught in quicksand. I look up. V is having just as much trouble as I am. Rach is already nearing the first flag.

I desperately want to scream a bad word at her, but I channel my mother and yell what she used to yell when she wanted to curse but couldn't because children were present. "YAHTZEE!" I scream.

The campers laugh. "You don't even know what that is!" I yell at them, already drenched in sweat.

"Water!" Rach yells. I look up, and she's waving a tiny flag along with her big one. "We have enough bottled water for a week!"

"YAHTZEE!" I yell up the dune at her.

Before I've even made it to the flag Rachel has already captured, I hear V scream, "Soap!"

I stop on the dune. I look up. V and Rach are going to capture all the flags, and I am going to cost us the victory. I am deadweight.

What's the point? I think. *I'm stuck. In the sand. In my career. In life. In everything.*

"Come on! Don't give up!"

Boys are cheering for me, their voices—some deep, some high, some cracking—echoing across the dune. I look around, studying their youthful faces. They are blissfully unaware of what awaits after summer camp: loss of loved ones, loss of dreams, loss of ideals, loss of self. The wind kicks up the sand, and the world looks as if I'm viewing it through a gritty, gauzy curtain. Just as quickly, the breeze dies, and the world is clear.

Why do I continue to view my life through the wrong lens?

"You can do it, Liz!"

I hear Billy's voice. I look, and he is standing just below me.

"It's not about who captures the flag," Billy says. "Never was."

He continues: "It's about teamwork. It's about fighting for yourself and your friends. It's about making people think differently about you. It's about finishing a battle you start."

Billy nods at me, and then at the bright ensemble of clothing I am sporting. I nod back.

"You have two more minutes," he says. "Go!"

I take one step and another, my feet churning. I turn my body sideways and climb uphill on an angle, like when I was young and used to go skiing in Boyne City, a northern Michigan resort. I step and grunt, step and grunt, and I don't actually look around until I hear, "We're here for you."

V and Rach are beside me. They take me by the arms, and we go up the dune.

Together.

When I look down, I am standing by a flag. I am near the top of the dune. Their hands are filled with flags. Mine are empty.

"Last flag is for you," V says.

I lean down and grab the final flag. Attached to it are the names and numbers of a local contractor, plumber, electrician and roofer, along with a note:

*Our wives, sisters and mothers
went to Birchwood.
It would be an honor to help you fix it up
in memory of your friend.
All labor: 50 percent off.*

I wave the flag at Billy, who is shouting at the top of his lungs.

It's about finishing the battle you start, I think.

And then three friends climb to the top of the dune.

The three of us lean down and pluck from the top of the dune the final, fluttering green flag emblazoned with a four-leaf clover.

We look at Billy.

"Four minutes and fifty-five seconds!" he yells.

We lift the final flag over our heads and shout in victory.

"THE CLOVER GIRLS!" we scream. "FOUR-ever!"

No one won, I think, looking at my friends, their faces red, arms and legs covered in sand. *We all did.*

We played Capture the Flag perfectly, just like Em would have wanted.

PART SEVEN

Sing-Along

SUMMER 1989

A deep, wide covered porch surrounds The Lodge on all four sides. An old railing designed with crisscrossed birch logs hugs the porch, and whenever a camper puts her hands on it, even now, she says she can feel the power and history in it.

More than anything, she swears she can feel it vibrate and hum, because it retains all the songs and memories the girls created over the decades at camp.

The Birchwood campers call this The Singing Porch. Every day, the girls take turns singing before and after dinner. Sometimes, they sing songs to help speed along the hoppers—which is what the dining room helpers are called—to get their meals finished a bit more quickly. Sometimes, after dinner—before the sun sets and they head down to the campfire to roast marshmallows and sing campfire songs—two bunkhouses each choose a side of The Singing Porch, and the campers sing songs in the round: "This Land Is Your Land," "Oh! Susanna," "Row, Row, Row Your Boat," "Frère Jacques," "Wheels on the Bus," "Fish and Chips" and "Rain Storm" when it is pouring cats and dogs. Most of the songs include snapping, clapping, rubbing hands together or slapping thighs, but they all have one thing in common: they bring the campers together and make them remember they are one.

The first song The Clover Girls actually sang at camp was "Land of the Silver Birch," the official camp song.

The second song they sang at camp was "Girls Just Want to Have Fun."

But they remember it very differently.

If you were to ask any of The Clover Girls what song was the first they sang together, they would all reply, "That's What Friends Are For."

They would not remember the transistor radio that played it, nor would they remember that anyone else was present. They believe they began singing it together, out of the blue, at the same time.

Every Sunday at camp, after dinner concludes and the campers gather on The Singing Porch, The Clover Girls start singing "That's What Friends Are For." For years, it became as much the camp song as "Land of the Silver Birch." All of the campers, no matter their age, would hold hands and sway like the clover in the field.

That song came to represent not just The Clover Girls but the friendships every girl made at camp.

And if you ask The Clover Girls what the last song they sang together at camp was, you would already know the answer.

They sang it for the last time—just the four of them—on The Singing Porch before they left to start their adult lives. They sang it to overcome the hurt they had caused one another and to remember why they became friends in the first place.

Because they made each other whole, in good times and bad times.

In the immediate years after The Clover Girls had disappeared from Birchwood, unbeknownst to them, campers would still sing "That's What Friends Are For" on Sunday nights. They would sway like the clover.

And when they would head back to their cabins and lay their hands on the railing, you could hear the youngest of campers whisper to one another, "I can still hear and feel The Clover Girls here."

SUMMER 2021
VERONICA

"I feel like I'm at the Ritz!"

"Hot water never felt sooo good!" Liz yells.

The shower house is filled with steam, and our happy chattering across the stall walls makes me feel as if I am at Birchwood as a girl once again. I scrub my body hard with our hard-won soap, as if I'm trying to wash away all the sand, dirt, husband drama and hurt we have caused one another.

But mostly the sand.

As a kid, you can play in sand all day long, jump in the lake, and it all seems to wash away.

As an adult, sand gets caught in every crevice and pothole, the puffy places and hidden spots that didn't exist decades ago. And then it follows you everywhere, into your clothes, your bed, finally your subconscious.

Just like resentment, I think, scrubbing even harder.

Get in a fight as a little kid, and you forget why you were mad the next day. Get in a fight as an adult, and it finds a place to bury itself and hide. Just when you think you've forgotten, it surfaces again.

Little did we know that while we were playing Capture the Flag, and then celebrating with a cookout at Taneycomo, Billy had already arranged for a plumber—assisted by a group of Billy's campers—to get the old shower house running like new.

Well, *new* is a rather optimistic word.

In a miraculously short amount of time, they were able to install a new hot water heater, repair some pipes and add insulation around them. Miraculously, things worked.

I wash the soap out of my eyes and look around my stall.

With a lot more work to go.

There are gaps in the logs, and a few in the roof, so big I have a clear view of the trees outside. The floor tiles are, let's just say, stacked directly atop the ground, and buckled where tree roots have thrust them this way and that. The earth is exposed, and mud flows freely in the stall along with all my sand. The showerhead is mostly rust. I'm wearing flip-flops because I don't want to die of tetanus. But Billy made a minor miracle happen: we can now enjoy running water the last few days we're here, and that's worth more to me right now than a million dollars and a case of Veuve.

Billy said it was his gift to us, but I wonder if it was his gift to Liz, or maybe Em. Perhaps even himself. Billy radiates kindness. He is a good guy.

I think of David, and feel more sand.

Based on what I'd just yelled about the Ritz, Rach starts singing "Puttin' on the Ritz," and Liz yells, "Five bucks if anyone can name who sang that in the '80s?"

"Taco!" Rach and I yell at the same time.

We laugh.

"I was just asking myself on the drive up here how I can forget to buy milk at the store, or the name of one of my clients, but I never forget the lyrics to an '80s song," Liz says.

"Ain't that the truth," I say, before humming the opening bars to "That's What Friends Are For." In seconds, the showers are filled with happy singing.

I turn off the water, grab my towel from a hook, dry off and head to the enormous mirror hanging over a row of little sinks. I turn on the faucet, which chugs and spews for a second. Dirt and rust spill forth.

Not everything is fixed, I see.

I turn it off and rub my hand over the foggy mirror. I stare at my face. For a moment, I can see myself as a girl. It is the face of a happy camper staring back, a face of pure joy, sunburned nose and freckled cheeks.

"I haven't seen you in a long time," I say, waving to my reflection.

The mirror fogs again and, just like that, my image is gone.

I head to the bunkhouse and dress. I am towel-drying my hair when Rach and Liz return. They are trying to sing, but their howls of laughter make them stop every other word.

On top of spaghetti,
All covered with cheese,
I lost my poor meatball,
When somebody sneezed . . .

"I can't." Liz laughs. She bends over and crouches toward the floor. "Stop! I'm about to pee my pants."

Rach cackles and rushes to a bunk to take a seat. "Me, too."

Their silliness makes me giggle and momentarily forget about my life, and soon the cabin is filled with more hoots than a forest full of owls.

I grab a brush and rake it through my auburn hair. "We sang all the time at camp, didn't we?" I ask. "We'd sing when we were being hoppers at mealtime, setting the tables, serving the food, cleaning up. We'd sing campfire songs. We'd sing on the porch. We'd sing before we went to bed." I stop and look at Rach and Liz, both rubbing aloe vera gel all over their too-red bodies. "Why don't we do that anymore?"

"You mean sing?" Rach asks, looking up at me.

"Yeah," I say.

"For fun?" Liz asks. "Or for a living?"

"Just because," I say. I walk over and take a seat on the bunk next to Rach. I rub lotion on my legs. "I mean, isn't it strange that we all sang constantly growing up? We sang in school, in class, at camp, in our rooms, in our cars, in the mall, to each other, to strangers. And then, we just stop as adults. Why?"

"We grow up," Rach says.

"That's such an oxymoron, isn't it? 'Grow up?' I mean, to grow up implies that we should continue reaching for things, be it our dreams or the sky. It implies that we continue to grow, which should mean amplifying our childhood joy, right? Why are we embarrassed to show emotion as adults? Why are we embarrassed to sing out loud? Why do we stop having fun?"

I look up and realize that Rach and Liz are staring at me, mouths wide open.

"Sorry," I say. "I'm babbling."

"No," Rach says. "You're right. Just look at me. I think showing emotion as a woman demonstrates weakness—and I skewer women when they do it—but it's a glorious thing that sets us apart from men. It's a reason I've been so lost for so long. I can fake emotion as an actress, but I'm reluctant to use it as a woman. Men just see it as a weakness when it's really a strength."

"And," Liz adds, "the more we're hurt, the more we hide our emotions and who we truly are inside. We bury all that, build a thick skin, so the blows will more easily glance off of us."

I nod. "Do you know what I was just remembering? David used to sing to me all the time. He'd sing up to my apartment window, he'd fill my answering machine with songs, he'd romance me in restaurants." I stop and shut my eyes. "What was the name of that Parisian singer he loved? The French Frank Sinatra, David called him? Charles Aznavour! That's it!"

The lyrics of a man never forgetting the face of the woman he loves come to me as if David is singing them to me in that little restaurant in Paris that overlooked Notre-Dame. We ate snails and octopus, drank a red wine so sturdy it could have served as our dining table, and he sang to me, tenderly, beautifully, so without embarrassment that the oft-haughty Parisians actually applauded.

I will never stop singing to you, he whispered.
But he did.

"Why don't you call him?" Liz says, ever practical. "The longer you don't talk, the more scar tissue develops."

I stare at her and nod, without getting up.

"Do you often go several days without speaking to him?" Rach asks directly. "Is this a theme?"

Her question pierces my heart. I can actually feel it twinge. I nod robotically.

"I used to work odd hours all over the world," I say. "Now he does the same. Sometimes, we'll go quite a few days without actually talking. We text all the time, but we don't talk all the time. There's a difference."

"There is," Liz says quickly. "Believe me, I know."

"And you've always trusted him?"

"Rach!" Liz yelps.

"It's okay, it's okay," I say. "We're all trying to be as honest as we can." I look at Rach. "I have. And he has always trusted me."

"But you're two different people," she says. "And genders."

I lift my wedding ring. "But this . . . this unites us. Seals us. Makes us one. You've never been married . . ."

Rach lifts her hands as if she's surrendering. "You're right," she says. "I've been the pro-vocateur too long. I'm sorry. I've just learned that men don't play by the same rules we do." Rach stops. "Because they don't have any. And because they don't have to."

I find myself nodding and thinking back over my life. I gave my heart to boys I thought I loved only to have them dump me as if I were an empty soda can. I had to watch my weight while men gorged without considering a calorie. I stayed at home for my family when I'm not sure doing the same would have even entered my husband's mind.

Our rule book *is* different.

I toss myself back on the bunk and sigh, like I

308

used to do at camp when the weight of the world was simply too much to bear.

"Oh, honey," Rachel says, rubbing my leg.

"David gives me one room to decorate," I say. "I know it's a midcentury house and that he hates clutter, but I'm starting to feel like I'm the clutter."

I feel the mattress dip. I look up, and Liz has joined us on the same bunk. She looks at me and smiles sweetly.

"I spent too much of my life going to bed next to someone that I knew in my heart was the wrong person," Liz says. "I spent a good part of my life asking, 'What if?' I never truly loved my husband, and I knew it. We were more partners of convenience. While you were talking about your husband singing to you, I remembered something, too. Mine would snore when he fell asleep, and his nose would whistle. It drove me crazy. To keep myself sane, I would pretend he was whistling a song, and it's only then I could fall asleep, thinking about how much we used to sing here at camp. I would dream my life was a musical and that a song could change the course of it. And then I would wake up and he would be snoring, and I'd be back in real life again." She stops and reaches for my hand. "But the big questions you have to answer are, Did you love David? And do you still love him? Can you forgive him? And can he change? If so, then there's a chance he will sing to you again, and you will hear it in your heart."

I've forgotten what it's like to have friends to talk to, listen to me, give advice.

And now to hold me.

"You never bowed down to anyone, V," Liz whispers as she rocks me. "You've always been confident. You've always been our leader. That's who you need to become again. And see how he handles that person."

"Thank you," I say. "Thank you both."

"We'll leave you alone for a while," Rachel says. "Take a nap. I bet you never do that."

"I bet none of us do," I say.

They nod. The screen door bangs behind them as they leave, and I can hear their footsteps in the gravel grow quieter.

There is silence. My heart hurts, and I turn onto my side. I lie very still for the longest time, stuck between falling asleep and the real world.

Out of nowhere, a chorus of Michigan peepers sings a throaty song in a round.

I smile.

Someone is singing to me.

And then I bury my face into the pillow and cry.

RACHEL

I am squirreling around in the shed. I scan a rusty shovel and a rake missing most of its teeth and then spot the kayak Emily got us. It is already covered in cobwebs. I just want to get lost in the day like I did as a kid. I don't want every minute planned and scheduled. I just want to be still, present, here.

Are all of us running from our lives? Or are we running toward something?

How can such strong women be so successful and still so lost?

Maybe Em knew we just needed a summer vacation.

I pull the kayak into the sun and lift my face toward it, feeling hopeful, which is what the lost need to feel more than anything.

In some point over the last week, the optimist has tumbled out of me, just like the bugs that tumble forth when I rattle the kayak.

What could this place become?

Who could I become?

A daddy longlegs skitters its way back to the shed. "I've worked with worse," I yell to it. "Way worse."

I drag the kayak all the way into the lake, up to my shins, and begin to wash it off.

Like most adults, it is hard for me to be idle. It is hard for me to still my mind. I must always busy myself, keep occupied, for I know that if I don't, I will dwell on the mess I've made of my life.

You may be successful, but you are not a success, young lady.

My mom's words from our horrific holiday reunion a few years ago ring in my head. I brought gifts, hoping for a peaceful Christmas.

My mom brought—as my dad liked to say—a can of whoop-ass.

My cell trills in my pocket constantly, and I keep ignoring it. I know that when I leave this place, I may not have any clients, but I may have earned back my soul.

Would you be proud then, Mom? I wonder.
What about you, Dad?

I toss handfuls of water onto the kayak and then turn it upside down. I drag it back to the shore and sit on one end facing the lake. My phone continues to vibrate, and I yank it angrily from my shorts pocket, lifting my arm into the air and thinking of throwing it into the lake. Reception at this camp is like controlling a hotheaded political candidate: you never know when it's going to go off.

I glance at the endless texts and voice mails that have come in the last few hours.

You're trending!

A text from my assistant catches my eye. I open it.

And not in a good way! it continues. Take a deep breath.

The last few years of my life have all centered around taking a deep breath. I take yet another one and click on the link.

It's a parody video by Eunice Unicorn, a comedienne and singer who became famous for her YouTube videos spoofing interviews with conservative political figures set to parody musical numbers. I glance at the number of views: three million and counting. My stomach drops, and I inhale yet again. I enlarge the video, turn up the volume and hit Play.

Eunice is wearing a Pure Michigan sweatshirt that she has bedazzled in seemingly thousands of sequins. She is wearing her trademark pink cat-eye glasses studded with rhinestones, her purple-gray wig, and enough pancake makeup to make you wonder if she's forty or a hundred and forty.

The video begins with the now infamous Ralph Ruddy video outside the bar. Part of me is instantly relieved that the focus of Eunice's biting satire is going to be on him. But after the footage of Ralph ends, the video shifts to yours truly. Eunice is seated on a set that looks very much like the one from *Red, White & You*, the national morning political talk show on which I frequently appear. She is seated in the same chair and spot as Chip Collins, the show's anchor. The TV show's graphics play, and Eunice turns to face the camera.

"I'm pleased to be joined today by Ralph Ruddy's spokeswoman, Rachel Ives, who also serves as campaign operative and spokesperson for many of the nation's leading conservative male candidates. Rachel, thanks for joining me."

Eunice has edited me into the video, as if I'm sitting right next to her, chatting. I mean, it's so insanely real-looking, I feel as if I might have been there, too.

"Ralph Ruddy is pro-woman," I say.

Oh, my God. She's using all my past interviews.

"As a woman, I wouldn't support a candidate who didn't see women as equals," I continue to babble. "Ralph believes women don't need a handout, we need hands applauding all we do."

"Then let's applaud your incredible efforts on behalf of women and our rights!"

Eunice applauds, her clapping echoing as if she's in an empty studio, and looks around, suddenly understanding that no one is applauding with her. It makes the whole thing—and my responses—seem that much more uncomfortable. And then, Eunice does what has made her famous. She takes a familiar song and rewrites the lyrics to parody the person she's interviewing.

Which is me.

"I am woman, hear me snore . . ." Eunice begins to sing.

The old Helen Reddy song, which my parents loved, I think. My heart stops, as I continue to watch her shred me apart in front of the nation, all of my old sound bites coming back to haunt me.

As well as my old sitcoms.

Eunice has edited old scenes from *Sorority Sisters* that show us tackling sensitive topics—teen pregnancy, sexual harassment, rape, access to health care—and me turning my back on my old friends, locking them in prison, laughing at them. All to the too-perfect lyrics of *I Am Woman.*

At the end of the video, Eunice looks at me and asks, "Any final words, Rachel?"

"I am pro-woman. I am pro-woman. I am pro-woman."

I keep parroting the words, over and over, staring directly at Eunice. It is chilling. It is heartbreaking.

No, I think. *It is accurate.*

Can you please handle this? I text my assistant. Put out a statement saying I thought it was funny. Nip it in the bud. Show them we have a sense of humor. Say that I love Eunice's sweatshirt, and it's nice to see her supporting the great state of Michigan.

I hit Send.

As soon as I do, I am furious at myself. I throw my cell down on the sand, pull the kayak back into the lake and jump in. The momentum propels me into Birchwood, and it's only then I realize I don't have a paddle, a way to go forward or get back to shore.

The perfect analogy.

And so I lean back in the kayak and float.

For a long while, my mind races, my brain jagged. I can only imagine what people are saying, the comments the media is making about me. I can only imagine how many more times the video will be viewed, how many times it's been shown on TV and laughed at by all the pundits. I can only imagine the calls my office is receiving. I'm never one to go MIA. I'm never one to back down from a fight. But this no longer feels like a fight. It's more like Rock 'Em Sock 'Em Robots, the game I played with my dad where red and blue robot fighters stand in the middle of a boxing ring and hit each other, the goal to be the first to knock your opponent's block off. The whole goal is to inflict as much damage as possible.

I've done that for too long. I've punched and punched with incredible anger and faux bravado, and still there is no victor. There are only losers, me being the biggest one.

When I played the game with my dad, we'd laugh and laugh, mostly because we swung and missed so many times, and because it seemed so silly when one of the boxers' heads would spring off after an uppercut connected to his jaw. But there are no winners in today's political boxing matches. The only ones getting hurt are real Americans.

All of us.

I stretch my legs out in front of me, lean back and shut my eyes. My instincts want me to steer, to open my eyes, to see where I'm going, but I fight that urge and let the wind carry me. My mind refuses to still.

I run numbers in my mind.

If I quit, I will lose my career, my reputation, my income, everything I have built for the last two decades. I have two homes. A staff. Health care coverage. I've done well, but it's not enough to carry me into retirement yet.

What do I do? Move back home with my mother?

But I'm tired of fighting. Especially for everything that goes against who I truly am. I have started by trying to make amends with and forgive my friends.

Can I do that with my mother? Can I forgive myself?

I think of Liz.

Life is not a musical, and a happy song may make you feel better for three minutes but it cannot change your life.

Right, Eunice?

The waves slap the side of the kayak, and the dull *thwak-thwak-thwak* of the water sings to me and lulls me into a more peaceful state. I think of my dad. We are playing games. I am waving to him as he heads off to work in the morning. I am eating cinnamon toast that my mom has pulled straight from under the broiler, the sugar and butter making a crunchy coating on top, the white bread soft underneath. I am singing campfire songs with The Clover Girls, giggling as we change the lyrics, my marshmallows sliding into the flames.

I awake with a start, whacking my knee on the kayak.

Ow!

I look around. I smile and shake my head. I'm back at the shore, exactly where I started.

In so many ways, I think. *And perhaps it's just where I need to be.*

At the beginning.

Where I started.

As the girl I once was.

I jump out of the kayak and grab my phone from where I left it in the sand. It trills in my hand and is filled with texts and voice mails.

But I know there is only one call I finally must make. Not to any candidate, or my office, or any news station, but to the person who realized I was a parody of myself long ago and did everything to help me from becoming one. The one who sang to me growing up and believed I could be anything I dreamed.

I dial a number I haven't called in ages. I still know it by heart.

My heart races as the phone rings.

"Hi, Mom," I say. "It's Rachel."

LIZ

You are my sunshine, my only sunshine . . .

I am singing the song to my mom that she always sang to lull me to sleep.

My mom's dull blue eyes dart around the room, thinking I must be somewhere close by. She no longer understands the concept of a voice over the phone. She can no longer register my face in front of her. But she knows this song, somewhere down deep in her mind, heart and soul, and she grins as I continue to sing, her eyes finally shutting, her head bobbing.

"Thank you," I say to Tammy, the late-afternoon aide who is holding up the phone I got for my mom. "I need to get back there."

"You need this time off," Tammy says very slowly. "You're busy 24/7. You *never* give yourself a break. You practically live here."

"How's she doing?" I ask. "Any change?"

Tammy turns the camera toward her own face. She is around my age. There are dark circles under her eyes, and I can only imagine the mental and physical toll such a job takes on her, how hard she works for so little money. Tammy shakes her head and gives me a faint smile. "Fading a bit more every day, just like the Michigan summer sunshine. We're losing a minute now every day. Soon, it will be dark all the time." She looks at me. "I'm so sorry. I know how hard this is."

I nod. "It's not just hard," I say. "It's agonizingly slow."

"We're keeping a good eye on her," she says.

"Any visitors?" I ask.

Tammy shakes her head. "Don't do that to yourself, Liz."

"How's Mrs. Dickens?"

She turns the phone toward her. "Wave, Mrs. Dickens."

She does.

I smile.

"I'll be home soon," I say.

"Enjoy the rest of your vacation," she says. "I'll call you if there's any change."

I hang up, feeling more disjointed than before I called.

Is that what you call this? A vacation? Is this a happy tune I'm singing? Or is it a goodbye to a friend? A girls' weekend, or a swan song? A wakeup call? Beginning of a new life?

I turn my face toward the sunshine. Oh, how my mom loved summer in Michigan.

I remember her taking any spare moment she could find during her busy days—when she was hanging the laundry, washing the windows, watering the flowers, picking up our toys scattered across the house, or cooking the casserole—to turn her face toward the light. It's as if she knew how fleeting it all was.

I remember what Tammy just said. "Fading every day . . . Soon, it will be dark all the time."

I look around, half hoping there is a closet— like the one in my mom's room—to hide in, but I see V and Rach painting their nails on the porch, and I walk over and begin to bawl.

"Oh, honey," V says, opening her arms.

I sit between them, and they scooch over until we're one big clump of a human, and they hold me until my tears subside.

"We're all taking turns crying today," I say, catching my breath.

I tell them about my mom's decline, my family's indifference and my growing resentment, and they listen and nod. When there is silence, Rach tells us about the viral video, the fallout with her family and the difficult, but hopeful, call with her mom.

"How did I get so lost?" she asks.

"We," I add. "How did *we* get so lost?"

"Do you think Em forgives us for ignoring our friendship for so long?" V asks. "For hurting one another?"

"I think she forgave us before she died," I say. "I actually think this plan of hers was not just about giving us a chance to forgive one another but for us to forgive ourselves before it was too late. This is all about finding ourselves in a place that we—and society—lost." I stop. "I mean, think of the silly things we've done here this week: Talent Night, swimming tests, Coed Socials, Capture the Flag . . . Why did we do them when we were at camp?"

"Boredom," V says with a laugh.

"To test ourselves," Rach says. "To unleash our potential and talents."

"Teamwork," V adds. "Make friends."

"And?" I ask.

They look at me.

"To just have fun," I say. "To just be a kid. To remind us—in this often too-busy, awful, hectic, hurtful, divisive, unkind world where we all want everything—that the most important things in life are still the simplest."

"I am finding myself," Rach says.

"Me, too," V says.

"I still need a guide," I say.

They laugh and reach out to hug me again. As if on cue, my cell rings.

"Devil phone," Rach says. "You get reception everywhere. I only get it when I don't want it."

I laugh and look. "Billy," I mouth.

"He can't hear you," V says.

"Hello? Oh, hi, Billy. We were just talking, painting our nails, doing all the *Sex and the City* things without, you know, the sex or the city."

His laughter explodes over the cell, and I hold

it back from my ear. The girls smile and start to paint their nails again.

"Well," Billy says, "I can't offer the city . . ."

Oh, my God, I think. *Is he offering me sex?!*

"And sex . . . well . . ." Billy fumbles over his words and actually giggles, like a schoolboy saying a dirty word. "I don't know what I'm saying. I'm sorry. You get me all tongue-tied, Liz. Anyway, I was calling to ask if you might be interested in going to The Smilin' Smelt . . ."

"That place is still around?"

"More popular than ever," Billy says. "And they still have their famous smoked chub Bloody Mary."

"Is this a . . ."

I stop cold. The word *date* practically hangs in the air like mosquitoes. V and Rach gasp.

"It can be a group thing," he says, his words coming out in a deflated tone.

No! I want to scream. I didn't mean I didn't *want* it to be a date. Me and my big mouth. He's not the only one that's tongue-tied.

"Sure," I say too perkily.

"Is eight o'clock too late?" he asks. "Younger boys will be in bed. Counselors can watch the older ones. And I can sneak out and pick you up."

"Sounds good! Bye."

"You sound chipper," Rach jokes, nudging me with her elbow. "Like a theme park character."

"Shut up," I say. "We have a date."

324

"Ooooh!" they both coo.

"No," I say, lifting my hand and gesturing at the three of us. "We. All of us. Group date. Like in eighth grade."

"Do we need a chaperone?" V asks.

"Ha ha," I say, jabbing my finger in their direction. "I already have two." I stop. "We're going to The Smilin' Smelt."

They shriek in excitement.

"Oh, my God! I always wanted to be able to order a Bloody Mary there!" Rachel says.

"Me, too!" V says. "They had the best food."

"Then this is worth staying another night?" I ask.

"For you," Rachel says. "Anything."

"For us, Bloody Marys!" V says. "Friday night par-tay!"

They stand and start jumping up and down, wagging their fingers in the air to dry their nails.

A few minutes before eight, we are standing in the parking lot by our cars, actually whispering to one another nervously, as if we're about to sneak off without permission with a group of local boys. Though it's still light, we see headlights blaring down the dirt road, which is cloaked in shade by the canopy of trees growing over it.

"A pickup?" V asks, her pretty eyes bulging.

"There better be a back seat," Rach says. "I did my hair."

Billy pulls up in an old Ford pickup that has the Taneycomo logo emblazoned on both sides.

"Hop in," he says.

No one moves.

"Do you ladies mind riding in the back?" he asks.

"Yeah," Rach says. "We do. We're not horses or hay bales."

"Listen," V says. "We don't mean to Bogart Liz. This is a date."

"Yeah," Rachel agrees. "Go have fun. Just the two of you."

My heart leaps, but I can see the disappointment in their faces.

"Are you bowing out because of me or the truck?" I ask.

They look at me.

Billy smiles. "I promise I'll go slow."

"Smelt!" they yell. "Bloody Marys!"

Their excitement is short-lived as the two of them, reluctantly and very dramatically, climb into the back of the pickup—taking a seat next to each other against the back of the window. I cannot contain my laughter as the truck bumps down the dirt road, and I turn my cell on them to record the journey. Rach's and V's bodies rise and fall with every pothole Billy hits. They scream and hold on to one another, briefly, before their hands fly back to their heads as if they can keep their hair in place in the open wind. Dust kicks up from the road, and V and Rach are hidden in dirt, just like Pig-Pen, until we reach the highway. When Billy picks up speed, their hair stands on end. They shriek and laugh, and point at one another, until they realize I am filming them. They flip me the bird.

"You will pay for this," V mouths.

"Having fun?" Billy asks.

"Too much," I say.

We chitchat about the wonderful weather and other completely lame topics until we get to the restaurant. We hop out, and Billy lowers the truck's gate and assists V and Rach out of the pickup. They both look as if they just completed a mud run.

"How do I look?" V and Rach ask at the same time.

I take a picture and show it to them. They shriek and run to find a restroom.

The Smilin' Smelt hasn't changed one bit since I was last here decades ago. The tiny restaurant, an expanded former wooden fishing shanty in the tiny resort town of Leland—known as Fishtown—sits near the falling waters where you can watch the salmon run in the fall. The restaurant is known for its smelt, a tiny fish that looks like a minnow, and its old neon sign hasn't changed either: a smiling smelt leaps out of the water, doffs its hat and then jumps on a dinner plate.

The restaurant is jammed, as are all places in northern Michigan in the summer. A line snakes out the door, but a man standing at a podium on the wooden walkway waves at Billy and motions him to the front.

"Good to see you, counselor," the man says.

Billy shakes his hand and looks at me. "I was his counselor at Taneycomo, not his attorney." He laughs.

"I could use a good one of those every now and then, however," the man says. "Although 'good attorney' may be an oxymoron."

"Hi," I say, extending my hand. "I'm Liz."

"Chase," he says. "Love your outfit."

"Thanks," I say, looking down at my clothes. I'm wearing a leopard headband and leopard top, a chain belt over tailored trousers, and slouchy boots. "I made everything, save for my slacks. They're from the Gap. I'm like Michelle Obama: high fashion and a little Gap."

"You should be a fashion designer," he says.

I wave off his compliment, as usual, but Billy says, "She *is* a fashion designer," and I blush.

"Cool," Chase says. "Let me show you to your table."

He leads us past a throng of people waiting in line, who groan audibly as we pass, before showing us to a small table for two overlooking the water.

"I made a reservation for four," Billy says.

"I know," Chase says. "*They* changed your reservation."

He nods toward the old, long, wooden bar—glossy in the light—where V and Rach are seated, Bloody Marys already in their hands.

"What?" I ask. "Why?"

Chase looks at them and then at me. "Let me see if I can get this right," he says. "They said, and I quote, that they didn't want to 'bogart' your date and have you 'wig out' because that would be 'so '87' so they said it was 'cool' to 'veg' at the bar so you two could 'scarf' some smelt and decide if you wanted to 'go together.' " He stops. "I think I got that right."

I laugh and look at them.

"Cheers, Betty!" they yell. "Enjoy!"

"I thought your name was Liz," Chase says.

" '80s slang," I say. "It's like speaking a second language."

He seats us at the table and for a moment, we watch the water rush toward the lake.

"What is it about water that calms us?" I finally ask. "I literally sell the lake to homeowners, and it never gets old."

"I think we realize it's bigger than we are and that it will be here long after we're gone," Billy says.

"Have you always been this wise?" I ask.

"No," he says. "I just packed your best friends

into the back of a pickup. That wasn't wise at all."

I look over at them again, their hair '80s big from the wind and too much hairspray. An older man who looks like he could be Rach's grandfather is chatting her up, while a group of women are clustered around V, asking for her autograph and taking pictures.

The waiter approaches. "Good evening," he says. "What will it be?"

"Two Bloodys and two smelts?" Billy asks.

"Why rock tradition?"

The waiter walks away, and Billy looks at me with a big smile and says, "Speaking of tradition, your outfit. Totally '80s. Like the way your friends speak."

I laugh and wave him off as I did earlier.

"You know, everything you're wearing is back in style. It's what all the girlfriends of the camp counselors wear on their date nights."

"Everything comes back in style," I say. "Winona Ryder on *Stranger Things*, for instance."

Billy reaches over and grabs my hand. I flinch and nearly knock over a glass of water. I grab it and then hold onto it tightly to mask my nervous energy.

"I want you to look at me for a moment. Be serious," he says.

"Okay," I say, a bit too dramatically.

"It's really good to see you again, Liz." He

330

stops and reaches for my hand again. I let go of the glass. He holds it tightly. I can feel my heart pulse in his palm. "I think Emily knew what she was doing."

I stare at him, blinking uselessly like a flashing yellow light on an empty country road, unable to speak. Thankfully, the waiter arrives with our drinks.

"Speaking of tradition," I say.

"Cheers!" Billy says.

"Can I even take a sip?" I ask, trying to get the drink within the vicinity of my face.

The drink is as big as my arm. Jutting out of the mammoth Bloody Mary glass are not just celery stalks and toothpicks of olives but skewers filled with cheese, sausage, bacon and pickles. But the biggest splash—quite literally— is a giant smoked chub, a whole fish, eye intact, leaping from the drink as if it's breaking water.

True Michiganders love smoked chub—just as they love smelt and whitefish—but the reactions of vacationers seeing the drink for the first time run the gamut from laughter to horror, guffaws to gasps.

"This is the most Michigan drink ever!" I say. "Cheers!"

I take a sip, and then another, before plucking the smoked fish from the glass and eating it in a few big gulps.

"You're the most Michigan girl ever!" Billy says, following suit.

When our fried smelt come, we eat them whole—skin, head and tail—and they are as delicious as I remembered. I try to pick at my fries as if I'm a light eater, but I'm starving after living off of coffee, s'mores and Jiffy Pop for days, and I gulp them down. Billy orders another round of drinks, and when they arrive, Billy looks at me and says, "To the next chapter of your life."

I lift my glass.

"What does it look like to you?"

I stare out at the falling waters and then at Billy. "I know what it looks like," I say, "but I don't know if I can actually design the whole fashion show."

"You can and you will," Billy says. "If you can make that outfit . . ." I chuckle, but Billy turns serious again. "I didn't know what my life would look like after my divorce. But I knew I wanted—no, *needed*—a new start. Things have changed so much since we were little—technology, travel, the way we interact, politics—but many things haven't. I see so many young men come to camp, just like I did as a boy, and even at the ages of ten or eleven, their path in life has already been cemented: they will be doctors like their grandfathers, or engineers like the men in their family have always been, or . . ." Billy stops and points at himself. ". . . attorneys like their fathers. I was doing the same thing for my children. We decide the paths for the next generation before they've even had the chance to figure it out themselves, to just be kids."

Billy continues: "Camp is the place where they're simply allowed to be kids again. To figure it out for themselves. To take our advice and maybe, hopefully, take it to heart. So many of the kids I grew up with now are unhappy adults, and their kids are unhappy, too. I just want the young men who come to Taneycomo to know that they can be—and do—anything they dream. The only things that hold us back are fear and ourselves."

I am nodding, and drinking, in agreement.

"My children have so little empathy for those around them, especially their elders," I say. "And I know much of that is my fault. I grew up wanting to be a friend more than a parent. I didn't get that from my husband, so I put it all into my kids. I gave in to their whims and wishes. I wanted to make up for all that my marriage lacked." I hesitate. "But I know I was a good mother. I gave my life to them, to my entire family, and I don't regret any of that for one second. This saddens me to say out loud, but I will, because I need to hear myself say it: my children are selfish. They will not be there for me, to care for me as I age. I know that. And I must accept that reality, as much as it crushes my heart. So I have to look at the next chapter in my life knowing that it will be me taking care of me."

I take a sip of my drink. "This time at Birch-wood has reminded me that family is comprised of more than those who are related by blood. Family should consist of those who know you, inside and out. And who is that?" I look over at V and Rach. Rach catches my eye and lifts her drink. "Friends. Friends are family. And I forgot that. You know, I found who I was supposed to be at camp a long time ago, and I think I'm rediscovering that all over again here. I spent much of my adult life worried about what every-one thought: my husband, my kids, my parents, my neighbors, my coworkers, my friends. And I spent my life giving every second to someone else, because I felt it was selfish to focus on myself. Mostly, I realize, I felt I wasn't worth it. I think that Bloody Mary well changes now."

I raise my drink. Billy clinks it. I can hear the ring tone of my cell over the din of the restaurant. "Mind if I check?" I ask Billy. He shakes his head, and I grab my cell from my bag. I take a deep breath as I look, thinking it is about my mother, but instead I see it's for my Etsy store. I click on it, and I have over a hundred new orders since I've been gone.

One hundred!

I scan the orders, from jewelry to blouses to bandanas. From women sixteen to sixty.

"Is everything okay?" Billy asks.

"I think it just might be," I say. "I think it just might be."

All of a sudden, the lights dim, and an elderly man in a pilled tuxedo jacket walks to a piano in the corner of the room. A shaky spotlight hits him as he sits.

"It's 9:00 p.m., which means it's time for the nightly sing-along!" he says, his gray mustache twitching. "I'm Frank DeMuth, and I have been for eighty-nine years."

The diners cheer.

"They still do this?" I whisper to Billy.

"They do," he says.

"And is that the same Frank?"

"It is." Billy laughs.

"He hasn't changed," I say.

"Every song we sing here at The Smilin' Smelt is sung in the round. This side of the room starts," Frank says, pointing toward the right side of the restaurant, "and then this side of the room sings," he says, pointing toward the left side and the bar. "We're a team. And if you can't sing, don't worry. Neither can I." The diners laugh. He tickles the ivories and smiles.

"I mean, nothing has changed," I whisper to Billy, "down to the act."

"Isn't it great?"

"And we already have a request," Frank says. "Ladies, where are you?"

335

The spotlight dances around The Smilin' Smelt. I look around the restaurant. V and Rach stand and walk, very wobbly, toward the piano, holding on tightly to one another. The crowd whoops and hollers, calling out Rach's name, and then V's.

"You know famous people," Billy says.

"Infamous people, you mean," I say.

There is a screeching noise. I look up to see V holding the mic much too close to her face. "Hello, Smelt!" she yells too loudly. The mic squeals again, and people put their hands over their ears. Rach grabs the mic. Some in the audience cheer as the spotlight illuminates her face even more; some boo. "I get that reaction all the time," Rach says to laughter. She continues, undeterred. "My best friend here and I want all of you to join us in singing a special song to one of our best friends. Liz, will you stand up?"

My face flushes immediately.

"Stand up," Billy urges, clapping.

I stand reluctantly, wave my hand, and sit.

"The song we're going to sing is inspired by one we heard Liz sing to her mother this morning. It's also inspired by our love of all things '80s. We're Birchwood girls forever!"

V shoots up four fingers into the air and yells, "The Clover Girls! Best friends forever!"

She is beyond buzzed, I think. *As in feeling no pain.*

Some older folks in the crowd applaud, remembering the camp.

V grabs the mic from Rach and takes a seat on the piano bench next to Frank, sidling up closely and sliding an arm around his back. "You know something we don't, don'cha, Frank?" V asks, her words slurred.

"Do I?" Frank asks with a wink.

"You do," V continues. "You know that life is like these silly songs you sing here. These sing-alongs . . ." She stops, searching for her words. Someone hands her a glass of wine, and she chugs a good part of the glass.

Oh, this is not good, I think.

Rach grabs the mic back.

"I think what my friend is trying to say is that these sing-alongs are a part of history that shouldn't be forgotten. They're like life—a continuum—that constantly goes in a round. We all act like life is a straight line but it's not . . . it's a circle. We start and end our lives the same way . . . as people who need boundless love and care."

I put my hand to my mouth.

"What makes all the pain and hurt worthwhile is the love and connections we create along the way. What makes it all worth the ride is friends . . ." Rach stops and leans toward V, putting the mic in front of both of their mouths.

"And sunshine," they say together. "Frank?"

Frank begins to play the piano, and I know the song immediately. In fact, I could name that Katrina and the Waves tune in two notes.

When we get to the chorus, the left side of the room is singing, "I'm walkin' on sunshine" and the right side is singing, "Woah-ooooah!" and I'm crying and laughing so hard my mascara is running down my face.

Rach and V walk over and grab my hands. We stand and begin to jump up and down, not as much dancing together as sharing a communal hug.

As we leap and spin and sing and sway, I think of my mom, of sunshine, and how a simple song can have such a profound impact on your life.

What is the mark I want to leave on this world? I think.

I feel another set of arms around me. I look over, and Billy is jumping with us, the spotlight on the four of us.

A four-leaf clover once again, Em!

I jump and laugh and cry.

And, for the first time in a long time, I feel as if I am, finally, walking on sunshine.

PART EIGHT

Color War!

SUMMER 1985

Emily looks right and then left. She hesitates and stops abruptly when she sees them, her milk carton tumbling off her tray. Liz, right behind, nearly runs into the back of her. Her sneakers release an ear-shattering squeak, and her green Jell-O slides to the edge of her tray.

"What are you doing?" Liz asks.

That's when Liz sees them.

"The Birches," Emily whispers without moving a muscle of her body. She indicates the girls occupying both ends of the table at the far end of The Lodge.

The camp elders, the "legends" from every clique—the Athletes, the Leaders, the Artists, the City Girls—would sit at the ends of all the long dining tables, and then greet campers who would stand before them, trays in hands, to pay their respects.

But the Birches claimed the long table by the windows overlooking the camp. It was where they could keep an eye on their minions. The table was also by the tray return and huge freezer stuffed with frozen treats, a place they could torture newbies.

Emily had already felt their wrath the very first day when she went to retrieve an ice cream sandwich and was stopped before she could return to her seat at the table.

"Pay your toll," one of the Birches said.

"What do you mean?" Emily asked.

She held out her hand. Emily paid with her ice cream.

When she returned empty-handed, sweet ol' Em actually coined the term "Birches" because she was too nice to say what she meant: those girls were bitches. They thought they were the prettiest, the coolest, Courtney Cox yanked onto the stage by Bruce Springsteen to dance with him in his "Dancing in the Dark" video cool. But they were really just mean.

"That burns my butt," V had said.

"They need to pay," Rachel added.

We had taken seats at the center of the end table because we didn't know any better. We didn't realize that "The Birches" occupied both ends.

"What do I do?" Em whispers to Liz.

"Just walk," Liz whispers. "Be confident. And don't give them your food!"

Em walks toward The Birches. Liz can see the tray shaking in her new friend's hands. One of the girls acts as if she's going to stand—like a basketball player trying to fake out a defender—but remains seated.

Liz sighs as Em passes. She moves quickly, keeping her head high.

The next thing Liz knows is that she is airborne.

One of The Birches extended her leg at the last minute into the middle of the aisle to trip her. Liz's tray flies out of her hands and bounces off the window. She hits the floor, hard, scraping her knees and nearly knocking out a tooth on a chair. When she looks up, a blob of Jell-O is trailing down the window like an alien.

"You're such a klutz," one of The Birches says.

"Yeah," says another. "We should start calling you Grace."

"A round of applause for Grace," a Birch yells across The Lodge, clapping with faux enthusiasm.

Liz sits up just in time to see Mrs. Nigh bee-lining across The Lodge, wagging a finger, already asking for an explanation.

But before she reaches the table, V and Rachel are standing in front of Liz, before The Birches.

"Look, it's Blair and Jo!" one of The Birches taunts.

Rach grabs the girl, lifts her from her chair and holds the front of her T-shirt. V nabs my Jell-O from the floor and drops it down her shirt.

"Our names are V and Rachel, got it? And that's Emily and Liz. You don't mess with them, and you don't mess with us."

Another Birch stands, ready to fight, but V scoops up another blob of green Jell-O and rubs it across her shirt.

"Remember our names, and remember our color. We are The Clover Girls."

The Lodge breaks into thunderous cheers.

The Clover Girls refuse to move from the center of the table. Everyone readies themselves for a camp war, but it never materializes. The Birches eventually find another table, knowing they—and their ways—are no longer in control. And that changes the culture of the camp: as The Birches and the other cliques leave camp, The Clover Girls remain firmly entrenched in the middle— not only at their table in The Lodge but in the entire camp—welcoming girls from every group to sit with them.

Other cliques try to rise up. One group starts the "I'm Over the Clovers" movement, but it doesn't stick: no one messes with Rach and V.

And green Jell-O.

SUMMER 2021
VERONICA

"Work, V!"

I position my body in an impossible angle, much like my moniker "V," and lift my chin. Wind machines are blowing my hair back from my face, and a half dozen assistants are holding reflectors at varied positions all around me.

"The only thing hotter than me are these!" I say. I pop a Flamin' Hot Cheeto into my mouth, then suddenly pop into my famed tiger pose and roar.

"Cut!" the director yells. "Excellent work, V!"

Nena's "99 Luftballons" suddenly blares in the studio, and a team of people rush up to retouch my makeup. I close my eyes as mascara is applied to my lashes. When I open them, I flinch. A raccoon, not a woman, is holding a tube of mascara. I shut my eyes again as gloss is applied to my lips. When I open them again, a raccoon is brushing my lips with a shimmery pink applicator.

I scream.

Scritch. Scratch. Scritch.

99 Luftballons . . .

I try to open an eye, but it is sealed shut. I

manage to pop open the other eye. Light blares directly into it. My head pounds and my stomach lurches.

On a scale of one to ten, my hangover is more along the lines of Studio 54.

I hear music and what sounds like a TV playing an animated cartoon. I tilt my head on the mattress—as much effort as I can make at the moment—and narrow my one working eye around the bunkhouse.

I scream, sit up, my other eye popping open, finally breaking through its mascaraed prison.

The door to the cabin is wide open. Two raccoons are going through our purses, which we've left—along with a trail of chip bags, junk food wrappers and our clothes—scattered across the floor. *99 Luftballons* is playing on a cell, and I wonder if a raccoon somehow turned on a phone—I vaguely recall us dancing to '80s music when we got back to Birchwood—or if we left it playing all night long.

One raccoon is leisurely eating chips from a bag, smacking its lips and chattering away in ecstasy, while the other is going through my bag like a purse snatcher, much like one had done with Rach's when we arrived.

Are you the same bandit who loves junk food and makeup? I wonder. *Em in disguise?*

The raccoon pulls my lip gloss from my bag, opens it, tastes it, squeals in horror, and tosses the wand over its shoulder. It reaches for my good mascara.

"Stop!" I scream. "Don't touch that! Get out!"

I can feel the bunk shake.

"Wha'?" Liz asks sleepily.

"I've got a gun!" Rach yells.

The raccoons scamper off as if Rach's threat has done the trick. I dangle my head over the bunk, defying the spinning of the room, and look at Rach.

"Really?"

"I don't," she says, rubbing her eyes. "But I'm used to saying it at political rallies. Something about a woman with a gun that gets folks all—pardon the pun—fired up. I've also had to say it to more than one of the men I represent."

"I can't imagine," I say.

"I can't either, anymore," she says.

I try to nod at her, but the room spins.

"You look like a raccoon," Rach says. "A really hungover raccoon that used to model."

"You don't look much better, sister," I say. "Or should I say, Twisted Sister."

Liz groans, and I can't tell if it's from my joke or her hangover.

It finally dawns on me none of us are in our regular bunks. I'm in a top bunk, Rach is in Em's old bunk, and Liz is somewhere down below.

Was I the most sober one last night? The only

one who could actually crawl into a top bunk? That's a frightening thought.

"Shut the door," I say to her. "You're closest. And I'm cold. And dizzy. And I don't want to get my makeup done by raccoons."

"Too late." Rach laughs.

"Oh, my gosh!" Liz says.

I lean over the bunk and look at Rach again, a puzzled look on my face.

Liz is murmuring now, her voice muffled by the bunk above her.

"Are you okay?" I ask.

"Yes. No. I don't know."

"Is your mom okay?" Rach asks, her voice slightly panicked.

"Oh, yes, yes. No, it's not her. It's . . . Just listen. I got this text from Em's attorney. She must have given him my number, since I was the last to stay in touch with her."

Liz begins to read:

" 'Dear Ms. Anderson: I am Raymond Wilcox, the attorney representing your friend Emily's estate. It has been nearly one week since you should have arrived at Camp Birchwood. Per the instructions detailed in her trust, and as noted to you, in order to inherit Camp Birchwood, you, Ms. Ives and Mrs. Berzini were required to spend a week there together. The only stipulation was that by the end of the week the three of you must have committed to the camp together. If any of you have chosen to leave or walk away, then the camp and its endowment will be turned over to the State of Michigan for future generations to enjoy. Emily asked that I arrive at some unannounced point within the week to assess whether you are still together and have met her requirements. If you, Ms. Ives and Mrs. Berzini have already departed, please let me know as soon as possible so I can begin the transfer of assets to the State. Should you have questions you may reach me at the number below. In advance, thank you for your time. Best, Raymond Wilcox.' "

For the longest time, there is silence.

"Has it already been nearly a week?" Rach finally asks. "I can't believe it."

"I feel like we just got here," Liz says.

More silence.

"Is someone capable of making coffee?" I finally ask. "I think we need to talk."

A half hour later, the three of us are huddled at our old spot in the center of the table by the window, holding on to our mugs of coffee as if they were life rafts. Rachel has started a campfire outside, and I watch the logs crackle. I think of my days at camp, of my childhood, my career, my marriage and my children, of Em and how quickly time fades, just like the smoke into the quickly warming Michigan morning. I stare at the fire, the warmth of the coffee making me feel just good enough not to die, the caffeine emboldening me just enough to say, "I think I want to keep Birchwood."

Rach looks at me, and Liz jerks upright, her coffee splashing out of her mug.

"Really?" Liz asks. "I mean, for real, real?"

I nod.

"Me, too," Liz says.

"Me, three," Rachel says.

"And I have an idea about what to do with it," I say. "More than just having it be a memory. How to bring it to life. How to bring myself back to life."

"Me, too," Liz repeats.

"Me, three," Rachel says.

We all stare at each other, mascara-smeared eyes wide.

"I'll go first then," I say. "I can't even believe what I'm about to say. I didn't even know if I'd come back here when I got Em's letter. I didn't know if I would stay. I didn't know if we would even talk to one another again. I don't even know if I'll have a marriage when I get home. But I came for Emily. I came because I remembered what this place—and all of you—meant to me. And that has changed me, no matter what. So . . . here goes."

I take a breath and continue. "I came to Birchwood with no self-confidence. I was a freckled, red-haired girl who didn't fit into the standard norms of beauty. I have a long-term vision of turning Birchwood into a girls' summer camp again, but with a different focus: a focus on body positivity, self-acceptance and self-confidence, so that girls can love themselves—no matter how they look—because that will change their lives forever. I want to run a camp with a theme of 'Don't Be a Super Model, Be a Role Model.' "

I look at Rach and Liz, who both look at each other. They squeeze their coffee mugs between their knees and begin to applaud. I blush. "Thank you," I say. "That means a lot." I look at Rach. "Next."

Rach takes a deep breath and plucks her coffee mug from between her knees. I can see that her hands are shaking slightly, but I can't tell if it's the hangover or nerves. When she begins to speak, her voice quavers—perhaps a first in Rach's lifetime—and I now know she is genuinely nervous.

"I want to help young women get into politics . . ."

Liz groans.

"Hear me out!" Rach says. "Please!"

"Sorry," Liz says. "Go on."

"I want to teach them how to volunteer, get involved in local politics, become politically active, teach them how to change the laws and how much their voice and vote matter. I want to nurture the young women of tomorrow to run for office . . ." Rach stops and begins to cry. "I screwed up. For too long. I need to make amends. I need to effect change. I have only a short time to make up for a lifetime of mistakes. I've harmed us . . . I've hurt women . . . our cause, our lives, our rights, and I need to make good on all of that."

I set my coffee down, stand up and walk over to hug Rach. She stands and holds on to me so tightly that I don't know if she'll ever let go. When she does, Liz reaches out her hand, and Rach grips it tightly.

"Last but not least," I say, sitting down again. "Liz?"

"I want to create a creativity camp," Liz says. "A camp that encourages the arts. Kids are never encouraged to see the arts as a viable career, and I'd like to change that. Kids have the most creative spirits in the world. What happens to that spark? Adults snuff it before it can turn into a flame because we believe we must be 'serious,' we must make money, we must 'act' like grown-ups. I want girls to channel their creative souls. I want to teach design. Rach and V, you could teach about the world of entertainment. Just look at someone like Reese Witherspoon: women need to be creating content and entertainment by women for women. This could start here at the earliest of ages."

Rach and I nod enthusiastically. "Great idea. I love it," I say. "In fact, I love all of them."

"All of these ideas are viable," Rachel says. "And there is no doubt girls would benefit from the power of attending such a camp. But as businesswomen, we all know this is going to take a great deal of time—and money—to make it a reality. We need to do our due diligence when it comes to the specifics of the camp—the financials, the business plan, the business structure, the remodel. Moreover, we're all in the midst of rather large . . ." Rachel clears her throat. ". . . ahem, life changes and decisions. We need more than another day or two to decide all of that."

"You're a hundred percent right," I say. "I don't know if I'll be married in a year."

"I don't know if my mom will be here in a month," Liz says.

"I don't know if I'll have a job next week," Rachel says. "What should we do?"

"I think we need to decide if we're actually going to keep the camp," I say. "We start there and then move forward. Or not." I stop. "As Em said, it will require us all to be here together for a few more days. Even more than that, it will mean committing to something long-term together: not just this camp, but each other. And that won't be easy. It will take patience and understanding and money and respect. It will require finally forgiving one another fully so we can start a new chapter. It will mean that we'll never be over The Clovers."

Rachel and Liz laugh, immediately getting my reference from the past.

I continue. "I mean, this has all been an emotional roller coaster. I think it's clarified a lot of things for each of us, and also muddied the waters even more in some ways. Our futures all seem a bit uncertain. But we can at least clarify one thing right now." I start to sing the old punk anthem. "Should we stay or should we go?"

Liz grabs her phone and starts to play the Clash's song. We all sing.

When it is over, another song comes on Pandora, and we all look at one another as if Em were one step ahead of us, as if she wasn't just directing the soundtrack of our lives from beyond but also every move.

"*99 Luftballons.*"

"This is war!" Nena sings.

"Color War!" I yell.

Rachel and Liz look at one another and then me.

"Totally brilliant and ironic," Liz says. "It's the only way to decide if we want to make a go of this. And each other."

She puts her hand out, and we put them atop one another's as if we were one going into battle against our rival.

Which could be each other.

It does seem too ironic to imagine: three friends competing against one another in Color War as we used to do as teams in camp. This will either solidify our friendship or prove that all of this— even staying an extra few days—just isn't going to work. Color War always has.

Has our time here together truly been real or just an imaginary high from our lives and our grief? Can we survive, not only a Color War but also each other's pasts?

And will we stand up for one another like we once did? Or will we turn on one another like we have done? Are we one team? Or divided individuals?

It's as if every moment has led up to this.

As if Em always knew that if she got us together it would come down to one final test.

I look at my friends.

I'm as equally hopeful and pessimistic about the outcome as I am about my own marriage.

RACHEL

For the last hour, we have been seated at our old spot in The Lodge, middle seats at the table closest to the big windows overlooking the bunkhouses. We have been singing and talking and trying to avoid the obvious: Are we the same girls who left here, or have the years and bad blood changed us?

I look out at the camp. Everything still glistens in the morning dew, the sun not high enough yet to burn off the moisture, and water drips off the bunkhouse roofs and trails over logs before evaporating into the chinking. The fire is dying.

Though there aren't countless girls rushing to and fro, the three of us have already managed to recreate the spokes in the dirt that used to run from the bunkhouses in every direction. I smile and look at The Lodge in the morning light. Dust motes float, and the old wood floor is covered in a layer of dirt. I sniff the air and swear I can still smell Love's Baby Soft.

Memories, I think.

Though I tend to remember all the positive things about camp, I also know my experience at Birchwood made me—as my mom and dad used to say—*ornery.*

When I got to be a senior counselor, I used

to make the newbies put lime in the latrines. I would put lotion in girls' shampoo bottles and baby oil in their conditioner. I'd eat all the hidden contraband they tried to sneak in—Chips Ahoy!, Oreos, Pop-Tarts, Tab—and tell them someone must have stolen it when they were ready to leave.

Did I become a Birch? Or was I just having good, clean camp fun? What does power do to us?

I was most ornery during Color War.

I look at V and Liz chatting in the light. Liz—ever the fashion designer and real estate agent—has a pad of paper at the ready in front of her, pen in hand, ready to jot down what Color War games we will play, what the rules will be, and how the points will be tallied.

Liz is no match for me. Nor is V. Not after all these years in politics. I know how to take an opponent down.

During Color War, Birchwood had two teams: Green and White.

And every summer, no matter how it was arranged, Color War was, quite literally, a war.

When The Clover Girls first arrived at camp, The Nighs and the counselors divided cabins into Green and White. We were Green from the get-go. However, this caused each team and each cabin to sabotage one another.

Warring teams put everything from whipped

cream to spiders in girls' bunks, causing them to lose sleep. Food was stolen, so Green might go a day without much sustenance. Lines were drawn, quite literally, in the sand: Cross it, and you will pay dearly.

Eventually, the Nighs divided teams randomly. When a camper arrived at camp, she picked a card: Green or White.

That only made the war worse, however.

Friends were pitted against one another, making girls sworn enemies and throwing bunkhouses into utter turmoil. Green girls refused to sleep in cabins with their competitors, and some counselors even tried to keep opposing team members awake all night so they would be sleep-deprived for competitions. At Taneycomo, the boys often got into fistfights.

Color War was the defining moment of camp. Electricity built in the air from week to week. It seemed as if the entire summer—no, the entire year—built up to those few days of competition. During Color War, tears were shed. Knees—and egos—were bruised. Hearts were broken. Legends were made.

And girls looked forward to it more than anything.

Especially me.

In the speech that kicked off Color War every year, the Nighs would tell us that life was often a contact sport, a competition, and that Color War was a microcosm of life. We needed to learn not only how to fight and win but also how to work together as a team as well as lose with grace and dignity.

Will we remember that now?

But after my father died, I felt lost, adrift, as if I had to prove my worth to him—and the world—every single day. So I became the ultra-competitor. I lived to win. At any cost. Especially during Color War.

How many times did my team win Color War?

I shut my eyes and search my memory banks.

Every year but one.

I look at V and shake my head.

Our last year at Birchwood. She outmaneuvered me during the rope burn, the final event of Color War. I will never forget it.

"Earth to Rach," Liz says, knocking me from my thoughts. "Do you need a chill pill?"

"Sorry," I say. "Hangover. Feel grossed out."

"Like, totally," V says, and we all laugh.

"Okay," Liz says, pen in the air. "Here is the list of traditional Color War games we played our last years here: hatchet hunt, dodgeball, tug-of-war, cracker whistle, sing night, and, of course, rope burn."

V and I nod.

"How do we play if there are just three of us?" V asks.

"And how do we score them?" I ask.

"So, I was thinking," Liz says, "that instead of a color, we're each a letter, just like you said when we first met at camp, Rach. Remember?"

"I do," I say.

"So," Liz continues, "it'll be E versus V versus R. Make sense?"

We nod.

Almost forever, I think.

"Maybe we focus on some of the games that make sense for the three of us to play, like dodgeball, tug of war, rope burn and cracker whistle? We've already done a talent night, and hatchet hunt requires too much effort."

We nod again.

"Some of the games, like tug of war and dodgeball, will require us to play each other round robin, like in a tennis tournament, to decide who will play each other in the final," Liz says. "For instance, me versus V in the first round. Winner moves on. Rach, then you'd play me . . ." Liz stops, waiting for her joke to register.

"Hey!" V says.

". . . with the round robin winners playing each other at the end," Liz continues. "And we'll score every game based on difficulty." She stops and turns the list toward us so we can peruse what she's written.

"Maybe," V starts, "one point for the easier competitions, like the cracker whistle, dodgeball and tug-of-war, and three points for the hardest one of all, rope burn. That way, if someone wins a couple—or all—of the earlier rounds, someone still has a chance at the end."

"What if it's a tie?" I ask just for effect, knowing it won't be.

"We'll figure that out," Liz says. "Agree on everything else?"

I nod, and she writes it all down on her pad of paper, as if it's the queen's edict.

Dodgeball = 1 Point
Tug-of-War = 1 Point
Cracker Whistle = 1 Point
Rope Burn = 3 Points

"So," I say, "since we're getting all of the rules down on paper, I want to get the biggest one of all clear: this is winner-take-all. Whoever wins Color War is considered the greatest Color War champion of all." I think of my dad and smile. "My dad used to do this at family reunions. When we'd play badminton, the winner would be crowned 'The Greatest Great Lakes Champion of All Time!'"

The girls laugh.

"May I suggest one more thing?" Liz says.

I look at V. We nod.

"That the idea of the Color War winner also gets the first and most serious consideration for how Camp Birchwood will be reinvented and relaunched."

Silly Liz, I think. *That means it will come down to me and V.*

"Agreed," I say quickly.

"Okay," V says.

"And may I suggest one final—and probably most important—thing?" V asks, her tone serious. "That no matter who wins Color War, we finish our time here at camp like Em wanted out of respect for her and our friendship? Let's promise not to resort to the behavior that drove us apart in the first place. Agreed?"

We look at one another. "Agreed."

"We're in this together," I say. "Even though someone wins, it's still The Clover Girls FOUR-ever!" I lift four fingers and then hold out my hand into the middle of the table.

Liz looks at V.

V looks at me.

We all look at each other.

And then V puts her hand on mine. Liz places hers on top. We raise and lift our hands once again as if we're going into war.

"Clover Girls FOUR-ever!" we say.

I look at them and smile.

As the old saying goes, *Nothing's fair in love and war.* And although I may love these girls like sisters, this is just like an election: war.

And I will win.

Because I always win.

And always will.

LIZ

My heart is pounding, and I feel exactly like I did as a girl during Color War: overwhelmed, klutzy, unathletic.

I was better behind the scenes, like Em: I preferred to make our team's shirts and pins. Em enjoyed cheering the other girls on from the sidelines. We both liked to strategize on paper.

Em and I were wonderful fans.

But we were reluctant competitors.

Every Color War, all of the campers were divided into two teams. But the Green and White team generals subdivided the girls on those teams as well.

Who was a great athlete? Who could run fastest, swim the farthest, throw the hardest? Who was the strongest? Who could gather the most wood, lift the heaviest limbs, cut the biggest branches? Who could get tackled, take a hit, get back up and fight on?

I was never a part of that group.

As a kid or an adult.

Standing here, ready to play dodgeball, I am instantly reminded that being a kid in the '80s was not as nostalgic as I too often make it. And being a semi-unathletic girl at a girls' summer camp was often downright mean.

And being a camper during Color War was, well, war.

I can't tell you how many times I cried, how many times I stormed off the field, how many times I told my counselors, parents and comrades I hated them, how many times I wanted to give up.

Kids are mean. Girls are downright awful. Especially to each other. Why? I'm still trying to come to grips with that.

We would often hear the tales of the Taneycomo boys who would fight over the stupidest of stuff: a prank; stealing a Twinkie; ribbing someone over his girlfriend; too hard of a hit playing football; or even two guys wearing Cubs and Cardinals T-shirts.

But boys let you know where you stood.

Girls? Oh, we play dirty.

Boys may hurt one another physically, but those bruises you can see. They're visible to the eye. And they heal quickly.

Girls hurt one another where it lasts the longest: inside. We bruise one another's fragile egos and self-confidence, and that *never* heals.

That is mirrored to us in society, and we repeat the cycle. There will always be a hierarchy. And even though I was part of the in-group here, I lived on the periphery.

And still do.

I look at Rach standing on the sand, stretching.

It's difficult for me to forgive how she often behaved during Color War. It's nearly impossible for me to forgive her for what she's done to women during her career in politics. But part of me admires her competitiveness and drive. She always forced herself into the hierarchy. She always set the rules. She always won.

I . . . I stop. *I too often took the easy way out, the path of least resistance, be it men, career, parenting, Color War.*

Why didn't I fight harder?

"Ready?" Rach yells.

I am not.

A hard red dodgeball hits me squarely in the belly.

Oooofff!

I lean over and groan.

Damn you, Billy.

We borrowed most of the Color War toys, tools and accessories from him and Taneycomo, and he promised me that today's dodgeballs were softer and more friendly than the cannonballs I remember being directed at my head and mid-section. They are not.

"1-0, Rach!" V yells.

"I wasn't ready," I say, standing back up.

"I said 'ready'!" Rach yells again.

Damn you, too, Rach, I think. *Color War Rachel is back.*

She is tossing a dodgeball in the air, catching

it, as if she's juggling. She is in a tank top and short-shorts, and her body is lithe and muscled. I forgot just how striking she really is until I see her in front of me out of her heavy makeup and spokeswoman garb. Rach is beautiful. V is beautiful. I look down at myself: I am average on a good day.

Perhaps that's why I wear what I do, I think. *To overwhelm my averageness.*

We have created our own dodgeball court by Birchwood Lake. I am standing against the metal wall of the storage shed. Rach is standing behind a line that has been drawn in the sand—*ah, the irony!*—a few yards in front of the water. She has five throws, and then I will get five throws.

"Ready?" Rach asks again, this time her voice dripping in sarcasm.

I nod, Rach pulls her arm back like a catapult in *Game of Thrones,* and she releases the dodge-ball.

I can see it clearly this time.

Traveling at warp speed.

Directly toward my head.

I dip my body and rush to the right, but Rach has thrown a curveball. It's as though the dodge-ball has a homing device on my noggin, and it strikes me directly on the temple.

I stumble toward the wall and lean against it. When I lift my head, I see stars.

"Are you okay?" V asks.

"Shake it off," Rach yells. "2-0."

I put my hands against the shed and shake my head, which feels as if it's filled with concrete. I stand and try to walk, stumbling a bit, and raise my hands.

"Good?" V asks.

I shake my head, unsure if I'm nodding or hemorrhaging.

"Ready?" Rach yells.

I stand lifeless. As she throws the ball, I simply fall to the ground. The ball whizzes over my head.

"Are you okay?" V says, rushing over.

"Strategy," I lie.

"Okay then," V says.

I try the same strategy, but Rach has already caught on. She whacks me two more times in the side. I miss her on all five attempts. Rach beats V in a close match, as I sit in a chair, happy to be a judge and cheerleader, and she takes a 1-0 lead in Color War. She races around the edge of the lake, whooping in victory.

V wins tug-of-war, despite Rach's physical strength and my—shall we say—slightly more voluptuous body. V has a determination, and once she dug into the sand, neither of us could move her even one inch.

And although Rach and V are now tied 1-1, I feel confident going into cracker whistle because not only do I love to whistle, I love food as well.

And I've made a living talking to clients over the phone while my mouth was full.

I'd forgotten how childishly simple and fun cracker whistle is: its only requirements are crackers and a mouth. Back in The Lodge, we set up stacks of saltines on napkins about 20 feet apart from each other on the newly cleaned floor. In camp, we played this as a team relay: one person would race forward, eat the cracker, whistle the song and return to tag the next in line. First team to finish won. Individually, we've decided to race against one another, but make the challenge a bit more challenging: at the first stop, we eat a cracker and recite the ABCs. At the second stop, we eat three saltines and whistle "On Top of Spaghetti." At the final stop, we must cram five crackers into our mouth and whistle the chorus to "Karma Chameleon" by Culture Club.

I asked Billy to serve as judge—to ensure that our renditions of the songs are passable with our mouths full—but he was busy, so he sent the clueless Bieber boy counselor I met a few days ago. We had to play "Karma Chameleon" for him a half dozen times so he understood what the '80s chorus sounded like. I'm still not certain he even knows what year it is.

"Um, yeah," he says, after we play it for him the seventh time on a cell. "I, like, don't get it. What's a Carmen Million?"

"Kar-ma Ku-me-lee-un," I over enunciate. "Do you know what Karma is?"

He shakes his head, his bangs covering his eyes.

And, obviously, his brain.

"Oh, wait," he says, and I brighten. "There's like a juice bar near where I live that's Karma something." He lifts his bangs and furrows his brow. "Like Karrot Karma or something weird."

"Okay, good," I say, trying like the dickens not to roll my eyes. "Do you know Boy George?"

"Who?"

He looks at me like I'm insane, and I realize I am trying yet again to explain to a young person who was famous from my generation.

"Are you ready?" I ask.

"Are you?" he asks.

We line up, and he yells, "Like, go!"

We sprint to the first cracker at the same time, shove it in our mouths and recite the ABCs. All of a sudden, the kid is totally into our insanity. He is standing directly in front of us, his head lowered, his hands cupped around his ears, listening intently. We all finish the alphabet at about the same time and head toward the second row. As Rachel and V shove three crackers into their mouths, I take just a second and fill my mouth with saliva to more easily dissolve the crackers. I put them in my mouth, make a sort of saltine chewing gum ball with my spit and begin to whistle "On Top of Old Smokey." I look over, and dry chunks of cracker are flying out of V's and Rach's mouths. They are going slowly, both beginning to laugh. I finish, the kid gives me the okay to move on, and I dash toward the final row.

I used to get half a can of Pringles in my mouth, I think. *This is nothing.*

I cram the crackers into my mouth and begin to whistle "Karma Chameleon." I see in my periphery Rach and V rush up to the final row, and I shut my eyes to block out their presence and all the pressure.

Karma karma karma karma karma cha-me-le-on, I whistle, crackers spewing from my mouth like a volcano.

I keep my eyes shut. This is my moment. I'm even sporting a hat like Boy George. I can feel his spirit cheering me on.

I finish and open my eyes, and the kid is waving his arms wildly, telling me I'm good, as if he wants me to win.

I glance to my right and left. Rach and V are still whistling. Well, sort of. Rach is choking on her crackers. It's probably the most she's eaten in weeks. V's cheeks are puffed, and she's out of breath.

I race to the finish line, a bench we've set up at the end of The Lodge.

"Winner, winner, chicken dinner!" I yell,

crackers still falling from my mouth. "We're all tied up, ladies!"

I hear a loud cheer. I turn, and Billy is clapping wildly, calling, "Way to go, Cracker Barrel!"

I jog over to meet him.

"Thisth isth a thurpristh," I attempt to say.

He laughs. "I knew you could do it," he says.

"What are you doing here?" I ask.

"I didn't want to freak you out with too much pressure. I couldn't stay away, though."

Out of the blue, Billy leans in and kisses me. It is the most romantic, unromantic moment of my life.

When he finally leans back, crackers are encased on his lips.

"You look like one of my grandma's casseroles," I say. "We have to try that again, okay?" I grab his hands. "But thank you. For that. For all of this."

Billy squeezes my hands. "You are such a good person, Liz. Do you know that?"

I shake my head.

"But life is a contact sport, Liz. Life is a competition. Remember that."

"You sound just like a camp counselor," I say. "Which is totally hot."

I lean in and kiss Billy full on the lips, nearly knocking him off his feet.

Behind me, I can hear V and Rach cheering.

"This is, like, so gross, Mr. Collins," the boy says. "On, like, every level."

Billy and I start to laugh. We look at the kid.

"And, like, why would anyone want to win a chicken dinner? That is so lame. I'd, like, want tacos and tickets to see Drake."

V and Rach bust a gut, and I shake my head, actually agreeing with him.

It's not a chicken dinner I want to win, I think. *I want to win Color War for once in my life.*

PART NINE

Rope Burn

SUMMER 1986

Every summer on the drive to camp, Rachel's mother would make her dad stop to collect birch wood. She could spot them, he used to joke, from miles away, like a hawk.

And she could.

She could see the white in the darkest of woods as easily as she could see lightning flash at night. Rachel's father would always joke about it, but he didn't mind doing it. He knew his wife thought the northern birch were more magical, even whiter, and finding the bark was like discovering buried treasure.

After Rachel's father died, she asked her mom the next summer to stop on the way to camp to gather birch.

"Oh, Rachel," she says. "What a beautiful way to honor his memory and our drives up here together."

The two collect a trunk full.

Just before her mother drives all the way into camp, Rachel tells her to stop about a mile or so from the parking lot. Thinking it is an emergency, her mother pulls over.

"Are you okay?" she asks.

Rachel reaches over and pops the trunk.

"What are you doing?"

"It's a surprise," Rachel says, jumping out of the car. "I want to make something for you, but I don't want the counselors to know. You know how they get when we try to sneak in contraband. Don't spoil it!"

Rachel's mother beams, hoping, believing that they are finally over their cold war since her husband's death.

She watches Rachel build a little canopy over the birch, and her heart soars.

"We've raised a good girl," she whispers to her husband.

When Rachel's mom returns to pick her up at the end of camp, Rachel is wearing the medal she won for being one of the generals to lead the Green team to victory in Color War.

"I was the one who brought us to victory!" she tells her mother. "It all came down to the birch. It's so easy to catch fire. Daddy taught me that."

"Where is my gift?" her mom finally asks. "The one you were going to make me from all that birch you hid?"

Rachel's face turns red. She hems and haws, forgetting the lie she told her mother before the start of camp.

"Rachel LeAnn," her mom finally says, using her full name, which she only does when she is angry or disappointed. "How could you?"

Rachel's mother refused to stop the next summer to collect birch, but when Rachel could finally drive to camp, she repeated her forest deception year after year and never lost rope burn again.

Until . . .

"I knew it!"

Rachel jumps and drops the armful of birch she is holding. Liz is standing a few feet away, watching her.

"You sneak!" Rachel yells.

"You're a good person, Rach," Liz says. "You don't need to win this way."

"Am I?" Rachel asks. "Am I a good person? I'm mean to my mother, and she still loves me. I'm mean to a lot of the new girls here. I'm mean to you. I'm not a good person, Liz. I'm not. The only way to get ahead in this world is to cheat, because life isn't fair, and it never will be. Being a good person didn't keep my dad from dying. Being a good person didn't make me almost kill Em. Being a good person means nothing. When are you going to learn that? Nice gets you nowhere. You're going to be a loser your whole life."

"Not true," Liz says, her voice shaking. "I will never believe that."

"What are you going to do? Narc me out?"

Liz turns and walks back to camp.

She never says a word about Rachel cheating, and the one Color War Rachel tries to be a good person and not utilize her secret stash, she loses to V.

SUMMER 2021

VERONICA

I am staring into the fire, waiting for my lunch—a hot dog on a stick—to cook.

In my early modeling days, I once starred in a Def Leppard video on MTV. Well, "starred" is a generous verb. I pretty much just strutted around a fire in high heels—*which makes a ton of sense when camping, right?*—and slid roasted marshmallows suggestively into band members' mouths before disappearing into a tent.

I'm actually humiliated to this day that I did it. My agent told me it would get me a lot of attention, and it did. I booked a ton of jobs because of it. Not because of any talent I displayed but simply because a lot of people saw it and liked how I looked.

I think back to what Rach said to me decades ago—the last time I spoke to her, actually—after I tried to talk to her about the ramifications of her newfound political career.

"Spare me, V! You're one to talk. A model who sold her body to hawk soda and potato chips to men. You set women back light-years. You're such a hypocrite."

She's right. And that's why I so desperately

want to win our final challenge, rope burn, so badly. I am still burning to be in control of my own destiny. I want the chance to shape young women, not have young women shaped by men— their bodies, minds, ideas, decisions, careers.

I look around the fire. The Clover Girls are quiet, lost in thought.

Friends are forever, I think, *but so are rivalries.*

For years, Rach and I were generals during Color War. If there's one thing that brought all the Birchwood girls together—and also pitted them against one another—it was rope burn.

I look at Liz and think of Em.

Like the Def Leppard video, I'm also embarrassed by how enraged Rach and I would get if Em or Liz wound up on our Green or White teams. They were incredible friends but terrible competitors. They were too nice, even when they needed to summon their most competitive nature. Most of the time, the two of them hunched over a notebook, writing down ideas and strategizing as if they were General MacArthur.

"I'm the general!" I screamed more than once at them, frustrated that they simply didn't follow my orders, compete without thinking, fight to the death for their team. And they always seemed okay losing.

"That's alright," they'd coo to our teammates. "We'll get 'em next time."

I hated to lose. At anything. I think that's why

I've been so frustrated in my life. I've had a successful career. I raised a wonderful family. I have nothing to compete for anymore.

That's not true.

My marriage.

Maybe we all need . . . I stop, stare into the fire and shake my head at my unintentional pun. *. . . a little fire in our bellies?*

I look at Rach.

She was the best general I ever competed against. It's no wonder she made it in Hollywood and then as a political consultant. She thrived in the two most cutthroat, competitive environments in the world. And she won.

Liz. Rach. V.

Here we are, all tied up, even after all these years.

I jump. "Burning Down the House" by Talking Heads suddenly plays on Liz's cell.

"How appropriate," I say.

"A little mood music," Liz says.

She lifts the pad of paper she's been writing on the last half hour and shakes it at us.

"I've set down the rules for rope burn."

"We know the rules." Rach rolls her eyes.

"Some of us don't play by them though, right?" Liz says.

I look at both of them, confused.

Liz glares at Rachel, and I've never seen—again, pardon the obvious pun—such fire in her eyes.

She wants to win this, I think. A small smile flickers on my face. *Game on, Liz.*

"None of us would be here if it hadn't been for Em's long-term planning," Liz says, her eyes flaring, her face red. "Have you two ever considered you may not have won Color War without our strategizing? Yeah, Em and I know you both thought we were total Dexters, but take a red! I mean, V, who organized our game plan and end-arounds that won Capture the Flag every year? Wasn't you. And, Rach, who pieced together all the clues so that we won hatchet hunt every year? Again, not you. Em and I may not have been the brawn but we were always the brains. And you never would have won without a head attached to that brawny body."

My eyes widen, and I look at Rach. Liz is furious. She's reverted to '80s speak.

Rachel shoots me a look.

"So, if I can continue without the eye rolls and indignation," Liz says, pushing forward, "I was thinking that after lunch we spend three hours gathering wood." Liz again glares at Rachel. "Then we all rendezvous back here at four o'clock. That gives us two hours to cut our logs and strip the branches, an hour to think about our stack and an hour to build it. By that time, it will be nightfall. Billy supplied us with three big ropes from his camp, and I've asked him and a few of his campers to help us hang them when it's time. But, before we do that, you know what we have to do?"

"Write up a detailed plan about how we place the rope into the lake to soak it thoroughly?" Rach asks.

I laugh.

"Bite me!" Liz says, standing so abruptly that the cell she's holding tumbles onto the ground, Talking Heads suddenly quieted. The pad of paper on which she's been writing falls into the fire, which bursts into flame.

"Both of you!" Liz continues. Her lips are trembling, and her cheeks are blotchy. She had the same reactions when she was a girl. I can tell she's near tears.

"You both always win!" Liz says, her voice rising. "Have you ever thought I want to win?" She stops. "Have you ever considered I *can* win?"

"You might . . ." Rach says.

"Might?" Liz says, her voice high. " 'Might win' means 'won't win.' 'Can't win.' Right?"

Rachel and I stare at each other.

"Your silence speaks volumes," she says. "Let's get this party started, then. Meet me at the lake in five."

Rach nods.

"Hot dog," I say.

Liz glares at me anew.

"I was being serious," I say, my heart racing

382

at all of her emotion. "My hot dog is done. Let me just scarf it down, and I'll meet you there. Okay?"

Liz waits a beat. "Okay."

Five minutes later, we are standing on the edge of the lake. Liz is in front of the ropes.

"Do you want to drown us, or hang us?" I ask.

Liz looks from me to Rach, as if she's seriously considering my question.

"One each?" she finally says.

I let go a relieved laugh. My world has been filled too long with too much unresolved anger and tension. It is not a healthy way to live.

"Political consultants are like roaches," Rach says. "You can't kill us."

We all laugh, our voices echoing across the lake.

"I thought you were done with all that?" I ask.

Rachel shoots Liz one of their twin glances, and the two talk in silence.

"Trying," she finally says.

Liz takes one end of the first long rope and hands the other to me. We kick off our shoes, stretch out the rope and walk into the lake.

"Get a sturdy rock," Liz says.

I pick a big, round, pale lake stone, covered in moss.

"How appropriate is this?" I ask, lifting it from the water. "Green and White."

I sink my end of the rope underwater, as Liz

does the same. I secure my end under the rock, and kick some more rocks and sand from the bottom of the lake over part of the rope just to ensure it stays put.

"Got it?" I yell.

"Yep!"

We head to the shore, and repeat the process with the other two ropes. When we finish, Liz looks at her cell.

"All of our wood must be gathered by four," she says. "Arrange it in three piles down here on the shore. Make sense?"

I nod as I put my tennis shoes back on.

"Thoughts?" Liz asks.

"I'm too scared to say anything," I say meekly.

Liz laughs.

"You should be," she says, before taking off running toward the woods.

Rach takes off sprinting in the other direction.

"May the best woman win!" I yell.

"I will!" I hear them both say.

For a moment, I stand alone on the shore. It's just me. In so many ways, it really just comes down to each of us, alone, trying to ignite a fire out of thin air, wanting to build a flame high enough that the whole world takes notice.

I turn back and look at the ropes under the water. My reflection ripples back at me.

I think of Em, here, alone, during some of her last moments on earth.

Maybe Liz is right.

Em's planning—her quiet spark—is the one we all remember. Her sweetness is her legacy, her goodness our gift.

Liz emerges from the woods, dragging a huge log, her T-shirt already soaked with sweat.

She drops the log, bending over to catch her breath. When she stands, she asks, "Are you okay?"

"I'm sorry," I say. "For years of crap." I stop. "For not appreciating you or Em enough. For influencing you to join my plot against Rachel. I'm still trying to get it right."

Liz tilts her head, walks over and hugs me so tightly, my breath hitches in my lungs.

"Thank you," she says. "Me, too." She looks at me. "Believe me, it's harder to be a nice person than a mean one. It's harder to be alone than with someone."

"You're not alone," I say.

"And you're not nice sometimes," Liz says.

I look at her and then laugh.

"Keep laughing!" she yells, letting go of me and running into the woods again. "I need the head start!"

Suddenly, she stops and turns.

"Hey," she calls. "Remember what we always did if the opposing team won rope burn?"

I look at her. "What do you mean?"

"The winning team didn't celebrate," she

says. "It cheered on the other team until its rope burned, too. It showed that we were still one. Friends."

I nod, and Liz takes off running toward the woods.

I hope I remember that this time, I think. *I hope we all do.*

And then I sprint in another direction, flying, my heart racing. The sunlight disappears as I head into the woods. I see a birch tree in the distance, shimmering white. I race up and touch it. It's dead. It's dry. It's perfect. I knock it over with three big shoves, and then tear it from the earth, as if I'm a warrior princess.

I drag it back to the beach and drop it.

I just don't want to be the loser at the end everyone is still cheering on, I think.

I turn and race toward the woods.

RACHEL

I am lost—in both life and the woods—and it is simultaneously exhilarating and frustrating.

While Liz and V have stayed close to the lake, I have gone out on my own—as I always have—in search of something more.

I have never been good simply being comfortable, in life, love or career. I have always enjoyed risk-taking. I have always gotten off on the adrenaline. I have always liked to push the boundaries. I have always enjoyed taking the path of *most* resistance.

I think it's because I've felt rudderless ever since my father died. Lost. Looking for a friend.

I think of Em, her arms around me in the lake.

I think of V and Liz helping me this week.

I think of them hurting me in the past.

Are we friends? Or are we destined to always be rivals?

Is there a path forward? Is this it?

I stop.

There is no longer a path. I can no longer hear Lake Michigan, or the shouts of Taneycomo campers. I am truly lost. But I am lost for a reason. I know I'll eventually get out of here. I can turn around and walk until I hear the roar of the lake, or keep going until I hear cars on the highway, or cross into a farmer's pasture. *But I need to find the perfect wood to burn. And it's here somewhere.*

I stop, turning, looking for a sign.

Before me, there is a clearing in the woods, and the sunlight shines in a perfect circle. In the middle stands a beech tree.

Biblically beautiful.

That's what my dad used to say when he witnessed something in nature—a magical sunset over the lake, or the sun breaking though clouds engulfing a mountain just enough to illuminate its peak—that was almost too breathtaking for explanation. That's what he would say if he were standing here right now with me.

Biblically beautiful, isn't it, Rach?

After my dad died, I used to believe in signs like this.

I used to look for them—and him—everywhere: cardinals in snowy white branches, hummingbirds—beaks buried in a mock orange bush—on a warm day, the squirrel I named "Harold" after my father that used to chatter at me from the oak that stood outside my bedroom window.

Even though your daddy is gone, he's still all around you, talking to you, my mom used to tell me. *Just pay attention, and you'll see him.*

But all of the searching and hoping and wishing and looking never brought my father back. No cardinal could tuck me into bed. No hummingbird could make pancakes for me on Saturday morning. No squirrel would be able to teach me to drive a car, give me away at my wedding, watch a Tigers game with me, or hold me so tightly that I felt safer than I ever would again my whole life.

And yet . . .

If there were anything that reminded me of my father it would be a tree. Sounds so silly to say, but my dad loved trees. He knew everything about them. And he taught me everything about them. My father ran our neighborhood and my school's Arbor Day campaign. He raised money and planted saplings all around our neighborhood.

I walk over, into the light, and place my hand on the beech tree. It is gray, strong and silent like my father.

Ironically, my father also taught me everything about firewood. He was the king of fire: our home had an original woodstove in it my father adored.

Wood-burning only! my dad used to say. *No gas! It's not real!*

We also had an old grill. Guess what he used to say?

Charcoal only! No gas! It's not real!

And in the corner of our backyard patio sat my dad's beloved smoker.

Wood chips! Never pellets!

He could sit by the fire, the grill or the smoker all day long, a Stroh's beer in hand, and wax philosophical about the best firewood, the best briquettes, or the wood chips that made his smoked ribs, turkey, chicken and brisket taste the best.

What was that poem about firewood he used to recite to me all the time?

I lean my head against the beech tree's wide trunk. It is cool and solid. I shut my eyes and try to remember. I can picture myself sitting in an old cane rocker next to my father in front of the fireplace, a quilt over my lap, a cup of hot chocolate in my hands.

Beechwood fires are bright and clear, if the logs are kept a year . . .

I can hear my father's voice, clear as the birds singing around me, and I smile.

Birch and fir logs burn too fast, blaze up bright and do not last . . .

I open my eyes, lift my head and then, for some reason, kiss the trunk of the beech.

"Thank you," I whisper. "For reminding me."

The tree does not respond. It simply listens to me as my father used to when I'd have a tantrum.

I trudge forward, away from the light and the beech, and head into the darkness.

The birch, I think. *I must find the birch. I must find the light.*

I pass tree after tree, bird after bird, and I cannot shake thoughts of my parents.

Do we intentionally turn our backs on how we were raised just because we don't want to be like our parents? Or does life drive the goodness from our hearts?

Was it simpler back then? Or have we all just made life too damn difficult?

I think of Liz, her children and her mother.

Liz is a good person. Even despite what she did to me, I know that. Her mother was a good woman. Why have Liz's kids strayed so much from those role models?

Does it pay to be nice?

I nearly trip over a branch.

Why did I stray so much from my role models?

I stop cold in my tracks. The semicircular stand of pines. The dry creek bed lined with massive ferns.

This all looks familiar, even after all these decades!

I race forward.

There is a huge thicket of brush, a tangle of overgrowth, burgeoning saplings, weeds, dead logs, moss.

I step through the overgrowth and begin to knock away the broken branches. It feels like I am somehow trying to unearth a chest of buried treasure at the bottom of the ocean. I pant, work, sweat, tossing debris left and right like a dog digging a hole.

And then I see it!

My long-forgotten stack of birch still remains somehow—miraculously dry!—surviving the snow, rain and the wind, as if it were waiting for me to return.

To test me.

I look at the stack and begin to estimate how much I can haul and how many trips it will take me in the time we have allotted.

I fill my arms and head toward the road about a quarter mile away that leads back to camp. I know I can make good time that way, and that no one will ever catch me.

I jump at the loud crack behind me.

"Liz?" I yell. "Are you following me again? Grow up, you narc."

There is a thundering crash.

I yelp and turn carefully, wondering if Liz—or a bear—is tracking me.

It is quiet. That's when I see a beech tree lying in the middle of the woods, not far from where I was just standing. I set the logs down and walk over. White spots cover the bark.

Beech bark disease. Poor thing.

As a consultant, and because of my father, I know that beech bark disease has greatly affected the majestic tree. Of the four dominant trees in Michigan's hardwood forest—along with maple, yellow birch and hemlock—beech is the biggest nut producer in the ecosystem, and its loss affects a wide variety of wildlife, from deer to black bear to birds. As the infected beech die and fall, they create a gap in the canopy, and other trees spring up to take advantage of the space and light to fill the forest floor.

I crouch and sit on the beech.

I have already snapped. If I walk away from everything I've created, will other opportunities spring up to take advantage of the space? Will light finally fill that darkness in me?

I touch the beech.

Weakened trees often fall without warning, even on days with little or no wind. It's known as "beech snap."

I again think of my dad. He's the one who taught me all of this.

No, he taught me everything.

So did my mother.

So did my friends.

I've just chosen to ignore it.

I look at the fallen tree. I look at my contraband.

Beech, birch?

Good, bad?

My entire adult life, I've jumped from fire to fire, trying to put them out. Now I just want to start one for myself.

What if I lose? How will I react?

V and Liz have good ideas, but I know that mine is the best. It has the most potential to earn money, to bring in high-profile donors and leaders, to garner loads of publicity, sustain this camp, but—most importantly—to change lives.

And I need this Color War victory the most for my faltering confidence. I need this win as a sign. Liz has a career, and V has a family. I will have nothing if I lose, and I cannot go back to the way things were.

But I cannot move forward if I don't stop acting like . . . I shake my head, chuckling at my childishly ironic joke. . . . *such a beech.*

I suddenly think of the mean girls clique from camp.

Or would it be Birch?

Another beech snaps, and I jump.

Just as quickly, my throat tightens, because I finally realize who and what it is.

It's the sign I've always sought but never found. Actually, two signs from two beech.

"Hi, Dad," I say. "Hi, Em."

I look around.

"Hi, me."

And then I stand, nodding my head with conviction at what I must do.

I leave the birch and head back toward camp.

I will do it on my own this time. I will do it my dad's way. Honorable. Fair and square. I will do it Em's way. I will do it the way Liz wanted me to do it. The way my mother wanted me to do it.

"May the best woman win," I say out loud, my walk turning into a jog and finally into a full-out sprint.

LIZ

Even though there is no fire yet, the air crackles with electricity.

Billy's boys have assembled three separate areas in front of the lake. Eight-foot-high poles hold up thick seven-foot lengths of rope that have been soaking in the lake. Water drips from the rope onto the sand below.

I scan the scene. The whole thing resembles something straight out of an '80s teenage rom-com. The boy I like has come to see me take on the popular girls. The entire school—in this case, Billy's campers—are here to cheer us on. They are holding wooden poles, some taller than the youngest boys, with handmade flags on the end that feature four-leaf clovers. I know what Billy—as the good camp director and man that he is—has tried to do: Green and White are one. There is no *I* in team. Emphasize that there won't be an individual winner tonight. We are—and will always be—friends. That transcends triumph.

And yet . . .

I look around. These campers may have very limited access to their cell phones while at camp, but they have obviously talked to their parents about tonight when they were allowed to if their buzzing and pointing is any indication. It seems as if the camp is pretty much equally divided into two teams: Rach and V. The boys seem taken by their beauty and fame. They understand, probably after a few online searches following conversations with their parents, that they are someone.

Me? There does not seem to be a lot of admiration for a caretaker and real estate agent from Holland, Michigan, who dresses in clothes they only see in old movies.

In sports, we often like to root for the underdog. We love it when David knocks off Goliath. But in life? We cheer for the winners. We love the famous. We envy the rich. We yearn to be the beautiful.

Beautiful.

I shake my head and study the beauty of our surroundings—dusk begins to fall, the sky turns bright pink, fireflies blink over the lake, birds dart over the water, log cabins sit in the distance behind us—and that makes it feel even more as if we're standing in front of a faux Hollywood backdrop, and the director is about to yell, "Action!"

I turn, half expecting to see John Hughes behind a camera. Instead, Billy catches my eye and gives me a secret wink.

I smile.

He is imbued with Em's goodness. Who would

go to all of this trouble—in the middle of his busiest time of year—for someone he hasn't talked to in decades? He told me he wanted to do this to show his campers the meaning of camp and the power of the lifelong friendships they make here.

But are we the best examples of that?

Billy also left me a note. He nudged it in the screen door of the bunkhouse, as if he were a schoolboy leaving me a crush note in my locker.

He wrote:

> What you've done for your mom, for your family, for your friends is a sign of what a good person you are. But in all of that goodness is a fighter, too. From all you've told me, I can see it in your every action: How you started your own business after your divorce. How you fight for your mom. How you fight to do the right thing. You can win this Color War. But don't do it for anyone other than you. Fight for yourself for once, Liz. Let the world see your talent, your spirit, your light and your drive.

I look over at Billy.

"You got this," he mouths, and gives me the thumbs-up.

I want this, I think. *But do I got this?*

If Vegas were placing odds on this race, I'd be the three-hundred-to-one horse. My track record is not great. How many times did I win rope burn? How many times did I win Color War?

Stop it, Liz, I say to myself. *What if I win? Is that what it comes down to, if I'm being honest?*

That I'm actually scared to win?

It's easier to lose. It's safer not to be the center of attention, on the front lines, because then all eyes are on you. I can hate on Rach and V all I want, but they took the risk and were rewarded. No one would have been there to save their butts if they'd failed. But, still, they jumped without a parachute.

I eye my stack of wood. I can do this. In fact, I'm really good at this. What everyone here doesn't realize is that for the past couple of decades, I've been a sort of rope burn apprentice. I've staged fires on beaches for clients to show off a house, to make the setting romantic and memorable, to give them a feel of summer in Michigan so real and so rich that they will jump at the storybook moment, no matter the price tag. I've gathered sticks and debris from the beach and started bonfires from wet wood countless times. And that extra effort has helped sell countless homes.

"Are you ready?" Billy yells, his voice startling me.

I look back. *Where the hell did he get a mega-phone?*

He sees my reaction and laughs.

"Coaches and counselors always have mega-phones," he says.

The Clover Girls look at each other, our faces intent.

"Three, two, one . . ." An air horn blasts.

Where the hell did he get an air horn?

Rach and V lunge forward, and I quickly follow.

We all begin to dig in the sand, directly under the ropes, like happy dogs on the beach. As soon as we have our pits, V and Rach race to their piles and begin to stack sticks and small pieces of wood.

I begin to empty my pockets. I have accumulated tinder, which is the smallest and easiest material to use to get a fire started. I dig out handfuls of wood shavings I made with an old knife I found in The Lodge, along with strips of cardboard and wads of paper. I make a small mound.

Rach looks over at me, wide-eyed. I smile and wink.

Her eyes blaze, and she moves at warp speed.

I grab my kindling, stacking twigs and small branches in a canopy over my tinder. I crisscross my larger pieces of firewood over that, almost as if I'm building a cabin out of Lincoln Logs. I begin to position my giant pieces of wood, which

I've stripped, vertically. Some of my logs are a couple of feet high, and I've notched them out at the top. I dig one into the sand so it's standing upright, and then I do the same on the opposite side of my fire pit. Slowly, I edge one big branch down until it's secured into the notch of the other. I repeat the same process on the other side, until I've formed what looks like the skeleton of a teepee.

I take a deep breath and finally look around. Rach and V already have small fires started, and they are blowing like crazy. V's fire is barely lit. It flickers and dies, and she blows and blows.

I grab the matches from my pocket. We are given only three. If they go out, or we don't get our fire started, we're doomed. I take a match, position it against a smooth stone I collected from the lake earlier, and strike it. The match explodes, and I hold it to my tinder. The wood chips spark, and then, there is a tiny blaze. I blow, easily at first, and then more forcefully, until I see stars. I grab another match and light another small pile of tinder.

"Go, Rach!" boys scream.

"V for Victory!" another group yells.

I look around. A group of young boys, chubby and red-faced, are cheering for me.

"Don't give up!" they say, as if they are telling themselves that because they need to hear it as much as I do.

I nod at them, and return to blowing on the fire.

I look over at Billy. He holds up three fingers, indicating we've been going three minutes. Rope burn seldom lasts more than eight minutes, so I know time is against me.

My fire is not as big as Rach's, which is a healthy blaze now, but I have better construction, and a bigger foundation of flames. I blow and blow, and my kindling catches. I throw more wood chips onto my fire, and my big branches begin to catch fire. Flames are leaping up the firewood, which suddenly burst into flame. I glance at Rach and V's fires. Only mine is beginning to lick the wet rope. I blow and blow and toss more kindling into the blaze. My face is red-hot, and the world around me looks as if it's melting. Everyone is screaming and jumping up and down, waving their flags. I keep adding more wood, feeding the fire, feeding my chances.

I look up. My rope and Rach's rope are now fully engulfed in flames. Rach is racing around her fire in a circle, manically, like a witch casting a spell, but I just stand still now, watching the world burn. I stare at my rope, then Rach's, then mine. And then I remember. I race over to the edge of my pile, grab a pile of dry leaves I gathered from underneath the bunkhouses, and toss them into my fire. I keep going back and forth and back and forth. I stop when I hear a loud sizzle. I look instinctively at Rach's rope, but I turn my eyes at the last moment. My rope splits, the poles easing, and the crowd erupts.

I won?

"I won!" I yell. "I won! I won! I won!"

I race over to the group of boys cheering me on and high-five them. When I turn, Rach and V are staring at me, mouths open, in shock.

I walk over to their fires and begin to cheer, like we were taught to do here at camp. I cheer until everyone's rope is burned. I chant and yell, but Rach's and V's heads are down. They aren't even watching. When their ropes finally collapse, they hug me half-heartedly, whispering, "Congrats, Liz. Really."

Billy rushes over and throws his arms around me. "I knew you could do it!"

Without warning, he blows the air horn and lifts the megaphone. "Winner of the 2021 Camp Birchwood Color War is Liz!"

I lift my arms, and when I turn, looking for V and Rach, I see their silhouettes walking back toward the camp. My heart shatters suddenly, like a vase thrown onto the floor, but then I shudder with a rage that burns as brightly as the fires still flaming behind me.

I have come out on top for the first time. And, now when it's my turn to celebrate, they turn away.

Despite all our talk, they have not changed one bit.

"I have some champagne," Billy says. "I kinda knew you'd win."

"Really?"

"I meant what I wrote. You're a fighter, Liz. You just needed to fight."

I stare at him and then lean in and kiss him. Boys razz us in the background.

"Let me get the boys back to their bunks, and I can meet you back here in a half hour, okay?"

I nod.

When everyone clears, it is just me, the lake, and three dying fires. I wait, believing in my heart Rach and V will return, apologize, celebrate with me. They don't.

"I won, Em," I say to my fire. "I won."

I take a seat on the beach and watch the fires slowly die. Even after all we've been through this week, this scene truly represents our friendship: quick-burning, intense, but always destined to flame out because we cannot put away our pasts. The glue that held us together is gone. There's nothing left to feed this fire any longer except memories.

"Hi!"

I jump.

Billy returns carrying not one but two bottles of champagne. He stands over my winning fire and pops a cork into it.

"Congrats!" he cheers. He fills a plastic mug

and hands it to me. He fills one for himself and takes a seat.

"How do you feel?" he asks.

"Sad," I say. "They didn't even stay to celebrate."

"They'll get over it," Billy says.

"Will they?" I ask. "Will I?"

I look at him. "No, they won't. I know them. It's over." I will myself not to cry.

Billy's face is ruddy in the firelight. "I'm so sorry, Liz."

"Friendships are such fragile things, aren't they?" I say. "We expect so much from our friends, and when they don't deliver, we're incredibly disappointed."

"We forget our friends are human," Billy says.

"They shouldn't be mean, though," I say. "What's the point in a friend if they can't be there for you when you need them most?"

"What's the point in being a friend if you can't love someone even at their worst?" Billy asks.

"Stop it," I say. "I can't right now."

I drink my champagne, much too quickly, and then pour another glass.

The fire slowly dies, just like Em's dreams for our reunion, my dreams for this camp, my friendships with Rach and V.

Everything.

I chug my champagne, and then have yet

404

another, the bubbles going straight to my head.

"I feel like one of the fireflies floating over the shoreline," I say, trying to change the dark mood. "Lit."

Billy laughs.

"Kiss me," I say.

Make at least one of my dreams come true before this all comes to an end and I have to return to the real world, I don't say.

"Hello? Hello?"

I open my eyes. It is morning.

Or I'm dead.

No, my head hurts too much to be dead, so I know I'm just insanely hungover. I sit up. There is a note beside me in bed.

What a night! Billy

Oh, my God, Liz! What did you do? Did Billy see me naked? A man hasn't seen me naked in a decade! The only person that's seen me naked recently is my trash man. By accident one morning. And, by the look on his face, he wanted to put me into the recycling bin.

I peek under the blanket.

Thank God!

I still have a bra and underwear on. But that doesn't clarify things.

Did we . . .

The night slowly comes back to me. The fight. The champagne. The kiss.

I rub my eyes, the light blinding me. I try to sit up but can't. The logs of the cabin spin around me. I hold my head as if that's going to stop the motion. That's when I realize the bunkhouse is quiet. I cock my head and listen. Nothing.

Where did they go?

Did they leave?

I want to sit up, but I have no motor skills at the moment.

"Hello?"

I hear a man's voice outside the bunk.

"Billy, what did we do?" I yell. "Get in here. And bring me some clothes. If I just had sex for the first time in ages and I can't remember it, I'm going to be furious."

"I'm not Billy," a voice at the door says.

I yelp and pull the blanket up to my shoulders.

"Who are you?"

"I'm Raymond Wilcox, Emily's attorney. It's been a week since you came to Birchwood."

It's been a week?

"I said I'd be arriving at an unannounced time, remember?" he asks.

"Your timing is impeccable," I say.

"Okay then," he says. "I'll wait outside until you're ready."

I throw on a hoodie and some shorts, down

some aspirin and chug a bottle of water, and head outside.

"I'm Liz," I say. "Elizabeth Anderson."

He extends his hand, albeit a bit warily. "It's nice to finally meet you in person," he says. "Emily said such wonderful things about you."

His last sentence is drunk with irony.

I think of last night, the world spinning.

"Can I ask you something? How many cars were in the parking lot when you arrived?"

"Three," he says.

I'm hungover and still hurt and angry, but his answer makes me want to cry.

"What's going on?"

Rach and V appear, and the sight of them in the flesh makes me incredibly and simultaneously happy and sad.

I introduce Mr. Wilcox.

"As you are aware, Emily's only conditions for you to retain this camp were very simple: spend a week together and reconnect. I take it the three of you have been here all week?"

We nod.

"And the three of you had a chance to reconnect?"

Rachel and V nod. I do not, but Mr. Wilcox doesn't notice.

"What an amazing testament to friendship," he says. "In all my years, I've never seen anything quite like it."

I look at Rach and V. They are smiling.

"Well, I will be in touch with specifics about turning over the estate to the three of you. I would suggest you contact your own attorneys, and work together as a group on how you would like to handle this now and moving forward. Perhaps you can start an LLC. What was that nickname Emily used for you?"

"The Clover Girls," V says.

"Clover Girls, LLC," Mr. Wilcox says. "Has a nice ring, doesn't it? Very northern Michigan. Very summer camp."

They nod.

"Oh," he says, eyes widening. "There is one last thing before I go. Emily left a gift for you. She wanted me to pass it along in case all of this worked out according to plan." He opens his briefcase and hands me a small wrapped gift with an envelope attached. "I'll be in touch and on my way. It was nice meeting you ladies."

When he departs, I still my shaking hands as well as possible to open the envelope. Inside is a letter in Em's handwriting. I begin to read:

My Dear Clovers:
If you receive this letter, then I know you've stuck it out together thus far. Congratulations! (I hope . . . LOL)
   Over the years, I've tried to stay in touch with all of you no matter how much

time has evolved and life has changed. And there's a reason why. YOU were my family. Family is more than blood. It's about being there for one another. Knowing you will always be there for one another. I hope you've learned what that truly means this time around. We only get so many chances to get it right.

It's ironic that I know so much about all of your lives, especially since I've kept a lot hidden about mine.

After my brother, Todd, died, my parents became different people. Their love for life—and me—just seemed to dry up. I know they loved me, but they just couldn't show it anymore. Maybe they were afraid of being hurt, or losing someone again, but they became shells of their former selves. That's why they sent me to Camp Birchwood. So that perhaps I could find not only what I was missing in my life but also what they could not fully provide: warmth, love, laughter, friendship.

I picked up the upstairs phone to listen in on a call my parents were having with Mrs. Nigh before they agreed to send me to camp.

"She needs to get away from the house," my father said. "Todd's death is haunting all of us. She needs to be outside, away from her books. She needs to run and swim and hike . . ."

"We will give your daughter what she needs most," Mrs. Nigh said. "Friends. And hope."

And she did.

You weren't just my friends. You were my family. You filled the void in my heart that my brother left. You would hold me when I would wake up screaming from a nightmare. You told me I could be anything I wanted. And I did. I became a librarian.

I know that all of you must think that I was alone for much of my life. And I know you must think how awful it must have been for poor ol' Em to die alone. But I was never alone. I had my books. I had my memories. I had all of you in my heart.

Despite our ups and downs, you were my hot air balloon when I needed one the most: you lifted my spirits when they were down, you carried me out into a new world, and you breathed new life and hope into me. There is a great difference between being alone and being lonely. I was never lonely.

V, you became the person you were

destined to be because of this camp and all of us. You are one of the world's bright lights. It wasn't your beauty that made you so famous. It was the soul that shined from within, that lit up those incredible eyes. You invited me to the popular table, you instinctively held my hand when you knew I was down, and you respected who I was. You never expected me to change because you loved who I was already.

Rach, I didn't save your life. You saved mine. You probably think I sank further into my books after the accident, but it was actually a wake-up call. I realized I was content with my life and friends. I was happy to be who I was. Sometimes a wake-up call doesn't mean reinventing and forgetting who you were. It means reinforcing and remembering who you are, and you did that for me. Your confidence made me confident. I dated in college. Can you believe it? I just never met the right guy. And yes, I was always scared that someone I loved might die, and I didn't know if I could handle that again. But I did put myself out there, and you need to know that.

And my sweet Liz, you taught me how to put on makeup, wear cool clothes and be unique. Do you know that all the kids who came into the library called me Hat Lady, and when they did I would show them pictures of Debbie Gibson and tell them all about '80s music and fashion and life before cell phones and Instagram? And they loved it! You reached out to me when I needed it most. You sent me books you knew I'd love. You wrote me letters. Your mom became a surrogate to me.

Yes, we all hurt each other. Sometimes intentionally, sometimes not. For the longest time, I regretted spilling the secret of what you did to Rachel, but I knew that I—we—could never move forward if we kept such lies hidden forever. The truth eventually comes out. And it's only then that we can heal. Even if it takes decades to achieve. Even if it takes a dying friend to show you how to live.

But we also helped each other, stood by each other and stood up for each other, and the good far outweighed the bad. What we all tend to forget is that our friends are human. They mess up because life is messy. But in the end, true friends forgive.

Oh, my Clover Girls, it wasn't coincidence that we met each other and found that four-leaf clover the very first day at camp. Have you ever considered it was our destiny? This camp was our paradise? We were meant to be together? That we have become who we are not in spite of each other but because of each other?

Life, I've learned, is not happenstance. You realize that when you're dying. Life is beautiful and ugly, awful and amazing, happy and sad all rolled together. But more than anything, it is oh so fragile.

We all grow up and are too often divided into two camps just like we were during Color War: There are those of us who dreamily remember their childhood days with misty eyes and shiny memories, and those of us who only want to shut the door on the past and lock away the hurt.

Camp Birchwood was both camps. Don't you see? That's life. You can't know where you're going if you don't know from where you came, hurt and all.

Before you leave camp, look at one another and forgive. Say "I love you" to each other. You may never have another chance. I will say it again: life is fragile.

I didn't die alone. I was never alone. Just like you're not alone right now. You were always with me in my heart. And you always will be.

I will love you FOUR-ever.

Em

My voice is shaking, and tears are streaming down my face.

I hand the letter to V and unwrap Em's mystery gift.

It is a plaque in an old frame with crackly green paint and wavy glass. A saying is painted on old construction paper, the edges yellowed and curled, hand-drawn clovers entwining the border.

A Friend Is Someone Who Knows
You Are Not Perfect
But Treats You As If You Are

I start bawling. Rachel takes the plaque from me and shows it to V.

"She made that our first year here," I say.

"Liz—" V starts.

"We feel so bad about last night," Rachel continues.

"Do you?" I ask. "It's too late for that. I've tried to forgive you, I really have, but you both walked away from me. When I needed you most. Em never would have done that. You showed me what I mean to you . . . what I've always meant to you . . . that I am less than you, and I always will be." I point at the plaque. "I suggest you read that again. God, we had Em fooled. We are not the people she believed we were."

"Liz," V says again.

I hear my ringtone and rush into the bunkhouse to answer it.

"Liz, it's Tammy from Manor Court. It's your mom . . ."

I throw my clothes into my bag and hurry out of the cabin, the screen door banging behind me.

"Liz? Where are you going?" Rachel calls.

I turn and look at her, unable to speak, knowing we are no longer connected, and she cannot read my mind.

I race to my car, the girls following.

"Liz stop," V yells. "What are you doing?"

"I can't do this," I say. "It's all a lie."

I drive away.

The last thing I see is Rach and V standing in the middle of the dirt road, and then the sign for Camp Birchwood, the logs that make up the letters barely clinging.

"Goodbye," I say, not just to camp but to my entire childhood.

PART TEN

Campfire Ashes

SUMMER 1985

"Do you believe in God?"

Rach, V and Liz look at Em. Every feature of her sweet face is illuminated by the campfire, and it gives her an otherworldly glow, light where shadows should be, and vice versa.

"I do," Rachel says.

"Me, too," says V.

"Me, three," says Liz. "We're Catholic, so I don't have a choice."

V and Rachel laugh at Liz's joke, but Em only nods.

The Clover Girls' first year of summer camp is ending, and they are seated around the final campfire for the Campfire Ashes ceremony. Mr. and Mrs. Nigh stand, and all of the campers grow quiet.

"Do you understand the historical significance of the campfire?" Mr. Nigh asks.

The older girls nod, but the first-year campers shake their heads and shift on the ground in front of the fire.

"It has great significance in cultures throughout the world," he continues.

Mrs. Nigh continues. "The campfire is communal; it provides light and warmth. It can protect us at night. It can boil our water. It can cook our food. It can keep us safe. It can provide a signal that we are one, or that we need help." She stops. "At Birchwood, a campfire is part of our tradition and is even more meaningful."

"It is a never-ending flame and circle," says Mr. Nigh.

"It represents eternal friendship," Mrs. Nigh says. "Tonight, we gather around our final campfire to celebrate the time we've spent together and to say goodbye. We will watch the flames burst and reach for the sky as we did this summer, and then we will watch the fire die, and bid farewell to Birchwood for another year. Tomorrow morning, we will gather here one last time to stir these ashes. We will give some to each of you to keep. Next summer when we all gather again, the ashes from the old campfire will be added to the new one, so the tradition continues."

She pauses.

"We are one, from year to year, eternally connected. Even in the dark, we know there is light to come."

The girls are riveted, hearts pounding. The only sound is the crackling of the fire.

"Like this fire, camp does not end when you leave here tomorrow," Mrs. Nigh continues. "Neither do the friendships you made. You will carry the warmth of all inside you until we meet again. You will remember the importance of tradition, doing what is right and the value of friendship as you go back into the world. But always remember that we are here for you. This circle can never be broken. The light can never be dimmed. But it's up to each of you to make sure that continues. Forever."

After the ceremony, the girls roast marshmallows, sing and say goodbyes in front of the fire.

The next morning, the ashes are stirred and then scooped into baggies—dated on the front in Magic Marker—and given to each girl.

The Clover Girls return to their cabin and begin to pack their belongings. As they do, Em opens her baggie, dips her finger in the ashes and makes a cross on each of their foreheads.

"It's not Good Friday, silly," Liz says.

"I know," Em says, trying not to cry. "But I just need to believe in something right now . . . you, me, us . . . that I'll see you again . . . that everything'll be okay until we meet again . . ." She stops. ". . . that you really are my friends, that the circle can't be broken and the fire won't ever go out." She begins to sniffle. "I have to believe that there will be light again next summer, or I won't make it."

The girls close in on Em and hug her until she can't breathe.

And then they leave their cabin together.

"Goodbye," V says as her parents gather her things.

"Goodbye," Rach says. "I'll call."

"I'll write!" Em says.

Liz stares at all of them. "It's not goodbye," she says. "It's never goodbye." She scans the camp one last time. "We'll meet again when the clover blooms, and a campfire burns so big and so bright that we can find our way back home again." She stops. "Even in the dark."

"Clover Girls FOUR-ever!" they yell.

SUMMER 2021
VERONICA

I sit on the edge of my bed and look at the souvenirs I've laid all around me in a semicircle on the comforter.

A friendship pin. A T-shirt from The Smilin' Smelt. A lake stone. A vintage Camp Birchwood coffee mug. White birch bark. A perfect pine cone.

I pull the last one from my suitcase, and my heart aches.

The outfit Liz made for me on Talent Night.

I lie back on my luxurious bed with a big sigh. For the first time in a week, my back and bed—unlike the bunk I slept in—don't creak. But something is off.

I am home. But I was home there, too.

The way I left both places was jarring. I went back to Birchwood with too much anger, too much baggage. I came home with . . .

I shift in bed, and all my souvenirs slide toward me, into the indention left in the mattress by my body. I finish my thought.

. . . too much baggage.

I think of Liz leaving camp, driving away, sobbing. Why did we hurt her? Why did we hurt each other again?

What did she do wrong besides win? Why can't I accept that? Is it my own insecurities that have made me question my marriage, my husband, my life, my friends?

I am exhausted, but the sickness I feel in the pit of my stomach is self-induced. I'm so ashamed of my behavior. I think of Rachel and what I did to her. I think of Em.

"Am I a good person, Em?" I say out loud, startling myself. "Am I?"

I secure the friendship pin to my top. I stare at my little rock, worn smooth from who knows how many years in the lake.

I've traveled around the world. I've returned from Paris with Chanel, I've come back with Gucci from Italy and Burberry from London, I've had cases of the best Rioja delivered from Spain. And yet these simple little trinkets from my days at camp are worth more than all of those combined.

Why?

They may not be worth much, but they are rich in memories and meaning.

I shut my eyes and see myself as a girl growing up in the 1980s. My imagination was my best friend. My world revolved around such little treasures like my bike, my Hula Hoop, my diary, board games—from Monopoly to Candy Land—tree swings. I would wake up early and skitter out of the house, roaming the neighborhood, coming home at dusk when I'd hear my mom yelling my name.

As a teenager, the mall became my playground. My heart would race every time I walked inside. I spent entire weeks at the mall, eating at Sbarro, shopping at Benetton, Lerner, Merry-Go-Round. I would meet classmates at Orange Julius, hoping older boys would talk to us. I would eventually work at Units.

Every summer at camp, we swam, canoed, played games, sang and talked.

None of us were glued to our cells. None of us were trying to influence strangers on social media. None of us could Photoshop our pictures, or connect with anyone other than who was standing directly before us.

Fun was free. Imagination was free.

I was free.

I sit up in bed and pull Liz's dress up to my shoulders.

I think of Talent Night and wearing this dress to the Coed Social, and I start to laugh.

"V?"

I jump. David is standing in the doorway.

"Why are you home?" I ask.

"Why are you?"

We look at each other and shake our heads. We know that asking *Why are you here?* is not a normal greeting for couples who haven't seen or spoken to each other for a week.

"When did you get home?" David finally asks.

"Not too long ago," I say. "Sort of a quick decision."

He cocks his head. "Lots of quick decisions lately." David hesitates. "Why didn't you call me?"

I shrug. "I didn't want to bother you. I know how busy you are."

He sighs. His face looks genuinely pained.

"What are we doing?" he asks. His voice is unsteady. "You're not happy. I'm not happy."

"I know," I say.

"I missed you," he says.

"Did you?"

"I did, V." He stops. "I love you."

"But do you like me?"

"Oh, V," he says, walking over to take a seat close—but not too close—to me on the bed. "What have I done to you? To us?"

"I just feel so . . . unwanted," I say. "I feel so . . . lost."

"V—" David starts.

"No, please, let me finish. I feel like I never get heard anymore. I feel like that one room in this house you've given me to decorate: I've just boxed my past away in there and forgotten who I was."

I touch the outfit Liz made for me and then glance at the friendship pin. "Do you want to know why I never talked about my friends? It's

426

because we hurt one other. In fact, we hurt each other so badly that we just gave up. We stopped talking and started believing in the worst in one another instead of the best." I look at my husband. "That's exactly the same path we're headed."

I look at my mementoes and continue. "But Em's death has, ironically, brought me back to life, David. I used to be a leader. I used to travel the world. I went from a kid with no confidence to someone whose face was instantly recognizable anywhere. And then I went back to being a sad little girl again. But I've finally learned that my true worth isn't tied to a dress size or what a man thinks of me. I had to learn to love myself all over again. And my friends helped me do that this last week."

David looks at me. "That's the woman I fell in love with, V. I hope you know that." He stops. "But I also realize my behavior has diminished you. I am too controlling much of the time because I feel like I'm about to lose control of everything. You, my career, my kids. It's all so tenuous, and the pressure nearly kills me some-times. My time is so limited, and I feel like I have to choose. And I've chosen my career to the detriment of you." He takes a deep breath and sighs. "You're a better parent than I am, V. Our kids adore you. You're a better person, too. Yes, you were—and still are—beautiful. And the first time I saw you I thought this gorgeous creature could never notice me, much less love me. But I didn't fall in love with you because you were a model. I fell in love with you because you were a model person. You weren't just beautiful. You glowed from the inside out."

I think of Em's last letter and nearly cry.

David studies a shaft of light on the bedroom wall and then looks at me for the longest time. "Our children are a reflection of you and not me, thank God. They are light-filled. And that gives me hope for the future . . . my future . . . our future."

I do not want to cry, but I do.

"This is going to take work," I say. "A lot of work. And mutual respect. And time."

"I know," he says. "But I want to try if you do. I can't imagine a life without you."

He reaches over and takes my hand.

The doorbell rings. David stands. "Probably something being delivered from work," he says. "I'm sorry."

"The world isn't going to change, David," I say. "We're the ones who are going to have to do that."

He nods, leaves and returns with a box.

"Not for me," he says. "It's for you."

I stand to look at it. "No return address," I say. "That's odd."

I open it. Inside is a homemade birch box. An

envelope is wrapped around it with string. The box is poorly constructed, almost as if a child had done it: glue in the seams, the sides at an awkward angle. I pull the string, which is way too big for the package, and open the envelope. A long, handwritten note is inside. It's from Rachel.

Greetings from Camp Birchwood!
I've never been the greatest of crafters, and this proves it! Em will always be the craftiest of The Clovers.

To say that I'm sad and disappointed in the two of us would be a massive understatement, V. Remember how we all felt when we learned Milli Vanilli lip-synced all their songs? Duped. Ripped off. Angry. That's how I feel right now, and I'm sure you have that same sick feeling in your own stomach, too. I've actually felt that way for a very long time about myself, and our time together made me realize I have to change. Now. Life is too fragile. Time is too short. And the only way to change the world is to start with yourself. Friends support one another. Just like the plaque Em made: A Friend Is Someone Who Knows You Are Not Perfect But Treats You As If You Are.

We didn't treat Liz like that. And we

haven't treated one another like that for a long time. That's why things fell apart.

What do you want out of life? I now know what I want.

I thought we all had rekindled the fire, but we blew it out once again, V. There's only one way to make it right. Open the box. Go on. Do it now.

I lift the lid off the box and recoil.

Don't worry. It's not Em (lol). Remember the Campfire Ash Ceremony?

Can you imagine how many ashes were passed along over the years? How many memories were created around those campfires? How many secrets were told? How many friendships started? Ours did. At our very first one. Our traditions, memories and friendship are forged in fire.

We ended a lot of traditions over the years. I've enclosed some of the ashes from rope burn just in case there's a chance we all can rise from them once again. I've decided that there is no Color War winner: We all are winners. All of our ideas are viable. Because we are all unique. All of our ideas are valuable. All of our ideas are needed more than ever today. But we can only do that together. Otherwise, it will never be what Em envisioned. A place where we can be a family, a place that—like these ashes—links one generation to the next.

Boom, didi, boom, boom . . .

Rach

I'm a wreck by the time I am done.

David puts his arms around me.

I show him the letter. I fill him in on what transpired. As I do, his eyes widen, and they again focus on the light moving on the wall.

"I have an idea," he says.

He grabs a pencil and pad of sketch paper he always has on hand, sits on the bed and begins to draw. David still puts pencil to paper to sketch ideas. He has long lamented that many younger architects no longer do this. It's a process that makes him feel creatively alive.

His pencil dashes quickly across the paper, and slowly the abstract lines become buildings, and a vision springs forth from the ash.

"Birchwood is a truly historic property," David says, his words spilling out, like they do when he's in what I term a "creative trance." "One of a kind. Those log cabins and that lodge. If we gave them some mid-mod elements . . . added lots of light . . . new tech . . . a juxtaposition of the new with the old . . ."

After a few minutes, he moves his hand, and my face breaks into a huge smile.

"Camp . . ." he starts.

"Clover . . ." I add. "Camp Clover. I can see it. I can really see it. Camp Clover. An old camp with new traditions."

"You've invested in my dream," David says. "I want to invest in yours."

"Really?"

"Can I tell you something I don't think I've ever told you?"

I nod.

"I went to a summer camp in upstate New York when I was a boy," David says.

"You didn't ever tell me that," I say. "I can't imagine you at camp."

"It was just one summer, because my family moved around so much, like we have, but I remember it vividly, mostly because I wasn't an athlete or extrovert. I drew. Kids thought that was weird. Anyway, this camp had a group activity called The Bucket Brigade. All of the campers were split into two teams, and we lined up in long rows that snaked from the lake to the center of camp. A bucket was filled with water, passed along the rows of boys to the very end of the line, and then dumped into a huge trash can. The empty bucket was passed back, and that continued until the trash can was full. When it overflowed, one team won." He stops and shuts his eyes for a moment. "I wasn't the strongest of boys. More book smart, like your Emily."

I smile and nod.

"You know, the first time that bucket was passed to me, it was so heavy, I dropped it. All the water poured out, soaked all the boys around me, and the empty bucket had to be returned to the lake. A lot of my teammates started mocking me. They asked the boys in front of and behind me to skip me the next time the bucket came. But the kid right in front of me said, 'No way. That's not how we do it. That's not a team. We win together. We lose together.' Next time that bucket came, he helped me hold it and pass it to the next guy. A few buckets later, I no longer needed his help. I learned I was just scared. All I needed was the confidence to do it. And we won. We won Bucket Brigade." He stops. "That actually changed my life. And the sad thing is, I don't even remember the kid's name who stood up for me, but I remember what he taught me. After all these years. That's why what you all have is so special. Because you all never forgot, and you should never forget. Because you all have the chance to change future generations."

David opens his arms, and we hold one another until the light slides away.

And then, out of nowhere, David begins to sing "She," the Charles Aznavour song he used to sing to me, and he does not stop until he has sung the whole song, until I am weeping happy tears, until I swear I can hear the Michigan peepers singing in round with my husband.

RACHEL

"You can't quit. I will sue your ass."

"Really? You? Sue me? Now, that's irony at its ironic best."

I stop and give my finest death stare to Ralph Ruddy.

"It's my business, and I choose to walk away," I say.

"What if I lose the election?"

"The world will be a better place," I quip.

"I'm not paying for your last month of service," he says. "Not paying," he repeats, before storming out.

I wave goodbye—to Ralph, my career, my income, my past—with my middle finger raised in the air.

Despite everything he's done, I've done, and everything he will likely do, Ralph will probably win. Politics too often is no longer about who wants to do what's right for our country, our state and our citizens. It's not about who's most qualified, or who truly wants to effect change that will better the world. It's about who's filled with the most hot air, who's able to bounce back the quickest from all the blows, who's able to inflict the most damage, who has the most cash in the bank.

I smile, thinking of the Romper Room punching clown I had as a kid. I would hit it, kick it, smack it, attack it, and it would always bounce right back up, a huge smile plastered on its face.

"So, that's it?"

One of my assistants, Gary, is standing in the doorway, his arms folded. He's all of twenty-one, an intern, poli sci major, student senate. Gary is fresh-faced and all promise. He's yet to be knocked around by either life or politics. Gary's beliefs are absolute, unwavering, and he knows everything about everything, and that's a nice little place to be when you're young, but I know that someday soon reality will greet him with a thunderous gut punch, and Gary will not bounce back. He doesn't have it in him.

"No, that's not it," I say. "This part of my life may be over but the next part isn't. Whatever that may be."

"How can you just quit? Walk away?"

I jerk upright. Old Rach would have gutted him. New Rach takes a breath.

"I've never quit a thing in my life," I say, teeth gritted.

But I know that's a lie. I quit on my friends. This old dog may have learned some new tricks, but she doesn't quite know how to utilize them yet.

"Sorry," Gary says, his voice hurt.

"No, I'm sorry," I say. "Emotional day."

He gives me a slight smile and nods.

"I'll be out in a minute," I say.

Gary walks away, and I turn in a circle to say goodbye to my office. I feel like a caged bird, and I can see that the door is open.

I'm ready to fly, Em, I think. *To where, I'm still not sure.*

I check my watch and exit, saying goodbye to my staff and my career. Most, I know, will be hired by Ralph and other candidates. I've done too good a job. I don't worry about their careers. I worry about their souls.

And then I walk out of the building, get in my car and head to the most important lunch meeting of my life. I park, take a huge breath and head inside the restaurant.

"Rachel!"

I stop cold in my tracks and then smile brightly. I wave crazily, like a first grader to her parents when she's on stage at a school concert, simply to cover my initial reaction to what I'm seeing.

My mother has had some work done.

A lot of work done.

She is sitting at the bar, sipping a glass of rosé, chatting with the bartender as if they're old friends. I walk over and hug her, tentatively.

"Hi, Mom! It's good to see you."

"You, too. How long has it been?"

My mother is not one to mince words. *Wonder where I got that from?*

"Too long," I answer, trying to calculate silently how many years it has been since we've actually seen each other in person. *Two years? Three years?*

"That disastrous Christmas," my mother says.

Ouch.

I don't respond, but she continues. "You remember that one where we discussed the election, and things got heated and your uncle threw a turkey leg at you. That one?"

Ouch again.

"Would you care for a drink?" the bartender asks.

"I ordered you one, but I drank it," my mom says with a laugh, winking at the bartender. Or she tries to wink. Her eyes are pulled back very tightly, almost like a trout.

"Aren't we getting a table?" I ask. "Having lunch?"

"Let's start with a drink, shall we?"

"I'll have a glass of very dry rosé," I say.

"Attagirl," my mom says.

When my drink is set before me, I lift my glass and say, "To new beginnings!"

"Indeed," she says.

"You've changed," I say to her, my voice and bravado wavering.

"No, honey. You did." She takes a sip of her wine and leans toward me. "So I had a little face work. I don't want to look like your grandma did

438

at my age. Women have choices these days." She gives me a wary look. "At least for a little while longer."

Ouch times three.

"It's me who doesn't recognize you any-more." She takes another sip of wine. "My own daughter. I don't even know her." I flinch. "I'm sorry to sound so mean, but I'm nervous, Rachel. Really nervous. I was so glad to receive your call from camp. I was so happy to hear your voice and listen to how you've changed, but I can't tell if it's real. Can you understand that? I mean . . ." She looks around the restaurant, and, for the first time, I realize people are staring, pointing, taking pictures. ". . . you're not exactly Dolly Parton."

"What?"

"Universally loved. You're more like . . ." My mom attempts to scrunch her face, thinking, but it doesn't move much. ". . . well . . . cilantro. Some people have a keen taste for you, and others think you're downright nasty."

"Which camp are you in?"

"I prefer parsley," my mother says.

"Truce," I say. "For today. I'm just here to talk."

"Today truce then," my mother says. She stares for the longest time at the throng of diners who surround us.

"We're becoming such an isolated country," my

mom finally says. "But look around. We cannot operate—we cannot live—in isolation. We cannot beat our chests, scream and proclaim, 'We are strong!' That's just fear and cowardice wrapped in bravado. Isolation doesn't make you bigger, it makes you smaller." She turns and focuses her eyes on me. "This was not the life your father and I envisioned for you, all of this one-sided, partisan nonsense. We were middle-class. We sent you to a nice school and a wonderful summer camp even though we didn't have a lot of extra money to do so. We did that because we wanted to open the world up to you. We wanted you to be surrounded by diverse people and view-points. That's the beauty of education, travel and experience: you're changed as a result of others' lives, politics, faiths, backgrounds and points of view. You're better because of them because you see the world in a completely different way. You understand there are more things that unite us than divide us."

My mom stops and takes another sip of wine. "Steeling myself," she says with a small laugh before asking, "I really just have one question: Did you believe what you were saying? I always felt like I was watching an actress portray my daughter."

"You were."

"Then why, Rachel? Why?"

I pick up my glass and study the wine for

the longest time. "I think I've never felt good enough. I've never felt seen."

"You?" My mom's staccato laugh is shocking.

"I think I've seen myself as being in competition with women my whole life rather than being in sync with them." I stop. It's hard to look directly at my mom, but I do. "I felt adrift after dad died. I felt like I needed to prove myself to him, or to me, or to someone, I don't know. I just wanted to fill that void. I wanted to be needed. And then, after my acting career crashed, I was considered a joke, and I didn't want anyone—man or woman—to be in control of my destiny again."

"But what about your soul? Who was in control of that?"

I lower my head and sigh deeply.

"I'm sorry, honey. I don't mean to be so harsh, but—as a mother—I'm just trying to understand. You're not the girl I knew. You haven't been since your father died, and that just breaks my heart."

"It breaks mine, too, Mom," I say. "I fought with you for so long. I was awful. I know that. I just didn't know how to deal with my grief. And that consumed me. I ended up distancing myself from my best friends, from all the women who tried to shape me."

I take a big sip of rosé and then look her in the eye.

"I have a lot to share with you," I say.

My mom swivels her stool my way and crosses her legs. "Share away."

And so I do. I tell her more than I previously had about Em's trust, Birchwood, Liz and V, our plans to reopen the camp. I tell her about my specific vision, about how I want to teach young women to get involved in local politics, become politically active, ensure their voices and votes matter and nurture them to run for office. I tell her about Dad and the trees, losing Color War and rope burn. I tell her about how I hurt my friends and Liz leaving.

"I lost," I say. "Everything."

My mom reaches out and grabs my hand.

"No, honey. You won." She gives my hand a little shake. "Everything. You fought the right way. I'm so proud of you. You just have to fight a little bit harder for your friends now."

"I'm trying."

"Your dad would be so proud of you."

I get goose bumps.

"I just want you to be proud of me, Mom."

My mom smiles at me. "*You* just need to be proud of you, Rachel. And that's a really hard thing to do, isn't it? Loving yourself? Some people never get there." She shakes my leg and continues. "But you can't run forever. You can't live with regret. Take it from an old woman."

"You're not old, Mom," I say. She gives me a

funny look. "Well, you don't look old, Mom."

She laughs. "Those are quite the friends you have there. Look at the impact they've had on you and your life, even though you didn't realize it at the time. And isn't it amazing the impact those who are gone, like your father and Emily, have on our lives? She was such a sweet girl. You know, she sent me a book a few years ago."

I sit up on my stool. "What?"

"Don't get in a tizzy. She sent me a biography of Ruth Bader Ginsburg. Sort of a sign of solidarity, I'm sure." My mom looks at me. My eyes are wide. "I think she just wanted me to know she was thinking of me. Anyway, she highlighted a quote in the book that I've always remembered."

"What was it?"

"RBG said, 'The true symbol of the United States is not the bald eagle. It is the pendulum. And when the pendulum swings too far in one direction, it will go back.'"

I smile. A lone tear trails down my face. My mom takes her napkin and wipes it away gently.

"I quit my job today, Mom. Walked away from everything."

"You buried the lede." My mom laughs. She lifts her glass and motions for me to do the same. "Congratulations," she continues, clinking my glass.

"Thank you."

"So," my mom says, polishing off her wine, "which way is the pendulum going to swing?"

I dash from my Lyft, an umbrella over my head to protect myself from the rain.

I tiptoe in my heels along the sidewalk and slide through the revolving doors. I stop in the lobby, lower my umbrella and look around. I take a deep breath to steady myself. My heart is racing, and I feel a mix of adrenaline and dread.

I take the elevator to the studio for *Red, White & You* and check in at the front desk.

"Please have a seat," the woman says. "Someone will be with you in a moment."

TVs fill the waiting area, which is worn and dated. I once thought TV was incredibly sexy and glamorous until I lived in front of a camera as an actress and spokeswoman. Sets are cheap, dressing rooms are minuscule, green rooms are dirty and dated. Everything is fake. All that you see on your TV is a tiny, carefully edited window that makes you believe something.

Growing up, most kids hated Sunday nights because it meant school was the next day. But I loved Sunday nights, because it meant I got to watch all my favorite shows with my family. Usually, we'd head to my grandma and grandpa's house for Sunday dinner, and then settle in the den to watch TV: my grandpa and grandma loved Lawrence Welk, my dad adored *Mutual of*

Omaha's Wild Kingdom, and my favorite show was *The Wonderful World of Disney*. I felt so safe curled up on the couch next to my family, or slumped into a beanbag chair with a quilt draped over me. TV doesn't make anyone feel safe anymore.

"Are you alone?"

I'm so lost in my thoughts that I jump when I hear a woman's voice. I look up. It's Dana, the producer.

Dana scans the lobby and looks at me again.

"Are you alone?" she repeats.

Her question unnerves me for some reason.

I am, I think.

"Just me this time," I say.

"No makeup?" she asks. "No assistants." I shake my head. "Oh, well, follow me."

Dana ushers me into a green room. "You're on in twenty." She begins to scurry from the room.

"Dana," I begin.

"Rachel," she says. "I'm busy. I really don't have time."

"I just wanted—"

Dana exits without a word. I set my bag down, shed my jacket and turn to look at myself in the huge mirrors. Rows of bare bulbs encircle them, much like my mom's old makeup mirror on steroids. The bulbs are so bright, it's like a slap to the face. I lean in and stare at myself. I don't even recognize who I am, or who I was.

I just know who I want to be.

I grab makeup from my bag. Old Rach would have gone full clown; new Rach just doesn't want to look like a zombie. A little mascara, some lipstick, foundation to cover the bags under my eyes . . .

Today, I have no notes. I have no rehearsed lines. I have only myself.

I haven't felt this nervous in ages, I think. *I haven't felt this naked and vulnerable.*

Dana's question ricochets in my brain: *Are you alone?*

"We're ready for you."

I follow a production assistant with a mic in his mouth who keeps whispering, "We're walking, we're walking."

I take a seat in a too-big chair that makes me look like Lily Tomlin's child character, Edith Ann. They do this on purpose in order to make the host, Chip Collins, look powerful and in control. Old Rach would have demanded a new chair. New Rach thinks, *Fill the space with your own strength.*

A team of makeup artists is redoing Chip's foundation and touching up his hair, which wouldn't move in a typhoon. When they leave, he looks at his notes but refuses to acknowledge me.

"And we're back in three, two . . ." Dana points at Chip.

"Welcome back, America, to *Red, White &
You*! Our next guest will be very familiar to you.
Rachel Ives has been a political spokesperson
for many controversial candidates over the years
and has earned a reputation for her, let's just say,
outspoken demeanor. She recently shocked DC
by quitting politics, and she's here to talk about
that decision."

I open my mouth to say, "Thank you for having
me," but Chip looks at me with a wicked smile
and says, "But before she does, we thought we'd
take a look at some of her greatest hits. And I
mean that quite literally."

A prepared montage begins to play, showing me
berating guests, challenging Chip, weaponizing
faith, belittling politicians. The blood drains from
my face, and I feel as if I might be sick. I look
over at Dana. She is watching me. A Grinch-like
smile grows on her face. Dana created this. She
did this as payback.

The montage ends with a clip of the viral
parody video that Eunice Unicorn made of me.

Chip turns to me for the first time. He is absolutely giddy. "Thank you for joining us today,
Rachel. What do you think of that video? Seeing
yourself over the years? Would you consider
those your greatest hits? Or your greatest hit
jobs?"

I am beginning to sweat under the lights and
the pressure. I blink and realize I look like a

deer in the headlights. They have me right where they want me. They want old Rach to come out fighting and screaming and spitting fire.

"I deserved that," I say, my voice calm. "I deserve anything and everything you throw at me."

Chip's face falls. I turn and look off camera. "Well done, Dana."

Her eyes grow wide, and she looks at Chip.

"Well," he starts. "I'm surprised by your reaction. Is this a new Rachel? Or am I watching a remake of the *Invasion of the Body Snatchers*?"

An assistant does a spit take off camera at Chip's remark. I stop, take a deep breath and look at Chip. "May I speak candidly?"

"You always have."

"I am embarrassed and ashamed of my behavior over the last few years. It's not who I am. It's not how my parents raised me. This has nothing to do with politics. Politics is a big business. It's a game. Most politicians, no matter the party, start out with the right intentions. They run for local office. They want to change their communities. They want to change the world in some way for the better. And then it goes off track. Things change as we grow older, bigger, more successful. We forget the people we used to be. We forget the people we used to know." I stop and look at the crew beyond the camera. "I don't know if your viewers know this, but I used to be friends with Dana, the brains behind *Red, White & You*. We grew up together on the sitcom I used to do. We wanted to change the world. Only one of us has." I nod at her. "The last time I was here, she asked me which side I was on."

"And?" Chip asks.

"That's the whole point, Chip. There shouldn't be 'sides.' There shouldn't be walls that divide us. Growing up, the dinner table was where my family talked, shared our lives, aired our differences, discussed our viewpoints. That table was made by my dad from an oak tree. It was solid and stable. But most of all, it was unifying. We all had a place at that table, and that's what we need to remind ourselves of. We all deserve a place at the table. There are more things that unite us than divide us. Simple things: family, friends, love, respect, a sunrise and sunset. We need to remember that. I forgot that for the longest time."

"But Rachel, you just can't undo all the things you've said in the past in a few minutes today."

"No, I can't. But I can try to make them right, over time. Starting now."

I begin to tell my story of going to summer camp and how I met my best friends. I talk about our lives, Em's death and her gift to us. I tell them about Campfire Ashes and how it united girls. "It wasn't the land Emily gave us, though, that matters. She gave us our collective hearts and souls back. Her final gift was that of purpose."

"How can we believe that you've actually changed?" Chip asks.

"Watch me."

I smile, and the show goes to commercial.

I take off my mic. Chip stands and actually shakes my hand. Dana throws her arms around me when I step down from the set.

"Sorry about the video," she says.

"Sorry about, well, the last decade or so."

Dana laughs. "I want in," she says. "Whatever your final plans are for your new camp. And, once you're ready, I will work to help women in power get involved, either financially or personally. I'd love to talk about media and politics, something like that. How's that sound?"

"Incredible," I say.

"If this all works out, maybe you and your friends can come back on right before the camp opens."

"Thank you," I say. "Truly."

"You're a different person, Rach. I can tell. What happened?"

I tilt my head and consider her question. "Girl power."

"Sounds very Spice Girls."

"Oh, that's way after my time. It's more Go-Go's."

She laughs. "Talk soon."

I grab my purse and take the elevator down to the lobby.

I pull on my coat, order a Lyft to pick me up and head out into the rain to meet the car. I open my umbrella but then remember the day The Clover Girls sneaked out from camp and then sneaked inside the local movie theatre to watch *Purple Rain*, thanks to the help of an usher who had a crush on V. We danced all night after that.

I lower my umbrella and turn in a circle, feeling like Mary Tyler Moore, Gene Kelly and Apollonia all rolled into one.

No, I think as my car pulls up to the sidewalk. *I just feel like me again.*

LIZ

"I missed you, Mom."

My mother's eyes remain shut, but her lids flutter when she hears my voice. I grab her hand, but it remains lifeless across the top of her body. I will myself not to cry.

It's amazing the clarity one gains when removed from a situation. I've returned from camp, just as I did as a girl, a different person. I am more mature, I am more confident, I have been hurt, and yet I have been healed.

I also know my mother's time is nearing its end.

Early evening sunshine streams through the window in her room. Mrs. Dickens is sound asleep, snoring, her head lolled to the side, but my mom is quiet. She is bathed in light. I tilt her head toward the window.

"Enjoy the sun," I whisper. "I know how much you love summer in Michigan."

I listen to her sleep for the longest time. Her breathing has changed. My heart shatters.

I know the drill.

In the years my mom has been here, many residents have come and gone, in this home and in this room. Aides, nurses and hospice workers have filtered into my mother's room, and I have become an expert on death.

"You will know," a hospice worker once told me. "The body is like a baseball stadium after the last out is made. Every living thing begins to stream out of it, it grows quiet, calm, cool, and then the lights begin to be shut off, one section at a time, starting with the feet."

I stand, walk to the end of the bed and check my mom's toes and feet. The skin is blotchy and mottled. I stand over my mom and look at her in the light. Her skin is cool, and the area around her mouth is blue.

I slip out of the room, head to the kitchen and return with a tray holding a plate of cookies, a glass of milk and a cup of coffee. I pull the chair up next to my mom, just like I used to do when I'd return home from camp. She would always have cookies baked, and she'd pour me a glass of milk and fill her coffee cup, take a seat at the Formica table and say, *Tell me all about your time at camp.*

"Let me tell you about my week at camp," I say to my mom now, putting the tray down on the nightstand, grabbing a chocolate chip cookie and taking a big bite.

I tell her everything, from the rekindling of my friendship with Rach and V, to our falling out over Color War and plans for the camp, to my burgeoning relationship with Billy.

"Remember Billy?" I say to my mom. "Remember how I always used to talk about him when I was a girl? It's the *same* Billy, Mom. The same Billy."

My entire life, my mother has been there for me, listening. For every momentous marker in my life, and for every tragedy—big and small— she has been my rock. When my hair didn't turn out right for prom—I mean, I quite literally fried it off with a crimping iron—she was there. When my marriage went south, she was there. When I tried to start a real estate career, she was there.

Who will be there for me now?

I feel my phone trill, and I clamber from the chair for my purse, pulling it free.

Text message from V.

> I feel awful about how things went down.
>
> Can we talk?
>
> I want to make it right. We need to make it right. I'm sick inside.

I am overwhelmed with emotion in this moment, and my anger rises to the surface, out of nowhere, like the waves in a sudden windstorm.

> With my mom. Not much time left. Not much to say to you anymore either.

V responds:

> I'm so, so sorry, Liz. Is that why you left?
> Anything I can do? Let me know. Sending
> BIG prayers and all my love.

I don't respond. I put my phone on the little nightstand, kick off my shoes and crawl into bed next to my mother. She is so tiny now in this bed, a baby bird in a nest, and there is more than enough room for me. I pull her into my arms.

"You have never left me, have you?" I stop. "You will never leave me, will you?"

She does not answer, and I know there are two answers to my last question: *no, she will never leave me, but she will be gone.* And I must carry on the final chapter of my life alone, without my greatest supporter, cheerleader and confidante. *How does one continue when the person that loves you the most, unconditionally, dies?* There is a hole in my soul so deep that I feel I can't breathe, much less wake up when she is gone and walk a single step alone without her.

"I will never leave you either," I whisper, kissing her cheek.

I fall asleep and dream that my mom is driving me to camp. We do all the things we used to do on the drive up from Holland: We get root beers and Coney dogs at Dog 'N Suds in Montague and then ice cream at House of Flavors in Ludington.

We stop at all the quirky little haunts along the way—the concrete statuary shops and Lake Michigan overlooks—and giggle, listen to music and talk about the important things in life, like boys. When I get to camp, Em, V and Rach are waiting for me. They rush up to me as I get out of the car, barely giving me enough time to slide my feet into my flip-flops, and yell, "You're back! You're back! We missed you!"

I look at Em. "Wait," I say. "What are you doing here?"

"Oh," she says, in her sweet Em voice. "I'm not here for you. I'm here for your mom. We all just thought it would be easier this way."

I look at her, and then Rach and V. I turn around. My mom is not at the trunk, pulling out all my stuff for the summer. I look inside the car. She is still sitting behind the wheel.

"Mom?"

"Oh, honey," she says. "I'm not getting out here. This isn't my stop."

I stand and look at Em. She strides past me and gets into the passenger seat. "I know where to go," she says confidently. "Don't worry. I'll be with your mom. And she'll be with your dad."

They begin to pull away, and I chase after the car, racing after it. Finally, I have to stop. Rocks are caught in my flip-flops, and the soles of my feet hurt.

"Where are you going?" I cry.

Em leans out the side window. "To summer camp," she says. "Forever."

I fall into the road, and V and Rach lift me up, hold me and take my hand.

"Where are we going?" I ask.

"To summer camp," they say. "Forever."

"Ms. Anderson? Ms. Anderson?"

I wake with a start. Someone is gently shaking my arm. I open my eyes, and Tammy is leaning over me.

"She's gone. Your mother is gone."

I sit up in bed. "What? What?"

"She passed away sometime this morning," she says. "With you beside her."

"Mom?" I turn and gently shake her, like Tammy did to me. "Mom?"

She is lying next to me, peacefully.

"I think she waited for you," Tammy says. "She waited for you to come home. She waited for you to be here with her." She hesitates and reaches out to touch my shoulder. "They do that, you know. Wait until it's just them and the ones they love the most to be in the room with them. They know."

Tammy hugs me. When she lets go, I heave and cry, burying my head in my mother's hair. I kiss her cheek and inhale her scent, as if I'll need to remember it forever.

"We'll give you a few minutes," Tammy says,

"and then we'll need to make arrangements."

She leaves, and I lie back down against my mother for the last time on earth. I pull her next to me and hold her, whispering, "I love you, Mom. Thank you for everything."

I do not let her go until a throng of people appears in the doorway. I stand and watch them take my mother. When I turn, Mrs. Dickens is awake, waving goodbye to my mother.

An administrator talks to me about what I need to do next, but all I hear is the voice of Charlie Brown's teacher. When she leaves, there is silence, a deafening silence, that grows so loud in my head, my ears ring. I stare at my mother's empty bed. I stare at all the photos I have placed around her room, to make it seem like home.

Home.

My mind circles back to camp. I think of Rach and V, our laughter and tears around the campfire.

Ashes to ashes, dust to dust . . .

I see my cell. I walk over, grab it and text my kids.

> I'm so sorry to tell you, but Grandma died this morning. I was with her. I'm devastated and need you. I haven't even been home yet. You should have been here. I told you she didn't have much longer. I will have to make a lot of

arrangements very quickly and will need lots of help. I will be here for the next few hours. Come ASAP.

I hit Send and stand, unable to move, as if my feet are set in concrete.

I look at my cell. A row of dots undulates.

Oh, Mom. I'm so sorry.

More dots.

First week of sports camp. I have to get Teddy to practice by eight. Then a play date for Sam. Then grocery. Hank is swamped at work right now. Can't say this was unexpected. And can't stop by this morning with Sam. Too much for him. Want to come for dinner tonight? Then we can talk?

I do not respond. I finally realize what I've known for a while: my family is dead. I sound like a monster in the wake of my mother's death. Yes, my children and grandchildren are healthy and happy, but they are gone. I have been alone for a long time now. Too long.

I stand there in the middle of my mother's room, twisting my phone in my hands. I don't know what to do with all of my grief and rage and loneliness, so I walk over to my mom's closet and begin to fold her clothes into neat little piles. I have zero clue what I will do with these, but I know I must busy myself. I begin to fold her belongings. Her name is written in my handwriting—which is really my mom's handwriting as we have such similar, signature writing styles—in the back of her gowns, sweats and pajamas. I suddenly think of camp again, of the days when Birchwood would send campers what they called "early bird shirts." Birchwood drummed up anticipation for the upcoming summer season by sending veteran campers limited-edition T-shirts, often as early as Valentine's day, to get their enrollment filled as quickly as possible. As a designer, I loved the T-shirts because they usually featured campers' names in a clever way. One year, I received a T-shirt that read:

You Can't Spell BIRCHWOOD without LIZ!

My name, Liz, was cleverly spelled out vertically on the T-shirt, the "I" in BIRCHWOOD comprising the middle letter of it.

I kept all those shirts. In fact, I still have them, and I know I will keep my mom's shirts as well. I have no idea what I will ever do with them . . .

Yes, I do, I think. *I know exactly what I will do with them. I will use them as a teaching tool for future generations. Even if my own family doesn't care, others will.*

My eyes wander back to my mother's empty bed, and emotion overwhelms me. I place her shirts on top of the dresser and race out of the room, out of the home, off the porch and to the edge of the little pond nestled along the far side of the property. When my mom was in decent health, before her memory went completely, we would come here and watch the deer drink every morning and evening.

At Birchwood, Rach told me how different trees reminded her of her father. V said birds reminded her of lost loved ones. For me, deer will always remind me of my mom: beautiful, quiet, protective of their children . . .

In love with the beauty of Michigan.

I hear a rustling, and a deer jumps into the clearing, looks around, and then high-steps toward the pond. A second deer, a beautiful whitetail fawn, spotted and soft, eyes as big as its body, jumps into the clearing. It seems spooked, but its mother looks back at it reassuringly, and it moves toward the pond and begins to drink.

"Hi, Mom," I whisper. "I see you. You will never leave me, will you?"

Tears fill my eyes, and I watch the world, somehow, continue, without my most important person in it.

I feel the ground shake behind me, and I hear

a car engine. The deer look up. I turn. A black car pulls into the parking lot. At first, I think it is someone from the county or the funeral home, but I see a familiar light and ride share logo in the window.

One door opens in the back, and then another. Two figures emerge, and I emit a yelp. The deer scamper into the woods.

Rach and V are standing in the parking lot. I wave. They drop their bags and come running toward me. They take me into their arms, a collective hug, and I sob until there are no more tears.

"What are you doing here?" I finally manage to ask.

"Your mom," V says.

"We had to come," Rach says.

"But camp. You left rope burn. I thought . . ." I babble.

"You thought we were best friends," V says. "And you were right. We all just needed to be reminded of that."

"Are you okay?" Rach asks.

"No," I say.

They put their arms around me, and we stand, staring at the pond. The two deer step back out and begin to drink once again.

"What do I do now?" I ask. "How do I go on? Where do I go?"

"Summer camp," V says, her voice soft. "Forever."

EPILOGUE

Letters Home

SUMMER 2022

Dear Mom and Dad:

It's SO weird to write you a letter. I was joking to my friends that I felt like a cavewoman, and I should be chiseling symbols to you on a stone tablet. But, as you know, they don't let us have our phones here, and they want us away from our computers, so I had to go old-school!

You know how much I didn't want to come here. I just want to apologize for yelling and screaming at you (and even refusing to get out of the car when we got here). I hate to admit when you're right . . . but you were right. The first week at Camp Clover has probably been the best week of my life (except for when we went to Disney).

But it didn't start out that way at all. I was too scared to talk to anyone, and I barely slept my first night. When I did, I dreamed that you were driving away and never coming back to get me. I missed my room and how Bailey snuggles up against me every night and keeps me warm and safe. I woke up and wanted to cry. A counselor saw my face and knew I wasn't okay, but I told her I was. At breakfast, I pretty much ate alone, even though I sat at a big table with all the girls in my cabin. I was about to go back to that counselor and ask if I could call you to come home, but a girl saw me standing outside my first activity—Creativity Camp—and asked me if I was coming. I nodded. She sat next to me, and we talked about our dreams and what we wanted to be, and then we made candles for Wish Night.

That's when everything changed! That night, I met the three girls who are already my best friends, and I know that we will be the rest of our lives. We're all SO different, but it's like the four of us were meant to meet, because each of us has a part that completes the group, almost as if the four of us make one perfect person. Their names are Violet, Ensley and Riley, and we're all from somewhere different! And you want to know how we met? They all had the same wishes as me! Can you imagine that? Strangers out there in the world that I never knew had the same dreams as me: to love everyone, no matter our differences, to be a good friend to those who need one, and to want to change the world with our talent and vision.

In a way, we are just like the candles we set onto the lake during Wish Night: Each individual burning brightly, but when we came together we created a single light so powerful that no one can ignore it.

And the weirdest thing of all? We are all in the same bunkhouse, Pinewood, one of the original, old cabins!

Oh! Let me tell you about them!

Violet is super smart. She always has a book, is always reading and always telling us about something we don't know. If you can believe it, she's even shier than me, but sweeter than a Starbucks Unicorn Frap.

Ensley is a dynamo! And she's so pretty I can barely look at her sometimes. It's like she's not of this world . . . like she should be in Game of Thrones or something. Ensley wants to be a star. She already acts and has done a lot of regional theater. She even did a commercial when she was five. You probably remember it . . . it was the one for that fabric softener called "Sleepy" . . . Anyway, she already has over 100,000 Instagram followers, and she likes me!

And then there's Riley! She's going to be a big director. She wants to change the way that movies are made and wants women to take charge of the business. I call her "Rileywood." She seems like an adult already, but in a good way, like an old soul. Riley doesn't take anything from anyone, and it's weird how much people already respect her and Ensley. Riley does these short movies and videos on TikTok, and one of her movies got like 20,000 shares! (I have a lot of apps I need to buy for my phone so we can all stay in touch! Just so you know!)

Oh! I forgot to tell you the biggest thing: the next day after Wish Night, we were all at our first bonfire. We were toasting marshmallows, making s'mores and singing camp songs when it hit me. I started to scream, and Ensley said, "Chill, girl." Violet laughed, but they saw that my eyes were totally wide, and I was pointing at the four of us around the fire. "Ensley, Violet, Riley and me . . . !"

Riley was like, "Um, yeah, we all know our names." Violet asked, "Are you okay?" and then I started pointing at everyone again. They thought I was joking around, but I stopped and looked at them, the firelight all on my face, making me look really creepy. "You're Ensley!" I said. "You're Violet. I'm Emma. You're Riley."

"We got it." Ensley laughed.

"No, you don't," I said. "The four of us! Our names! The first letters of our names . . . E-V-E-R! Friends Forever! Get it! ForEVER!"

We all looked at each other, and that's when they understood it.

Ensley got real quiet and started pointing at everyone, like I just had.

"Tu es une rêveuse, tu es une rêveuse, tu es une rêveuse, et je suis un rêveuse!"

"Um," I said. "Are you okay?"

"It's French," she said. "I study French. And it all makes sense now! Dreamer in French is rêveuse! The first four letters of that are our names! R-E-V-E . . . we're friends forEVER AND we're all dreamers! From now on, we'll call ourselves Les Rêveuses!"

Then she taught me how to say it without me sounding like I was choking on something.

We ran up and told V, Rach and Liz—you know, the "OG"—the actual Clover Girls who started Camp Clover—and they started laughing and hugging each other and singing some old song about friends. And then they told us all about their friend who died and how the camp came to be. They told us how they got their nicknames and how long they'd been friends (and even a time when they weren't, if you can believe that).

We all decided that we want to be just like them when we're older. In fact, we've already made a pact: We've all agreed that, one day in the future, when we're really old (like you and them, lol!) we are going to all live together and have our own camp for girls, just like V, Rachel and Liz. No boys allowed (we can talk to them, but they have to stay all the way on other side of the lake at Taneycomo! That's where Liz's boyfriend is!). It would be PERFECT! Camp will be our forever home, where we'll take care of each other, always bring out the best in each other, always make each other laugh and feel safe. Most of all, we'll know each other better than anyone, and we'll always be there for each other, no matter what. Until then, we will support each other's dreams forEVER and be friends forEVER!

Every night here, before we go to bed, the bell chimes, and the entire camp sings "Land of the Silver Birch." It's so eerie and beautiful, and the way everyone's voices echo over the lake gives me chills but makes me feel safe.

Blue lake and rocky shore,
I will return once more,
Boom, didi, boom, boom,
Boom, didi, boom, boom,
Boom, didi, boom, boom . . . Booooom.

And then Les Rêveuses all say good-night to each other. Each of us says, "Sweet dreams, dreamers!" Sometimes, the other girls laugh at us, but we don't care anymore. Because every time we do that, right before I close my eyes and go to sleep, I understand why you both wanted me to come to camp. So I don't feel all alone. And I'll never be alone as long as I have friends. That's why you sent me here, wasn't it? To make friends.

I have friends now. And they make me feel happier and stronger and braver every day.

I love you, Mom and Dad. And I love Camp Clover! See you in August!

Em

ACKNOWLEDGMENTS

In many ways, my childhood was much like a summer camp. I spent summers with my grandparents at an old log cabin in the Missouri Ozarks. I slept on a cot. I spent summers fishing, swimming, canoeing, building campfires, roasting hot dogs and marshmallows on sticks, singing songs, telling stories and doing crafts—from making bark lampshades to building creek stone planters.

I did go to camp, too. I attended church camp and, one summer, a tennis camp, not the easiest of camps for a chubby kid with little range of motion.

In *The Clover Girls*, I write of traditional camp activities, from sing-alongs to swimming tests, color wars to candles on the lake. Those are important memories and traditions for kids, activities that build confidence. Mostly, however, the greatest thing about camp—and just being a kid—were the friendships. More than anything, I remember the friends I had as a kid. We shot bottle rockets into caves, played until the sun went down and my family had to call me in for dinner, ate ice cream when it was hot and stuck our bodies waist-deep into the freezer at the old general store to fish out grape Nehi.

As I grew older, it seemed a bit harder not only to make great friends but to retain them. We grew up so fast. We moved away from one another. We changed. We got jobs. We married, had families, became "responsible." Too often—and too easily—friendships fade. So do childhood dreams. I ask why we let that happen in *The Clover Girls*. I love the journey of the best friends FOUR-ever, "The Clover Girls," in this book and how they reclaim their childhood joy, dreams, themselves and each other.

The heart of this novel is as big as summer, as warm as the sand on a beach and as hopeful as a day of sunshine with nothing to do. I hope Em, V, Rachel and Liz stay in your hearts like your best friends. They remain in mine.

And to my best friends: thank you for being you and letting me be me. As my mom always used to say, "A good friend is like a lightning bug. They light up your life when you need it the most and least expect it." She was right. I would not be as bright as I am today without my friends lighting the way.

And I would not be where I am without my "team," whom I am proud to say have become some of my best friends.

Writing a book may be a solitary act but publishing one is not. *The Clover Girls* is my eleventh(!) book and sixth novel, and not one would have been possible without my agent,

Wendy Sherman, who has been on my side since day one of book one.

To my wonderful editor, Susan Swinwood: thank you for pushing me to make this novel as great as it could be!

To the entire publicity, marketing, art and sales teams—Roxanne Jones, Samantha McVeigh, Pam Osti, Lindsey Reeder—at Graydon House Books/Harlequin/HarperCollins, THANK YOU for your talent, tireless enthusiasm, expertise, hard work and belief in my work. I feel like I'm finally "home," and having such support, safety and nurturing is a dream for any author.

My foreign rights agent, Jenny Meyer, is always an unsung hero.

Carol Fitzgerald of The Book Report Network is not only my website guru but also my sounding board.

M.J. Rose and AuthorBuzz: thanks for your hard work, talent and creativity.

To all the independent bookstores and book-sellers across the US, thank you for your endless support, and keep hanging tough in these tough times. I'm proud to send every reader I come across your way.

To all the libraries, thank you for being the hearts and souls of our communities.

To Gary, dream nurturer, dream maker and dreamer: you are my everything.

To my Sigma Pi fraternity brothers and beloved

Little Sisters and Sweethearts from Drury College: we were the original '80s group of friends, and whenever I hear Wham!, Madonna, Prince, The Outfield and "99 Luftballons," I think of you and smile. (And want a beer!)

To my friend Trish: you were and still are the model who originated the Tiger Pose! (Kitty, Kitty!)

To my dear friends Judy and Kathy: thanks for your friendship, love, gardening tips and personal stories that helped inspire the novel and the character of Iris! (This note should have been in *The Heirloom Garden*, but I'm saying it here now!)

The lyrics I refer to in the novel are from the traditional camp song "Land of the Silver Birch," which friends from Michigan and Canada grew up singing at camp.

And to all of you: it is a dream to wake up every day and write the types of novels I do, and that would not be possible without your incredible love and support. You buy my books. You read my books. You inspire my books. And you have become my friends because you share as much of your lives with me as I do with you. You understand that the world needs stories of hope more than ever these days. You realize that stories inspired by my grandmas' heirlooms, lives, love and lessons are important. You know that stories that honor our elders, family memories and traditions are necessary. And you know that books that remind us of what's most important in life never go out of style. You are my "Clovers" and "FOUR-ever Friends," and I am honored to write novels that speak to your hearts, minds and souls.

I'll see you this fall with my first winter-and holiday-themed novel, *The Secret of Snow*. I can't wait to bundle up and go on a snowy journey with you!

XOXO,
Viola

DISCUSSION QUESTIONS

1. A major theme of *The Clover Girls* is friendship. Who are your best friends? Why are they? How did you meet? What have you gone through together over the years?
2. Did you attend summer camp as a kid? If so, what kind: sleepaway, day, church, sports? Was it a good experience?
3. Do you remember the friends you made there? Do you still stay in touch with any of them?
4. What were your favorite activities at camp? What did you learn? What helped build your confidence as a young woman? Discuss.
5. Do you think it's easier or harder to make and maintain friendships as an adult? Why or why not?
6. In the novel, I explore why women are often at odds with or do not support one another. Why do you think that is? Are women taught to be wary of or competitive with one another growing up? How can women support and empower one another better in life, work and society? Discuss.
7. Have you ever had a falling-out with a best friend? What caused it? Did you try to regain that friendship?

8. Has a close friend died? How did that impact you? How did you celebrate his/her life?

9. Who we are as children—and the dreams we have—is another theme in the novel. Why do we too often lose or forget who we were when we were younger? Do family and society change us and our dreams too much? How do we recapture that?

10. Family is a foundational theme in every novel I write. Liz's children and family are not supportive of her, from helping care for their grandmother to supporting their mother when she needs it the most. Is your family supportive of you in times of crisis? Why are some people incapable of caring for others, especially the elderly or infirmed?

11. V, Rachel and Liz are all successful but not happy. Why do you think we too often pursue the wrong paths? Are we changing for the better or worse as a society in regard to that? Discuss.

12. What defines summer to you and your family? What are your favorite summer activities and traditions, and why?

| Books are produced in the United States using U.S.-based materials | Books are printed using a revolutionary new process called THINKtech™ that lowers energy usage by 70% and increases overall quality | Books are durable and flexible because of Smyth-sewing | Paper is sourced using environmentally responsible foresting methods and the paper is acid-free |

Center Point Large Print
600 Brooks Road / PO Box 1
Thorndike, ME 04986-0001 USA

(207) 568-3717

US & Canada:
1 800 929-9108
www.centerpointlargeprint.com